LEANING INTO THE WIND

MEMOIRS OF AN

IMMIGRANT PRAIRIE FARM BOY

By Larry G. Jacobsen

First published by 1st Books 11/11/04

ISBN: 1-4107-6805-8 (e)
ISBN: 1-4107-6804-X (sc)

Printed in the United States of America
Bloomington, Indiana

This book is printed on acid-free paper.

Acknowledgments

I owe a debt of gratitude to a number of people whose assistance have been vital in writing this book, but any and all errors belong solely to me. However, **the book is a memoir** and its contents therefore depend on my memory of events which may at times differ from those of others.

First I want to thank my sister Inger who not only edited substantial parts of it, but also helped to twig my memory about a number of occasions that I should not otherwise have recalled.

I have taken most of the photos in this book, or scanned them from old family pictures in my possession. However, in many cases I have taken photos with the kind cooperation of museums or I have reproduced them from other sources. In these cases, I have attributed them to their source. I want to express my thanks to those who have made this possible.

I especially want to thank the following two people:
- Darlene Fisher of the E.I.D. Archives in Brooks, Alberta spent over two hours guiding me through their archives.
- Shawna Duckett of the E.I.D. Historical Park in Scandia, Alberta, who led me enthusiastically from one exhibit to the next during my visit there.

I also want to acknowledge the Heritage Acres Antique Threshing Club who collected the farm equipment that is on display near Pincher Creek, Alberta and the Brooks Museum that also collected equipment as well as household items from the thirties.

Finding underground mining photos has been a challenge, but a few people gave me access to the limited ones that they had. I am especially grateful to Britannia Mining Museum for the photos that I was able take of its mining equipment. Dennis Llewellyn of the Nelson Chamber of Mines in Nelson, BC was very helpful in this regard. I also want to thank Andy Wingerak, Peter Murray, Don Ormrod, Larry Finnbogason and Joel Ackert, who generously provided me with photos as well.

The family pictures were all scanned from photos in the author's possession.

Table of Contents

INTRODUCTION

This did not start out to be a book. It came into being gradually as I tried to tie together brief anecdotes I had written about some of the colorful characters I had met during my early working years. I considered a short book on my mining experiences, but I could not find enough material to interest any but a few ex-miners like myself. It finally dawned on me that I might write a memoir

As I began writing, more and more memories came flooding back and eventually my story grew to over 131,000 words. There are still many memories coming back that will not get into this book, for at some point I had to say; "Enough!"

I grew up on farms in BC and Alberta during the Great Depression and the Second World War. Since leaving the farm, I have worked in logging, mining, construction and the oil and gas industries - as well as two brief stints in sales. During these careers I have met many colorful people, some of whom have helped shape my character.

My life has been interesting and like the proverbial cat, I have been blessed with at least nine of them, for I have escaped from that many accidents that should have killed me. You will find accounts of these events in Part V of this book.

Our civilization has changed more during my years on earth than in any previous person's lifetime. The young people of today cannot begin to imagine what life was like on the farm sixty or seventy years ago. When I was a small child few rural people even owned radios. Today everyone in the Western World has at least one or more television sets.

During my youth we travelled mostly by train or by Greyhound bus. Today most of us fly and there are very few passenger trains still in operation. Greyhound today earns more from parcel freight than it does from its passengers.

The pace of industrialization has accelerated beyond belief. I bought my first computer in the 1979. The computer I am now using is my eleventh one. It is several thousand times as powerful as my first one, but cost only a quarter as much in 1979 dollars. Without the help of my computer, printer, digital camera and scanner, I should never have produced this book.

Canada has changed as well. When I grew up its inhabitants (except for the aborigines) were almost all white and had their roots in either

Europe or the United States. We now get more non-white immigrants than Caucasians. Whites in Canada may well become a minority.

We have left the countryside in droves and moved into the cities and towns. The rural population today is insignificant and has lost much of its political power.

Farming has been revolutionized! Until the nineteen thirties farming in Alberta was still powered mostly by horses but they were replaced by tractors during the late Thirties. The farming methods of today would have been unimaginable during my childhood. Then it required at least two men to farm a quarter section of irrigated land. Today with computerized sprinklers, large farm equipment and chemical weed control, etc., one man can farm several quarter sections.

During my early childhood, few people owned cars. Today many families own at least two and their teenage children often have their own as well. My parents did not have to buy car insurance until well after I left home. In Canada today, you can no longer drive a car without it.

I never made nor received a phone call until after I left home. Even then it was with a crank phone on a party line shared by at least six other families. Long distance calls to other countries were unheard of. Today my older grandchildren even have there own cellular phones and I can phone my children in Phoenix for seven cents a minute.

When I grew up, country folk did not lock their doors. Children walked to school from as far away as four to five miles. Today that is unthinkable! All rural children are now bused to school, and even in the city, many parents drive their children there from fear of them being molested or perhaps even kidnapped.

Poliomyelitis was still a dread disease during my childhood, (we all knew someone who had suffered from it) but today it is almost forgotten. Vaccination for it, as well as for Smallpox, Diphtheria, Typhoid Fever and many other diseases became routine during my childhood. Because of the recent mapping of the human genome we can look forward to new treatments for many other diseases in the foreseeable future.

My work has led me to live in many places in the West. Like the rolling stone, I may not have gathered much (financial) moss, but I have had a wealth of colorful experiences which I will share with you in this book.

PART I

THE EARLY YEARS

Chapter 1 – Denmark

Denmark is a small country that covers 43,094 square kilometers - about one third larger than Vancouver Island. Its geography however is very different. Unlike Vancouver Island, it has no rugged mountains, but is made up of flat or gently rolling terrain. The highest point is a hill in Jutland called "Himmelbjerg" which translates into Heaven Mountain. The top of this grand peak is a mere 500 feet above sea level.

Denmark has changed a lot since I was born. My grandparents were farmers, as were a great many other Danes of their time. Farms were then very labor intensive and a large segment of the population was therefore rural. Today that has changed. As in Canada and the U.S., farms have been consolidated into large holdings that are operated by corporations employing few people. The vast majority of Danes are now urban dwellers who buy all of their food in supermarkets, just as we do here.

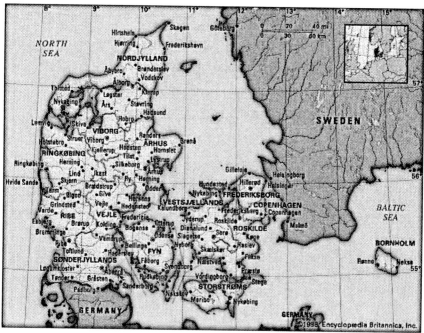

MAP OF DENMARK

I was the third of twelve children and the last to be born in Denmark. The next four were born in BC and the final five in Alberta. The first eight of us were all home births, but after Mother almost bled to death with number eight - Eva, the rest were born in the Brooks hospital.

I visited Denmark in the spring of 1999 and was astounded by the size of the farms and by the wind turbines dotting the countryside. I was surprised to learn that Denmark was the world leader in wind technology – that the huge wind farms in California are generally based on Danish design.

Life in Denmark today is much like that in Canada and the USA, but with one important difference. The people tend to me more physically active than we are. The number of bicycles in Copenhagen astounded me. There were bikes everywhere! It was not just the young people who were riding them, but elderly men and women as well. We learned that there were supposed to be free loaner bikes available at handy locations, but did not see very many. I suspect that like here, useful things are subject to theft.

These days every schoolchild in Denmark must learn at least two foreign languages, but many of them learn more than that. It is therefore not surprising that almost all Danes are fluent in English – it is usually the first foreign language they learn. I found that only a few of the older people had difficulty with it.

I do not believe that the standard of living is any higher in Denmark than in Canada even though their GNP may be higher than ours. The minimum wage is twice what ours is, but everything costs at least twice as much too.

Dad (lower right) at age 6 with his family

The first six children in our family all sported the second name - Boesen. That was our paternal grandmother's maiden name. I have often wondered why a woman's maiden name was incorporated into the family name, since I don't think that was customary in Denmark. One clue to the

3

puzzle came when my father told me that he did not know that his father was born out of wedlock until he visited Denmark when he was well into his seventies. In Danish society during his youth, such topics were taboo.

My paternal grandfather was born in January, 1849 one year after the German army overran a part of Denmark. His father was supposedly an Austrian officer. I don't know whether his conception was the result of rape or of a love match, but possibly the latter. Growing up the son of a single mother in those days would have put him at a huge disadvantage. Our paternal grandmother was a huge woman with massive hips who may not have been particularly marriageable. On the other hand she was

Dad at age 18. 6 months of army training was compulsory

possibly the daughter of a family with some means. This would certainly have enhanced her suitability to a prospective groom! I suspect that in marrying a penniless young bastard, her family would have made certain stipulations; e.g. incorporating her maiden name into the family name. Father's family moved a number of times while he was a child because his father made a living by rehabilitating farms. He would buy a rundown farm, operate it for a few years while he made improvements to it, and then sell it. Father was born in the Slesvig-Holstein area while it was still under German administration, (some of this area reverted to Denmark after WW1). He went to German speaking school for his first 3 years - before the family moved north to the Ribe area, where everyone spoke only Danish.

Dad had six older siblings, Katherine, who was born in 1890, followed by Hans about a year later. Next came the first set of twins - Helene & Thorvald (Thorvald died as a baby). The second set of twins was Helga and another boy, also named Thorvald. This Thorvald had meningitis or some similar disease as a baby. He never learned to speak and was never toilet trained. He died at the age of twenty. Dad (the youngest) was born on January 14, 1897, so his mother had five pregnancies in less than seven years.

Dad remembered when his oldest sister first worked away from home as a maid for another farming family. On a visit back home, she told

Mother's parents when they were young

them that in the house where she was working, the family all ate from separate plates. In Dad's family the food was served in a large bowl, and everyone ate from that same bowl. It was not long before they too ate from separate plates.

Mother's grandfather was a tenant farmer who rented the land on which both she and her father were born. Some time after her father took the farm over, he purchased it – a rare accomplishment then. The farm was about 36 acres in size - probably an average holding then. His typical crops would have included grains such as wheat, rye, barley and oats. Root crops were also very important and would have included potatoes, carrots, sugar beets and turnips. They fed both turnips and sugar beets to the livestock, as well as selling them, or eating them. Mother's father learned to improvise and take much of the brute muscle out of his work because he was small and had a slight build. She told me that he was continually finding new ways to make his work a little easier.

The farm-house was built in the shape of a quadrangle that enclosed a courtyard in its middle. The building included the living quarters, a smithy, a chicken coop, and a barn, as well as equipment and produce storage areas - all under the same roof. My grandfather, my mother and I were all born in this house. When I made my first visit Denmark during Christmas of 1978, I got to sleep in it again for the first time in fifty

The house where my mother, her father, possibly her grandfather and I was born. Photo was taken from within a completely enclosed courtyard.

years. When I visited Denmark for the second time in 1999, I discovered that the farm were no longer in the family. The house was no longer a part of the farm either and has now been converted into a couple of apartments.

Mother was born on December 6, 1899, the second of three girls – her name was Asta. Her older sister was named Kirstine and the younger one was called Valborg. She also had a younger brother who died of pneumonia before he reached his first birthday. It was when Kirstine married Dad's brother Hans that Mother first met my father. They were wed three years later - on September 1, 1922.

Both of our parents were reasonably well educated compared to most Danes of their day – they had both attended "Folk High-School" for a year. My father also went to Agricultural College for a year. After our parents married, Dad tried tenant farming for several years, but was not able to make a go of it despite his agricultural training. My

Kirstine & Mother are in back row. Valborg is sitting between my grandparents.

older sisters, Gerda and Ester were born during this time - in 1923 and 1924 respectively. Dad finally gave up farming there and emigrated to Canada in April of 1928. He sired me shortly before leaving, for I was born the following December.

The church where I was baptized was built before Columbus sailed to America. After the Reformation it was taken over by the Lutherans from the Catholic Church.

Mother, my two sisters and I followed Dad to Canada in April of 1929.. Mother's younger sister, Valborg came along to help Mother cope in the new land and especially during the long arduous trip.

After a sea voyage of fourteen days, we landed in Halifax on May 16, 1929 and were greeted by a snowstorm. The sea voyage was followed by a train trip of seven days in a "settler's coach." I of course don't remember anything about the trip for I was not quite five months old. However, I am sure that Mother never forgot it, because I was sick with "whooping cough." My sisters Ester and Inger both insist that it was Ester, not me that had whooping cough. They may be right, but I have a clear memory of Mother telling me that I had it.

6

Chapter 2 - Edgewater

I was the oldest of five boys in a family of twelve children and was given a Danish name that caused me endless embarrassment until I changed it at the age of 22. My two older sisters, Gerda and Ester were 5.5 and 4.25 years older than I was. This was the first and last age gap in the family, caused

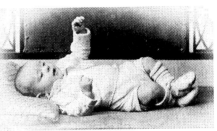

he author at 5 months.

in part because Mother had a miscarriage. After I was born, the next nine babies were born over a sixteen-year period.

Until 1937 when I was eight we lived near a village called Edgewater, on a 20-acre farm, half of which Dad had cleared. The farm was a little more than a mile from the village and about ten miles north of Radium Hot Springs, BC. Our parents built a three-room house on that farm, containing a kitchen, a living room and one bedroom as well as an attic, which we reached via an outside ladder. By the time child number seven arrived, we must have been very crowded in that house.

It was impossible to feed any family, and especially a large one on such a small piece of land, so Dad worked at various jobs in the woods. The man, who had sold us the farm, also owned a logging operation. My father and the other recent immigrants worked for this man felling trees, making railway "axe" ties, etc. This was during the early depression years and they soon found themselves continually short changed on their paychecks. After a short time, even this work dried up.

Father next worked in "Relief Camps" on road construction during the summers. Relief camps were one of the government's methods of alleviating the Great Depression that lasted

Our Edgewater house. My two older sisters slept in the attic. It was accessed via an outside ladder. Our water was carried from a well some 250 yards away.

until the war broke out in 1939. In return for their labor, the men in the camps were provided with free room and board plus a few cents each day in pocket money. Mother and my two older sisters tried valiantly to maintain the farm during Father's long absences. I can remember us having a vegetable stand beside the highway during the summer. We sold potatoes, carrots, peas and chickens to the tourists who stopped at the stand. The chickens were caught and butchered while the tourists waited. My sister Ester remembers with revulsion how one tourist just yanked the head off with a quick twist on one such hapless chicken.

Mother's younger sister, Valborg had accompanied us to Canada for the express purpose of helping my mother. She shortly met a Danish man named Anfred Pedersen who she married a year and a half later. They returned to Denmark immediately after their wedding. Our parents were therefore the only

Anfred fits me with an ingenious hat.

representatives of their respective families to remain in Canada. One of Valborg's sons came and spent a year in Canada during the fifties - after I had left home, but then returned to his native land again. A well situated some two hundred yards away from the house was our source of domestic water. We fetched the water in a couple of three-gallon pails, which were placed on the floor beside the stove. One of my earliest memories was of my sixth birthday. Some of our neighbors were visiting and I was busy doing my own thing. I remember pretending to be a truck and shuffling

Inger and I were good friends during early childhood, but she was usually the boss.

backwards from the living room into the kitchen without looking behind me. The next thing I knew, I had plopped myself down in a full water pail. I got soaked!

I remember Father sending me into town to post a letter one afternoon when I was six or seven years old. In the forenoon there had been a bunch of Hereford cattle adjacent to the fence bordering our yard. My sister Inger and I had been taunting them by sticking our

8

tongues out at them. I was terrified about leaving the safety of the farm for I was sure that the bulls would be waiting to get even with me. However, I was not able to tell Dad this, so off I went - very slowly.

The walk into town was a little over a mile. There were three or four farmhouses situated along the first half-mile stretch, but from then on there was nothing but forest on either side. Coinciding with the end of the farmed area was a deep wooded ravine adjacent to the road. When I reached it I could hear a rapid thumping noise emanating from the bottom of the ravine. I later learned that this is a sound a grouse makes when drumming, but I did not realize this at the time. I just knew that it was a bear! It must have taken me well over two hours to inch past this dreadful place, but eventually I did reach the post office, which by then was closed.

The postmaster and his family lived at the back of the post office. They took me in, fed me dinner (this was the very first time I tasted canned pears) and drove me back home. I was never able to satisfactorily explain to my father how a trip that should have taken me one half hour each way, consumed the entire afternoon. Not only that, but I had lost the letter as well, in which was a five dollar bill. The five dollars I lost would be worth well over $300 today and its loss must have been very serious for someone as poor as us.

In 1935 when I was six, my maternal grandfather visited us for the summer. He gave me a three tier pencil box that later made me the envy of all my school friends. No one else had a pencil box with more than two levels. I kept that pencil box for the entire (10) years I attended school after which I passed it on to a younger sibling.

Grandfather also brought a dollhouse for the girls. This dollhouse was unlike anything I have ever laid eyes on, before or since. It was a two-story structure that measured roughly 24 inches long by about 16 inches wide. On the main floor was the kitchen and living room and an upstairs were two bedrooms. All the furnishings were realistic and the house was lit by electric lamps that actually worked. They had beautiful lace covered shades with cut glass decorations hanging from them. The table was set with miniature, but real dishes. Each bed was covered

1936 – We are now 7 children. Mother is holding Julie. The author is on the left. Ester is not in the picture.

9

with a real duvet. Inside the house was a mother doll and a baby doll – each fashionably dressed and sporting real hair. I believe the mother doll had a blue dress overlaid with lace. My sister Inger tells me that there was even a "maid doll" that was dressed in a black dress and also wore a green apron and a cap. Everything inside this dollhouse was minutely detailed and built to scale. I have no idea where that dollhouse is now, but my sisters had it for many years.

The author's maternal grandfather pitching hay – circa 1935.
From a photograph restored by his sister Eva Manly

I can also remember that Grandfather had a garden hoe custom made. It had a very slim blade that made weeding the garden much easier than with the typically shaped hoes one regularly sees in the stores. It was especially good for cutting the weeds that were in close proximity to the plants. We still had that hoe when I left home a dozen years later. Inger tells me that she is now its proud owner.

Grandfather died the following year after returning to Denmark - five days before turning 75. His father had died three days before turning 75. I believe that for some strange reason he was convinced that he would not live any longer than his father had done.

The Halloween when I was still six, Mother dressed me up as an old crone. I accompanied my two older sisters on their rounds to two or three of our nearest neighbors. We had no flashlights in those days, and there were of course no electrical lights of any kind. I do not remember, but we may well have taken a barn lantern along on our foray to the nearest farmsteads, which ranged from a quarter mile to a half-mile away. The year following, I was dressed up as a chimney sweep. My face was blackened with soot and I was equipped with a broom made from a stick with some slim willows tied to one end of it.

I started school the autumn before I turned seven. Gerda and Ester had tried to teach me English at home, but I was not interested. Nevertheless, except for the first day or so, I don't remember having any language difficulties. One thing that undoubtedly helped was that Danish is somewhat related to English.

Once I was in school, Mother also taught me to read and write Danish. She had taught Gerda and Ester as well, but did not carry on the tradition with my younger siblings. Being able to read our Danish and other Scandinavian books helped me get an early appreciation of my roots. After my sister Inger grew up, she taught herself to read Danish. She later spent a year in Denmark and attended Folk high-school during her stay.

At Edgewater, we were a part of a small Danish community of perhaps a dozen families who were all recent immigrants. We naturally visited back and forth quite a bit, but because of the size of our family, we children had special rules. We were not allowed to accept second helpings. This applied especially to cakes and other desserts. I remember one neighbor lady who would say to us; "I know that your parents won't allow you to have a second helping, but that rule does not apply at my house." I don't remember, but I think Mother did not object too forcefully when we sometimes gave in and accepted second piece of cake there.

Around the time when I was six or seven, one of our neighbors asked me what I intended to be when I grew up. I replied; "I think I will get married." These turned out to be prophetic words. They caused quite a laugh at the time and our parents never forgot it. Little did anyone then guess just how enamoured with marriage I must have been, for I eventually married four times!

During my childhood, before Christmas each year, our maternal grandmother sent money to Mother to purchase presents for us. We would each make a wish list of items that could be purchased from the Eaton's or Simpson's catalogues for about $0.50 each. My first jack-knife was one such Christmas present.

The summer after I turned seven, Dad bought two gopher traps for me. A neighbor, who lived a half mile away, had a fox farm. He bought all the gophers I could trap. I don't remember how much he paid me for them, but it might have been a penny each. A cent then had the purchasing power of more than fifty cents today.

In the winter it was customary for us to take our sleighs along to school each day. One half mile from our house there was a long hill with a blind curve half way down. We were allowed to ride our sleighs from that curve to the bottom of the hill because from there we would be able to see any oncoming traffic. One morning I ran a ways to get well ahead of my two older sisters. As soon as I reached the crest of the hill, I threw myself down on the sleigh and away I went. When my sisters reached the brow of the hill, they were somewhat surprised that I was already out of sight. They probably suspected what I had done, but thankfully, they didn't tell Dad or Mother.

Sometimes we would get a good thaw followed by cold weather. When this happened we could walk on top of the crusted snow without breaking through. This made for ideal sleighing on the hills on our farm. It had its dangers though. I remember my sister Inger breaking through the crust. and suffering a number of bruises and cuts from the hard edges of it. Sleighing and skiing in those days was much healthier for us than now. There were no T- bars, rope tows or chair lifts to transport one to the top of a hill. In order to ski or sleigh down a hill, We first had to climb it.

Four of my siblings were born in Edgewater, but my only memory was of the last one. My sister Julie was born at home on March 8, 1936. What I do remember, was waking up early one morning to the squalling of what I thought were cats fighting. By this time the doctor had come and gone and I found instead that I had a new baby sister and it was her bawling that had awakened me.

While Julie was a baby, we had a visiting missionary. He was allowed to use the little Anglican Church in the village to show "lantern slides" of some far away country. After the slide show we all walked over to the nearby community hall, about two hundred yards away for refreshments. After we arrived at the hall, Mother discovered that Dad had forgotten Julie at the church. Such were the hazards of having so many children.

Irene Geddes, the granddaughter of local millionaire, Dr. Geddes, was my classmate. I will never forget being invited to her birthday party. At that party I got to both see and ride a tricycle and a "pedal" car for the very first time. My own toys and those of the other children, with whom we normally played, were very modest in comparison. The only purchased toys I remember having at the time was a wagon and a male doll named Per (contraction of Peter). However, we invented other toys. The one I remember using the most, was just an ordinary tree branch. I would stand astride the thick end of it and pretend that it was a horse. I used various gaits to simulate a horse walking, trotting or galloping. If a piece of string was available, I tied it on for reins.

I remember finding a discarded truck tire that was large enough in diameter for me to curl up inside so that I became a rolling wheel. We had a root cellar in the yard, which formed quite a large mound. One of my favorite pastimes was to have one of my playmates roll me down off this mound. It was a little like rapid and continuous somersaults, but much smoother. The sensation was quite unlike anything I had ever experienced and it also tended to make me a bit dizzy. For some reason, I could never persuade anyone else to try this form of entertainment.

The wagon I had was one my mother had purchased for me when I was two. One day when she was giving me a ride on it, I fell off, on to a sharp piece of metal, where the wagon's tongue was attached. The resulting scar on my chin remained a prominent facial feature for all the years I was a child. After I grew up it gradually became unnoticeable.

It is a warm summer day. I am six years old and Inger is five. The two of us are visiting Nils and Ditte (pronounced dee'ti) Nielsen. We are frolicking in a shallow marshy pond (nude of course) together with Ralph and his sisters. I can barely imagine the horror that this kind of activity might spawn in today's age of political correctness. The water in the pond is warm and it is teeming with snails, water spiders and other creatures common to such a pond environment. I remember Ditte bringing us milk to drink accompanied by a tray of open face sandwiches. They were buttered pieces of heavy brown bread liberally sprinkled with sugar.

The Nielsens have raised a tame deer that they acquired when it was a fawn. I am not sure how they got it, but believe that they rescued it from some kind of trouble it had gotten into. I remember seeing them coming down the road in their buggy with both the deer and their dog cavorting along behind them. Not only was the deer tame, but it was the dog's playmate as well. I don't recall how long they kept this deer, but I suspect that it did not survive the hunting season.

Not far from our house was a small poplar grove. In it we found young trees of suitable sizes which we bent down so that we could ride on them. Sitting astride such a tree, our feet would just barely touching the ground, we could propel ourselves into the air some distance, then return to earth for another push with our feet. In this manner we could ride the tree up and down. When the tree eventually lost its resiliency, we broke in a new one. We could ride such trees solo or double, depending on the size of them.

We had a neighbor whose son Ernst was a year younger than me. He was tough! As a six-year-old, he tramped barefooted in wild rose bushes to show off to us. His family shortly moved out to Lulu Island, and I never saw him again. When he was about twelve or thirteen, he fell through the ice on a pond and was drowned.

I remember another neighbor who had a son a year younger than me named Ralph. In our Danish community, each family took turns hosting an "in the home" church service each Sunday where they sang hymns and read scripture. We children were allowed to play outside as long as we did not disturb the service. We soon discovered that we could easily make Ralph cry by making faces at him. He would stand surrounded by us and slowly rotate while bawling loudly. Next, to the consternation and mortification of his parents, he would run into the house and repeat his performance in the middle of the meeting room. He was probably hoping that we would be punished for making him cry, but that never happened.

The Christmas when I was fourteen, (We had by then moved to Alberta) I came back to Edgewater for a visit and stayed with Ralph's family for a week. Whenever his mother misplaced something she tended to say something such as; "That's funny, I can't find it." Ralph would instantly retort; "If it's funny, we had all better laugh!" I honestly don't know how his mother stood having him around. I remember on an earlier occasion when I was visiting Ralph, that his exasperated mother broke the handle of her hairbrush while spanking him with it.

One day during that visit, the two of us went to Radium Hot Springs. Being December, there was snow on the concrete surface adjacent to the pool. Naturally we were soon throwing snowballs at each other. However, it was impossible to connect since all one had to do was duck under the surface whenever a snowball came too close. I can still vividly recall the tingling sensation on the soles of my feet whenever I got out of the hot water and ran barefoot in the snow. That was the last time I saw Ralph. I met his sisters many years later when they were both married and living in Victoria. However, the last I heard about Ralph was that he had become an academic at some university.The last summer in Edgewater, (1936) Dad came home from the construction camp with a car! It was a black 1923 Dodge convertible for which he had paid $50. He took us for a ride up to Brisco and back. I remember seeing a forest fire burning across the river from Brisco. At the time it seemed to me like a very long trip, but it was not more than a dozen miles each way. The highway surfacing in those days was gravel for it would be many years before there were paved roads anywhere in the province.

I vividly remember leaving Edgewater and moving to Alberta. My father had rented a boxcar into which he put our furniture, the car, some farm implements, the animals we were taking with us and a bunch of hay with which to feed them. Father was allowed to ride in the boxcar in order to tend to the animals. However, my two older sisters also rode in the boxcar, occasionally hidden, so that my father would not have to buy their fares.

The rest of us rode the train to Calgary and the Greyhound bus from there to Tilley. On the trip up the Columbia valley from Edgewater to Golden, we rode in a coach hitched to the tail end of a freight train. The coach swayed a lot on the soft, and unstable roadbed and I soon got motion sickness. I promptly brought up all my breakfast and had a miserable ride for the sixty miles to Golden. From Golden to Calgary we rode on a regular passenger train. We stopped for two days in Calgary where we stayed with Danish friends. I can still recall the garden shovel my mother purchased for me at the Eaton's store. I kept that little shovel for many years.

Leaving Edgewater in April 1937 (waiting for the train)
Gerda and Ester have already gone with Dad.

Chapter 3 - Tilley

Southern Alberta weather has a feature unique to this area. Warm, dry Chinook winds periodically sweep across its plains. In the winter this provides a welcome relief from the cold and we usually looked forward to it eagerly. A Chinook generally heralds its coming, by creating a cloud formation in the southwest that we referred to as a Chinook arch. Whenever a Chinook hit us, the temperature would often climb from well below zero, up into the mid forties to low fifties (Fahrenheit) within a few hours. The temperature could drop just as precipitously! Often, when a Chinook was in the offing it would cause a feature called Fata Morgana, also known as a mirage. When this happened, we could usually see the settlement of Scandia some thirty miles away. On rare occasions we could even see the Rocky Mountains which were normally visible only from at least sixty miles farther to the west.

The weather in southern Alberta does not tend to be too extreme. Typical winter lows might be from 0° to –10° F. We did not experience –20°F every winter. However, some winters could be severe. I remember one winter in the early forties when the temperature dropped to –40°F for a few days! In January of 1947, the winter when I turned eighteen and worked in Scandia, we had temperatures dip to –52°F and remain below –40°F for over a week. One saving grace was that when the weather turned cold, there was seldom any wind.

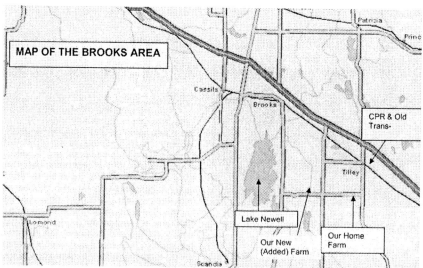

MAP OF THE BROOKS AREA

Kinder's Farm

It was raining heavily when we arrived in Tilley in late evening just after Easter in 1937. The roads such as they were, were almost impassable. Mr. Skanderup, an acquaintance of our parents, met us at the bus station. He took us to stay overnight with acquaintances some eight miles from town. During the drive, he would occasionally have to stop and clean the mud out from between the chained-up tires and the fenders. The roads had no surfacing nor decent drainage of any kind and the heavy clay balled up between the tires and the fender until it became impossible to keep on driving. For me the trip seemed to last an eternity because I had an ear infection.The following day we children were parcelled out to several families for a few days while Gerda, Ester and our parents prepared the house for occupancy. It was a draughty old farmhouse situated on 13 acres of land Dad rented from Mr. Kinder for the summer, while he looked for a suitable farm to buy.

The house we lived in during that first summer was poorly constructed and had been empty for some time. There were many cracks in the walls through which not only light, but dust and insects entered as well. Mother, Gerda and Ester cleaned it up as well as they could before we moved in.

Not long after we had moved into the house, a severe windstorm came up. The powerful wind picked up huge amounts of soil from the freshly tilled fields. It became so dark in the house that we had to light lamps to see. Outside the visibility was almost zero! When the storm finally blew itself out the following day, there was sandy silt everywhere, both inside and outside the house. Because of all the cracks in the walls, the silt had gotten inside, into, and onto everything. It covered all the dishes in the cupboard. It was in and on the beds. It was on the windowsills and in the pantry. It also covered the floors in a thick layer. Mother and my two older sisters must have had to clean for days to restore the house to a liveable condition.

That first summer - from Easter to early October, we attended a rural one-room school called Bethany. It had the same name as the Lutheran church being constructed nearby. We had to walk almost two miles to get to it. I promptly found out that academically I was at least a year ahead of my Grade II classmates. The teacher continually called on me for answers when no one in her Grade III class knew them. Nevertheless, it did not occur to her that she should skip me ahead a grade. Furthermore, using me to make her class look dumb did nothing for my popularity with the other students.

One day we discovered some fish in a nearby ditch that crossed under the road through a culvert. Dad and two other men immediately went over to see for themselves. The ditch was so narrow where it exited from the culvert that my dad was able to stand astride it. While one of the other men poked a pole into the culvert from the other end and rattled it around, my father was able to grab fish after fish as they came out. The image of my father catching and throwing fish up on to dry ground has remained with me. I don't remember how many he caught, but they kept Mother busy canning them for the rest of that day and the next. It turned out that they were Suckers – bony fish, at which most people turned up their noses, but to us they represented free meat.

Our parents had some friends that lived at Standard – about one hundred miles to the north. They invited us to visit them that summer, so one day we were all packed into the 1923 Dodge car together with a lunch and drove off to see them. Our typical speed was between 15 and 25 miles per hour, so the trip took all afternoon. We stopped along the way for a picnic lunch at Duchess. This was the only time I can remember Mother ever buying bread and jam in a store.

One day on my walk home from school, I took my usual shortcut through the neighbor's field. I followed an irrigation canal and encountered a skunk - the first I had ever seen. I ran home, found a big stone and a heavy stick, then returned to kill the skunk. It was still there, so I threw the stone at it, but missed. I then ran up to hit it with my stick, but the skunk fired before I could get there. Its spray caught me squarely in the eyes. It burned like pepper and I was temporarily blinded. I completely forgot about any further warfare and headed back home. When I got there, my smell preceded me and caused quite a stir. I can still remember Mother giving me a bath in the galvanized wash tub while she tried her level best to scrub the smell out of my face and hair. She decontaminated my clothes by burying them in the ground for seven days and I suspect she would have liked to do the same with me. At school I was ostracized until the end of the term - about as long as it took for the smell to wear off. No one wanted to sit anywhere near me!

That fall Father bought a quarter section (160 acres) of land some miles to the east where we attended a rural two-room school called Renfrew. We could not move until the crops had been harvested on the land we had rented, as well as on the farm we were buying. We therefore continued to attend Bethany School

One neighbor who lived just down the road from us had a daughter a year younger than me. When we first arrived she promptly became my girlfriend and we had decided to get married when we grew up. This infatuation lasted until the day she betrayed my sister Inger and me. During a school recess, she called Inger and me over to the woodshed. There surrounded by some other children and us, she ordered one little girl to drop her pants. Afterwards she told everyone that Inger had done the dirty deed. We were treated as pariahs after that! A few days later I was lured over to Kinder's place after supper by an older schoolmate named Chubby. He, his older brother and their hired man held me while they lowered my trousers and smeared my penis with equipment grease. They made some suggestions that I did not understand, but it had probably to do with facilitating sex next time some girl's pants were lowered. Inger and I were immensely relieved when we left the Bethany school and moved to the Renfrew school.

The New Farm

The new farm was 4 miles south, and ¾ of a mile west of Tilley. Tilley was a small village in which there was a blacksmith shop, one hotel with a beer parlour, two cafes, Mellon's Red & White store, McLaughlin's General store, a post office and a couple of garages. There were also three grain elevators, a butcher shop, a barber shop and a school. The nearest town was Brooks – 14 miles northwest by west from Tilley. It was much larger than Tilley and also boasted banks, a lawyer and a doctor. It was home to a provincial experimental farm and it was also headquarters for the local irrigation district. The nearest city was Medicine Hat, about 54 miles southeast by east from Tilley.

In all the years I lived at home, we went to Medicine Hat only once – and that was to get our confirmation class photographed. However we did get to Brooks at least once a year – to attend an annual church picnic each fall. We all looked forward to this because the picnic was held in the Town Park. Our parents never bought fresh fruit because it was too expensive, so being able to stuff ourselves with a variety of plums during the Brooks outing was especially appreciated.

When we arrived in the area, the roads could hardly be called roads at all. They consisted of flat driving surfaces with most of the topsoil removed and delineated by shallow ditches on either side. Whenever it rained the surface would at first become as slick as a bar of wet soap. Then as the rain penetrated deeper, a vehicle's wheels would leave deep ruts in it. After the rain was over and the road had dried, these ruts would harden and leave a very rough driving surface that was seldom graded. A few years after our arrival the main roads (including the one past our farm) were raised and gravelled. That was a welcome change!

19

The farm we bought turned out to have poor soil that was difficult to work. The soil was a heavy clay, commonly referred to as "gumbo." It was also very sticky and when it rained or when we were irrigating, it would build up under our rubber boots making them very heavy. At which point a good kick could dislodge it. Walking in the mud became a sequence of several steps followed by a kick with one leg, then a few more steps and a kick with the other.

The house on our new farm was called a "CPR" house. The Canadian government had given large tracts of land to the Canadian Pacific Railway (CPR) adjacent to its right-of-way in return for building the railway across Canada. It had later constructed the irrigation system that became known as the Eastern Irrigation District (EID). Shortly before our arrival, they had given the EID to the farmers. Because they had been losing a lot of money on it they were also obliged to include a goodly sum of operating

May 4th, 1938.

Mr. Peter B. Jacobson
TILLEY, Alberta.

Dear Sir:

L.C. 1272

With reference to the contract covering the NW¼ 36-16-13-4 which you took over by assignment from W.J.P. Hyssop, we have to advise that the total amount outstanding under this contract is $1553.76. The original contract issued to Hyssop called for a purchase price of $1726.41. Of this amount Hyssop paid $172.65 leaving the above balance outstanding. The contract we propose to issue to you will be taken up where Mr. Hyssop left off, two payments of $86.32 each and eight payments of $172.64 each will take care of this balance. The first payment of $86.32 will be due on the first of December, 1938. The land contains 129 acres irrigable and 31 acres non-irrigable. We are writing the contract as above outlined and same will be submitted to our Board of Trustees for approval at their next meeting.

Yours truly,

G.A. Robertson
Business Superintendent.

GAR/B

Land Title for our Tilley farm.

20

money before the farmers would accept ownership of it. When the CPR constructed the system during the early twenties, it had also built a number of houses to make the land more attractive to settlers. Our house was one of those built by the CPR.

Dad bought the farm from a Mr. Hyssop who had bought it from the E.I.D. I never found out how much money Dad paid to Hyssop, for he got a tractor and plow together with the farm. I just learned recently that he had taken over Hyssop's "Assignment" (mortgage) and that of the original price of $1726.41, Hyssop had paid just 10% of that amount before he sold it to us.

The House

The farmhouse sat at the edge of a large garden that was bordered on the north and the east by a wide shelter-belt of Russian Poplar. These trees protected the house from the cold winds that

A typical farm-yard shelterbelt. Photo taken by the author.

occasionally lashed down at us from the north. The house itself consisted of a living room, kitchen, bedroom and a pantry on the ground floor plus two bedrooms on the second floor. There was also a cellar under the house where we stored our canned goods. For a family that had as many as 10 children at home at one time, this was indeed a very small house.

None of the houses at that time were insulated and ours was no exception. They were all constructed with two by four-inch framing. The outer walls were sheathed with shiplap lumber covered with shingles and a layer of building paper in between. The inner walls of the house was plastered and the only insulation was the so-called dead air space between inner and outer walls.

With the onset of winter we installed storm windows on each of the windows and also banked dirt against the bottom of the outer walls to help keep the house warm. We heated the house with bituminous coal, which we bought from an open pit mine near the Bassano dam. It cost from $5 to $6 per ton delivered. We burned this coal in a heater in the living room and in the kitchen "range." The upstairs bedrooms got their heat through a trapdoor from the living room below, but they could still be quite chilly by

The CPR House: 9 children in the family in 1939.

morning. Our kitchen range looked much like the one in the photo, (at the end of this chapter) except that ours also had a hot water reservoir, which provided us with lukewarm water whenever the stove was lit.

One daily chore was bringing in coal for the cook stove and the heater and taking out the ashes. Both units discharged their smoke through a brick chimney at the centre of the house. One problem we had with it was that whenever the wind veered into a specific northerly direction, the chimney would not draft well and the house then filled with smoke. Eventually when I was about fifteen, Dad promoted me to "brick layer" for a day. I climbed up on the roof and extended the chimney by two to three feet. This eliminated the smoke problem, but my construction job stood as mute testimony to my inexperience as a bricklayer. The new section of chimney was neither quite straight nor quite vertical.

Farmhouses at that time were lit by a variety of lamps. We used a coal oil lamp or lantern where a low-grade light was adequate. We generally used these in the kitchen and in the barn. In the living room where we read, knitted or darned socks during the long winter evenings, much better lighting was required. Some people used pressurized gasoline lamps and other people such as us used the same type, but burned kerosene in them instead. Both kinds used mantles and produced a reasonably bright light, but they had to be pressurized frequently with a built-in hand pump.

There was a root cellar and an outside toilet about one hundred and fifty feet south of the house. Past them lay the

Typical kitchen range, missing warm water reservoir. *Photo taken by the author courtesy of the E.I.D. Historical Park in Scandia, Alberta.*

22

stock pond. During the summer, we got fresh water from the irrigation ditch that ran along the north side of the garden, but during the winter we had to rely on stored water from the stock pond to meet our needs and that of the livestock. Off towards the west and southwest two hundred feet from the house was the barn, the pigsty and the chicken coop. Having these outbuildings so close to the house assured us of being constantly harassed by flies except during winter.

One of the chief breeding places for the flies, was the manure pile behind the barn. From there the flies entered the house in hordes. They were everywhere. They flew around inside the house. They crawled on us. They crawled all over the table as well as over the food on it. As soon as the food was uncovered, the flies were on it immediately. Whenever we expected visitors, we first sprayed the house with insecticide. We also hung strips of flypaper in several places, but despite our best efforts, it was a losing battle. The barn and other outbuildings had been built far too close to the house.

Each fall we filled the stock pond just prior to the water being turned off in the irrigation ditches. The water in the stock pond was of reasonable quality until after it had been covered with ice for a period of time. As the winter progressed, it became infested with large numbers of organisms that rendered it unpalatable as well as very smelly.

Another problem with the water was that the cows drank from it directly. The manure left by the cows naturally leached into the water and did nothing for its quality. One year we had the stock-pond dredged and enlarged. We dug a well at one end of it, lined it with wooden barrels and connected the well to the stock-pond with a sand-filled tube. We also mounted a hand pump on top of the well. This improved the water quality for a while, but the sand gradually disappeared and the water quality quickly deteriorated again.

Eventually, we constructed a concrete lined cistern beside the house for storing our drinking and cooking water. It was a welcome change, not the least being the fact that we also installed a hand pump inside the kitchen, on the counter beside the sink. This made it unnecessary to go outside to fetch our drinking water. Our water for laundry, washing floors and dishes continued to be taken from the ditch in summer and the stock pond in winter.

On wash days we normally had about seven machine loads of laundry. The day began with me armed with two pails, carrying water that we heated in a "boiler" on the kitchen stove. We not only needed hot water for the washing machine, but for the rinse tub. It was not unusual for us to

Typical pump mounted beside the sink.
*Photo taken by the author
courtesy of the Brooks Museum.*

go through 18 or more pails of water during wash day. Whether the water came from the irrigation ditch or the stock pond, I still had to carry it well over one hundred yards, something I never looked forward to. I now tell my friends that we had running water on the farm – I ran for it!

The washing machine was hand powered. It had a flywheel on top, which powered the agitators inside the machine. We pushed a lever back and forth and propelled the whole apparatus. After each load was washed, we ran it through a hand-operated wringer into the rinse tub. There we rinsed the clothes by hand and then fed them through the wringer once more. From there we hung the clothes on the clothesline to dry. I don't believe we needed, nor used any kind of bleach. The sun provided all the bleaching necessary.

In the summer time the clothes dried quickly after which they were taken in and ironed. In the wintertime they froze solid on the clothesline, but the frost removed most of the moisture from them. We removed the remaining moisture from the clothes when we ironed them. I used to admire the way my mother could hang out clothes and take them in during bitter weather without ever complaining about the cold. It was one job that she could not do while wearing mitts.

Bedbugs

We had not been in the house long before we made a very unpleasant discovery. The house was infested with bedbugs! Despite our best efforts to eradicate them, they would remain the bane of our existence for many years. Bedbugs live off humans and other warm-blooded mammals by sucking their blood. They raise welts that are much larger than those caused by mosquito bites and they are also itchier. It was not long before we were perpetually covered with these welts. Fumigating to kill the bedbugs became an annual affair

Each summer, we camped outside for a couple of days while we fumigated the house with burning sulphur. First we took out all the food, as well as enough clothing, bedding, and cookware for the event. We then burned pails of sulphur in the house for a day. After we had ventilated it for another day, we moved back in. Meanwhile we cooked and ate outside. During the night we slept in the hayloft. After about three weeks we would repeat the procedure in order to kill any bedbugs that had hatched since the first fumigation.

The house would be quite liveable for a few months, but by the following spring it would again be as bad as ever. Sometimes Mother painted kerosene on the bedsteads, but I don't remember that this helped control the bugs. It was not until the end of World War II when DDT became available that we finally won the battle against these pernicious insects. Mother bought 20% DDT Barn Spray and painted the baseboards of every room, as well as each bed frame with it. Before long, there were no more bedbugs. Today this chemical has been outlawed in most countries, but without it, we should never have gotten rid of those horrible pests.

Our First Winter in Alberta

1938 began in an auspicious way when most of us got Scarlet Fever. Mrs. Follis, a former nurse who lived two miles away diagnosed it and came over and helped us. Then my sister Eva was born - on February 15th and my mother almost bled to death before the doctor from Brooks finally arrived. All the earlier children had been home-births, but after this near miss, my mother had her final four in the Brooks and Medicine Hat hospitals.

That spring we experienced the worst blizzard of the century. The latter part of March had been very warm and the snow was all gone. On March 29th or 30th a blizzard struck! It lasted two days and when it was over it left huge snowdrifts in its wake. Many of the local ranchers suffered heavy losses of cattle and sheep. A few people who were caught out in the storm died as well. We had a snow drift behind the house that was over six feet in height. We children loved it because we were able to dig a large cave in it.

At school there was a large drift adjacent to the swings. My male classmates and I took turns swinging as high as we could and then sliding of the swing seat and landing in the drift. It was such great fun that we kept on doing it as the drift melted. One day when I landed on the (by then) bare ground, my chin crashed into my knee and knocked several of my front teeth loose. They were eventually okay, but that was the end of our jumping from the swings.

Living in Extreme Poverty

We were very poor those first years, so poor that my mother sewed my sisters' dresses out of flour sacks, sugar sacks and cotton pea sacks, which she first dyed. One fortunate aspect of having a large family was that the clothes could be passed from one sibling down to the next. Mother sewed all of our clothes at first, but eventually she refused to sew the boys' overalls and bought them instead. She did continue to sew all of the girls' clothes, who as they grew older learned to sew their own. I was lucky - being the oldest of the boys – I did not have to wear any hand-me-down clothes or footwear.

During the summertime none of us wore socks in our boots. Not only did we not consider them necessary, but they would of course have added to Mother's darning load as well. When I was around fourteen or fifteen someone shit in Dad's rubber boot. I never learned who was responsible, but we all suspected Gerard. Dad was livid when he (quite literally) "put foot in it!"

Singer sewing machine like Mother's. Photo taken by the author courtesy of the Port Coquitlam Heritage Society.

Mother had brought a tabletop sewing machine with her from Denmark. She operated the machine with a hand crank. It made sewing slow and difficult because it left her with only one free hand to handle the cloth. One day a Singer Sewing Machine salesman dropped in to see us. My father told him that there was no way that we could afford a sewing machine, nevertheless the salesman insisted on demonstrating it. When he was ready to leave, he wanted to leave the machine with us, but of course we demurred. He kept insisting that he would leave it for the time being and retrieve it the next time he came, so Dad finally gave in. Meanwhile he assured Mother that she was free to use it since it was a "demo" anyway.

Next time the salesman showed up, he again insisted on leaving it. My father told him that he was wasting his time – that we could never afford it. The salesman said that was okay, that we could pay for it if and when we had some spare money. The sewing machine was a treadle operated machine that came with its own cabinet complete with drawers in which were stored all the needed accessories such as needles, bobbins, thread and the oil can etc. My mother's sewing production must have increased substantially because each time the salesman dropped in our protests became weaker. I have no idea how long it took, but we did eventually pay for it.

While we were youngsters, we went barefoot during the summer, but this was not at all unusual. Most of the other children in the area did so too. When we did wear boots, it was always without socks until the weather turned cold.

Preparing the annual fall Eaton's order was an exciting event. In addition to overalls, I remember mother buying a winter mackinaw for me as well. We purchased all of our footwear from the catalogue too. We boys all wore boots that probably cost $2 - $3 a pair. During the winter we also wore overshoes over top of the boots to protect them. We did not have dress footwear, but had to polish the work boots every Saturday afternoon to prepare them for wearing to church on Sunday morning.

During our second winter in Tilley, my father got a license to gill-net fish in Lake Newell. He brought home several hundred pounds of Whitefish and we practically lived on them for the following year. We had a hired man during that summer and he must have been a saint to put up with all the canned fish Mother fed him.

We churned butter from the cream our cows produced. I would regularly have to carry butter and eggs over four miles to the grocer before going to school. The money from these products paid for most of the essentials we purchased from him. During the worst times, instead of eating our own butter, we used lard because it was cheaper. We even tried to make our own flour by putting wheat through the feed grinder a number of times. This did not work very well because no amount of grinding turned out flour fine enough for baking.

We had a strict rule about eating in our house - we had to finish our main course before we were allowed to have dessert. As the later children were born, the enforcement of this rule was gradually relaxed. We older children resented very much that the younger ones were treated more leniently than we had been. Another rule applied to the sharing of cake or dessert within the family. Whoever cut the cake or divided the dessert got the last pick. We each learned to divide the cakes and desserts with mathematical precision so that we would not to be stuck with the smallest portion if we were the server.

When Mother baked cakes or cookies, we youngsters vied for the privileges of cleaning the mixing bowl. We wiped the dough off the inside of the bowl with a finger and then licked the dough off the finger. I don't remember when it happened, but Mother eventually acquired a rubber spatula called a "kitchen maid" with which she could clean the mixing bowl much more thoroughly. We children were very disappointed. From then on, there was practically no dough left in the bowl for us to clean up.

The diet in our family relied heavily on potatoes and vegetables as well as on home made bread and fatty pork. Breakfast invariably relied on oatmeal – the old slow cooking variety. Our school lunches consisted of a couple of sandwiches - one with jam and the other with headcheese. I have long since gotten over my aversion to oatmeal porridge, but my older sister Ester still refuses to eat it.

In a family as large as ours, we consumed a lot of bread – all of it home baked. Mother started the yeast in the evening to have it ready for the following day. In the morning after breakfast she prepared the dough and set it above the warming oven to rise. She punched it down at least twice during the day and then put into baking pans to rise one last time. In the evening after supper she finally baked it. We all looked forward eagerly to the bread coming out of the oven, for we could then have warm buttered bread covered with jam or honey. Normally Mother baked at least eight very large loaves at a time and this usually lasted us for most of the week. She baked both white as well as brown bread, but we all liked the white variety better because it was much lighter that the brown bread.

1939

Nineteen thirty-nine was a fateful year. The king and queen visited Canada during that summer and it was also the year that World War II broke out. Dad took us out of the potato field and into town to see the royal pair as their train came through Tilley. Our classmates and most of the townspeople were there as well. We were thrilled when the King and Queen stepped out on to the observation platform of the train and waved to us as they sped through town. The school, had previously, issued us miniature Union Jack flags. We all waved these flags furiously as the train with its important passengers sped by.

Later that summer I was in the field with my dad one day when I saw my first airplanes. There were seven of them, and my father told me that we would probably soon be at war with Germany. From that time on, we saw planes frequently because there were training bases not too far away. The planes usually flew in pairs or in very small groups and often at very low altitude. One evening one of them crashed on Jens Jensen's farm two miles away. When we visited the site a couple of days later, much to my disappointment, the wreckage had already been removed. On another occasion we did see the wreckage of a plane that had gone down on Alex Crumka's farm just south of town.

One important change the war brought to us was the rationing of sugar, liquor and gasoline. We were not much affected by it, yet except for Dad we all stopped putting sugar in our coffee. During late summer, extra supplements of sugar were allowed for canning. Because our family was so large, we were able to buy a 100-pound sack of it at one time. We were probably the only family in the area that ever did this.

Food Preservation

Electrical power did not arrive in our community until some years after I had left home. Food preservation was therefore an important activity in every farm household. Butchering for the family was usually done in the late fall or early winter when fresh meat could be preserved by freezing it outside. We hung some of the meat in bags on the north side of the house where it would quickly freeze and remain so until it was used. We canned some of the meat, but the pork hams and bacon sides were all salted and later smoked. We never did have a smokehouse, so my father brushed it with "liquid smoke," which appeared to produce the same end result.

We grew all of our own food except for a few staples such as flour, salt, sugar and spices. Since we had cows, we were never short of dairy products. We churned butter, which we sold to the local grocer. My mother made cottage cheese regularly and this was the only kind of cheese we ate. We had a Danish friend who made real (regular) cheese and I remember us having some of that once. When we were in the direst straits, we did not even eat our own butter, but used homemade lard instead. Our chickens supplied us with both eggs and fresh meat, but again, we usually ate the eggs sparingly because they were saleable. The chickens we ate were of course never plump young ones, but old laying hens or old roosters.

Our gardens in addition to supplying all of our vegetables also boasted raspberries, two black currant bushes and two crab apple trees. We generally had some strawberry plants as well, but the rhubarb plants were our main source of fruit. We used them for

A washtub & wringer
make a great pea shelling machine.
Photo taken by the author
courtesy of the Brooks Museum

29

making both desserts and jam. We often mixed in a few strawberries with the rhubarb to make that jam more delectable, but I don't remember us ever having pure strawberry jam. Next to the rhubarb, the black currants supplied most of the fruit for Mother's jams. We always canned the crab apples and used them for dessert. We also grew citrons, which we canned and ate for dessert. In addition to making jams and canning desserts, we also canned peas, tomatoes and beans regularly. We made large quantities of pickles from beets, cucumbers and vegetable marrow. Canning was a very important activity in every household, but especially so in ours. The vast majority of the jars we used were of the two-quart variety. It was a major undertaking to pick, shell and can enough peas to last us through the winter. When we discovered that we could use the clothes wringer to shell the peas, our productivity took a quantum leap. We scalded the pea pods then fed them through the wringer by the handful. The pods proceeded through the wringer, while the peas were ejected back into the tub from where we could scoop them up with ease.

Dad did the butchering for many of the Danes in our community. He was typically rewarded for his service with the pig's head, from which my mother made headcheese. Eventually Mother rebelled and demanded that he ask his friends for something more substantial in value than just a pig's-head (which they would probably have discarded anyway). I came to loathe head cheese and it was many years after I had grown up before I could even think of eating it again. The only animals we butchered for our own consumption were old sows and occasionally an old cow. All our good animals were sold to the slaughterhouse in Calgary. My father loved fat pork, but I developed an aversion to it, and eventually it got so bad that I could no longer eat it. This infuriated my father who was convinced that I was just being picky about my food, (a major crime in our house). I suspect that my body was rebelling against it and that was why I could no longer make myself eat it.

Ailments

When someone in the family got a communicable disease, it usually spread through the entire family. This was the case when we all got Scarlet Fever. The only "childhood disease I missed was the "Mumps" and I did not get "Red Measles" until I was twenty one years old. In a large family such as hours, colds and flu were not rare. If we did not feel like going to school or doing some specific chore, we sometimes feigned illness. Of course our siblings could be counted on to accuse one of "just pretending" on such occasions.

I have never been one to walk in my sleep, but it did happen once. I was feeling under the weather and I was very tired as well. I awoke one morning from a feverish dream still fresh in my consciousness. I dreamed that I had been doing the chores and milking the cows had been especially vivid. When I got out of bed and went down into the kitchen, there on the floor was a pail partly filled with fresh milk.

Chapter 4 - Farming

Plowing and Seeding

The first operation on the land each spring was plowing it. One sight I shall never forget was the large number of seagulls following behind the plow. As the plow turned the soil over, they feasted on the exposed worms and bugs. Another thing I will never forget is the pungent smell of that freshly turned soil.

A 2 bottom plow. Most tractors pulled at least a 3 bottom machine. *Photo taken by the author courtesy of Heritage Acres Antique Threshing Club, Pincher Creek, Alberta.*

After we finished the plowing, we harrowed the field and leveled it with a "float." The float made it easier for the irrigation water to spread over the ground, but it also contributed to soil drifting when the winds came up. Today many farmers no longer plow the land, but seed it without any preparation.

Seeding was the final operation, but sometimes we waited for the weeds to sprout first so that we could eradicate them with the cultivator before seeding. This delayed the crop for at least three weeks, but it ensured that the weeds wouldn't be quite so bad. Today the farmers control the weeds with the use of herbicides.

Before seeding, we first cleaned the seed-grain and then treated it with a fungicide so that it wouldn't rot in the ground. To clean it we fed the grain through a hand cranked "fan mill." This operation blew off the chaff, while the vibrating screens removed most of the weed seeds as well as the broken grain kernels. I believe that the fungicide we used contained mercury. We mixed it into the cleaned grain

A typical 16' wide seed drill. Photo taken by the author courtesy of Heritage Acres Antique Threshing Club, Pincher Creek, Alberta.

shortly before seeding it, for treated seed is unfit for consumption by either man or beast.

We seeded the grain with a "seed drill," a machine that did a sixteen foot wide strip at a time with rows about eight inches apart. Seed drills were often equipped with an attachment for depositing fertilizer at the same time. The use of chemical fertilizer had begun shortly before I left the farm. Most farmers typically applied around 50 pounds per acre. Today the farmers use about 300 pounds and obtain twice the yields that we did.

After seeding, we constructed temporary irrigation ditches. This operation took three to four days. Once the irrigation was finished and the crops ready to harvest, we filled these ditches back in to facilitate harvesting.

Irrigation

South-eastern Alberta is a semi desert that has an average annual precipitation of only 10 inches; not nearly enough to grow grain or any other kind of produce. The area depended entirely on irrigation so Lake Newell was established to provide water storage for that purpose. It lay about a dozen miles west from the edge of the Tilley community and the water was diverted into it from the Bow River at a dam near Bassano.

The 100'wide Bantry Canal brings water from Lake Newell to the Tilley and other areas.. Photo taken by the author.

The lake seemed huge to me because it stretched much farther than my young (the) eyes could see. Its actual size is about 16 miles in length and half that at its widest. There were large numbers of Pike in this lake (also called Jackfish), as well as Whitefish and Suckers. There were also several varieties of waterfowl including seagulls, pelican, snipe, killdeer and a number of duck and goose species.

When we arrived, there were no screens at the lake's outlets, so we often found fish (especially pike) in our field ditches. Not only were they fun to catch, but they were also a welcome addition to our diet. We children were very disappointed when the District installed screens at the outlets from the Lake. For from then on, there were no longer fish in our ditches.

The water was delivered to the communities through large canals. From there it was delivered to individual farms by smaller, but permanent canals. It was up to the farmer to construct both the permanent and the temporary ditches needed to distribute the water on his land. Situating the temporary ditches properly required some farmers to survey them in with a level, but Dad was able do it without using any instruments except his eyes. These ditches were "V" shaped with the excavated material forming a continuous levee above the surrounding ground. We flooded the fields by temporarily damming the ditch with a square piece of canvas attached to a five or six foot pole. The water was let out of the ditch via holes cut in the ditch banks at regular intervals. Each ditch occupied a strip of land about 2 yards wide. Since the ditches were typically spaced from 30 to 40 yards apart, they took up a sizeable portion of the arable land.

A control structure that helps allocate the water into smaller canals. *Photo taken by the author*

Today flood irrigation is becoming a thing of the past. Most of the small canals are gone and the water is brought to the fields in underground pipes. Most farmers now use sprinklers instead. When I visited the area recently, I was amazed at the number of "pivot systems" in use.

A pivot system consists of a vertical pipe riser in the middle of the field. Long pipe sections joined together and mounted on wheels pivot around the riser. Such a system typically waters an area one half mile in diameter. Some systems have auxiliary systems that do the corners of the field. Everything is controlled by computer, and once started up, requires no labor to maintain.

Field irrigation ditch with a canvas dam. *Photo taken by the author courtesy of The E.I.D. Historical Park in Scandia, Alberta.*

The canals and main ditches were permanent structures. They required maintenance to keep them free of water willows, reeds and other growth that diminished their capacity. All ditches that brought water to more than one farmer were the responsibility of the District. Permanent ditches for the farmer's convenience were his own responsibility. Chopping down and burning willows was therefore an ongoing project each winter. When the work was for the District, it created paid employment and this was always a welcome source of cash.

Depending upon the amount of rainfall, most of the farmers in the district irrigated the fields once or twice during each season. Where we lived we got less rainfall than our neighbors who lived farther west. Furthermore because of the high clay content of our soil, as well as the topography not being as flat, we typically had to water our fields one more time than our friends to the west had to. A man could irrigate between five and ten acres per day, depending on his ability and the amount of water available. On our farm, we therefore spent most of the summer irrigating. By the time we had finished the first irrigation, it was time to begin the next.

Irrigating was not particularly hard work, but it required long hours every day and the mosquitoes made the work uncomfortable. Our area was probably the worst mosquito breeding ground in Canada, due to the stagnant water in the borrow pits along the main ditches. During the early morning and late evening these insects swarmed around us in dense clouds and made life especially miserable. They plagued not only people but the livestock as well. When the insects became particularly bad, we often lit smudges (smoky fires made from burning dried manure) in the pasture. The cows and horses were quick to discover the benefit of standing in the smoke to escape the insects.

One aspect of irrigating was the never-ending drama provided by the waterfowl. Sea gulls always attended in large numbers to feast on the worms and mice driven to the surface by the water. There were also killdeer, snipes and other waterfowl present most of the time. Whenever a sea gull caught a mouse, an aerial show would ensue, as all the other gulls tried to steal it. Invariably the first gull would be forced to drop its prey, which would not fall very far before another gull would snatch it. This scenario would then be repeated – often several times before one of them finally swallowed the mouse. I never once saw a mouse consumed by the seagull that originally caught it.

Horse drawn mower. *Photo taken by the author courtesy of Heritage Acres Antique Threshing Club, Pincher Creek, Alberta.*

Grain & Alfalfa

When we first moved to Alberta, the farmers in our area grew mostly wheat. After the war ended, it became increasingly difficult to sell, so the government instituted incentive programs to cut down on the wheat acreage. One of these incentives was to pay farmers to "summer fallow" the land (cultivate the land to rid it of weeds while not growing a crop on it). Wheat quotas were also used. As a result of these and other measures, the farmers gradually began to switch to other crops.

Horse drawn rake. *Photo taken by the author courtesy of Heritage Acres Antique Threshing Club, Pincher Creek, Alberta.*

Alfalfa had always been an important crop because it was needed to feed the livestock and to regenerate the soil. However, alfalfa seed became increasingly important as did seed peas. Another crop that attained importance was flax. Flax though, depleted the soil more than any other crop we grew. Barley and oats also began to supplant the wheat acreage, but they too became increasingly difficult to sell. This led to more and more farmers getting into the livestock business. Calves (and sometimes lambs) were purchased in the fall and fattened during the winter for sale the following spring or early summer. In this way the farmers were able to dispose of a fair amount of their feed grain. By the time I left home, we no longer grew very much wheat and fed much of our grain to the livestock instead. One benefit of doing this was the ability to utilize frozen and other low-grade grains that had poor commercial value.

In addition to providing hay for the livestock, the most important function of alfalfa was to restore nitrogen to the soil and to displace weeds. The alfalfa was always seeded together with a cover crop – usually of oats to protect it during its first season. It would then be harvested two to three times each summer for three years, at which time it was plowed under and the land returned to grain production.

Now-a-days alfalfa is baled and stored as soon as it has been windrowed and sun dried. There is little physical work involved, but that was not the case when I grew up. We first cut the alfalfa with a horse drawn mower and later with a tractor attached one. Next the newly mown hay would be raked into windrows and then the windrows were made into mini-stacks by hand. After the alfalfa was properly cured, it was loaded, hauled on hayracks and stacked by hand. This was labor intensive work and it was therefore not too many years before stacking machines displaced the old methods.

A John Deere grain binder. It cuts the grain and ties it into bundles. *Photo taken by the author courtesy of the Brooks Museum*

In the early years our neighbor, Art Burton and Dad typically worked together, first stacking the hay on one farm and then on the other. My father was a very powerful man. Whereas the neighbor needed to take two forkfuls to load a mini-stack, my father invariably could do it in one forkful! The first year or two we hauled the hay to the stack with two horses hitched to a hayrack on wheels. There the hay was deposited and spread on the stack entirely by hand. Later on, we still used the hayrack, but without the wheels under it. Instead we used four horses to skid the hayrack on the ground. This made loading it easier since it was about three feet lower than it had been on wheels. The biggest saving in labor was however done at the haystack. Instead of pitching off the hay by hand, we rolled it off using two ropes that had first been placed on the floor of the hayrack before loading it in the field. My dad, standing on the stack, would take the ends of these two ropes and set a pitchfork down on top of them to help him hold them. The other ends of these two ropes were joined and connected to a larger rope which the horses then pulled to roll the load off the rack in one fell swoop and up onto the haystack. Using this method, there was virtually no limit to the height we could build a stack. To control the load as it came rolling up onto the stack, Dad steered it by letting a one or the other rope slip as needed. Once the load was up on the stack, I got to spread it while the men went for another load.

It was not too many years before all stacking was done by machine. Later when I worked in Scandia, my employer had a buck rake that was pulled by horses. This rake brought the hay to the stack where another machine threw it up on to the stack. A Tilley farmer named Kirchner invented a stacker that was pushed in front of a tractor. It not only brought the hay from the field, but also placed it on the stack.

During the winter we replenished the hayloft in the barn from the field stacks, and in later years when we fattened beef in our feedlot, we took the hay directly from the stacks to feed them. Generally we also sold surplus hay right out of the stack to cattle ranchers for $3 - $5 per ton. The later in the winter we sold the hay, the higher the price we tended to get for it.

During our first years in Alberta, the farmers all cut the grain using binders. The binder cut the grain and tied it into bundles. We then set the bundles upright into stooks where it finished ripening before it was threshed. The grain was threshed when a threshing crew became available.

When the threshing crew arrived, they loaded the bundles on to hayracks and hauled them to the threshing machine, which separated the grain from the straw.

A threshing machine like this was used before combines took over. *Photo taken by the author courtesy of Heritage Acres Antique Threshing Club, Pincher Creek, Alberta.*

The grain was hauled to the elevators in town for immediate sale, or stored in granaries on the farm for later disposal. The straw was blown from the thresher into large stacks that we either burned or saved for livestock bedding. In later years when the combines replaced the threshing machines, the straw was spread in the fields and we children had no more straw stacks on which to play.

A typical threshing crew consisted of about twelve men. The number varied, depending on the size of the thresher and the distance the bundles had to be hauled. There were usually six to eight teams of horses hitched to hayracks bringing the grain to the thresher. These men were often assisted in the field by a couple of men who "floated" from one wagon to the next. At the thresher there was also a man who did nothing except

Threshing stacked grain on our farm circa 1948. *From the author's collection.*

help unload the wagons. The straw was blown on to a stack and the grain was augured into a hopper from where a trucker hauled it to the elevators in town. The threshing machine was often owned in common by several farmers. One of these men would be the designated foreman - in charge of tending the machine full time. A tractor powered the thresher via a long heavy rubber belt. A typical crew could usually clean up a quarter section in two or three days, depending on the yield.

Feeding a threshing crew was a major event for every housewife. Some of the crew-members would sleep in the hayloft overnight, but even those who went home at the night would be back in time for breakfast by 6:00 AM. Since it was hard physical work the men had huge appetites. At midmorning the wife brought or sent coffee and cake out to the crew in the field, and then went on to prepare the noon meal. At mid afternoon, she would again send out coffee and cake before going on to prepare supper, which she usually served around 6:00 or 7:00 PM.

A typical wife with no grown children would as a rule enlist the help of another farm wife for those important days. In addition to cooking for a large crew, she would also have to milk the cows and do the farm chores. The food not only had to be plentiful and good, but she also had to bake and serve cakes and pies as well. Pies were cut into four pieces, not six, and it was not uncommon for a man to eat two pieces of pie at a meal. The pie consumption alone was therefore be quite substantial. An old Hungarian farmer once told me that his people had a saying; "No pork, no work. No pie, goodbye!" It is little wonder then why Mother used to marvel at Mrs. Sickel, the neighbor lady who not only did the farm chores and the cooking all alone, but even helped pitch bundles for an hour or two each day. She must have been one well-organized and tough little lady!

Potatoes

Dad grew several acres of potatoes every year and he always picked the weediest area on the farm on which to grow them. The idea was to clear the area of thistles and wild oats through the intensive cultivation the potatoes required. This gave us lots of work to do. We first tilled the potatoes with a horse drawn single row cultivator and then followed it up with manual hoeing. When I became old enough, I walked many miles behind a horse drawn cultivator. We used this cultivator not only for

Potato planter. *Photo taken by the author courtesy of The Brooks Museum*

loosening the soil and cutting the weeds between the rows, but also for "hilling" the potatoes. Even with the cultivator having eliminated most of the weeds, the work of hoeing the remaining weeds was still a daunting and tiring task.

Wherever potatoes are grown the Colorado Potato Beetles flourish. These beetles suddenly appear in huge numbers when the potato plants near maturity. If not exterminated promptly, they quickly eat the leaves, making the plants unable to nourish the developing potatoes. It is therefore important to kill the beetles as soon as they appear. I no longer remember what insecticide we used, but we borrowed a hand-operated sprayer and I would walk up and down the rows and carefully spray each and every plant. If memory serves me correctly, I would have to do this twice each

A potato digger similar to one we often borrowed. Photo taken by the author courtesy of The E.I.D. Historical Park in Scandia, Alberta.

season. Considering that the potato plants were about two feet apart in the rows, which in turn were three feet apart, a little arithmetic suggests that for each acre of potatoes, I would have to spray more than 7000 plants.

Potatoes thrive better in a sandy-loam type of soil. It is important that the soil drains well and the sand content of the soil is therefore important. The reason we hill the potatoes is to promote drainage and to make sure no potato is exposed to sunlight. Sunlight turns a potato green and unfit for consumption. Our soil was a heavy clay gumbo that did not drain well, so many of our potatoes became very knobby. Such potatoes were classed as culls and had little commercial value. One labor intensive job I had each winter was hand sorting all of the potatoes into Grades 1, 2 and culls. The culls consisted of the knobby potatoes as well as those that had been cut, or were too small. These were saved for our own consumption and for seed potatoes for the following year.

Planting potatoes and harvesting them was a labor intensive job. In the spring the seed potatoes had first to be cut into pieces with each piece optimally containing two eyes (each eye will become a single sprout). Our plantings the first years consisted of walking behind a plow and depositing a piece of potato every two feet in the furrow left by the plow. We carried the potatoes in a pail that had to be replenished each time it was emptied. For a skinny runt like me, this was back breaking work. In later years we were able to borrow a mechanical planter each spring; nevertheless, preparing the seed-potatoes was still an arduous chore.

Compared to harvesting the potatoes, seeding them was a snap! Our early efforts consisted of plowing them out of the ground. We, on our hands and knees would then rummage through the soil and extract the potatoes, place them in pails and dump them in a heap from which to gather them later. The problem with using a plow was that it was not only difficult to find them, but the operation cut a lot of potatoes in half, turning them into culls. In later years we were always able to borrow a potato digger to replace the plow. The digger separated the potatoes and the tops from the soil and dropped them on top of the ground. From there we could then pick them up into pails as before. I once visited a large well run potato farm during the harvest. The digger they used there was much larger and more modern than anything I had previously seen. A person stood on a running board on each side of the digger and removed the tops and dirt clods. As with the older diggers, the soil fell away from the potatoes through the course screening. The clean potatoes were then directed into burlap sacks at the rear of the digger where a man tied the 100-pound bags and dropped them off on to the ground for later retrieval.

As soon as we had harvested the potatoes, we would immediately sell some of them. Because all the potatoes in the countryside were harvested at about the same time, there would be a glut on the market and hence a very low price for them. It was therefore necessary for us to store them and then sell them periodically during the winter. Our root cellars could not contain all of our potatoes so we usually stored many of them in the field. There we covered them first with a layer of straw and potato-tops, and then with soil to protect them from the cold weather. Whenever the weather was warm enough and when there was room in the cellar, we would retrieve the potatoes from this temporary field storage.

As the years passed, potatoes became a more consequential product in the area. In order to raise awareness and to educate the young people, 4H potato clubs were formed. My sister Inger and I both became members of such a club. In return for writing winning essays on potatoes we both won trips to both Duchess and later to Calgary. There we were further educated on the care and cultivation of this important crop.

Farm Tractors

This tractor is similar to our McCormick Deering. *Photo taken by the author courtesy of Heritage Acres Antique Threshing Club, Pincher Creek, Alberta.*

When we first arrived in Tilley, Dad often used his old 1923 Dodge car to pull the farm wagon in the field. The car was built like a tractor as far as the driveline was concerned. However, eventually we could no longer buy parts for that old car, so we used the undercarriage to make a rubber tired wagon. We replaced the Dodge with a 1926 Chevrolet sedan. My father tried to pull equipment with this car too, but soon learned the hard way that this car was not built like a tractor!

Another aspect of the Chev was that we could never keep brakes in it. I learned to drive it when I was fourteen years old. At that time I had already been driving the tractor alone for over a year. Driving a car without brakes is different! When you come to where you want to stop, you must slow down, then shift down into low gear and turn off the ignition at the right moment. Done correctly, and with the judicious use of the clutch, you can stop the car pretty much where you wish. However, this does not work well in an emergency when you have no time to plan the stop.

One day on the way home from church I was following behind another parishioner. A pickup truck was coming towards us from the other direction, when without any warning; both vehicles came to a stop (the drivers wanted to chat). I had no time to do anything but try to make it through the gap between them. I almost made it too, but I creased the running board of the car I had been following. This was my only mishap during the years I drove that car. I did not tell my dad about it, but he heard about it soon enough from the neighbor whose car I had damaged!

In 1937 when we arrived in Tilley very few people had tractors, but still farmed with horses. Within a few years things had changed dramatically. Our neighbor, Art Burton, continued to farm with horses for several more years, but he was the exception. When we bought the farm, its price included a "McCormick Deering 15-30" tractor and a three-bottom plow. Most of the other farmers bought John Deere Model D tractors. They were much lighter, easier to steer and had more power than ours. Those early tractors all had steel wheels with big steel lugs on them. In one respect they were better than the rubber tired tractors that came later – they didn't compress the soil the way the rubber tired ones did. However, their top speed was around four miles per hour. Moving them from one farm to another was therefore slow.

By the time I was fourteen, my father had me do all the mechanical maintenance on our tractor. I of course did this work during the off season – usually in winter during a Chinook. The steel was always extremely cold to the touch, and I couldn't keep my small hands warm, so I hated the job. My tools did not include such modern ones as sockets and ratchets, but only open end or box-end wrenches, pliers and a crescent wrench. One annual job was to change the connecting rod bearings as well as the piston rings. It was a tedious job with the tools I had, and I swore then that I would never be a mechanic. Over the next few years, I worked on every single part of that old McCormick Deering tractor. From those experiences I did get a pretty fair mechanical knowledge of tractors which later stood me in good stead.

Our second tractor was a small John Deere Model B "row crop" tractor with rubber tires. It could pull only a two-bottom plow, but was powerful enough for all of our other implements. Still later we got a larger John Deere row crop tractor (Model G) as well as an old Model D to replace the McCormick Deering. This was after my dad acquired 80 acres of raw land at the edge of the district some 7 miles to the west. During the fall, after the crops had been threshed, it was customary to begin plowing the fields if the weather held. One fall when I was only nine or ten, my father got me to ride on the plow in the evenings after I came home from school. He wanted me to assist him in raising and lowering the plow at the field corners, but I suspect that he just wanted my company. It worked okay until I got my heel severely pinched in some moving part of the plow. Mother would not let me ride the plow after that. After I turned eleven, I began driving the old "McCormick Deering 15-30" under Dad's supervision. It was

John Deere Model B "Row Crop" trac-tor. Photo taken by the author in 2001 near Kamloops, BC.

a heavy, clumsy and an awkward machine to handle - far too much for a skinny little runt like me. I was not able to drive it alone until the summer I was thirteen. From then on I spent more time at home on the farm than at school. During grades eight, nine and ten, I attended school an average of ninety days each year. Today that would no longer be allowed.

Miscellaneous Farm Work

When I was thirteen and my sister Ester, seventeen, we not only cut and stooked all the grain on our farm, but we loaded, hauled and stacked it too while Dad was away, working on the threshing crew. By stacking the grain we protected it from the weather and also eliminated the need for about seven to eight men and their teams to haul it to the threshing machine. Furthermore, our grain could be threshed after the others were finished with theirs - even after winter set in. Threshing late in the season when not much work was going on, guaranteed us lower prices for the threshing crew.

In the fall during and after the threshing, it was customary to burn most of the straw stacks. It made for quite a sight to see burning straw stacks dotting the countryside. We children had mixed feelings about burning the stacks because they were great fun to play on.

During spring and summer I usually drove the tractor or irrigated the fields. During these times I was relieved of doing the chores - my mother and/or younger siblings did them instead. During the winter though, in addition to the outside work, I would often have to help in the house as well. At these times my father would do some of the chores because he was not busy in the fields. When my younger brothers got old enough, they too helped me with the chores.

After all the snow was gone in April, and the fields were bare, we sometimes got a light overnight snowfall. The following day the gopher mounds would be highly visible because the gophers when cleaning out their burrows would spread fresh dirt on top of the white snow. I would then have to stay home from school and poison them. I mixed the gopher poison (made with strychnine) with oats and placed a spoonful of it well down in each burrow out of the reach of any birds. Gophers like weeds were an ongoing problem on the farm.

We usually kept only one house cat, but had several other cats in the barn. Twice each summer the female cats had kittens, and since we could not allow the cats to multiply we had to dispose of them. It was a distasteful job that usually fell to me. The standard method was to place them in a burlap sack accompanied by a brick or two, and drown them. Veterinarians were not available then, but even if they had been, no one in those days would have considered their services for a chore of this kind. Spaying pets was then unheard of in our society.

Growing up on a farm during my youth entailed a never-ending routine of milking cows and feeding the livestock. I also had clean the manure out of the barn, pig sty, and chicken coop. Feeding and milking was done twice daily, while cleaning out the manure was done once a day. My day typically began with milking two or three cows and then letting them out into the pasture. I then came into the house and ran the milk through the "cream separator," (to remove the cream from the milk), before eating my breakfast. After eating (if I wasn't in school that day) I would go out and tend to the other animals. I carried chopped grain to the pigs amid much squealing as they fought for space at the troughs. Next I carried water for them from the stock pond in two five gallon pails, shoveled manure into a wheel barrow and wheeled it on to the manure pile, spread fresh straw in the stalls and in the pig sty. Lastly, I brought water and grain to the chickens, but 1 did not have to clean the chicken coop every day.

Even after tractors became commonplace, the farmers retained a few horses for doing odd jobs on the farm. These included hauling hay, hauling grain to the threshing machine and spreading manure. A few farmers also kept a saddle horse each. Everyone bred a few cows to provide the farm with milk products and beef. Most farmers also raised at least enough pigs for their own consumption. No one went without chickens and many raised a few ducks and geese as well. This ensured that there were always animals that had to be watered and fed. No one could go away for a period of time unless they first made arrangements for someone else to look after the animals during their absence. This has all changed now. Today the only livestock in the area is to be found in the feedlots or on the large pig farms. The farmers now purchase their milk and eggs, and no one does his own butchering anymore.

Chapter 5 - Livestock

Our Teams

Just before Easter the year that I was 14 my dad borrowed a team of horses from a neighbor named Wester. One day the horses got out and disappeared. I spent the Easter holidays in the saddle scouring the surrounding prairie for them while riding from forty to fifty miles every day. The country was gently rolling and I can remember wondering what I would find over the next rise, and then over the next one, etc. Of course the only thing I found was more of the same. Occasionally I encountered an abandoned farmstead that the "dust-bowl" had claimed some years earlier. Once in a while I found a farm still occupied.

One feature every "dry farm" had in common was a windmill used to pump water from a well. The water was extremely alkaline and very hard for me to drink. Too much of it would cause diarrhea for anyone not accustomed to it. During that week I also encountered the occasional sheepherder and his flocks of sheep. These men seldom saw another human being and some of them found it difficult to socialize.

Eventually we got word that the horses had been found. They had returned to the farm at Jenner, where they had been born - some 30 miles away. The weekend following the Easter holidays, I rode over to Jenner and brought them back.

On another occasion I borrowed a team of horses from a neighbor named English. I hitched the team up to our rubber tired wagon, and then drove to our nearby neighbor to pick up some milk for my mother - our own cows were dry at the time. The team was spirited and not well broken and on the way home they took off as fast as they could run. They were going full out and I could not even begin to slow them down. Even though the road was fairly smooth, the milk sloshed out of the pail and on to the wagon floor. There we were, thundering down the road with me sliding all over on the slippery wagon floor trying to stay on my feet. When we came to our gate, the horse on the right wanted to turn in, but I was able to keep it going straight ahead. Turning in at that speed would have tipped over the wagon.

Finally, after running flat out for two miles, I was able to bring them to a halt. I turned the wagon around and drove back home, where hitched them up to a hayrack. Since it was now time for lunch, I tethered them to a fence post while I went in to eat. Unfortunately, they managed to break the rope and take off yet again. This time they ran all over the farm, back and forth across ditches, destroying the borrowed hayrack in the process. My father had to replace it at substantial cost so he was very angry with me.

A few days later I was raking hay with them when once again they took off. This time when I was unable to stop them, fearing that I might fall off in front of the rake where they would drag me to death, I somersaulted myself backwards off the rake and let them go. This time I was lucky. They did not damage the rake or anything else. That was the last time we ever borrowed that particular team.

We later bought a team from a Mr. Follis. These horses were each a cross between a Percheron (work horse) and a Standard Bred (saddle horse). They were tall rangy animals – a gelding named Monty that had been broken for riding as well as for harness, and a mare named Alice. I did not particularly like to ride Monty because it had a very rough gait. Alice had been broken for harness only and I never tried to ride her. This team just loved to run. I often hitched them up to our rubber tired wagon for going to Church or some other place. They could keep up a 12 mile-per-hour pace for many miles without tiring and were a joy to drive!

Ester's Horse

My sister Ester had a saddle horse, which she left at home on the farm after she went to work in Calgary. His name was Prince, he was white and of medium size and build. He was so gentle that small children could walk around him, over him, and even under him with no fear of being hurt. I often rode him, sometimes to bring in the cows for milking, sometimes on errands, and sometimes to visit friends. I seldom bothered using a saddle or bridle because a halter and rope was enough to let him know where I wanted to go.

Riding Prince with just a halter rope did sometimes present problems - he liked to chase cars! Without a bridle I could not control him if he wanted to go. If I was riding him on the road and a car passed us, I could be assured of a short burst of speed from him as he tried to keep up with the vehicle. It did not matter in which direction the car was going either.

One afternoon after school I was riding over to see someone a couple of miles away. I was just past the Renfrew School when I saw an old convertible full of people coming towards us. Knowing what Prince would do, I urged him into a full gallop hoping that he would not turn around and chase the car. We arrived at a small ditch at the cross-roads just as the car came abreast. Instead of jumping the ditch, Prince came to an abrupt halt and I slid up his neck right to his ears. Before I could recover and get back to my normal place on his back, he had turned and was in full pursuit of the car. The car occupants had a great laugh at my expense as they waved and yelled at us. This went on until we had raced behind them for almost a half-mile and Prince was ready for a breather.

One Sunday afternoon after church, our parents had some friends and their young children over for lunch. After the meal we took turns riding Prince, (using only the halter and rope). It was a lovely sunny afternoon – perfect for such a pastime. When my turn came, I vaulted onto Prince's back, kicked him in the ribs and away we went. I was coming back towards the house at a full gallop when all hell suddenly broke loose under me and I found myself flat on my back on the ground. Prince immediately stopped, stood there and looked me in the eye as if to say; "you are sixteen and old enough for a bit of horseplay." From that day on, it occasionally bucked me off when I rode him bareback, but it remained as gentle as ever with young children.

Cows

Cows have a definite "pecking order." The boss cow always leads the herd wherever it goes. This may be into the pasture or into the barn, or sometimes for the sheer joy of it, anywhere but where you want them to go. In the wintertime, we usually kept the cows inside the barn during very cold weather. They would leave the barn only for their daily drink at the stock pond and would be very pleased to get back into the warm barn as quickly as possible.

Chinooks often terminated prolonged cold spells. In such instances the cows obviously enjoyed the freedom of getting out after being cooped up in the barn for days or weeks on end. They would not be at all anxious to return to the barn at milking time. I remember on some such occasions going out into the field to bring them in for the milking. Typically they offered no resistance and would follow the leader right up to the barn door. And that was where the fun began! The leader would stop right at the door, turn its head and look me square in the eye - I could almost see it grin. Then at that moment it would take off at a gallop with the others behind it, to the far end of the field half mile away.

After one or more tries with the same results, I would catch, saddle up Prince and ride out for the cows on horseback. As soon as the cows saw me on Prince they immediately ran for the barn and directly into their appropriate stalls. It seemed to me that they just needed to have some fun with me after being cooped up in the barn for so long.

One occasional problem on the farm was that of cows getting into the alfalfa field. This was especially bad in the early morning when there was dew on the alfalfa. This sometimes resulted in a bloated animal. If this happened the animal could be saved if it was treated quickly enough, but if not, the results were always fatal. Our treatment consisted of punching a hole into the affected stomach (a bovine has four of them) to relieve the gas pressure. Before doing that we might try to force a few ounces of kerosene down the animal's throat to make it start burping. There was also medicine available that would alleviate the symptoms if administered soon enough. Our neighbor, Harry Burton was not a vet, but he had some practical experience and he kept a small stock of veterinary medicines and we sometimes fetched him if he was available.

When a sheep or cow becomes bloated, it lies on it side with its legs sticking straight out and its eyes rolled back with the pupils out of sight. Its stomach becomes so distended that it feels as though it might burst. We lost a number of animals in this way, and apart from the financial aspect of it, it was never pleasant. We always skinned the animal and sold the hide, but that was small comfort. On a number of occasions we were able to treat the animal in time to save it from this horrible end.

There were always a number of cats on the farm. In cold weather they spent most of their time in the barn where the heat emitted from the cows and pigs would significantly warm the air. It occurred to me one day that it would be much warmer for a cat to sit on a cow than on the barn floor. So I took one cat and placed it on top of the most tranquil cow. The cow got a bit perturbed and this frightened the cat so that it jumped off. However, after I repeated this a few times the cow settled down and the cat quickly discovered that it was much warmer there. It was not long before the other cats joined it on its new perch. Being cats, they often jumped on to the wrong cow, and were frightened off. Over time though, the other cows also got used to it and soon all the cats were sleeping on top of any cow in the barn. If a new cat came along it would soon be indoctrinated, as would any new cow that was brought into the barn.

Pigs

Pigs were always important animals on our farm. We raised them to use up our oats and barley and to bring in cash. We shipped them to the Calgary slaughterhouse when they reached a weight of around two hundred and fifteen pounds. We did not have a scale, but could accurately estimate their weight with the use of a tape measure. When a pig's girth reached 41 inches just back of the front legs, it was ready to ship.

We never kept less than one brood sow and usually at least two. When new pigs were born, it was not uncommon for the sow to accidentally flop down on top of, and smother one or more of them. This was especially likely to happen if it the sow was feverish from birthing. Dad had the

49

blacksmith build him a narrow cage of steel bars. In this cage the sow could no longer flop down on its side and kill its, offspring. From then on, we did not lose any more piglets to this cause.

When pigs are born they come complete with razor sharp incisors. This is often a problem for the sow. The little pigs in their eagerness for their share of the sow's milk often bite the teats severely. Dad therefore always cut the offending teeth while I held each pig in turn. There would be a lot of squealing, but it did not hurt the pigs, and the sow's teats would soon heal up too.

It was common for some of the chickens to feed in the pigsty. They could usually find bits of grain that the pigs had missed. They would sometimes also find undigested grain kernels in the pig manure. With the ongoing proximity of the chickens to the pigs, it was inevitable that sooner or later a chicken would be accidentally killed. Pigs eat anything and a dead chicken does not last long. Being very intelligent animals, the pigs quickly make the connection and given the opportunity will begin killing chickens at every opportunity. When this happens, the chickens must be kept clear of the pens until all of that batch of pigs have gone to market. Otherwise the pigs will learn from each other and no chicken will be safe around them.

Chickens & Turkeys

We always kept a number of chickens on the farm – both for laying eggs and for providing us with fresh meat. We raised only New Hampshires because in addition to being good laying hens, they also were also much meatier than Leghorns. They were housed in a chicken coop, but allowed the freedom of the farmyard. This sometimes caused slight problems in the spring when the hens tried to establish nests in the shrubbery and hatch chickens instead of just laying eggs.

Mites were one pest we always had to contend with in the chicken coop. They got especially numerous during the winter, when the chickens stayed mostly indoors. I painted all the roosts with used engine oil to kill them whenever they got really bad. This helped for a while, but never for long.

One spring we placed some pheasant eggs under a brood hen and let her hatch them. She soon had three pheasant chicks that could outrun her from the day they were hatched. That poor hen ran itself ragged chasing after the chicks that were running off in three directions simultaneously. Those pheasant chicks stayed around the yard for the following year after which they disappeared.

In later years we also raised a few turkeys. We sold most of them but did eat a few of them ourselves. They like the chickens were allowed to forage all over the yard. Turkeys like chickens do not like to get wet, yet to my great surprize on a hot day I once saw them all swimming around in the stock pond.

Symbiosis In A Pigpen

Dodging hungry tusks
Not averse to chicken dinners
A beak goes up and down
Up and down
Plucking undigested grain kernels
From excrement oozing up
Between claws soon to appear
On a dim sum tray

Chapter 6 - Country Life

Religion

Mother was always deeply religious and Dad appeared to be so during my early childhood. My earliest memories include those of Mother singing a bedtime hymn and reciting the Lord's Prayer before tucking us in each night. She continued to do this for the younger children all the years that I was at home. My father did not get on very well with some of the leaders of our church, but he kept attending for a while anyway. In later years, he finally stopped going completely and as far as I know, never went inside a church again, except for weddings and funerals.

Most of the neighbors were recent immigrants. The majority of them were Slovak. Some were from Hungary and a few were of German extraction. The Slovaks and Hungarians were all Catholics, a religion, which we Lutherans considered as ungodly, more so because its adherents went to dances.

All of the other Danish families lived farther to the west and closer to the Lutheran church of which we were all members. The construction of this church was completed not long after our arrival in Tilley. It remained the focus of our social life for all of the years that I was at home. When my father eventually stopped attending church services, it became my duty to drive the family to church each Sunday morning. During the winter we used the team and the wagon to get to and from church. We attended Sunday-School classes from 10:00 AM to 11:00 AM followed by the regular service which ended at about 12:30 PM.

Except for our parents, the members of the congregation were all "Evangelical" Lutherans. For them, alcoholic beverages were absolutely taboo! Going to dances was unthinkable and was seen as already having one foot in Hell. I learned many years later that a few of our church leaders did not mind having a beer or two if they were away from home where no one knew them. Our parents did not see anything wrong with drinking in moderation, but they did not themselves drink because we were too poor to afford it.

When I was about eleven, we were being taught about Jesus' parents coming back and finding him in the temple amazing everyone with his knowledge. My ego must have been very healthy, because I remember thinking; "what's the big deal, I could do that!" One tenet of our Lutheran faith was that unless you believed in and accepted Jesus as your "personal"

Saviour, you would burn in Hell forever. I vaguely remember when I was about twelve, asking my Sunday school teacher how a loving God could condemn to Hell someone, who had never heard of Jesus. To me it seemed grossly unfair and not the deed of a loving God. I was told that God would somehow ensure that everyone got a chance to learn about Jesus. How this might come about was of course never explained.

When my sister Inger was fifteen and I was sixteen, we were both confirmed (in the Lutheran faith) at the same time. From then on we were expected to attend "Young People's meetings each Sunday evening. Included in our activities, were asinine games that established the popularity pecking order. The essence of these games was some person choosing another, who would then repeat the process. Inger and I were always chosen after all other choices had been exhausted!

Inger's and my "Confirmation" class. Inger is farthest left in 1st row and I am far right in back row. From the author's collection.

In preparation for confirmation we had to attend Saturday classes for several months each year for two years. Our minister, who was well beyond retirement age, regaled us with far-fetched stories intended to impress us with God's power and wrath. For me it had the exact opposite effect! Being naturally timid, challenging him or quitting was never an option for me, but my low opinion of organized religion sprang from the seeds implanted in me during that period.

The summer when I was sixteen, Dad let me go to the Sylvan Lake Lutheran Bible Camp for a week together with the other young people from our church. There I met two lovely seventeen year old girls, a preacher's daughter whose name I don't remember, and a girl named Anna who originally came from Edgewater, but was now living on Lulu Island in BC. It was her younger brother Ernst mentioned earlier who tramped barefooted in the rose bushes. One day I invited the two girls for a boat ride. I had no sooner rowed them out on the lake than I was afflicted with severe flatulence. I was mortified! There was nothing for it but to row them back to shore before I embarrassed myself beyond redemption. I had been eating "All Bran" for breakfast each morning not realizing its amazing properties. I did not get another chance like that again, and would probably not have had the courage to ask them out even if I had.

Once each summer we had a church picnic at Lake Newell. During this event we were able to rent boats and go fishing. I will never forget the sight of Pike, so fresh that the pieces were still wriggling in the frying pans. Mother brought along a chocolate cake on one such outing to Lake Newell. Mr. Bayer, the chap who owned the boats, made coffee for us and we of course shared our sandwiches and our chocolate cake with him. Mr. Bayer had an employee who also shared in the lunch. This man proceeded to spread a thick layer of strawberry jam on the chocolate cake! Mother was not only incensed, but dumbfounded as well! She made some of the best chocolate cake in the district, and could not imagine that it needed more than the icing she had already applied to it.

Danish Christmas

The Christmas season for us in the Danish community was the most important time of the year. Its observance began on December 24th and lasted until "All Kings" day on January 7. The week from Christmas Day until New Year's Day was the core of this season. It was spent visiting back and forth with friends. No outside work was done on the farm during this week except that of feeding and tending the livestock.

Preparation for the Christmas season in our house started with the baking. Mother began by making her special Christmas cookies and cakes early in December. We had a meat grinder equipped with special plates that we used to extrude the cookie dough into traditional shapes associated with our Christmas. We children vied for the privilege of feeding the grinder and shaping the cookies. Many of these cookies were very similar to Shortbread cookies – whitish, easily chewed and very rich. We also made ginger cookies that were brown and quite hard. As I grew older my preference changed from the white to the more flavourful brown cookies. The one kind of cookie that we especially liked were the little cube shaped ones, which literally translated, were called "pepper nuts." These were made from the same dough and were used to fill the paper baskets hanging on the Christmas tree.

Birthday parties at our house were held on a Saturday or Sunday afternoon when there were no regular school classes. The celebrant was always allowed to invite his or her best friends to it. This did not to apply to me when I got older because of conflict with church activities. We produced a Christmas pageant each year and performed it on the Sunday during the Holy Week. Rehearsals were held on every Saturday and Sunday afternoon from late November until Christmas. Since I was born on December 9th, these rehearsals got in the way of me having a party for my birthday because we had to rehearse instead. I resented this very much and felt cheated.

Christmas Eve was much more important to us in the Danish tradition, than Christmas Day. We had our big dinner on Christmas Eve, while on Christmas Day we ate leftovers. We opened our gifts on Christmas Eve and since we were not brought up to believe in Santa Claus, there were no stockings to hang. We always knew from whom the gifts came, even when the odd one was labelled "from Santa Clause." A well-to-do farming couple, named Soren and Dagmar Petersen, were good friends of our family. They had a long-standing habit of playing Santa to the younger children in our family.

My earliest memories of Christmas are from Edgewater, where I vaguely recall us accompanying our father into the adjacent woods to cut a tree. After we moved to Tilley, we had to buy our annual tree. We brought it into the house and set it up on its stand on the morning of December 24th to allow it some time to warm up. We did not decorate the tree until after dinner when those not engaged in washing the dishes helped do it.

Christmas dinner was a gala affair. The table was covered with our best, embroidered damask tablecloth and then set with the fine china from Denmark. During dinner, we feasted on roast chicken, (turkey in later years) roast pork, caramelized potatoes and gravy, red cabbage, carrots, cauliflower, peas and lots of home made pickles. The desert was an almond rice pudding called "ris-ala-mande" on which we applied liberal amounts of prune sauce. Normally, we younger children were not allowed to drink coffee, but on this occasion, all such prohibitions were suspended.

After the dinner was over, some of the older children washed the dishes and cleaned up. The others helped Dad and Mother to decorate the tree. We had brought many of our Christmas decorations with us from Denmark, but we made others by hand. We had brought pine and fir cones with us from Edgewater - these we painted silver or gold. We also wove paper baskets, which we stuffed with candy or cookies and hung from the tree. The most important feature though, was the candles! They were placed in the special candleholders that we clamped on to the tree branches. These candles came in a variety of colors and were about three to four inches in length and perhaps a third of an inch in diameter. We had to place them carefully so they would not set fire to the tree. My sister Inger recalls that we kept a pail full of water near the tree in case of emergency. I can remember that after every Christmas we would read a newspaper account of a house burned down somewhere on the prairie due to a Christmas tree fire.

After the tree was fully decorated and the candles lit, it was a wonderful sight to behold. We then encircled the tree, joined hands and sang Danish Christmas songs as we slowly walked around the tree. We children were always in a hurry to get this obligatory exercise over with so that we could get down to the serious business of opening our presents.

My sister Ester remembers that in Edgewater, the younger children were put to bed for a nap in the afternoon so they could stay up late without getting too tired. She says that Dad and Mother decorated the tree while she or Gerda read to us younger children in the bedroom. After the candles were lit and the other lights turned out, we were let out. She remembers our eyes sparkling as brightly as the candles on the tree.

Christmas Day was anticlimactic. We were always obliged to attend church, which of course interfered with enjoying our gifts. Books were an important element in our family life and we usually got several of them at Christmas. On a typical afternoon or evening we were unusually deaf to Mother's requests since we would either have our noses buried in books, doing jig saw puzzles or playing board game such as Snakes and Ladders and Ludo.

After New Year's Day, life slowly reverted to normal. We were back in school on the first weekday after January 1. Socializing tapered off and the usual farm work of hauling hay, grinding grain and cleaning the barn could no longer be ignored. The Christmas tree was taken down on January 7, and that marked the end of the festive season.

Renfrew School

The school we attended consisted of one large building which had about 40 - 45 students in grades 1 to 4 and a smaller building with about 30 students in grades 5 to 9. Grades 10 and 11 were also taught when we first arrived, but discontinued. However, Grade 10 was again taught the last year the school was in operation. In addition to the school itself, there were two outside latrines as well as a barn and a shed for wood and coal. The barn housed the horses, which some children from outlying areas used to get to school.

I attended this school for eight years - the remainder of my education. It burned down the following year and from then until the end of the term, my younger siblings attended a temporary school in the village of Tilley, where the hall at the hotel was partitioned off for this purpose. Soon after that, the other rural schools were closed as well and all the children in the district were bussed to a newly constructed six-room school in Tilley. Previously it had been necessary for students to live in Brooks and attend the High School there if they wanted to complete Grade XII.

When I first came to Renfrew School at age eight, one of our school recess activities was playing marbles. I was not allowed to "play for keeps," but of course we all did it anyway. In those days a box of Cracker Jack popcorn always contained a marble so this treat was highly prized, but the only time I ever got a nickel to buy a box was at the annual school sports day.

Another pastime was wrestling – the object was to pin the opponent to the ground while sitting astride his torso and pinning his arms. I was the perpetual loser in these contests and could not even compete with the boys who were a grade behind me.

Dirty words were taboo and were promptly reported to the teacher especially if overheard by a girl. Jack Taylor was a couple of years older than I was and when another boy called him "Jackass," he thought it was a dirty word and promptly complained to the teacher. To us the word "ass" referred to the buttocks and was hence a dirty word as were all words pertaining to our private parts.

The boys in my family were all late developers. When I turned fifteen, I did not yet weigh one hundred pounds! In school I hated sports because I did so poorly in them. Each year we had an annual "sports day" where the students from all four schools in the district competed. Participation was mandatory, so I could not opt out. The main events included running, high jumping and broad jumping. It was the worst day of the year for me as I was always last in every event. I had one classmate named Ronald who was a year younger than I was. He was academically challenged, but sports were his forte. He also came from a large family (eleven children) and they were all athletically gifted. He could outrun and out jump everyone, not only in his own age group, but even those two years older than himself as well. In those days we did the high jump in a sitting position. Ronald could clear a bar that was set above his own height. I have often wondered how high he might have jumped using the modern techniques together with a bit of coaching.

The Renfrew schoolyard occupied about three acres, and being surrounded by fields, often had gophers inhabiting it. They did this at great risk, because anytime a gopher showed up, we boys would soon drown it out of its burrow and kill it. We carried water from the school pump in anything we could lay our hands on, including our lunch pails. Few gophers survived more than one or two recess periods! For a time we also collected a bounty for gopher tails.

One of the things the boys at school especially liked was embarrassing the girls. Once when we had an evening event of some kind, three of boys got a willow tree a few feet long. They went to the girls' outhouse and poked one end of it into the pile of feces. They then turned the tree end for end and embedded it in the stinky mound to a depth that left the upper end just below the seat level. We never did find out if anyone got to sit on it or not, but just the idea that a girl would get her buttocks smeared was enough to titillate us.

One year while my sister Ester was still attending Renfrew School, we held a bazaar to raise money for some school project. Ester sewed and contributed a pair of pajamas for the event, which the mother of one of the Slovak students bought. Unfortunately for the daughter, they had no idea what pajamas were, or what they were used for. She wore them to school the following day and was mortified when the rest of the students had a huge laugh at her expense. Needless to say, she did not wear them to school again!

The most popular past time except during winter, was playing "scrub." This was akin to "Softball," (also called Fastball) but with slightly different rules. There were no sides. A fielder progressed through various positions towards the batting station each time a batter was put out. Once someone like Ron got to bat, he usually stayed there until the end of the recess. Because I did so poorly in all of the sports, I often stayed inside during recess and read anything I could get my hands on. We had a limited library at Renfrew, and it did not take me very many grades before I had read every book in it.

One day when I was in Grade 6, I inadvertently let out a long drawn out, high-pitched fart. I was embarrassed and quickly turned to see how

Vincent, the boy behind me would react. To his consternation, my reaction caused everyone in the classroom to assume that he was the felon! The whole room was in an uproar for a few minutes. Even the teacher could not keep a straight face. Vincent was some teed off with me! Of course no one believed him when he tried to say that I had been the culprit. To give you some idea of the magnitude of this event, I can honestly say that in all my years in school, I never ever heard anyone else fart.

During the early years I attended Renfrew, we always had a weekly art class. Seared into my memory was the humiliation I suffered in Grades III and IV. There our projects were invariably watercolors with scenes of purple mountains and green trees with unrealistic drooping branches. The teacher would arrange all of our work along the blackboard ledge in order of merit. Mine were always ranked last or second last! I don't recall anything about the art classes of later years until my one moment of triumph. In grade VII the teacher taught us to do pencil shading. I drew my brother Frank and he was clearly recognizable! This was the only time I can recall that my artistic results weren't mediocre.

Until I was in Grade VI or VII we had a school fair in Tilley each fall just before school resumed. One year I baked oatmeal cookies and baking powder biscuits and entered them at the fair. I won second prize for the cookies and fourth for my biscuits despite having forgotten to put salt in the biscuits. When school resumed the following week my classmates accused me of entering my mother's baking. I suppose they may have been jealous, but it bothered me a great deal to be accused of cheating.

One year we had a teacher (Mr. Edwin Parks) who was interested in music. He enlisted a Mrs. Woods to help coach us. With her help, we competed in the district music festival being held at the Duchess school. Those performing well enough there were able to go on to compete at a higher level. Inger and I were both able to go to Duchess to sing, but we were not good enough for the next level. Mrs. Woods, our coach, was married to a British Boer War veteran who was much older than her. Their children were not only good athletes, but also the best singers in Tilley. Hubert was the oldest but I did not know him well because he was about three years older than I was. Audrey was a year older and Charles was a year younger than me and was one of my best friends. Those of her children who competed at Duchess went on to the next level. I don't remember how they did there, but I do remember being startled by the power and quality of Hubert's singing. Many years later when my youngest brother joined the RCMP, none other than a Sgt. Charles Woods interviewed him!

One item on the curriculum in grades 5 to 9 was memorization. We were required to memorize a minimum of 150 lines of poetry from our "readers." I liked this requirement because I found it easy and usually completed it sometime in October. Another assignment was writing short compositions weekly. While I had Miss Claire for a teacher she stipulated that if anyone got a mark of 7 out of 10, they would not have to write an essay the following week. Anyone who maintained that grade would have to write only once every three weeks. During her term I was able to meet that challenge and wrote only once every three weeks. I liked that because this gave me more time to read whatever I liked.

When I completed Grade IX, I had to get special permission to write the mandatory provincial exams because I had attended school for only 86 days that term. Dad kept me at home the following year to help him full time on the farm. However, the year following that, Grade X was available at Renfrew, so I returned to school in mid October after the harvest was over. There were just two of us in the class, John Figeckski and myself. Just before Easter the following spring, I was struck in the eye by a foul tick off the bat while playing ball. My eye hurt so badly that Mother insisted that Dad take me to see the doctor in Brooks since there was none in Tilley. It was my first visit to a doctor. He cleaned out my eye, bandaged it up and told me to keep it bandaged for three weeks while the scratches healed.

After my bandages came off, my father decided to keep me at home for the rest of the term to help put in the crops. Nevertheless, when the end of June came, I decided to go and write the exams. I did not have a chance to study before the first exam (physics) and got only a "B." However, I got "A"s in all the other subjects. My elation was short lived because the Department of Education in its wisdom decided that since my attendance including my "Harvest Leave of 20 days" amounted to only 116 days out of a mandatory 150, they would award me only 22 of the 30 credits the courses were worth. I thought this most unfair since my marks indicated (at least to me) that I knew my material. It killed any thoughts I had of continuing high school even if Dad could have afforded to let me go. That fall I went to Scandia to work for a farmer there for a little over a year. However, I returned to work for my father for the summers of 1948 and 1949, before leaving home permanently.

Early (Paying?) Jobs

It is threshing time and I am eleven. Dad keeps me out of school to work in the grain hopper of the threshing machine. My job is to level the wheat in the hopper and especially to keep it well away from the grain spout. One day I momentarily got careless and the wheat backed up into the spout and plugged the auger. The foreman had to shut down the threshing machine and clean it out. He repeatedly asked me if I had let the wheat back up into the auger. I was afraid to admit it so I insisted that I hadn't. My pay is fifty cents a day. It is paid to Dad who records the money owed to me in a notebook.

One of our permanent ditches is getting plugged up with vegetation. Dad gives me the job of shaving off this growth so that the ditch can carry more water. He promises to pay me by the foot. I don't remember how much I earned, but it is added to my account.

On another occasion Dad sends Frank and me to pick potatoes for Mr. Orval, a farmer who lives two and a half miles away. I don't know whether or not we knew how much Dad was paid for the two of us, nor how much I earned. However, he adds the amounts to our accounts. I also remember Mr. Orval shouting at me for not working hard enough.

On still another occasion I was helping a nearby Hungarian farmer for a couple of days. I stayed at his place overnight and shall never forget sleeping in a bed on top of and under a feather tick. It was very cozy, warm and comfortable. It was so soft that it felt as though I was sinking into a soft fluffy cloud.

Later, when I was a teenager, my father took contracts by the acre to "stook" grain. Frank and I stayed out of school and helped him with this. The two of us together could barely keep pace with Dad. He collected the money for our work and supposedly credited it to our accounts but I don't remember ever being paid.

My first steady (part time) job paid $7.50 per month for lighting the fire in the school furnace each morning. It had previously been done by a grownup living nearby, who also did the janitorial work. It had then be the duty of the students to tend the fire during the day. Unfortunately for me, when I got the job, it was assumed (and decided) by the teacher that I should be responsible for the fire all day long. I took a lot of flack whenever the classroom got too cold. I held this job during grades 8 and 9.

Bee Keeping

When I turned fifteen, my father thought I should become a Beekeeper so I could provide honey for the family. I wrote to the Alberta Agricultural Department and ordered literature on the subject – then spent the winter studying it. With the money Dad advanced to me, I next bought materials for making two beehives and ordered two 2-pound packages of bees from California. Each box contained about 12,000 bees.

A basic hive consists of a rectangular box that is about 24" x 18" by 12" deep and open on both the top and bottom. The box is set on a base and a cover is placed over its top. A dozen honey combs are suspended inside this box. The bees are first housed in a single box, but as their numbers increase, another box is added on top of the first one. Up to 3 separate boxes to store the honey are added (as required) once the honey season is underway.

A new honeycomb is made up of a frame in which a sheet of reinforced wax has been inserted. The bees must first build their honeycombs on this structure before they can store honey or the queen lay its eggs in them.

I assembled the two hives and eagerly awaited my bees. They arrived in early May via the Post Office in a pair of light wooden boxes that had a screen making up one side. The queens were in small separate boxes attached to the larger ones.

I don't remember how I coaxed the bees into their respective hives, but I believe that I placed the box containing a queen bee inside each hive and that the bees then had to eat their way through some food to liberate her. I had to feed the bees with syrup, made from sugar and water, for a number of days until the first flowers came into bloom.

Each hive began with about 12,000 bees, but this number could grow to 60,000 if no other queens were allowed to develop. With normal conditions, such a hive could produce 200 – 300 pounds of honey during the summer.

The bees if left alone, will produce other queens once their numbers have increased above certain limits. It is up to the beekeeper to inspect the hive regularly and to destroy any queen cells that appear. If he fails to do this, a new queen, when she appears, will promptly leave the hive with a large number of bees to establish her own hive somewhere else. This activity is called "swarming." If this happens, the original population is decimated and hence the honey production is much decreased. It is therefore vital that the beekeeper, prevent this from happening.

Because I never managed to find all the queen cells during the two years that I kept bees, they always swarmed. My honey production therefore never exceeded 90 pounds per hive. My lack of experience coupled with my nervousness around the bees was undoubtedly responsible for this. In retrospect, I realize that I should first have tried to work with a professional beekeeper for at least a short time to get some practical experience.

Beehives have two natural enemies on the prairies – ants and skunks. Ants will invade the hive, kill the bees and steal the honey. Skunks will eat the bees as they emerge from the hive. Their longhaired fur protects them from being stung.

Guarding against ants was relatively easy. I would check for anthills in the vicinity and kill the ants with calcium cyanide which I could buy at the local store without any permits,. To kill the ants, I poked 3 or 4 holes into the anthill with a broom handle, placed a spoonful of cyanide down each hole and then covered each hole with a piece of paper held in place by some dirt on top. The moisture inside the anthill would soon combine with the calcium cyanide to produce deadly cyanide gas that quickly killed all the ants. Guarding against skunks was another matter, but I was fortunate that our dog, Brownie kept their numbers in check.

Some beekeepers are able to work around their hives without any protection against bee stings. I did not try to do this, but always wore coveralls over my regular clothes as well as a bee veil and special gloves. In hot weather it was very uncomfortable to wear all those clothes. I also used smoke to pacify the bees by blowing it into the hive before taking the top of to inspect the combs for queen cells. Nevertheless, I was always very nervous while working with them and often managed to get stung. Sometimes a bee found its way inside my veil, I found this very disconcerting.

When the summer if over it is customary to kill the bees. It is possible to insulate the hives and to feed the bees through the winter, but it is not economically feasible. It is easier and cheaper to buy fresh bees each spring. To kill them I place a spoonful of Calcium Cyanide just inside the entrance to each hive. The moisture from the colony activates the cyanide, which quickly kills off all of the hive residents.

I now borrow a honey extractor from a Mr. Gleddis who lives just north of Tilley. It consists of a hand-cranked centrifuge inside a large tank. It will accommodate four honeycombs at a time. I set the extractor up in the kitchen and bring in the hive boxes. I have a special knife for removing the wax seal from the combs. I dip it in boiling water, then make one pass along the comb. I dip it in the water again and make another pass. It is slow sticky work but I soon get the wax off the first four combs. Commercial beekeepers have steam assisted wax removers that work much better and don't have to be reheated for each pass.

I place the four combs into the extractor and begin cranking. The honey comes out of one side of the combs but not the other. I try to crank a little faster, but that does not help. I finally realize that I have to reverse the combs in the extractor – after all, it is centrifuge and it can only expel the honey from the sided facing outwards.

From then on the work goes much better, but it is still a sticky, messy job! Honey is not easy to clean off anything. When I am finally finished, I have eighty-five pounds of it, which Dad buys from me for $0.10 per pound. The amount is entered into Dad's account book.

Contracting

When I was fifteen or sixteen, Dad got an idea for earning some money by salvaging barbed wire from fences that were no longer needed. Barbed wire was in short supply due to the war and what was available was of poor quality – it stretched too easily. The old "used" wire, being of much better quality was easily sold. Dad discussed his idea with Mr. Charlesworth, the auctioneer in Brooks and made an agreement with him to split the profits from the salvage and sale of such wire.

There were a number of farmers in the Standard area who no longer wanted fences. By removing them we were doing them a favour. With the fences gone they could farm closer to their boundaries and thereby add a few acres to their cropland. Each fence consisted of three strands of wire, and since most quarter sections had from one to two miles of fence each, this amounted to nearly four miles of wire per quarter. At 320 pounds per mile, a quarter section could produce .64 tons of wire each. Our only out-of-pocket costs would be our travel, hotel and meal expenses.

Dad and I took the Greyhound bus to Standard to get a head start on laying down wire before the auctioneer was scheduled to arrive. On our trip up there we had an interesting (and hair-raising) experience. Because a bridge was being replaced on the highway, the bus driver had to take a detour. It was his first trip on this new stretch of road, but since the detour was smooth he sped along at 60 miles per hour. Everything went fine until we crossed a canal bridge. The approach to it had a gentle rise, so the driver did not reduce his speed. You can imagine his and our surprise, when all four wheels of the bus suddenly left the ground! It turned out that the other approach dropped off sharply and the Greyhound bus was actually airborne for a second or two.

When we arrived at Standard we stayed mostly with friends and spent a few days laying down several miles of barbed wire. Mr. Charlesworth then came up with a flat deck truck equipped with a hand operated reel in the back. Dad and I took turns reeling in the wire as Mr. Charlesworth backed the truck up along each fence. The auctioneer had no trouble selling this wire at auctions, but when it came to splitting the proceeds, he paid us by the day for our labor instead. Since there was no agreement in writing, there was nothing we could do but chalk it up to experience.

Chapter 7 - In Lighter Vein

Hijinks

My brother Frank seemed to be Dad's favorite son. He appeared to be able to get away with things that I could not. Nevertheless he and I, being just three years apart, did a lot of things together. We shared a bed on the second floor, which we reached via a ladder in the pantry. When Mother baked cookies she stored them in a one-gallon jar in this pantry. Frank and I had a habit of stopping on the way to bed each night to steal one cookie each from the jar. We felt that such a small number would not be missed, but of course after a week of this, the loss would be quite noticeable.

On one occasion Mother had baked a spice cake in preparation for hosting the "Ladies Aid" meeting the following day. The next morning when she went to put icing on it, the spatula broke through to empty space below. It turned out that Frank on the previous evening, when we were out, had tipped the cake out of the pan. He had then scooped out and eaten a good part of it before returning it to the pan. Fortunately Mother had time to bake some cinnamon buns before the Ladies Aid meeting convened that afternoon.

When Frank turned fourteen, he was allowed to use Dad's .22 calibre rifle. One day he was out shooting gophers together with the neighbor's son, Joe Sickel. He was chatting with Joe while leaning on the .22 with the muzzle resting on his foot, when he accidentally pulled the trigger. The bullet hole through the shoe was well back and he first thought the bullet had gone through his foot. Fortunately, he had merely grazed his third toe and chipped the bone. Nevertheless, it was a very painful wound and he could not walk without limping. To explain his limp, he told our parents that he had sprained his ankle. I became his doctor and dressed his toe each evening before going to bed. It was not until many years later that he finally told our parents the truth about this incident.

On another day when he was alone home, after removing the pellets from a shotgun shell, Frank threw the shell into the cook stove to see how big a bang it would make. It made a bang all right! It blew all the lids off the stove and blackened the ceiling and walls of the kitchen with soot. This time he did get a thorough dressing down from both Dad and Mother.

Our parents did not let us go out roving at Halloween, fearing that we would get into trouble. I did get out once when I was about fifteen and joined a group. We promptly went to the Renfrew School and tipped over both outhouses there. This was usually the extent of Halloween vandalism in our district. The next day at school I was also part of the gang that had to set them upright again.

As children we used to collect pieces of binder twine, from the straw stacks, which we used in a variety of ways and we had a large pile of it hanging in the porch. One day when Frank was searching for something in the porch, he lit a match to better see, and accidentally lit fire to the twine. Fortunately I was able to extinguish the fire before it got away on us, but we were lucky that he did not burn down the house.

One evening when we were still both teenagers, Frank and I walked the four and one half miles into Tilley to play snooker at the pool hall. On our way home we passed by Sinclair's garage whose owner had, in Dad's opinion, not only overcharged him for work on his tractor, but had done such a poor job that it had to be redone. To get even with him, we stole a radio, a spotlight and a fountain pen from his unlocked office. When we got close to home, we hid the loot in the willows beside a permanent irrigation ditch on our farm, but directly across from our neighbor, Sickel's house. It happened that one day the girls there were hunting for pheasant eggs along this ditch when they found the stolen items. They immediately blamed the theft on their brothers. I don't know what the outcome was, because by then, I had left home and was working in Scandia.

Hunting

One feature of the irrigation country was the number of game birds that flourished in the heavy growth along the canals and permanent ditches. These areas were overgrown with willows, sweet clover and other lush vegetation - perfect cover for Ringneck pheasants. The larger of the waterways were usually bordered by water filled borrow pits heavily vegetated with cat tails and other reedy growth that provided habitat for a variety of waterfowl. In addition to the game birds, there were also many other birds as well as skunks, weasels, garter snakes and even coyotes. It was a great place for a young farm boy to grow up.

Like every other boy growing up on a farm I became proficient with firearms. Like most others I soon owned a .22 rifle, and later a shotgun. If my memory serves me correctly, it was not necessary for me to have a hunting license for game birds as long as I hunted only on our own property.

Our area was so noted for its pheasants that people' came from far and wide to hunt them every autumn. Whenever my father saw a hunting group trespassing, he would send me over to order them off our property. On one occasion when I did this, one of the hunters immediately apologized and told me that they were just trying to find a wounded pheasant that had landed on our farm (this was a pretty lame alibi). He then asked me what my name was. When I told him, he asked if we were Danish. I answered in the affirmative, and he then said that he too was Danish, that his name was Tem Kjaer and that he was the "Fish and Game Inspector" for Alberta. He then introduced another man named Fisher who was also an important game official, and a third hunter who was a lawyer, also from Calgary. Mr. Kjaer next insisted on meeting my parents and they shortly came over to the house during the lunch hour.

From that day on, Tem was an annual visitor to our farm during the hunting season. He invariably brought other well-known people with him. One time he brought Bing Crosby. Another time he brought the world famous opera singer, Lauritz Melchior, who also became a repeat visitor. Once when Melchior burst into song in the local beer parlour, he was promptly told to cut out the noise! I have often wondered what his reaction was to having his singing called noise. I unfortunately did not get to meet either Crosby or Melchior because by that time I was no longer at home.

Being an avid hunter myself, I went hunting during the season when time allowed it. However, I lacked one important aid – a hunting dog. We did have a dog, named Brownie. It was a cross between a Collie and a Fox Terrier (and was of course mostly brown). One day I decided to see if I could train it to be a hunting dog. That turned out to be a strategic blunder. Brownie could indeed flush the pheasants, but it got so carried away with the excitement of the chase that it would not heed my calls and stay within shotgun range. It kept chasing up pheasants all over the farm, but too far away to be of any use to me.

Since that first fateful attempt at training the dog, I was never again able to hunt alone. The moment it saw me with a firearm it would get extremely excited in anticipation of the fun it would soon have. I of course tried my damnedest to leave the dog at home, but it would stay behind only until I was out of sight. It then sneaked ahead of me, and scared up pheasants, but so far ahead I would be forced to abort my hunt. I left home the following year and was spared further frustration in my hunting endeavors.

My father was convinced that since we fed the game birds, we also had a right to eat them. It became my job to provide the odd pheasant for the table regardless of whether or not the season was open. In the summer when I was mowing alfalfa, the mower would often kill a hen pheasant sitting on its nest. These birds were never wasted for I took them home so we could eat them. In the wintertime when we were fattening cattle in the feed lot, it was pretty easy to pick off the occasional pheasant in the feed lot with my .22 rifle.

Some time after I had moved away from home, the local Mountie came to investigate a report that we had shot pheasants out of season. If he had bothered to look behind the root cellar, he would have found lots of pheasant feathers. Perhaps he was not really too interested in finding evidence with which to prosecute a poor family that occasionally augmented its meagre diet with a pheasant or two.

Recreation

I got my first skates when I was about ten. The stock pond was close to the house so that was where I learned to skate. There was also a large slough called "Burton's Lake" on the adjoining farm a half mile away, where we were allowed to skate. This body of water was over one third of a mile long hence the wind often blew the snow off the ice for us. On one occasion when the wind was blowing, we fashioned sails from some canvas and poles. With these makeshift devices we could reach fair speeds on our sleighs.

Skating rinks as they exist today were completely unknown to us at the time. Sometimes the "Young Peoples" group from the church would sponsor a skating party. No hockey sticks or pucks were allowed at such gatherings, and I for one never had the opportunity to learn to play hockey.

During the winter when there was little farm work other than caring for the livestock, we had a lot of free time. It was common in those days for our weekly newspaper to publish books in serial form. We invariably took turns reading these stories aloud for the benefit of the other family members who were knitting, darning socks or crocheting. If no stories were available in the paper, we would read from books. Today I realize that the most important trait I developed at home was reading. Many years later at the age of 43, I was able to enter graduate school despite my lack of formal education. I credit my reading habit for the opportunities I was able capitalize on years later.

At the time when the war was coming to an end, the price for fur was quite high. One fur-bearing animal in plentiful supply was the Jackrabbit. It was therefore natural that I spent quite a few hours hunting them with my .22 rifle. After their numbers on our farm declined I once got permission to hunt on the farm of family friends. I remember using my sister's horse, Prince to ride over there. It was probably just as well that she did not get to see her horse covered in blood from transporting a half dozen jackrabbits back home.

On occasion either a skunk or a weasel would raid the chicken coop. At such times it became important to trap the offender before too many chickens were killed. One problem with trapping a skunk in the yard was the obnoxious stink raised when it was trapped. We therefore tried to keep down the skunk population before the problem arose. Skunks liked to set up house underneath buildings when possible. Granaries were often mounted on skids, which left space underneath and hence attractive to skunks. The best method I learned later for catching a skunk in such a place was with the use of barbed wire. A length of barbed wire was doubled back on itself and twisted into a spiral to make it rigid. When I found a skunk under a building, I pushed the wire in close to the skunk, while constantly turning it. The barbed wire soon caught the long hair of the skunk and wound the animal tightly into a ball. A skunk cannot spray without its tail in the air so it could easily be killed without creating a stench.

Early in its career, our dog Brownie had tackled a skunk and was ill rewarded for its efforts. Eventually the smell wore of, but Brownie kept on attacking skunks. It must have learned from its earlier mistake, because no skunk ever again sprayed it. With Brownie around the skunks did not raid the chicken coop much anymore.

My brother Frank and I were always looking for things to do in our spare time. We had some old batteries lying around that we decided to smelt. We burned used engine oil in an empty coffee can with a rag for a wick to produce the heat we needed. With this apparatus we were able to smelt the lead in the battery plates and cast them into various desired shapes.

One Sunday afternoon, a family friend came over for a visit. He and my father went out in the field looking at the crops. His wife and daughters were in the house and his son Eric was helping Frank and me smelting lead. We were deeply engaged in this activity when we saw the men returning from the field. Since I did not know whether or not we were allowed to do this, I quickly tipped over the fire can, but instead of tipping it away; I tipped it towards myself. The burning oil splashed on to and inside my boot causing a huge blister all the way down the front of my foot. That was the end of lead smelting for a while. Quite possibly there were no more old batteries to process anyway.

Army Cadets

When I was 15, an army sergeant came to the Renfrew School and recruited a number of us for the Army Cadets. He supplied us with uniforms and taught us how to march, switch step, present arms, etc. He also took us out to Lake Newell and gave us a lesson in shooting with a 22-calibre rifle.

The following summer I was allowed to attend Cadet Camp at the Sarcee Army Base south of Calgary for two weeks. There were a number of boys from Brooks attending, but I was the only one from Renfrew. We got to see both a four-inch cannon and a two-inch mortar demonstrated.

The food was served in a "mess" tent on tin plates and was not very good. My one powerful memory of that tent was the strong smell of Lysol and bleach, which we used, in large quantities to disinfect everything. The camp latrines consisted of long open pits with poles erected over each for us to sit on while we did our jobs. These pits were regularly sprinkled with liberal doses of quicklime, but they still stunk horribly.

One evening we were allowed to go into Calgary. It was a six-mile walk to 17th Avenue Southwest, which was then the southern boundary of the city - the nearest streetcar ran on 15th avenue. Today Sarcee has long since been swallowed up by Calgary, which has a population 16 times as large as it was then.

I was visiting with some of the boys from Brooks one night when they bet a fellow that he couldn't blow out a candle while blindfolded. The candle was set on the floor and as soon as he was blindfolded, a kid named Archibald dropped his pants. Meanwhile they were directing the kid with the blindfold to blow farther this way or that. When they ripped off the blindfold, he found himself blowing into the hairiest ass I have ever seen.

I might have enjoyed my stay at the camp, except that my tent mates saddled me with embarrassing nicknames. I have a congenital drooping eyelid that was especially noticeable while I was a child. It ran in the family – both my maternal grandfather and a younger sister were afflicted with it too, but not to the same degree. My parents named me "Uffe" after a Danish king who, I believe ruled around 800 AD. (Pronounced oof'i with a soft i) This name was not common – even in Denmark, and in our area it was unique. Nobody except other Danes could or would pronounce it properly. At Sarcee I soon became known by such epithets as "Cockeye," "Fuckeye," "You-Fuck-I," etc.

On Sex

During our teen years, my brothers, our pals and I were totally preoccupied with sex, but in our straight-laced society, it was a taboo subject. I don't remember exactly how old I was when I discovered how to masturbate. No one told me about it – I reasoned it out for myself and with some experimentation coupled with fantasizing I achieved my goal. I'm not sure, but I think I probably passed my discovery on to my brother Frank. Later, I had a friend who used to say; "Ninety percent of all guys "pull their wire," and the rest are liars."

On the farm we were very much aware of sex because we saw the roosters doing it all the time and on occasion we also got to see the pigs and the cows copulate. Our friends and we used to say that we wished that we could do it as often as a rooster and for as long as a boar.

When I was twelve, I was with my parents visiting friends whose daughter, was a year older than me. We were sitting in her room chatting when she asked me; "Do you fuck?" Without thinking, I replied; "No." She then said; "Neither do I." When I confided this to my friend Gordon a few years later, he told me how stupid I had been for she did indeed put out.

One of the fantasies I often indulged in as a teenager was that I was suffering from some exotic disease where only the sex act could save my life. I pictured the girl that I most admired being given the choice of sacrificing her virginity to save me, or letting me die a horrible death. Knowing that she was pure, but also kind, I visualized the mental torment she would experience before capitulating to my needs.

PART II

AWAY FROM HOME

Chapter 8 - Alberta

Art Nelson

I was seventeen in October of 1946 when Dad got a job for me with Art Nelson – a farmer in nearby Scandia. The name, "Scandia" is a shortening of Scandinavia and as the name suggests, many, if not most of its inhabitants were of Scandinavian descent. Art told my dad that he would pay me $70 per month plus room and board, but he did not tell him that it would be for only one month. He lowered my wages to $45 per month at the end of my first month, saying that this was the going rate for winter work.

Mr. Nelson was a stocky man of above average height with brown curly hair and was thirty-five years old. He had immigrated to the Winnipeg area from Sweden in 1930. There he worked on a farm during the great depression. He said he was much better off than most. The government paid the farmer $5 per month to hire a man and they paid the man $3 per month to work for the farmer. In his case the farmer was well enough off to pay Art the entire $8.

When I came to work for Mr. Nelson, he had been married for a year or two and had a son named Leroy who was then one year old and already weighed thirty pounds. His wife Esther was in her middle twenties and was also of Swedish descent. I recently had the surprising experience of meeting a former school classmate of Leroy's fifty-five years later.

A Manure Spreader. *Photo taken by the author courtesy of the EID Historical Park in Scandia, Alberta.*

Art owned a 400-acre farm, of which 300 acres were irrigated. It bordered on the Bow River and was seven miles from the village of Scandia. He grew mostly grain, but also had a substantial acreage in alfalfa. Hence there were a many haystacks on the farm.

When I first arrived, Mr. Nelson started me on the tractor, doing the fall plowing. Once the weather turned cold, my work changed to doing regular farm chores such as milking the cows, feeding the livestock, hauling hay and spreading manure in the field.

I lived in a small shack (bunkhouse) that I heated with a wood and coal cook stove. Mrs. Nelson served my meals to me in the family kitchen, but I was not invited to spend any of my free time there even though Mr. Nelson had told my father that I would be treated as one of the family. The only family affair I was invited to join was accompanying them to church on Sunday mornings.

Getting up in the morning when the weather was cold was an unpleasant experience. The fire in the stove always died out during the night and by morning the temperature in the un-insulated bunkhouse was often below freezing. One day I had a brain wave! I decided to leave my clothing in the oven figuring that it would retain enough heat to keep my clothes warm until morning. That was some idea! When I got up the next morning, I discovered that my clothes were totally ruined. They had not caught fire, but they were so charred that they fell apart when I handled them. Even my boots were ruined. They had shrunk to half their previous size. I had to wear my dress clothes while doing the chores that morning. Mr. Nelson then took me into town where I replaced my ruined wardrobe. He had a great laugh at my expense.

A cream separator. The cream is separated from the milk by centrifugal force and comes out of the top spout. The milk comes out of the bottom spout. *Photo taken by the author courtesy of the Brooks Museum at Brooks, Alberta.*

I typically began my day by feeding the livestock, milking three cows and running the milk through the cream separator before breakfast. After breakfast I harnessed up his team of mules and either hauled hay in from a stack in the field, or loaded and spread manure in the fields. Occasionally the two of us ground grain for animal feed. I carried on this kind of work all day except for a break at lunch.

My workday ended with me doing the chores again and then coming into the house for dinner. During the long winter evenings, I read anything and everything I could lay my hands on. Since I did not have a radio, I had no other entertainment.

After Christmas Mr. Nelson told me that he would not need me for the following two months, but that a Mr. Brockelsby would hire me during that time providing that I agreed to the same wages. He explained to me that they assumed that $45 per month was fair because that was what the Canadian government had required them to pay for the German war prisoners who had recently worked on the farms.

Brockelsby

Mr. Brockelsby was seventy years old and his son Leonard was forty. They had come to Scandia from Iowa ten years earlier and began by buying a few old cows with impeccable lineage - taking a chance on getting a calf or two from each of them. It was a risky gamble, but in this way they had managed to get superior bloodlines at prices they could afford.

At the Brockelsby farm they housed me in an old granary that was heated by a wood and coal heater. Mr. Brockelsby farmed a quarter section of land and worked together with his son Leonard who also farmed a quarter section of land (160 acres) nearby. When I worked for them they jointly owned a herd of forty Aberdeen Angus purebred cows, a few bulls and forty calves. My job in addition to milking two cows was "halter-breaking" the calves. They normally did this chore in the late fall after the field work was over, but this year they had neglected it until I came to work for them in the new year.

The calves had to be halter broken so that they could be led around in "show-rings" at livestock shows. We usually brought four or five calves into the barn at a time, fitted them each with rope a halter and tied them in the stalls. My job was to take them out to water twice daily, feed them and currycomb them. It was a challenging job leading them to water because the calves were quite wild at first.

Because we were halter breaking them two months later than normal, the calves were that much bigger. The first few times we led a calf to water, it required the efforts of all three of us to control it. Younger calves had tended to panic and fight against the rope during their first few days in the barn and would got their necks rope burned in the process. This made them much easier to handle. This year's calves being older were calmer in the barn and hence did not suffer from rope burn. They therefore had plenty of power with which to resist our efforts to lead them around. Nevertheless, after the first couple of days I could usually handle them on my own and after a week's work they became docile

There were a couple of incidents that enlivened our days. Since we heated everything with coal, we generated substantial ashes. We deposited these ashes on a pile in the middle of the yard. One morning after a

76

Chinook, the entire yard was like a skating rink. When we led the first calf to water, it was quite a contest. Neither the calf nor we had very good footing - until it managed to get on to that ash-pile. Our attempts to dislodge it were comical. It instinctively knew better than to leave the ashes where it had sure footing. We on the other hand had to get off the pile and on to the ice where we had no footing at all. Despite the use of an electric cattle prod, it took us an hour to dislodge that calf.

On another morning as I was leading a calf to water on my own, a moment's inattention on my part allowed the calf to get its head turned directly away from me (a real no-no). I did not have a chance to hold it so away it went. I had enough presence of mind to hang on to the rope. It galloped across the yard dragging me along flat on my stomach. I was finally able to stop it when it dragged me across the hitch of the threshing machine.

Mr. Brockelsby in addition to being a farmer was also an amateur blacksmith of some ability. He owned a forge (which I cranked) and made his own cold chisels. In the summer he sharpened his own plowshares as well. He was an impatient man who yelled at me a lot. When I cranked the forge, I could never do it at just the right speed. Since I did not have the experience to judge the heat of the fire, I did not know when to speed up and when to slack off the airflow. His son Leonard on the other hand was a joy to work for. He was not only patient and polite, but very kind and friendly as well.

Although I lived in the bunkhouse as I had done at the Nelsons, I was in all other respects treated as one of the family. The Brockelsbys had two daughters - one was married to a Murray and the other to a Swanson, who both farmed nearby. We visited back and forth with these families every Sunday and they always included me in their activities. We usually played cards during these visits and I learned to play Norwegian Whist and Pinochle that winter. After I returned to work for Art Nelson in the spring, I continued visiting the Brockelsby clan regularly.

Once during a visit to the Murray family, we ate meat from an antelope that they had shot that afternoon. After dinner we popped corn and played cards for the rest of the evening. I became violently ill that night, and had severe diarrhea and vomiting all the next day. The fresh antelope meat probably caused my distress, but I unconsciously associated it with all the popcorn I had eaten. It would be many years before I got over feeling nauseated by the smell of fresh popcorn at movie theaters.

Larry G. Jacobsen

Art Nelson again

I went back to work for Art Nelson again on March first of 1947. There I worked for $45 per month until mid April when he raised my wages to $70 again. My work continued much as before, but during Easter He left me alone while they went away for two or three weeks.

My day started with lighting the fire in the kitchen stove, then milking the cows, followed by making my breakfast. One morning after milking, I returned to the house to find it on fire! The stovepipe where it entered the brick chimney had gotten so hot that it had ignited the ceiling. I was able to get into the attic with a pail of water and quickly douse the fire, but it was a near thing. If I had been just a few minutes longer with my milking, I would surely have burned down the house. I did my best to hide the damage with paint, but some of the wood above the stovepipe had been deeply charred and no amount of paint could hide that. When Art Nelson returned, his only comment was; "I see you had a fire."

My first job that spring was painting the house before we started plowing and seeding. Both the roof and the walls of the house were covered with cedar shingles. I did not find painting the roof too difficult, but the walls were a different matter. Painting the bottoms of the shingles and gaps between them on the vertical walls was tedious painstaking work. I wore out several paintbrushes from poking them up into the shingle bottoms and into the gaps between them. Those weathered dried out old shingles consumed a heck of a lot of paint, but the house was transformed.

I don't remember a thing about putting in the crops that spring, nor irrigating them later. I do remember that Art had a large acreage in alfalfa and I do remember haying.

Mr. Nelson not only purchased hail insurance that spring, but he decided to get triple coverage by insuring with three different companies. He must have been prescient, for hail destroyed all his crops that summer. I suspect that he made more money from the insurance than he would have done if he had actually harvested those crops. Nevertheless, we still had a lot of haying to do, because the alfalfa produced a later cutting.

I purchased a saddle horse for $65 from a local schoolteacher that same spring. It not only included the saddle, but a colt as well. Art Nelson did not complain about the grass my horse ate, but he ordered me to shoot the colt since he did not think it was worth anything. I enjoyed that horse very much because it made it easier for me to get around and visit my friends. It also allowed me to explore the Bow River area in my free time. On several occasions I rode it all the way to Tilley to visit my family.

78

In the fall of 1947, Art Nelson purchased a hay baler because it was easier to sell hay that was baled. It also brought a higher price. He had the hay he had put up that summer and from the previous summer as well.

There were six or seven men on the baling crew. Two to three men on the stack forked the hay into the baler; two men tied the bales and one to two men stacked them. The farm tractor powered the baler by means of a belt. The person inserting the wooden blocks to separate the bales also controlled their size. This same person inserted the tie-wires through slots in each block, to a man on the other side who then tied them. With a bit of experience we were able to size each bale to the one hundred pounds that we strove to maintain.

Except for tying the bales, it was hard (hence warm) work, so we switched jobs whenever someone got cold. I very much enjoyed this job and reveled in the ease with which I was able to handle bales that weighed almost as much as me (I then weighed less than 120 pounds). When we finished baling all of Art Nelson's hay, we baled the hay on the farms owned by some of the crew-members as well. By Christmas time we had finished all of the baling and I decided to find work in BC instead of staying there for another winter.

Chapter 9 - British Columbia

The East Kootenays

I returned to Tilley and spent Christmas with my parents and before heading to Invermere, BC to look for work. Instead of taking the train to Golden, I went through the Crowsnest Pass to Cranbrook. From Cranbrook I rode in a lone coach hitched to the rear of a long freight train. This coach was very old. It had an antiquated heater that burned charcoal briquettes. Instead of upholstered seats, there were wooden benches bolted to the floor. It was probably the same kind of "Settler's Coach" that had carried us from Halifax to Edgewater in 1929, and from Edgewater to Golden in 1937

The worst part of the ride was the stopping and the starting at each station. Each time the locomotive came to a stop, the freight cars would slam into one another. The passenger coach being last got the worst of it. When its turn came, it would go from a fair speed to a violent stop. Each time the train started, the reverse held. The coach then lurched from a standstill to an instant speed of several miles per hour.

I met an eighteen-year old guy named Peter Young on the train who was on his way home to Invermere. He and I hit enjoyed the trip and especially the discomfiture of the conductor. We had quite laugh at this man, who despite his experience was nevertheless caught off guard once. He was going out the forward door of the coach, when it came to a sudden and violent stop. The conductor flew a few feet and slammed into the rear end of the freight car ahead of him.

When we got to Invermere, Peter took me to meet his family. They were just going out "curling" and I came along to see what this sport was all about. The curling rink was outdoors, on Lake Windermere. I had never before seen curling stones, and I was not particularly impressed by the game.

When I arrived in Invermere, there was a picture of a local Aboriginal man named Jimmy Joe together with a dead cougar on the front page of the local paper. This intrepid young man had spotted the cougar up in a tree. He climbed up the tree armed with only a jackknife tied to the end of a pole, and stabbed the cougar. The cat came down, out of the tree, ran about eighty yards and dropped dead. I was told that this same fellow had previously skated down a coyote on Lake Windermere and strangled it with his bare hands.

There was a man named Simon Ronacher who logged in the Invermere area. He also owned both a planer mill and the hotel in nearby Athelmere. This was a prosperous arrangement for him. On payday his beer parlour was one of the few places where the men could cash their paychecks after work. Naturally this did not hurt his beer sales one bit. I was told that the cheques were actually issued to the employees in the beer parlour, but I don't know if this was really true.

Simon Ronacher's wife ran the hotel. There was a story going around that the men's toilet in the hotel got plugged one day. While she was busy with a plunger trying to unplug it, a big logger walked in and said; "I know how that toilet got plugged." Mrs. Ronacher whirled around and demanded to know how? The logger then continued with; "That's a two inch pipe, isn't it?" "Yes," she conceded. "Well, a man with a three inch asshole sat on it, that's how." retorted the logger.

I immediately began asking around for work and soon I found a job at 70 cents per hour with a man named Kon Feller. He owned a small logging operation seven miles out of town where he was sawing ties for the CPR. He lived in a large house on a small farm and he provided me with a furnished shack in which to live while I worked for him. It was not much in the way of living quarters, but not much worse than I was used to back on the farm. Kon had three young sons aged from ten to fourteen. The oldest one usually helped out at the mill when he was not in school.

The mill was located about two miles up the hill from the house. There we cut eight foot long logs and skidded them to the mill, each of us using a single horse. If a log was too large for a lone horse to pull, we harnessed the two horses together for the job. Kon had two other employees as well when I first arrived, but they soon left for better paying jobs. He asked me to feed and tend the horses before and after work and promised that he would pay me additional time for doing this.

My job with Kon Feller varied a lot. On some days His son and I felled trees and cut them into logs with a crosscut saw. On other days we skidded these logs to the mill. Whenever we started the mill up, Kon was the sawyer and I was the "tail-sawyer". My job as tail-sawyer included stacking the slabs in one pile, the ties in another and the lumber in still others. Whatever was left over after making ties out of a log was usually cut into 2x4s and 2x6s. The ties were two sizes; Number two ties were 6 inches by 8 inches by 8 feet long and weighed over 100 pounds. Number ones were 7 inches by 9 inches by 8 feet long and usually weighed 120 pounds, but with some being much heavier. Since I weighed only 120 pounds, packing these ties away from the saw was heavy work, but it was not nearly as bad as loading them into railway cars.

Whenever we hauled a load of ties into town, we had to load them into either box-cars or into steel gondolas. It was not too hard to pull the ties from the top of the load up on to a gondola, but as we got to the bottom of the load, the work became brutal. We would have to reach down over four feet, drive a pickaroon into the tie and then drag it up to the level where we were standing, before stacking it in the car.

I enjoyed working with Kon Feller's oldest son, but I soon discovered that his youngest was filching food from my shack. On my next shopping trip I bought some castor oil. I then made a plate of fudge candy into which I mixed the laxative. The following day the youngster had to ride into town to get the mail. That trip took him much longer than usual – he had to dismount a number of times because of diarrhea. I had no more problems with my food disappearing after that, and his older brothers got quite a kick out of the incident.

Between the farm and the mill were two hills. The upper one was probably ¾ mile in length. It was steep and had one sharp curve on it. From the bottom of this hill to the top of the lower hill was about ¼ mile, which in turn was ½ mile long. When I arrived, in Invermere, I bought a pair of skis. I did not get ski poles since they cost too much and I did not consider them necessary. I wore laced up rubber boots, which afforded me very little control over those skis.

On Sundays, the boys and I would go skiing. We walked to the top of the second hill and tried to ski down without falling. The road consisted of two icy ruts on which were some occasional horse droppings. We knew nothing about ski wax, but it was in any case not needed because the skis slid quite well on the ice. The problem was when we hit the horse droppings. They were very effective brakes, and we seldom stayed upright when we hit them. The sharp curve in the road was another formidable hazard. It was impossible to stay in the original rut on that curve. If I began in the inside rut, I would immediately slide over into the outer one. If I was already in the outer rut, I would instantly be into the trees and have to fall down or collide with them. It was not very often that we could make it from top to bottom of that hill without falling, but when we did, we had enough momentum to carry us over to the second hill. This gave us a total run of 1.5 miles!

My recollections of skiing down those hills include memories of arms and legs flailing in all directions as we rolled, tumbled and somersaulted down the hill after falling. The amazing thing was that we never got hurt. That did not happen until we tried ski jumping down at the farm. We made a ramp using some ties and planks and skied over it. We did not know that the landing area should not be flat. After one hard landing on my tailbone, we all stopped ski jumping.

Kon Feller shut down his operation during Easter of 1948, and went to Alberta to visit relatives. I caught a ride with them as far as Cranbrook where I got a bad tooth extracted. My old friend Gordon Nielsen from Tilley was in Cranbrook, so I promptly looked him up. He was not working and we soon decided that he should come back to Invermere with me. We stayed a couple of days in Cranbrook and caught a ride to Kimberley to see someone he knew there. By this time we were both out of money so we decided to head back to Invermere. After breakfast I first went to the bank and asked them to wire some money to me from my account in Brooks, but when it did not arrive by closing time we had to leave because we had no place to sleep and no money for food.

We left Kimberley when the bank closed. We had not eaten since early morning and were already hungry but we did not have any choice but to hit the road. During the first part of the afternoon, it was not so bad, for we got a couple of short rides. But as the evening wore on, no one picked us up. To make matters worse, Gordon had a suitcase that seemed to weigh a ton. We took turns carrying it, but I still developed a painful stitch in my side.

We were both wearing oxfords, but since the road was paved and bare, it was pretty good walking. When we tried to build a fire and rest, we got colder from wading around in the foot deep snow than we gained from any fire we managed to start. To feed the fire we had to dig in the snow for branches which tended to be too wet to burn well, so we finally gave up on that endeavor. Meanwhile the soles of my shoes started to peel back from the toe. It got so that I had to kick each foot as I took a step so that the soles wouldn't double up under my feet.

It was a very long night! We were tired and hungry and our sides ached miserably. I knew that there was a hotel at Canal Flats and I kept telling Gordon that once we got there, we could curl up on a chesterfield in a nice warm lobby and get some rest.

We finally reached Canal Flats – at five the next morning. We had to leave the highway and walk a mile to get to the village. We did find the hotel there and the door to the lobby was open as expected, but we found it was just as cold in the lobby as outside. Instead of a chesterfield there were just a few wooden kitchen chairs, and that was all!

After resting and freezing in the hotel lobby for an hour, we decided to hit the road again. But now our luck changed. We barely reached the highway when a logging truck picked us up. After the driver dropped us off, we walked for perhaps another hour and then got a ride all the way to Invermere. In Invermere I had an account at the grocery store, so it was not long before we were stuffing ourselves with cinnamon buns. After buying some more groceries, we headed out to Kon Feller's place and reached it by noon. We calculated that during the past twenty hours we had walked over thirty-five miles.

Kon Feller came back after a three week holiday. He immediately hired Gordon and we stayed and worked for him until it was time for me to go back and help Dad on the farm as I had previously promised him. During the time we were waiting for Kon Feller to return we went hunting and shot a deer (out of season) to help keep down our grocery bill. We also bought a bottle of whiskey and I got drunk for the first time in my life.

Back on the farm it was customary to pay the hired help in the fall after the crops had been sold. During the summer the farmers gave the hired men small advances with which to buy tobacco and other necessities. When I went to work for Kon Feller, I did not ask for my pay, but took advances for buying groceries, as I needed them. That was a blunder! When I left in the spring to go back home, he paid me for only 5 to 6 hours a day. He rounded my time to the nearest quarter hour and allowed me nothing for tending the team nor driving them to and from the mill. Then to add insult to injury, he wrote a letter to my father suggesting that I had been doing some high living. I think this was to explain to Dad why I came home almost broke.

Back on Dad's Farm

During that summer of 1948 my father, acquired 80 acres of raw prairie land seven miles to the west. We irrigated it with recycled water, which we pumped from the adjacent spill ditch. The soil on this new land was of good quality and never having been farmed, was very rich. Compared to the home farm, this soil was a treat to work.

That same year my saddle horse and Dad's team of horses got out when a gate was left open. They were never found. During this era, just after the war, there were people in the business of rounding up unclaimed horses that ran free on the prairies. They sold them to meat packers who in turn butchered them and shipped the meat to Europe. I suspect that our horses met that fate – no one bothered looking for brands on the animals they caught.

That autumn, my brother Frank, who was then seventeen, left home and found a job near Invermere. He returned shortly before Christmas at which time he suggested that I come back to BC with him. My parents decided that this was a good time to celebrate Christmas with old friends in Edgewater. Dad owned a 1947 International pickup truck, and since it could accommodate just three people, and since Frank had a return ticket to Golden, one of us would have to take the train. Frank and I flipped a coin and I took the train.

On the morning I left Frank drove me to the station at 4:00 AM. An attendant flagged down the train, which did not normally stop at Tilley. I had earlier agreed to pay Frank $3.00 for my share of the ticket and gave him the money at the station.

My train ride to Golden was uneventful and I arrived there early the following morning. When I went to buy a ticket for the Golden-Cranbrook Stage Line (a limousine), I discovered that I did not have enough money. At first I thought I must have lost my money on the train, so the stationmaster wired ahead to see if anyone had found it, but no such luck. I had no choice, but to start walking and hope for a ride. It turned out later that I had, in the dark, mistakenly given Frank my $20 bill in place of a $1 bill.

It was December 24th and the weather was mild with a few snowflakes falling. I was wearing oxfords, but no overshoes since I had not expected to walk. The road was not overly slippery, but my shoes had leather soles and with each step I took, they would slip back just a little. This slipping was much worse when I was walking up hill. There was practically no traffic and it began to appear that I might have to walk the entire sixty miles to Edgewater. Meanwhile an older chap caught up with me. He was a very fast walker, and there was no way that I was going to let him out-walk me, so I kept up to him. When he left me at Parsons, we had walked twenty-four miles in six hours! By now it was late afternoon, but I continued to walk for another hour before my luck finally changed. First a middle aged female schoolteacher picked me up, and later I got a ride with a salesman from Investor's Syndicate. This man took me all the way to Edgewater. From there I had a mere one-mile walk to Niels Nielsen's farm. When I arrived Frank and my parents were already there. I immediately asked Frank to see his wallet. He was some surprised when I plucked out my twenty-dollar bill which he did not even know that he had. I had arrived a bit late, but not too late to enjoy a wonderful Christmas dinner on a very empty stomach.

After Christmas we found that the mill where Frank had worked was now shut down. I wound up getting a laborer's job with the Paradise mine at their mill site near Invermere and Frank went back home with Mother and Dad.

The Paradise was a high-grade silver-lead-zinc mine located at an elevation of nearly 8,000 feet above seal level. The mill-site was located eight miles below the mine and 5,000 feet lower, beside Toby Creek and about twelve miles from Invermere. They were readying a fifty-ton per day concentrator for production and I wound up digging ditches for water lines in the frozen soil. The temperature was –30° F, but where the snow lay undisturbed, the frost had not penetrated more than a couple of inches. However, any place where a dozer had compressed the snow, the frost was down three feet.

This was my first job in a camp. The food was excellent and I was enjoying the work until my skin began to itch. My body gradually became covered with a rash and the itch from it was driving me nuts. I was there for about three weeks when Mr. Jack Crowhurst complimented me on my work but apologized and said he had to lay me off. I returned to Tilley, and before long, everyone in the house had the same rash that I was suffering from. We finally went in to Brooks to see a doctor. He diagnosed the rash as "Scabies." I had probably gotten it from sleeping on unwashed sheets in the camp. It was quite a job to get rid of the scabies. The easy part was applying the ointment the doctor prescribed. The hard part was boiling all of our clothes and bedding.

My First Mine

I worked for my father again during that summer of 1949, but in October I went back to work at the Paradise mine. This time they gave me a job as a "mucker" inside the mine. My first day underground was spent shoveling ore off the track and into a 1-ton mine car. There was an ore-pass nearby where I dumped the car after filling it. I was able to load and dump twenty loads of muck that first day. When the mine foreman asked me how many cars I mucked, and I told him twenty, his retort was; "Not enough!" I soon realized though, that he was only joking.

The foreman's family lived with him at the mine. He had a three-year-old son who often came unaccompanied to the bunkhouse. There some of the men delighted in teaching him to swear and use foul language. The boy was finally kept at home after the men instructed him to ask his mother if she was getting enough. (His father reputedly had a very small dick).

A couple of days after I came, they put me to work with a young miner named Harold Pretty. I later found that this man had worked underground for less than six months and was hardly qualified to be called a "miner." Our job was to re-timber an old drift (tunnel) to make it safe. Normal practice required us to scale down the loose rock before timbering under

A timbered drift. *Photo taken by the author courtesy of the Britannia Mining Museum at Britannia Beach, BC*

it. Mr. Pretty did not believe in doing this because we would then have to hand muck the rock off the track. It was while I was working with Harold that I used up Life #2, (See Chapter 26 - "This Cat Had More than Nine Lives."

I turned 21 on December 9th while I was at the Paradise mine. I had the strange experience of being chased by a bull in my dreams every single night for the whole month. I have since read quite a lot of Carl Jung's work on dreams, but it has not helped me understand this weird episode.

Joe Fryea was the next miner I worked with. He had worked underground for over six years, but unlike Mr. Pretty, he was safety conscious. While I worked with Joe Fryea, we drove drift using a "leyner." This was an air-powered drill mounted on a bar and arm. Our light was produced by carbide lamps, which were notorious for going out. We were forever cleaning their nozzles and re-lighting

A 1 ton "end dump" muck car hooked to an air powered locomotive. *Photo taken by the author courtesy of the Britannia Mining Museum at Britannia Beach, BC*

them. One day Joe became so enraged that he hurled his lamp down the drift as far as he could throw it. After he cooled down, he retrieved it, straightened the bent reflector and re-lit it. Surprisingly, it worked much better after that.

There were two McKenzie brothers working at the mine and Fraser, the younger one was my roommate. They came from Inverness on Cape Breton Island, Nova Scotia and Fraser was the same age as me. I don't recall much about them, but I do remember some colorful experiences they related.

Larry G. Jacobsen

A "Crank Leyner" similar to what Joe Fryea and I used. *Photo taken by the author courtesy of the Britannia Mining Museum at Britannia Beach, BC*

Fraser told me he was walking home late one night and in the process had to go by the local graveyard. It was a dark moonless night and as he came abreast of the cemetery, he heard the sound of subdued voices coming from a nearby grave. He could distinguish words such as; "You can have that one and I'll take this one." He immediately pictured God in discourse with Satan dividing up the souls of the dead!

Eventually he got past the eerie place and arrived home safely. The next day the local newspaper carried an account of a jewelry store robbery of the previous evening. What Fraser had heard was the thieves divvying up the loot in the relatively safety of the graveyard.

His older brother had worked for a time at an Insane Asylum. He told me that he was walking across a field one day where some of the inmates were haying, when one of them began chasing him with a pitch fork in hand. Fraser, his heart pounding ran for the safety of the asylum, but the inmate kept gaining on him. Finally, when he could run no father, the inmate caught up, tapped him on the shoulder and said; "You're it!" He had been playing "tag."

I was introduced to Poker at the mine. For all the brains I thought I had, I was a remarkably slow learner, but that did not stop me from becoming addicted to the game. Joe tried to dissuade me from playing, but I was too stubborn to heed his advice. I lost most of my pay checks while I was there.

One evening I experienced a mild case of food poisoning. I began having cramps a couple of hours after dinner and remained rooted on the toilet with diarrhea and vomiting late into the night. I must have had a fairly weak stomach, for no one else had symptoms nearly as severe as mine.

One Saturday afternoon in late November, a few of us went to Invermere together with the only miner (an ex sailor named Gallant) who

88

owned a car. It was snowing heavily at the mine, but as we descended from the higher elevations, the snow turned to rain. We did not stay long in Invermere, but bought some beer and a set of chains for Gallant's car before heading back. At the mill camp we stopped and partied with the cat skinner before heading back up the hill at 1:00 AM.

It was still raining heavily at the mill-site, but we did not get very far before we were into the snow. By the time we had gotten half way up the hill, we had torn the chains apart and could drive no farther. The road had a grade of 25% and the snow was by now over two feet deep, so at 3:00 AM we abandoned the car and started walking. We were all physically fit, but it still took us a full four hours to walk the last four miles to the mine. The company shut the mine down in early January because they could not keep the road open with the equipment on hand so we all went job hunting.

During that same month, the liquor store in Invermere burned down. It was a popular event with many of the residents, because the more daring of them were able to salvage cases of liquor from the burning building. While they were engrossed in this, some of the teenagers were stealing it from their cars and stashing it elsewhere. It was some time before the local residents again needed to buy liquor.

Meanwhile, we had heard that the city of Toronto was driving a tunnel for a subway so we took the train there. I accompanied Joe Fryea there together with another young man named Kenny. When we left Cranbrook, the temperature was –40°F. When we arrived in Toronto, it was raining and the grass was green. It was the first time I had ever seen green grass during winter. The subway turned out to be an open excavation and did not require miners. I had no more money left, so Joe gave me $50 - enough for a bus ticket to Tilley. I did get to see one boxing match in the Maple Leaf Gardens while we were in Toronto.

The trip back west via Greyhound was through Detroit, Chicago and Minneapolis and back up to Winnipeg. North of Chicago I saw sleet for the first time. The road was so slippery that the bus had to crawl at a mere five miles per hour for a while. I saw a tandem axle fuel truck in front of us that was trying make a turn, but kept going straight ahead. When the driver stepped out of the truck to see what the problem was, his feet shot out from under him. He would have gone flying had he not been holding on to the door handle of the truck.

From Minneapolis to Winnipeg the temperature was –30° F and in Winnipeg the wind was howling down the street at Portage and Main. I was not dressed for such weather. I had also missed my connections due to the icy roads near Chicago and I now had a choice of either spending

24 hours in Winnipeg, or twelve hours there and twelve hours in Swift Current, Saskatchewan. I chose the latter because I had no money for a hotel room.

The trip across Saskatchewan was in temperatures that dipped to –60° F and it was the only time I have ever been cold in a Greyhound bus. Eventually I arrived in Tilley after a trip that took three days instead of the normal two.

Dickson & Tilley Farms

That spring I worked for my sister Ester's husband, Henry for six weeks helping him put in the crop near Dickson, Alberta. While I was there, I had my first date. I borrowed Henry's pickup truck to visit a young woman I had first met at the Sylvan Lake Bible Camp some years earlier. Her name was Ardis Knorr and she was in her first year of teaching in a small nearby school. I was so entranced by her, but also so timid and shy that I remained tongue tied the whole evening and did not have the guts to ask her for another date.

After leaving Dickson I returned to Tilley and worked for our former neighbor, Art Burton for the rest of the summer. We did not discuss my wages until the time came for me to leave that fall when I asked him for $135 per month – the same as my father was paying his hired man. Art did not want to pay me this amount because he was paying his full time man $125 per month. He maintained that since I did not have the same amount of experience as this other man, he could not pay me any more than him. I did not consider myself less experienced for I believed that I produced more than anyone else that worked there. I argued that since I was able to irrigate twice as much per day as anyone else, he should at least pay me the higher rate during the irrigation season, which he then did.

Chapter 10 - Final Goodbye to Farming

The East Kootenays Again

My brother Gerard had come to BC and found a job at Moore's sawmill in Edgewater. He promptly wrote to me to come out there. I arrived in Edgewater in October and was immediately hired. Gerard was living at a boarding house owned by Mr. O.P. Nielsen, and I soon shared a room with him there.

The Moore sawmill cut about 20,000 board feet (fbm) per day and employed about a dozen men in addition to the foreman. While I was there, I worked at every position except that of "sawyer" and "Edgerman." I also worked for a few days at the planer mill as well as loading lumber into boxcars. We worked forty-four hours a week and our wages were $1.10 per hour.

We had a one-hour lunch break each day during which most of the married men went home to eat. A few of us brought our lunches with us and ate them at the mill. One of the men who stayed at the mill to eat was an older man named Jackson. He was a born storyteller and he would forget to eat while relating an adventure. When we noticed this trait, we soon learned to prompt him for another story as soon as he had finished the one he was telling. He seldom got to eat much of his lunch after that.

One weekend there was a dance at the Edgewater community hall. I prepared for it by ordering a twenty-six of rum and a thirteen-ounce bottle of "Drambuie" for the event. At this time I knew absolutely nothing about mixing drinks – we all drank it straight. Whenever I invited someone out for a drink, I would offer them swigs out of each bottle. I soon learned that they would drink the rum, but not the Drambuie, so I drank it myself. Meanwhile, I was of course sharing my friends' bottles as well.

It was not very long before I got sick. I left the hall and started on my walk to the boarding house. I remember vomiting in the snow and I remember falling down, but I did get home. When I entered the house, O.P. Larsen said; "I see you made it home." I replied; "You bet!" I also made it up the stairs – well almost up the stairs. I collapsed on the second step from the top. O.P. and another boarder came and put me to bed. I was aware of all they were saying about me, but I was paralyzed and unable to move or say anything. This was my first real hangover, but it was a nasty one!

I got two black eyes while I worked at Moore's mill. The first one was an accident that occurred one evening when another young fellow and I were horsing around. The second one I deserved. Gerard and I often played rummy with a middle-aged boarder whose nickname was "Liverlips." Liverlips was not very bright, but he was big and must have weighed at least 250 pounds. There was no money involved in the game, but we started to cheat, just to frustrate Liverlips. He finally caught me slipping a card to my brother. I was sitting in a low wicker chair and before I could get up, he rained a number of punches on my face. I got a lot of sympathy, but also some teasing over that incident. Those were the only black eyes I have ever endured.

Pacific Diamond Drilling

In early 1951 while I was still working at Moore's sawmill, a gentleman came up from Vancouver and stayed briefly at the boarding house. His name was Cy Keyes, and he was the owner of Pacific Diamond Drilling Co. His company was doing foundation testing for a potential dam at Brisco, BC for the British Columbia Power Commission, (the fore-runner of BC Hydro).

While he was staying with us, he taught me how to play cribbage and according to my landlord, cheated me regularly. I believe that I wound up paying for all his cigarettes, but then he offered me a job. I shortly went to work for him on his churn drill as a driller's helper.

The job consisted of drilling an eight-inch hole to bedrock or to a depth of two hundred feet, whichever came first. An 8-inch diameter casing was first driven some distance and then the material inside the casing was liquefied and bailed out. Undisturbed core samples were taken ahead of the casing at regular intervals as well. If bedrock was encountered, a diamond drill hole was then drilled fifty feet into the rock to provide core samples of the rock.

There were two three-man crews operating the drill on ten-hour shifts. The foreman was an experienced diamond driller named Chuck Morley. He and his wife lived in a tent right at the job site. Mrs. Morley prepared the crew's meals in a cook tent and was assisted by one of the driller's wives. I was shocked by the women's bawdy language during my first meal in the tent. I had never heard women swear or use foul language before. Back in the farming community where I came from only a few men used such language. There had not been much swearing at Moore's sawmill either. It was too noisy, and at lunch time most of the crew went home to eat.

We finished the Brisco job shortly after my arrival. Since I had a driver's license, I became the truck driver and hauled the equipment to our next job at Saint Mary's Lake near Kimberly. To reach the job site I turned off at Marysville and drove about fifteen miles up to the lake via a road that was not much more than a trail. On my first trip I almost had an accident. As I came around a sharp corner, the truck suddenly left the road and plowed straight ahead into the trees. Fortunately for me there was no ditch and I was able to stop before hitting a tree of any size. When I crawled under the truck to see what the problem was, I found that the tie-rod had come off on one end. Its ball joint was completely worn out! I was able to join the two parts with some wire and that held everything together until I got back down the hill to Kimberly. There I was able to replace the worn parts and continue back to Brisco for another load.

The Crowsnest Lumber Company owned a saw-mill on the shore of the lake and housed their crew in an adjacent bunkhouse. When we arrived we were able to rent space there for all of the crew except two. So Frank and I stayed six miles downriver at the McGuinness logging camp for a few days until we too moved into the sawmill camp. This turned out to be an unforgettable experience for both of us, but especially for Frank.

The McGuinness Logging Camp

No one seemed to know much about him. He had worked at this camp longer than any of other the men I spoke with, some of whom had been there for several years. He spoke infrequently, kept to himself and apparently had no friends except for the team of horses with which he worked every day, and in whose company he spent his evenings.

His name was George Longcott and he was 70 years old, but in remarkable condition for his age. He had been called "Longcock" for so long that some of his coworkers believed that to be his true name. Some even insisted that this was the name that appeared on his pay checks.

He was the type of chap that would have drawn attention anywhere, even in a logging camp. He was a tall lanky man with a fierce visage - not the kind to invite idle chatter or probing into his background. His head was topped by a large unruly mass of hair that had probably been black in earlier times, but was now a mixture of grey, white and black. It was unkempt and he wore it long at a time when this was very uncommon. He had a beard that was at least twelve inches long and was just as scraggly as his hair. He also had a huge walrus mustache, which completely covered his mouth and blended in with his beard. It was impossible to tell just exactly where one ended and the other began and his mouth was completely hidden by them. It became visible only at meal times or on the rare occasions when he spoke. He reminded me of a painting of Moses delivering the Ten Commandments.

George wore clothes typical for a logger - a woolen plaid jacket, woolen trousers held up by heavy suspenders, and a plaid shirt, as well as woolen Stanfield underwear commonly called "long johns." In George's case there was one major difference. He reputedly put on a new suit of long johns each autumn and kept it on until he discarded it the following spring. Needless to say, one could often smell George's presence.

Frank had been away from home for over a year. He was in some ways worldly, but in others still quite naive. For a seventeen-year-old though, he was very mature. He was a gutsy young fellow who dearly loved partying and having a good time. He also appeared to be very popular with the opposite sex and had at least one steady girlfriend back in Creston.

Frank's father had farmed a small orchard in Creston before being killed in World War II. His late grandfather had been a cabinet minister in the coalition government of BC and had acquired his wealth during the nineteen twenties smuggling liquor into the United States during Prohibition.

As camps go this one was not particularly noteworthy. The food was excellent, at least it seemed so to me. It was placed in large serving bowls on a table, which stretched from one end of the dining hall to the other. The food was passed from one person to the next and one had better help oneself the first time around because no one wanted to interrupt their eating to pass it a second time. Such requests were usually met with smart retorts such as; "shut up and eat you dinner."

Much of the food had colorful, but logical as well as highly descriptive names. You would hear commands such as; "pass the iron cow," (canned milk), "send down the cackleberries," (eggs), "have some CPR strawberries," (prunes), "pass the mush," (oatmeal porridge) etc. Until I learned this new jargon, I was sometimes rebuked for being too slow in responding.

Back in 1951 there was very little mechanization in the logging camps. The loggers felled and bucked the trees with crosscut saws. It was brutally hard work and the men ate huge amounts of food to fuel their bodies from one meal to the next. I have never since seen anyone eat such prodigious amounts at every meal!

We quickly discovered that each worker had his own place at the table and that newcomers had better wait until everyone else was seated before choosing their seats. I learned the hard way that taking someone else's place at the table was not tolerated. The chair's rightful owner came and stood at the table glowering at me until someone nudged me and whispered that I was sitting in his chair. It was no fun to find my self with proverbial "egg on my face," but for Frank at least, the worst was yet to come.

It wasn't until the first morning at breakfast that Frank got to meet George Longcott up close for he was seated directly across the table from him. Not only was he treated to the smell that emanated from him, but he soon learned that George had other eccentric habits as well.

George began his morning repast by partially filling his breakfast bowl with oatmeal porridge. He next diced up a few fried eggs and stirred them into the porridge. After that he crumbled up two slices of burnt toast and stirred them in as well. He then cradled the bowl in his huge gnarled hands and raised it to his mouth. Accompanied by a cacophony of slurping sounds he sucked in the unholy mess while straining it through his beard in the process. When he was finished his beard looked awful! Poor Frank! He was mesmerized, his gaze riveted by the performance. He completely forgot his own food, and sat entranced by the sight of porridge, crumbs and pieces of egg profusely embedded in the mustache and beard of the man across the table from him. He could not in any event have eaten his own breakfast for he came dangerously close to bringing up the little he had already eaten.

From that day on, Frank ate sparingly at each meal, keeping his gaze focused intently on his own plate. Not once did his curiosity allow him to look up until he had finished his food and escaped from the table. Fortunately for him, we stayed in the logging camp for only few more days before we were able to move in with the rest of our drill crew at the sawmill camp.

On the St. Mary's Lake job we had to drill four holes about one half mile downstream from the lake. One hole was in the middle of the river, one on the far (south) side and two on the north side. We constructed the drill site in the middle of the river by creating a small gravel island and connecting it to the shore with a makeshift log bridge. Unfortunately, it was now April and the weather had suddenly become very warm.

We had almost completed the first hole when the river suddenly rose several feet overnight. The island was being inundated and our log bridge was in danger of being swept away. We were able to retrieve the drill casing, abandon the hole and get the drill back to shore by morning. It was a near thing for by this time the river had risen over five feet! It took several days, but eventually we had a dozer push a substantial dike out from the cut bank on the far side of the river and we were able to re-drill this hole without further incident.

One day a former employee came out to visit us while we were drilling. He passed a bottle of whiskey around, and before long the driller was slightly inebriated. While he was pulling casing pipe out of the hole, he caused it to vibrate and gyrate wildly about. When I grabbed the pipe to steady it, I promptly got a fingernail smashed between the pipe and the derrick. I did not realize until much later that my finger was actually broken, so it was small wonder that it hurt so much.

On the job we were not well equipped and one luxury we did not have was a gasoline pump. We regularly used a hose to siphon gasoline out of a barrel and into a pail to fuel the drills and the small pumps. One day while performing this chore, I had a larger siphon hose than usual. As I sucked on it I felt the gas starting to come, but I sucked once more, just to be sure. As I did this, the gas erupted into my mouth, into my stomach and down my windpipe! I immediately began a sneezing bout such as I have never before, nor since, experienced. I sneezed several times a second for at least ten minutes before it eased up even a little bit. Over the next hours my sneezing slowly abated, but it not stop for the rest of the day and continued far into the night. I have since learned that getting gasoline in the lungs is very dangerous and often fatal.

Spillimacheen

When we finished at St. Mary's Lake we moved the diamond drill to Spillimacheen. Chuck Morley was driving, Ed Litviak was in the middle and I was sitting next to the door on the passenger side when I began to notice a rotten smell. I was wondering who was responsible until I noticed that whenever I took a drag on my cigarette the smell got worse. It finally dawned on me that it was my smashed finger that was creating the stench. I got out a nail clipper and my knife and slowly cut the blackened fingernail off. There was a

A small diamond drill similar to the one I operated. Photo taken by the author courtesy of the Britannia Mining Museum at Britannia Beach, BC

deep groove under the fingernail and it was full of rotting pus! My finger eventually healed, but it was many years before that groove filled in and my fingernail was able to grow out to the end of my misshapen finger.

At Spillimacheen I took over as the driller on the diamond drill and Ed became my helper. We stayed at a motel where some of the Giant Mascot mineworkers were also living.

On July 1st Chuck, Ed, and I decided to try to find an old abandoned silver mine somewhere near the head of the Bugaboo valley. No one was sure just how far it was and everyone had a different opinion about it. One of the men from the Giant Mascot mine named Robinson had an open 1928 Dodge car and he agreed to drive us out there. Robinson had been shot down while serving in the RCAF during World War II and now had silver plates in one leg. He walked with a pronounced limp, but it did not seem to slow him down very much.

The Bugaboo Spire. *Photo taken by the author.*

We left Spillimacheen at 7:00 in the morning and proceeded up a BC Forestry road where we found a small crew working on the access. They had opened up the first 12 miles of it, but from there on it was slow going indeed. It took us four hours to travel the next 13 miles. We had to stop frequently to cut down willows and small trees growing in the middle of the road. In some places we even had to corduroy our way across mud holes. Twenty-five miles from town we came upon a cabin belonging to a local guiding outfit. From there it was impossible to drive any farther, because there were big trees lying across the road.

About four miles before we reached the cabin, the car's clutch suddenly came apart. We found that the "throw-out" fork had gotten disconnected, so from that point on, Robinson shifted gears without using the clutch.

The Bugaboo valley was a stunningly beautiful area, which aside from the primitive road, was still untouched by human hands. It was densely covered with fir, spruce and pine, as well as a number of deciduous trees. It would be many years later before logging would make a significant impact on this pristine valley. There were numerous little waterfalls cascading off the perpendicular cliffs that lined the eastern side of the valley. The Bugaboo was a small river, full of glacial silt, which meandered its way down the broad valley. West of the road was the Bugaboo Spire, a mountain used by climbers for training purposes because of its sheer walls. It was not very high, but it had perpendicular walls. A few years earlier a party of four climbers on it had been killed when they were struck by lightning.

We stopped at noon to eat the lunch that the wives had packed for us. It was a very light lunch indeed – not nearly enough for four men who had toiled mightily to clear the road to get this far. Nevertheless we decided to hike up to the end of the valley which appeared to be not too distant. By 4:00 PM we had reached a glacier, but were not anywhere near the summit. We had not yet seen any signs of old mine workings, so we decided it was high time to head back home. On the way up the valley, and back, we had forded a creek several times, so our socks were wet, but we did not take the time to dry them out. For me this turned out to be a very poor decision.

We got back to the car by 7:00 PM and began the long drive back to town. We had not gotten very far, when with a loud bang the engine quit and the car skidded to an abrupt stop. We found that the clutch throw-out fork was jammed between the flywheel and the housing. We managed to free it, but could not get it out. Each time we freed it, we could drive for only one or two hundred yards before it would get caught in the flywheel again, bringing the car to a screeching halt. Nevertheless, we kept persevering until it became obvious that we would never get home that way.

We then decided that we would have to remove the fork one way or another, but we had practically no tools with us. There was a plate underneath the car just forward of the flywheel. It appeared that if we could remove this plate we might be able to extricate the throw-out fork. I had brought my Husquarna 270 rifle along, so I shot the four bolt heads off. We were able to remove the cover but alas, it turned out that there was no room to get the fork out this way either. There was nothing for it but to hoof it back to town! We had already, in addition to opening up the road, hiked about 14 miles that day. Now we had to walk another 23 miles to get home.

It was 9:00 PM when we abandoned the car. We had not eaten since noon, so we were all weak with hunger. By this time Robinson's leg was giving him a great deal of trouble as well. Still he limped gamely along. I left my camera in the car, but took along my rifle.

We were hiking along briskly, and it was just getting dark when Chuck, looking back, saw a cougar following us. It slunk quickly into the bush, but before long we saw it on the trail behind us once more. I fired a shot back in its general direction and from then on we saw no more sign of it.

We reached the Forestry's camp at 1:00 AM. We awakened the crew, who fed us some canned sausages, bread and coffee. What a relief that was because we were by now all suffering from severe side pains from walking on empty stomachs. We were soon on the road again, but Robinson was at the end of his endurance, so we left him at the camp and continued on our way.

By this time my heels were getting very sore. When I removed my boots, I found that each heel was entirely covered with a large blister. It was my own fault for not having taken the time to dry my wet socks. It was not too painful to set my feet down, but it was agonizing to lift them up. I tried a number of things to ease the pain, but nothing worked. I even tried walking backwards down the hills to keep the weight off my heels, but to no avail. It became an exercise of taking one painful step at a time, and then another and another.

We arrived back at the motel at 8:00 AM and went straight to bed. Not one of us even considered going to work that day. The Forestry crew delivered Robinson back to town later in the day, so he too missed a scheduled shift. We never did find out where that mine was. All we learned from our adventure was where it was not.

It was not very long after this that I drove the flatbed truck to Vancouver and rolled it on the Cascade section of Highway 3 (See "Chapter 26 This Cat Had More than Nine Lives"). After delivering the truck to the company in Vancouver, I got on the Greyhound bus going back to Golden. It was a long rough ride, for once we left the concrete pavement at Chilliwack, the road was very rough. It took us the afternoon and all night to reach Revelstoke.

I arrived in Revelstoke the following morning at the same time as the train from Vancouver. I was dreading the ride over the Big Bend Highway, so I applied for a refund on the unused portion of my bus ticket and took the train from there to Golden. I saved enough on my bus ticket, to pay for the train ride. Not only did I save money, but I also arrived at Golden four hours earlier than the Greyhound bus!

During our stay at Spillimacheen, we were held up waiting for drill bits more than once, but we still had to pay for our board and lodging. Finally, when we had been idle for a whole week I quit. Ed Litviak quit too and we travelled to Creston where we stayed at the motel he had recently inherited, but was still being held for him in trust.

Larry G. Jacobsen

The Moyie Forest Fire

We were getting bored, and we were also running short of cash, when in August a forest fire broke out south of Cranbrook in the Moyie area. In those days the Forest Service forcibly recruited workers in the bars and on the street. For some reason we were being ignored, even though we walked boldly about not caring whether or not we got picked up. Finally we went to the Forest Service and volunteered our services.

We were hauled up to Moyie in the back of a big truck, from there we hiked ten miles to the fire. Each of us was given a pack-board and expected to carry some supplies along in to the camp. My load was a five-gallon can of gasoline, which was no fun to carry because the contents sloshed around inside its container. The trail to the fire led up over one mountain and down the other side. I soon found that going downhill, though not requiring as much energy, was much harder on the knees. When we reached the camp that evening, the fire was pretty much under control. We were assigned to tents and each given a couple of blankets, but after supper I was sent out on fire patrol along the creek.

I was walking on the ground near the creek when I came to a large log. I hopped onto the log and continued to its far end where I stepped off expecting the ground to be a couple of feet below me. I was surprized when I plunged down six feet through a heavy thorny growth. I had never seen such plants before, and when I asked what they were, I was told; "Devil's Club!" It was such an apt name that I never doubted its veracity.

Things were quiet at the fire and some of the crew had already been sent home when a strong wind came up. During the next two days the fire burned off an area three times its original size. We kept busy with pulaskis (a combination mattock and axe) digging fireguards along the burn boundary. When our camp ran short of food, some of us hiked across two mountain ridges to the base camp for supplies. Since there were no helicopters available in those days, the Forest Service supplied the base camp via parachute drops. From there the food was distributed manually on foot.

We stayed on that fire for three weeks and I think we were paid $6.00 per day (24 hours @ 25 cents per hour). After the fire was out, while Ed and I were hitch hiking back to Creston we got a ride with a man who said he was the manager of the Van Roi mine near Silverton. When I mentioned to him that I had previously worked underground, he suggested that I should come to work for him at the mine.

PART III

MINING AND

CONSTRUCTION

Table III-1 — Mining Glossary

Blasting caps	Small detonators used to initiate the explosion of dynamite
Cage	A vehicle used to transport workers (or materials) up or down a shaft – powered by a hoist.
Chute	A timbered structure at the bottom of an ore pass that allows the muck to be loaded into mine cars when it is opened.
Diggers	Clothes a miner wears underground.
Draw-point	The bottom of a stope from where the ore is drawn.
Drift	A horizontal tunnel.
Electric caps	Caps that are set off by an electrical current.
Face	The end of a drift or a raise, where we drill the next round.
Fan pipe	A rigid or collapsible duct used to blow fresh air into the mine to displace smoke and other noxious gasses.
Galvanometer	A small instrument that measures the resistance of a blasting circuit in ohms.
Heading	A drift or raise working place
Hoist	A large electrical powered single or double drum hoist used to transport men and equipment up and down a shaft.
Jackleg	An air-powered drill attached to an air-leg used to drive drifts.
Jumbo	A self-powered vehicle fitted with two or more air or hydraulic operated drills -usually used in large tunnels or for "long-holing.
Locomotive	A battery, trolley or diesel powered unit used to pull the mine cars into and out of the mine.

Man-way	The portion of a raise or shaft isolated from the rest of it by timber and equipped with ladders for the workers' access.
Muck	Broken ore or waste rock.
Oiler	A small steel oil container inserted into the airline – used to mix a small amount of oil into the air that powers the air tools.
Orebody	Different from a typical vein in that it is often of significant size in three dimensions.
Ore-pass	A raise with a chute at the bottom from which the muck can be drawn and loaded into cars.
Powder	Dynamite
Primer	A stick of dynamite with either an electric or fused cap inserted into it.
Raise	A steep tunnel – usually over 45 degrees and driven from the bottom up.
Rock bolts	Steel bars drilled and cemented into the rock to stabilize it.
Round	A cycle at a heading – drilling, blasting and setting up or mucking out
Safety fuse	A black cord containing black powder that burns at a rate of about 90 seconds per foot of length. It is attached to, and used to set off a blasting cap
Scaling	The act of prying down loose rock that might endanger those working under it.
Shaft	A steep or vertical tunnel driven from the top down.
Sinker	An air powered drill used for sinking shafts.
Skip	A metal bucket powered by a tugger and used to hoist materials up a raise.
Skipway	A wooden slide on which the skip slides in the raise or shaft.
Slickers	Water proof outerwear.
Slusher	A double-drum hoist used to power a scraper to move muck along a drift and into an ore-pass.

Stoper	An air-powered drill used to drive raises.
Tramming	Hauling muck
Trolley	An electrified cable used to power a locomotive - similar to that once used by streetcars.
Tugger	A single drum hoist used to power a skip to hoist materials up a raise.
Vein	The rock containing the ore, often quite extensive, but not very thick.

Table III-2 - Operating Mines In BC During The Early Fifties

Ainsworth
- Kootenay Florence
- Yale Lead & Zinc

Barkerville-Wells
- Caribou Gold Quartz
- Island Mountain

Bridge River
- Braelorne
- Pioneer
- Britannia Beach
- Britannia

Hazelton-Skeena Crossing
- Silver Standard
- Red Rose

Hope
- Giant (Giant Mascot)

Invermere
- Mineral King

Kimberley
- Cominco's Sullivan Mine

New Denver-Silverton
- Van Roi
- Standard
- Mammoth

Princeton-Hedley
- Copper Mountain
- Hedley Nickel Plate

Rossland
- Bluebird

Salmo:
- Canadian Exploration – Jersey Mine and the Dodger tunnels
- Reeves McDonald
- Cominco's HB
- Sheep Creek Gold

Sandon-Kaslo
- Court Province
- Deadman
- Silver Ridge
- Silver Smith
- Sunshine Lardeau
- Utica
- Viola Mac
- Whitewater
- Wellington

Spillimachine
- Giant Mascot

Stewart
- Premier
- Dolly Varden/Torbrit Silver
- Polaris Taku
- Chief
- Bull

Texada
- Vananda
- Empire Iron

Chapter 11 - Mining:
The Early Fifties

Introduction

Back in the early fifties, there were numerous underground mines operating in BC. (See Table III-2 at the start of this section). This is no longer the case. To the best of my knowledge there are practically no underground mines still operating here. Cominco's Sullivan mine at Kimberley closed in 2001. The Great Bear mine west of Telegraph Creek closed after the price of gold fell below $300 per ounce. The Yukon is no better off. During the fifties there were a lot of underground mines operating there too, but none today. Because of these changes, the underground miner in Western Canada has become virtually extinct. The few miners left are generally in their sixties or older.

The Mine & Its "Dry"

Every underground mine in BC was required by law to have a "mine dry." This was a building that contained a set of common showers, probably a locker area for the men, often a lamp room as well as the mine foreman's office. It also had washing machines in which the miners could wash their diggers (underground clothing).

The locker area included a locker for each man and a three or four pronged hook on which to hang his underground clothes between shifts. The clothes hook was attached to a rope, which was threaded through a pulley, suspended from a high ceiling. The clothes were raised to the ceiling for drying, and lowered to shoulder level for access to them. The other end of the rope was in some cases secured inside the locker. When the clothes were raised to the ceiling the warmer air there dried them between shifts – hence the name "dry" for this building.

The shower area was usually one big room within the dry containing a number of showerheads. Here the crew all showered together when they came off shift.

The foreman and the shift bosses used the office from which to give instructions to the miners before they headed into the mine. Here the miners also picked up sharpened drill bits, small tools, or on occasion purchased new slickers or boots.

The lamp room contained a charging area where the miners' lamps were recharged while they were off shift. Here the miner picked up his assigned lamp from the charging rack. He hung the battery on his miner's belt and placed the lamp on his hard hat. The battery provided enough power to power his lamp for eight to ten hours, depending on its age. On his miner's belt he often carried a crescent wrench and a powder punch as well.

A miner's diggers (work clothes) consisted of heavy woolen (usually grey) underwear called "long-johns," woolen socks, jeans, long sleeved work shirt, and his "slickers," also called oilers. When the miner had donned his underground clothes," he picked up his lamp, proceeded to the Shift boss' office and picked up his drill bits and any instructions pertinent to his work. The miner then boarded a "man-car," and rode into the mine. An electric locomotive, powered either by a set of batteries or by a live overhead copper line (similar to that used by city trolley busses), pulled the man-cars.

The miner was let off at his general work area after a ride of up to a mile or more. From there he might have to climb a hundred feet of ladders, or ride a cage in the shaft, to the level on which he was working.

In B.C. the underground rock temperature in a typical mine was around 50° Fahrenheit and varied only near the mine portals or at substantial depth. This was a comfortable temperature in which to work because one was not likely to perspire too much, and yet it was not so cold as to be uncomfortable, unless one sat around for too long. Rock temperature increases about 1° F for each one hundred feet in depth. The bottom levels at the Pioneer Gold Mine near Braelorne were 5000 feet below the surface, and hence about 100° F.

One feature in many BC mines was that there were a number of different levels with the ore fed from the various levels through ore passes down to the bottom level from where it was hauled out to the surface. Both the top level and the bottom one often had exits to the outside. This created a chimney effect, which facilitated great ventilation for most of the year. In the winter when the air outside was colder than the air inside the mine, it entered the mine at the bottom level, rose to the top as it was heated by the warmer rock and then exited at the top level. In the summer when the air outside was warmer than the rock inside, it would enter at the top, fall as it cooled and exit at the bottom. The greater the temperature differential between the air outside and the rock inside the mine, the faster the air would move through the mine. Only when the temperatures inside and out were equal, would there be poor (or no) natural ventilation.

There were two general types of mining; production and development. Production mining entailed drilling and blasting in stopes that had already been developed by others. Development work consisted of opening up new mining areas. This work usually consisted of driving "drifts" (horizontal tunnels), or "raises" (steeply inclined tunnels). A Prima-Donna miner would always opt for development work because it generally paid better. Development mining also required superior knowledge and organization as well as harder work.

Production (Stope) Mining

In the larger mines, the stopes were usually mined using "longhole" drills or in some cases, diamond drills. The holes were typically two and one half, to three inches in diameter and drilled to depths of fifty to one hundred feet. When I worked at Remac, the longhole machines there weighed a little over 300 pounds each, and there were two of them mounted on a bar with two arms with one miner per machine. After I left mining, these two drills were often mounted on a single hydraulic "jumbo" and operated by a lone miner. Loading and blasting the longholes was done by either the drillers, or by full-time powder men.

Development Mining

In the early days every miner had a helper - also called a "nipper" or "chuck tender." In later years in some mines, a miner often worked alone while in others, two miners would work together. In the Reeves McDonald mine where I spent seven years, a development miner invariably worked alone. If he was driving a drift, he had a cross shift (someone on the opposite shift). In a raise this was not the case. There if his bonus earnings were below his expectations, there was no one to blame but himself.

During most of my mining career (1951 to 1964) we worked just two shifts; 8:00 AM to 4:00 PM and 7:00 PM to 3:00 AM. The only exceptions to this were the slusher and tramming crews. They often worked a three-shift schedule in order to supply the concentrator with a steady supply of ore. For the miner, the gap between the shifts provided time to ventilate the mine after the blasts and before the next crew arrived. In some mines the general ventilation was provided for by nature and augmented by fans and ventilation tubing, while in others it was done entirely by nature. At the work heading itself, the gasses were displaced using compressed air left blowing between shifts.

Carbide Lamps

At the Van Roi as in many other small mines that flourished during the fifties, we had no electric lamps, but used carbide lamps instead. A new carbide lamp could produce as bright a light as a two-cell flashlight, but as the reflector tarnished, it lost that brightness. The lamp contained two chambers, a lower chamber for the carbide, and an upper one filled with water. A manual valve on top of the lamp controlled the amount of water dripping down into the carbide. More water produced a larger flame and less water, a smaller one. The water mixing with carbide, generated acetylene gas used to produce the light. The gas was ejected through a nozzle in the middle of the reflector where it was burned to produce the flame that emitted the light. Adjacent to the nozzle was a spark striker used to light the lamp. It was identical to those found on cigarette lighters.

Carbide lamps were notoriously temperamental. The valve controlling the water flow was not very sophisticated. Trying to get a flame with a constant size was difficult. However, the biggest problem was with the nozzle. It was easily plugged with dirt, especially while drilling, when mud often splattered it. It was necessary to have on hand an assortment of fine wires for unclogging the nozzle. Cleaning the nozzle and getting the lamp re-lit was a constant and irritating problem, one that would have tried the patience of the biblical Job!

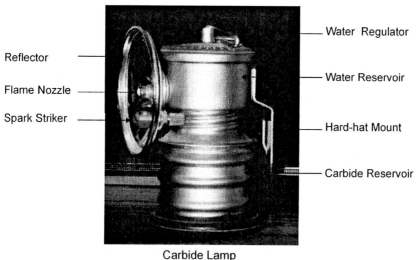

Carbide Lamp
Photo taken by the author courtesy of the
Britannia Mining Museum, Britannia Beach, BC

Another problem with the carbide lamps was the heat generated by the flame. I would hate to count the number of times I was cursed for burning my partner's neck when we were timbering. Being curious, I tended to lean over my coworker's shoulder when he was marking a timber cut to see exactly what he was doing, and would sometimes get too close to his neck with my lamp.

The Miner

Today there are virtually no underground mines left in western Canada. Almost all western mines are now large scale "open pit" operations, where the work force employs huge modern equipment that even small women can (and do) operate. The people described in the following section are therefore men of a bygone era. The old time miners were a very special breed of men. They worked hard and they played hard. An important part of that play included hard drinking. The men worked hard because they were usually on some kind of incentive system. The more they produced the more bonus they earned. A good miner could oftentimes more than double his base pay. In order to do this he sometimes ignored safety rules and took chances. It is not surprising that until recently, the mining industry had one of the highest accident rates in the country. Not only could mining be dangerous, it could also require brutally hard work. The Gardner Denver stoper (drill used in raises) I used for much of my mining career weighed 140 pounds. Longhole drills weighed in at over 300 pounds, and we sometimes manhandled them alone. On top of these problems were the foul gasses that often permeated the work place. It was small wonder that many miners played hard. They had much in common with the loggers of the past too, in that they often lived in remote camps where women were a rarity. When they came into the city they often stayed drunk until their pay had been used up or stolen, at which time they headed back to another camp.

There is an old story about the man who came into town after working in a camp for eight months and saving all his paychecks. His order of priorities was first to get drunk, then find a woman and get laid. He quickly accomplished his first goal and in the process met a hooker. She promptly accompanied him to his hotel room, where she slipped a "Mickey" into his drink and stole all his money. When he awoke, he was obliged to go back to the camp he had just left. When his friends questioned him about his experience, his remark about losing his money was; "Oh well, easy come, easy go."

As far as miners are concerned, not everyone working in a mine is a miner. To them the term, "miner" applies only to someone who actually drills and blasts the rock in the mine. The others who work there, e.g. trammers; timbermen; helpers and surveyors, etc., are not miners! A miner deriding an inept miner, often called him by such names as "farmer" or "calciminer."

During the past few years I have made it a point to try to find some of the men I knew from my mining days. I have been fortunate in being able to locate a number of them, but my wife complains that we spend far too much of our time reminiscing about the men who are now dead. One interesting feature of these departed acquaintances is the number of them that died in mining or drunk driving accidents. On the following pages I have included stories about some of the miners I have worked with or known.

Chapter 12 - The West Kootenays

The Van Roi Mine

After fighting the fire near Moyie in the summer of 1951, Ed Litviak and I were hitch hiking back to Creston when we got a ride with a Mr. Bill Wilson who was the manager of the Van Roi mine near Silverton, BC. When he learned that I had previous mining experience, he suggested I come and see him when I was ready to go back to work. I shortly travelled to Silverton and went to work as a laborer at the mine. A Swede named Carl Anderson was the mine foreman. He started me on a jackhammer, but after a few days, put me to work with a man named Rae Thomas as a miner's helper.

The Van Roi mine contained lead-zinc ore with a very high silver content. Some of the ore had been found in kidney type formations and one stope had in earlier times produced silver worth $1 million. In 1951, the little ore we mined came from small, scattered pockets that were difficult to find. Veins in an established ore-body were usually fairly easy to locate with diamond drill holes because they tended to be quite extensive, but small pocket formations were totally unpredictable.

There was a small camp at the mine with most of the men living in tents and the others commuting from Silverton and New Denver. These tents had wooden floors and were heated with oil fired stoves. I was fortunate because I was given a room above the camp kitchen and did not have to stay in a tent. I shared my room with George Gower, a young man who was a two years younger than me.

Cocktails for Two

George Gower hailed from Medicine Hat, Alberta. He was different from most of the other men, in that he had completed high school, was an avid reader and was more curious about the world than most.

George liked to imitate the fictional Detective Marlowe by speaking out of the side of his mouth in a tough guy fashion. He also liked to convey the impression that he had been around a lot – which may indeed have been true. He frequently regaled me with stories of his exploits when on drunks in Vancouver. The following is one such story, and knowing George, and some of the old tramp miners that I later encountered, I suspect it may have been true.

George was in Vancouver in the company of an older miner who I shall call Fraser. George told me that he kept pestering this fellow with wanting to know what a cocktail was. In those days the only drink you could buy in a public place was beer. If you wanted hard liquor, you purchased it at a government liquor store and drank it at home or in your hotel room. George had read about cocktail parties in the Readers Digest, but had only a poor idea what a cocktail was.

Fraser finally tired of his endless questions, made up a list of ingredients, gave it to George and sent him shopping. The only liquor on the list was a bottle of Johnny Walkers Black Label Scotch whiskey. It took George much of the afternoon to complete his shopping, but he finally returned to the room with paper bags containing his purchases.

Fraser first pulled the bottle of Scotch from its bag and poured two water glasses two thirds full of the amber fluid. He then set the bottle down on the table, turned to George and said; "So you want to know how to make a good drink, do you?" "Yes!" replied George eagerly. Fraser then picked up the paper bags with all the remaining items, carried them over to the open window, and hurled them out on to the parking lot, some three floors below. Turning to George, he handed him a glass of whiskey and said; "Here, drink this. This is a good drink!" George never again brought up the subject of cocktails with Fraser.

George (Ten Day) Armstrong

Ten Day was another colorful miner I met at the Van Roi mine that fall. He did not work in the Van Roi proper, but at the nearby Hewitt Mine, also owned by the Van Roi. Under the supervision of Gus Engberg, and together with three other men, he drove drift. We saw them every day because they changed clothes in the same mine dry as the rest of us.

I got to know George because he was a good friend of Rae Thomas, and sometimes came to Rae's house. As can be surmised, he got his nickname; "Ten Day" because he had a habit of changing jobs frequently. Like so many other miners of the era, he was a heavy drinker who did not let work get in the way of pleasure. Furthermore, with so many jobs available then, other pastures usually looked greener.

George lived with a woman who was three years older than him. They seemed to hit it off well, probably because she, like he, was also a nomad. They eventually got married after fifteen years of living together in a common-law relationship and they were still married when I looked them up in the fall of 2000.

I found George by coincidence. I was at the Starbuck's coffeehouse in Coquitlam one day and got talking to a couple sitting next to me. The woman mentioned that she had an uncle who had mined all over BC, and it turned out to be George. What a small world!

I made a point then of looking George up and going to see him. His wife Ruth was travelling in Britain on her own despite being 89 years old. George's health was still pretty good considering he was 86 and had been heavy drinker. He had been to "Detox" to dry out a number of times during his life.

When I next saw George a year later, he was on chemotherapy and therefore not feeling too spry. Ruth was again travelling on her own, this time in Ontario. It was shortly after this visit that Ruth came home and suffered an aneurysm. She had a "living will" that stipulated that no one was to prolong her life in such circumstances. She died two weeks later, just 10 days short of her 90th birthday. I got to meet a large number of family members and friends at the funeral get-together.

I had asked George about his children on a couple of occasions, but he did not seem anxious to talk about them. He finally told me that he did indeed have two, but they did not know he was their father. He had married at the beginning of the war and had two children; the second one was born just before he went overseas. When George returned in 1945, he found his wife living with another man. George immediately left the area and his wife told the children that the man she was living with was their father. When George eventually got his divorce, he did not have the heart to tell his children that he was their real father, because they would then realize that their mother had lied to them. I suspect that this hurt George more deeply than he ever cared to admit.

Although his formal education did not amount to much, George has nevertheless written a number of poems, some of which I find interesting. His writing style reminds me of Robert Service. Its appeal lies in that it is aimed at the common person. Anyone who is familiar with the breed of miners, of which George was one, can readily identify with it. The two poems reprinted below give some insight into his character and talent.

George (Ten Day) Armstrong;
1914 - 2002.
Photo taken by the author.

John Barleycorn

It was one of those days when a man often strays
Too wide on the old straight and narrow
My heart it was heavy, likewise were my feet,
And the wind chilled my bones to the marrow.

My friend that morn was old John Barleycorn.
I'd met him on several occasions.
He was a man of great cheer,
and men came from far and near.
Just to listen to his friendly persuasions.

We drank to our health, to our fortunes and wealth
We drank to the future and present.
The sun it shone brighter, my feet became lighter
And everything seemed rather pleasant.

It was getting quite late as I entered my gate
I had trouble locating my room
And the face of old John flittered hither and yon
Like a banshee escaped from a tomb

I located my bed and pillowed my head,
I regretted the day I was born.
Life seems so darn cruel after fighting a duel
With the old fellow John Barleycorn.

I could hear voices quite near
and they seemed to appear
To belong to persons long dead
I tried to arise and I opened my eyes
Just to clear the cobwebs from my head

They were playing a game,
draw poker's the name.
There were two drawing cards, and one dealt
They were playing for keeps
and it gave the creeps
For the tension could almost be felt.

One sat by the door, I'd seen her before,
She had a face that a mother could love
I tried to retrace where I'd seen that dear face.
But the cobwebs were still up above

The one that was dealing gave me the feeling,
she cared not who lost, drew or won.
Yet her face seemed to wear the look of despair
They were playing for keeps not for fun.

The other old witch wore her hair in a switch
As they wore in the dark middle ages.
How the girl by the door
could face this old whore;
Was nothing less than courageous.

The old hag was death, the chill of her breath
Seemed to cut the quick like a knife
Fate the other dame, was a gambler of fame
And the sweet girl was known as life.

The old hag drew one; she had two pair or a run
The sweet girl drew the limit of three
The hag says he's mine, you're drawing too fine
By God! They were playing for me.

I lay back on my bed, and I covered my head
I returned to my land of wild dreams
There were men of weird shapes,
there were tigers and apes,
And banshees emitting wild screams.

I open my eyes and to my surprise
I was holding the soft hand of life.
You've won! You've won me!
I cried over and over.
And I kissed the dear face of my wife.

I was upright by now,
wiping sweat from my brow.
Then I wandered over to the table

I knew what to expect; and I drew up erect
And summoned all the strength I was able.
One hand was face up the other face down
The pack was pushed to one side
Fate only plays cards when she's out on the town
This time she just went for the ride

The hand I could see, held two pair and a three
A three flanked by aces and eights
The other was a draw of the famous McGraw
And one of his inside straights
I went back to bed; and I lay my head
On this lady's soft warm arm
I knew in this state that I could not tempt fate
And those banshees would do me no harm

I was out of the fog, I slept like a log
I felt like a soul that's reborn
And a sadder and a wiser man
I rose the morrow morn.

Old Buddies

It was getting near dark as I strolled near a park
When a voice whispered out of the night
It was a voice quite clear
yet with a faint ring of fear
Say buddy, can you spare me a light?

Now buddy says he; we were buddies you see
As we sailed to Dieppe at the dawn.
We were buddies in Brighton,
we were buddies when fightin'
To clear out the Jerries in Caen.

If you'll tarry a spell, I've a story to tell,
A story that's common as sin.
I have to relate it, yet somehow I hate it
But if you'll light up a fag I'll begin

He gave me no choice - the sound of his voice
Seemed to hold me in kind of a spell
It took me back home, back to school and a poem
Of a mariner with a strange tale to tell

(My buddy will now relate his story as in the first person)

I'd been on a bender and walking down Pender
As free as a bird in a tree
I had no money that's true.
Twas a small thing I knew
In this land of the brave and the free

I could have put in some sack time,
but this was a slack time.
My rent came due yesterday,
I've had troubles before, yes troubles galore,
And I worried not where I would stay.

I could sleep in the Sally or down Hogan's alley.
I wasn't stuck by a long shot you see
Great Northern's a cinch C.N.R. in a pinch
And if need be I'd go P.G.E.

I took me some cover to think this thing over,
And my mind wandered back o'er the years
I was back there in Blighty,
the home of the mighty
In the dark days of blood, sweat, and tears

The war it was ended. The land we defended
Was more than thankful, and free
Now the nightmare was over,
let's get on with the chore,
It's at home where we wanted to be

So we sailed by and by to this land where the sky
In our minds was always pale blue.
No troubles and strife, and with children and wife
Was the land of God's chosen few.

We were met at our stations
by friends and relations
We were feted in newsreel and press
The high brass of course, was out in great force
The P.M. he gave an address

We are proud of you men you'll ne'er want again.
You've laid down your lives for our land
And we owe you a debt that we will never forget
The land's yours on which you now stand

I awoke with a scream
and like a man from a dream
My mind was still in a haze
And as the horror passed by I realized why
And I reckoned oh! oh! Thirty days

The cops says to me you'd better come see,
Our modern Bastille from within
It's a shame with a place and all that spare space
There are fellows left out to seek sin

The judge says (you've no right)
to traverse by night,
Our streets without justifiable cause
I could throw you in jail or just grant you bail
Then he stopped, thanks be for the pause

But if you have a remark before you embark
On this trip with an escort of police
Your plea I have heard, but I'll give you my word
Speak up now or else hold thy peace

I related aloud what the P.M. had vowed
My words were razor sharp honed
I'll admit I must go, but I'd like you to know
I was inspecting some land I once owned

Some men are given a chance for a liv'n
Some men seek livelihood strange.
But if we have help to extend,

please think of my friend
And look after our own for a change.

①Reprinted with the kind permission of George Armstrong.

Rae Thomas

Rae Thomas was twenty-nine and just over six years my senior when I went to work with him. He was raised in Selkirk, Manitoba and had one quarter Native ancestry. He had survived the Second World War without incident despite being in the army from its onset to its end. He stood about five foot eleven, had a fine build and was pretty strong. He also had a penchant for becoming quarrelsome when drunk, which was not infrequent. This led to Rae getting into occasional fights. He had recently been married and lived in Silverton, six miles from the mine and rode to work each day in the company bus.

I had worked with Rae for only a few weeks, when he invited me to his house in Silverton for dinner. Since I had nothing better to do during the long (two-day) weekend, I gladly accepted. (We normally worked five days one week and six the next). After that, I became a regular visitor at Rae's house, and sometimes baby-sat Linda when Rae and Doris went out for an evening in the local beer parlour. Doris already had a one-year-old daughter named Linda when she married Rae. When I met Doris she was pregnant again and gave birth to twin boys on September 30, 1951.

Rae, like most of the miners I knew, liked his liquor. His problem was that once he had a few drinks, there was no stopping him until he had been drunk for two or three days. During these episodes, he could get very mean and unreasonable. Doris confided to me that one night when he came home from the bar, he started to choke her. She was able to grab a clothes iron (the old fashioned ones you heated on top of the stove) and hit him on the head hard enough to knock him out. When he asked her the next day how he got the ugly gash on his

Rae and Doris Thomas on their wedding day in 1950. Photo courtesy of Rae and Doris Thomas

121

forehead, she told him that he had fallen and hit his head on the corner of the stove.

One day Rae and I were starting a new raise off an existing one. We drilled and blasted out a section to create a new face. After the blast we had time to scale the loose rock and to set up the staging for the night shift before leaving for the day. On our cross shift were two Campbell brothers from Cape Breton Island in Nova Scotia. That night a large slab of rock fell on them killing one and hospitalizing the other (Frank) with several broken bones.

During the early fifties, there were two whorehouses in Nelson. They were next door to each other at 608 and 612 Lake Street and were an important destination for miners coming into town. While I worked at the Van Roi, I came to Nelson just once and I was determined that I would not return to camp without visiting one of the two houses.

I arrived at 608 Lake Street in the early evening and was shown into the living room where some older men and a few women were sitting around drinking. The hostess immediately asked; "Would you like a drink?"

Me; "Yes please."

She; "I think I'll have one too. Would you like one Mary?"

I wound up paying for three expensive drinks, two of which may have been only tea. One of the women (Laura) then took me to a bedroom and we both stripped. I was embarrassed, for it was the first time since I had grown up that a woman had seen me naked. I found the act disappointing. Laura was anything but sexy and I was so self-conscious and embarrassed that I did not enjoy it very much. However, when I got back to work after the weekend, I was able to brag to Rae that I had been to 608 Lake Street.

Rae with first of three sets of twins in October 1951. *Photo courtesy of Rae and Doris Thomas*

In late November a couple of other miners convinced me to quit and go with them to Vancouver. Before long, I had to lend them money (which was of course never repaid) and soon I had none left. Fortunately, I was able to land a job as a "miner" at the Red Rose mine some thirty miles from Skeena Crossing, BC.

The Silver King Aerial Tramway at New Denver, BC. It was similar to the one we used at the Red Rose Mine. *Photo taken by the author courtesy of Silverton Historical Society.*

The company advanced me the fare. I flew to Prince Rupert and took the train to Skeena Crossing where a mine vehicle picked me up and took me to the mine. The Red Rose mill was at the foot of Roche De Boule Mountain and the mine was four miles up the mountainside via a narrow road with numerous "switch-backs." The ore was transported from the mine down to the mill by an aerial tramway.

It was a "haywire" place! We had no electric power in the camp, and used candles for light. There was no hot water for showers. In order to wash, we had first to melt snow and heat it over the cook stove. Most of the crew worked long hours trying to thaw and insulate the water system. The mine, contrary to the Labor regulations, did not pay them overtime as was required.

On December 31st I walked down to the mill and caught a ride into New Hazelton with one of the truckers. I promptly phoned the Silver Standard mine and was told to come to work the next day. That evening I went to the New Year's Eve dance after which I caught a ride back to the mine with Charlie Campbell, the mine manager. It was a long, cold trip that took us the rest of the night. The temperature was –30° F and the gas line in Campbell's pickup kept freezing up so we did not get back to the mill until breakfast time. I walked up to the mine, packed my clothes and sent them down on the aerial tramway. I then walked back down the hill and quit. When Charlie Campbell saw that I was leaving, he blew his top! "Here we take you into town and back, and while you are there, you hustle up another job," he snarled.

I started work in the Silver Standard mine the following day and stayed until late April, when I returned to the Nelson country. It was a good mine in which to work and it was my first real experience as a miner. I enjoyed a good social life too for New Hazelton was only six miles away, and we attended dances there regularly.

When I came back from the north, Rae and Doris were living in Nelson, but Rae was not working. He and I decided to go looking for work on the coast. We took the Greyhound bus to Vancouver, and after a few days of partying there, we found a job in a hydro electric tunnel being driven near Bridal Falls, between Chilliwack and Hope. The contractor was Northern Construction and the work was being done for BC Electric, the for-runner of BC Hydro. Access to the portal was via a tramway that ran up the steep mountainside on a set of rails. Riding up and down on that skip was not for the faint hearted. Today one can still clearly see the scar left on the mountain side fifty years ago.

The tunnel was horseshoe shaped and measured nine feet wide and ten feet high in the arch. It had been advanced about 8,500 feet from the portal when we arrived and was a very dirty place to work! We were blasting an average of two and one half times during an eight-hour shift. We had a reversible fan system that sucked out the smoke after the blast, and when finished, it was reversed to blow fresh air back in. The problem was that the fan was never given enough time to complete its job before it was reversed, we therefore got a lot of smoke blown right back to us. Another problem was that after a blast, a lot of gasses resided in the pile of broken muck. Before loading out the muck, we first watered it down to drive out the gasses, but we never had enough time to complete the job properly. We were then exposed to the noxious fumes as we mucked (loaded) out the round. Everyone on the crew carried a pocketful of ammonia capsules which we sniffed constantly to alleviate the blinding headaches we suffered every day from breathing the gas laden air.

We used four "jacklegs" to drill the round - one driller with a helper on each side, and two drillers with one helper (me) in the middle. The middle drills worked off a flatcar while drilling the upper holes, and off the track for the remainder. The rock was granite and the drills frequently jammed as the chisel bits got stuck in the holes being drilled. One of the drillers was a big Finlander, who instead of just lifting the drill leg off the flatcar to take the tension off the drill steel ordered me to hammer the drill off the steel with a chuck wrench. While I was thus engaged, he jerked the drill up and down as he tried to pull it off. One day I swung and missed! Instead of hitting the drill, I hit the Finlander right across the nose. I managed to check my swing enough so that I did not break it, but the blow brought involuntary tears to his eyes. Fortunately the noise of the other three drills easily drowned out the diatribe that followed. I can only imagine some of the things he must have called me. (In a tunnel such as this, with the deafening noise from the machines, all discourse had to be done via sign language).

On our first weekend off, ten days after beginning work in the tunnel, Rae and I took the Greyhound bus to Vancouver. Rae wanted to visit a cousin who lived on Lulu Island. To get there from downtown Vancouver we took a streetcar to the Marpole area. From there we walked across a bridge and down a country road for another four miles to the farm. At that time, except for the village of Steveston, there were absolutely no urban dwellings south of Vancouver.

After our visit we walked back to the bridge and via another streetcar, returned to the downtown area. Since we had to wait a couple of hours for the next Greyhound bus, Rae decided we should have a few drinks first. However, when the time came to catch the bus, I was unable to get him out of the bar. It was two days before we finally returned to camp. The next morning the superintendent promptly told me to pick up my pay check and not to bother coming to work. I suspect that hitting the driller on the nose played a part in that outcome. Rae was not let go, but he refused to go back to work because I had been fired, so he quit and we headed back to the West Kootenays again.

We got off the Greyhound bus in Trail and went to the Union hiring office for the Waneta dam. This dam was under construction on the Pend'Oreille river at its confluence with the Columbia River south of Trail. We told the agent that we wanted jobs running wagon drills (the forerunner of airtracs). His only jobs were on jackhammers, so we declined. I then called the Emerald mine at Salmo and was immediately promised jobs in the "Dodger" tunnels they were driving there. We were heading back to the bus depot, when we heard a fellow yelling at us. We turned around, and there was the business agent running to catch up with us. As soon as he got his breath back, he told us that he now had jobs for both of us on wagon drills. Rae curtly responded; "You don't pay enough."

A miner's battery and lamp together with the belt he carried the battery on. *Photo taken by the author courtesy of the Britannia Mining Museum at Britannia Beach, BC*

In 1952 the mining industry was in its heyday, and the Salmo area was no exception. This was largely due to the war raging in Korea, which caused a great demand for metals. It was therefore especially great for job hunters in the mining industry. There were three medium sized lead-zinc mines in the Salmo area. Cominco operated the HB mine six miles from town. Placer Development ran the Emerald mine eight miles away, and American Metals owned the Reeves McDonald mine twenty-two miles south of town, on the Canada-U.S. border. In addition to these three, there were some small mining operations in the area as well.

When we arrived at the Emerald there were over 600 men employed there of which 350 stayed in the Dodger tunnel camp. A number of men commuted from Salmo on the Emerald Mine's busses and the rest of them lived at the Jersey town-site adjacent to the mine.

Rae rented a house in a small hamlet north of Salmo called Ymir. I found living quarters in the Dodger tunnel camp where I was temporarily housed in a tent which accommodated four men. The tent had a wooden floor and was heated by an oil-stove. This stove was temperamental and sometimes had minor explosions, spewing soot over everything inside the tent.

When the temporary nature of my stay in the tent began to look as if it was becoming permanent, I rebelled. It happened one morning when I awoke covered in soot. I was black! The sheets were black! All my clothes strung from hangers in the tent were also black. I stormed into the office and told them I was quitting unless they moved me into a bunkhouse right now! It turned out that the only reason I had not been moved earlier was because the staff was just too busy (or lazy) to get around to it. I had a room in a bunkhouse within the hour!

One Saturday evening after my first payday, I caught a ride into Salmo with some other miners. As soon as we left the camp, someone pulled out a bottle of rye whiskey, opened it and threw the cap out the window. The bottle was passed around until it was empty. Since we still had a mile or two to go, a second bottle was opened. Its cap too was thrown out the window. Again, the bottle was passed around and we were not allowed to leave the car until it was empty. That was one of my early lessons on how miners drank.

While I was living in the Dodger camp I had a strange experience. Whenever I worked "graveyard" shift, I usually found it very difficult to sleep - until around the end of the week when I would be so tired that I could sleep for a few hours.

One morning I had just come off a graveyard shift and had my breakfast. I grabbed a blanket and a book and settled down to read while getting some sun at the same time. I was lying on the blanket reading my book and smoking. I had taken a drag on my cigarette but when I went to bring the cigarette to my lips for a second puff, I found I had dropped it. I looked to pick it up, but discovered there was nothing left of it except a long ash lying on the blanket. I had not been aware of either falling asleep, nor of waking up, yet I had obviously been unconscious of time for several minutes. I have since read that sleep deprivation can cause short memory blanks, but this episode must have lasted at least ten minutes.

The food in the cookhouse was awful. The breakfasts were the worst. The eggs were so old that the yolks would harden while the whites stayed runny. What's more, they stank! One nice aspect of the camp was that there were eight young single women working in the cookhouse. I soon learned that these girls were so sought after by all the men that some of them considered themselves God's gift to mankind. I dated one of them a couple of times and decided not to bother again. Before long I found room and board in a private home in Salmo and moved out of the camp.

The woman I was boarding with in Salmo had a son-in-law named Floyd Fleming who also worked in the Dodger Tunnels. When Floyd came off "graveyard" shift one morning, he found that someone had stolen his brand new shoes. He had purchased them the previous day and had paid a lot of money for them. He wrote out the following note and pinned it to his clothes hook;

"Will the thief who stoled my shoes please return them."

That evening I added the following line to his note;

"Your shoes fit very well, I really enjoy them. Thank you, the Thief." Floyd was incensed! He never forgot that incident.

A few years later, Floyd was working at the HB mine in an ore pass raise when he slipped and fell down the raise. The raise had a number of knuckle-backs (90 degree turns) in it. They were there for the purpose of smashing up the rock on its way down. They smashed up Floyd pretty well too for his fall took him through two of those knuckle-backs. He did survive and eventually went back mining.

One forenoon Rae came to Salmo to see me. We were to go to work that afternoon at 4:00 PM. After a few beer in one of the two pubs, he said; "Lets go to Remac (Reeves McDonald mine) and get a job there." By this time he owned a 1949 Ford Coupe. We got in his car and drove to the mine at Remac. They told us that the mines had a policy of not hiring each other's workers, but that they did indeed need men. They intimated that if we first quit our present jobs, they would hire us immediately. Rae then decided that since we were already at the US border, we should go for a drink at Metaline Falls. This small town was in Washington State, only 14 miles south of the border. Once we got to Metaline Falls we had a couple of beer, next we purchased a "Mickey" of Seagram's "Seven Crown" rye whiskey and headed back north. We drained the bottle on our way back to the Border and by the time we got to the Emerald mine, we were both pretty drunk.

We were at the mine in plenty of time for shift, but Rae said; "Let's quit!" The office clerk told us to come back for our paychecks the following week. No amount of arguing helped. He said that it was just not possible to prepare them on such short notice. Rae lost his temper and began swearing at the clerk! He reached through the clerk's wicket and grabbed him by his tie. Yanking the man's head through the opening, he yelled; "I want

Rae in a wheelchair (July 2000).
Photo taken by the author

my F--king check right now!" It had an amazing effect. We were both paid off within fifteen minutes. (I learned much later that we were also both blackballed from ever working at that mine again).

We drove the four miles down the mountain and reached the highway just as the Emerald bus carrying the afternoon shift was turning off the highway to go up the hill. The bus stopped and out jumped Doris, madder than a wet hen. She stooped down beside the road and grabbed a big stone. Then swearing like a trooper, she smashed one segment of the windshield, one side window and one vent window on Rae's car before he could get out and stop her.

Rae, Doris and their children at their Golden Wedding celebration on July 8, 2000.
Photo taken by the author

Rae and I started work at Remac the following week. He continued to live in Ymir, but I moved into the bunkhouse at the mine. We both spent the winter there, but the following spring the mine shut down and I left the area for a couple of years.

I returned to Salmo in the spring of 1955 and again worked with Rae, this time at the HB mine for Cominco. This time I boarded with Rae and Doris until I got married in October. I then moved into a company house at Remac, which had recently reopened. During that summer I often baby-sat their son Brian, (their latest arrival). Rae was by now settling down, but he still went on the odd binge. It appeared that Doris got pregnant every time Rae got drunk. Whatever the reason, in addition to Linda, the twins and Brian, they had six more children including two more sets of twins! They might perhaps have had even more, but fate finally stepped in!

In January of 1964 Rae was working at the Velvet mine near Rossland. He and three other fellows were riding to work with another miner named Willie McLean. Willie failed to slow down for one switchback (believing the previous one to be the last one before getting to the mine entrance road). The car shot off the end of the switchback, down the hill and over a cliff. It turned out that Willie had put some large boulders in the trunk for ballast to improve the car's traction on the snowy roads. When the car came to an abrupt stop at the bottom of the cliff, the rocks hurtled through from the trunk, mortally injured Willie and fractured several of Rae's vertebrae. Rae became a paraplegic and has been in a wheel chair ever since. He is able to hobble around a little on crutches, but depends on his wheelchair for most of his locomotion. To many people, such a blow would surely have killed all initiative, but for Rae, it was the turning point in his life. It brought out the best in him as well as the toughness that was always there. First of all Rae quit drinking, next he spent four years in legal battles with the insurance company before finally collecting from them. An attorney named Bob Ross successfully sued Willie McLean's insurance company for gross negligence and collected $57,000 including interest. After paying his legal and medical bills, Rae was left with only $28,000. However, in 1968 this was still a fair chunk of money.

After Rae got his car outfitted so that he could drive it, he got a job with the Canadian Paraplegic Association and for many years was their representative for both BC and the Yukon. Doris and Rae both became heavily involved in community volunteer work and in 1992 were both awarded the Governor General's medals for those contributions.

As this is written, Rae and Doris are both in their late seventies. They still reside in Ymir, but their children are scattered about – mainly throughout BC. Their eldest daughter, Linda now works for the WCB in Kamloops. One of their two oldest sons, Richard enlisted in the Canadian army. He distinguished himself by advancing from the rank of Private to that of Colonel, a most unusual feat! The other son, Raymond, recently went back to school and got a diploma in Forestry after injuries forced him to quit tree felling for a living. The third eldest son runs a tugboat that transports log booms on the Columbia River near Castlegar. One granddaughter graduated from mechanic's school and is now a licensed mechanic in Regina, Saskatchewan. Their other children are in a variety of occupations.

Len

When I met Len he was married to Linda, the eldest of the Thomas children. I never knew him well, but he told us about his most embarrassing moment, which I will share with you here.

Len was on a drunk in Vancouver when he climbed on to a city bus one day. There was standing room only, and everyone was jam-packed together. As he stood there hanging on to the overhead support, he noticed that his fly was open. Trying not to attract attention, and looking around in a nonchalant way, he hurriedly pulled up his zipper.

Standing in front of him was a huge woman wearing a muskrat fur coat. As the bus halted at its next stop and she moved to leave the bus, Len felt a tug on his trousers. She felt it too and turned around to see the long hairs of her coat caught in Len's zipper. With a look of disgust and utter disbelief, she tore away from him and left the bus. Len was left with a number of muskrat hairs sticking out of his zipper and the nearby passengers staring at him in amusement. He was instantly sober and got off at the next stop even though it was not his planned destination.

Bert Savage

I met Bert at the Dodger Tunnel camp, but never got to know him very well. I was told that he was quite a scrapper. One day when they were returning to the mine from a visit to Priest River, Idaho, they stopped at the edge of the road to relieve themselves. One of the other men got into a bit of an altercation with Bert who promptly hit him and drove him over the embankment. The hapless man tumbled down the steep slope, bouncing off boulders and stumps. I saw this fellow the next day and there was not a square inch of his body not covered in bruises.

On another occasion Bert was on a ship coming to Vancouver from Prince Rupert. He and his buddy, Lee were both very drunk and very loud. They did not know that there were two nuns in the adjoining cabin. When the steward knocked on their door; he said; "Please be a little quieter – there are two sisters in the cabin next door to you. Bert not grasping that he was referring to nuns retorted; "Tell them that we are two brothers." Bert and Lee were moved to the other end of the ship the following day.

I met Bert again in Victoria a dozen years later. He was selling cars for the Chevrolet dealer there, and I bought a new car from him when I began selling Real Estate.

Doc Fraser

One of the hazards of entering a beer parlour back in the early fifties was that of running into a tramp miner looking for a handout. Of course they never asked for anything but a loan, but only a fool would expect to have it repaid. Some of them had the audacity to maintain that even if they didn't repay you, it still came out even in the end since they too would lend money when they were working, (which of course never happened).

The New Grand Hotel in Nelson was one of the miners' favorite hangouts. (It was later renamed the Nelson Hotel, but is today called the New Grand once more). One day when I walked into the beer parlour there, I had no sooner sat down, than I saw Doc Fraser heading towards my table. Fraser was a notorious bum who never worked and sponged off any miners who happened his way. Since I had already lent him money, I did not want to be tapped for another "loan."

Acting on inspiration, I jumped up and walking swiftly towards him and said; "Doc, you are just the man I want to see. Can you lend me a ten spot?" Fraser was completely taken aback. He couldn't get away from me fast enough, and I was left to finish my beer in peace.

There was a story going around about how Doc Fraser got his nickname. It was said that he was drunk and walking down the street in Sudbury one day when he noticed an unattended car window open and a black bag sitting on the front seat. Thinking that there might be some money in it, he took the bag. Later as he was walking along the street, a woman came running out when she saw he was carrying a doctor's bag. She implored him to come in and see her sick child. Fraser had one look at the infant and said; "All that kid needs is a good dose of Castor Oil!" The child almost died and Fraser got two years in jail for theft and for impersonating a doctor. From then on his acquaintances all called him Doc.

Wally Bunka

During the summer while I worked in the Dodger tunnels, I met two young men who worked at the adjacent Jersey Lead Zinc mine. One was Ray White, who was still only seventeen, but had been the junior ski jumping champion of BC the previous year. The other was Wally Bunka, a fellow I would get to know even better a few years later. They were both working in the Emerald mine and were on opposite shifts from each other on a two-shift basis. I was working in the tunnel on one of three shifts, so we did not see each other much during the week.

Shortly after we first met, the three of us were walking down Baker street in Nelson one weekend, when one of three young girls behind us said, "Hi Larry." She said her name was Dixie, and she must have heard one of my friends address me, for I had never seen her before. Before long we had talked all three of them into coming with us to the dance in Ymir. I never again saw the girl that Wally dated that night, but Ray began to date the other girl regularly. Her name was Grace Sinclair; she was sixteen and her father was a policeman for CP Rail. From that day on, I dated Dixie occasionally as well.

Wally Bunka decided the two of us should buy a car, so he and I pooled our money for a down payment and bought a 1938 Dodge sedan for $500. That car provided us with a measure of independence we had not had before. We no longer had to rely on public transportation or on friends to get us to Nelson or Trail on the weekends. Getting dates was so much easier too, because we could take our dates to dances at Ymir or Playmor. Playmor was a dance hall 20 miles west of Nelson that brought in "Big Name" bands on occasion. I remember dancing to Frankie Carle and his band there before they became famous.

One weekend when Wally and I went into Nelson, we booked a room at the North Shore Motel and stocked it with liquor. We next went to the dance in Ymir where Wally picked up a young woman who we took back to the motel with us.

It turned out that Wally knew the man who was in the adjoining room so we were soon all partying together. The other man was sitting on his bed playing a guitar and we were all singing. Then I noticed that both Wally and the girl were missing. The next thing I knew, the girl clad only in panties came running from the bathroom screaming, through our room and into the next. Behind her came Wally, chasing her stark naked, his dick swinging from side to side. Our guitarist immediately turned up the volume on his amplifier to drown out her screams.

At that moment there was loud persistent hammering on the door and a woman's voice yelling; "Turn off that radio and get those women out of there or I will call the police!" Wally hurriedly dressed, picked up the near naked girl and carried her out the door, past the gaping motel owner, to the car. The guitarist helped me to pack up the booze and just as we went out the door, we saw Wally driving away. We assumed he was just getting the car turned around, but when he did not return, we carried our clothes and our booze down to the highway where we sat eating garlic sausage and drinking wine. It was at least a half-hour before Wally returned with a satisfied look on his face. When we dropped Wally's date off at her house, it was already getting daylight, so we barely stopped the car as she got out, for we knew nothing about her, and were nervous about whether or not she was of legal age.

We returned to the mine and Wally, who still had the girl's panties, hung them on the antennae of the first car he came to. That caused quite a stir, for the owner of the car had been dating one of the girls from the cookhouse. When this girl saw the panties on her boyfriend's antenna, she promptly broke up with him for it just happened that he had been out without her the previous night.

Ray White

Ray was frequently invited to Grace's home for Sunday dinners and I was sometimes included in that invitation. Grace's mother was both friendly and outgoing, but her father was silent and aloof. During the ensuing months, Ray got into trouble more than once on account of being drunk. However, as soon as the local police found that he was the guy who was dating Grace, they would immediately let him go.

One weekend I ran into Ray while I was in Nelson. He invited me to his room at the New Grand Hotel where I saw Grace and another girl. Ray was already drunk, but since it was a beautiful day we prevailed on Ray to come with us to the lakeside-park. We got to the park and Ray immediately changed into his swim trunks. We watched in horror as Ray walked towards the pool while stunning the people around him with his foul language. He could hardly stand up, but he climbed to the highest board and as we watched with trepidation, made a perfect dive.

The next thing we knew, Ray had disappeared and we were unable to find him, so we headed back to his hotel, more than a mile away. When we got there we were surprised to find Ray was already in the room and having yet another drink. Suddenly Ray leapt up off the bed and yanked the sink off the wall. Water spurted from the broken pipe like a geyser so I quickly hustled the girls out of the room and on to the street where Ray soon joined us. Ray then decided that perhaps he had better report the broken waterline to the hotel management. By this time the water was an inch deep in his room and spilling out into the hallway

Ray was shortly in jail again, but again the police turned him loose. The ceiling of the beer parlour was a mess. It was sagging from the flooding he had caused so the hotel sent Ray a bill for the damage, but later cancelled the charges. They were in the process of remodeling the place anyway. Perhaps they also realized that it would be difficult to collect any money from Ray.

Grace of course denied having been in Ray's room, but in our haste to leave, she had forgotten the new blouse she had just purchased and her name was on the bill of sale. The next time Ray had dinner at the Sinclair's; Grace's taciturn father who was always short on words anyway didn't even say Hello or Goodbye.

Remac

Late that summer I left the Dodger Tunnels to go to Remac. Wally Bunka kept the 1938 Dodge but the dealer repossessed it when he missed the payments. Since I was also on the hook for the car, I paid it off, but took out a 1951 Chev in its place.

At Remac we had single rooms in the bunkhouse – an unheard of luxury in those days. Before going to work each day we had to prepare our own lunches and a table covered with bread, butter, jam, lettuce and a variety of cold cuts was at our disposal for that purpose. The only interesting thing I remember about this was that a miner named Jack Keller made unusual (and unappetizing) sandwiches for his lunch. After buttering both slices of bread, he smeared each with strawberry jam. He then proceeded to put in a thick layer of sardines before joining the slices of bread into a sandwich. When I phoned Jack's home in 2001, (he now lives in Creston), I asked his wife if this was the Jack that liked sardines on top of strawberry jam. I was reassured that I had indeed found the right Jack.

After leaving Remac in March 1953, I drove to Kamloops to visit Ray White. He was working in a logging camp, but took a few days off to visit with me. We spent the next three days partying before he headed back to work. I never saw Ray again, but during the seventies I learned he was selling trucks in Vancouver. We conversed briefly on the phone but never did get together.

At Remac I met some new friends including a guy named John Blondeau. (John was one of my old friends I recently looked up. I had good visits with him and his wife at their home in Riondel in 1999 and 2002).

I had recently met a pretty and shapely young auburn-haired hairdresser named Audrey. While Audrey was perhaps not overly exciting, she was still nice to be with. She was hard working, thrifty, kind and intelligent. In short, she was the kind of person that you would look for as the mother of your future children.

One Friday night, John, and I were sharing a hotel room in Nelson for the weekend. I had a date with Audrey and John was planning to attend a party at a private home on the shores of Kootenay Lake. Two young women were temporarily minding this home while the owners were in California for the winter.

Audrey and I first went to dinner, then to a movie. I took her home early since she had to work the following day. We planned to meet for lunch the next day and she invited me to her mother's house for Sunday dinner. I felt very good about how well I was doing since this was the first time that I had been invited to meet her family. Our relationship was moving along at a most satisfactory rate.

When I returned to the hotel, there was a message to call John. On the phone I could hear a loud party in the background. John said; "We need you here because we are short one man, and furthermore, I need a ride back to the hotel." I was not one to refuse John a ride so off I went.

I found the house without difficulty. It was a large imposing structure built on a spectacular property fronting the lake. Fruit trees flanked the road down to the house. Behind the house was a lovely sandy beach and a large garden surrounded by tall stately Firs. It was an impressive place.

When I entered the house, a party was in full swing. There were bottles of beer and liquor everywhere. Some couples were dancing; others were necking on the sofas while still others were doing some serious drinking. My friend introduced me to his friends, including one young woman named Sally. Sally was about eighteen, with a decent figure, but a sour looking disposition and a face that only a mother could love. She must have been standing behind the door when God passed out the looks. I was set up to be this girl's escort.

It was a long evening! I found everything about Sally repulsive. Though I tried valiantly to hide it, she could not help but sense my revulsion. We spent a miserable two hours (it seemed an eternity) trying to be polite to each other. The evening must have been just as dreadful for her as it was for me.

On Sunday afternoon Audrey duly introduced me to her mother and her two brothers. She explained that her sister Irene was expected shortly. On the table was a gorgeous roast turkey surrounded by mouth-watering roast potatoes and assorted vegetables. We were about to dig into this scrumptious feast when the front door opened and in walked Sally. Audrey called her over and said; Larry, I would like you to meet my sister, Irene. Irene (Sally) gave me a withering look and curtly replied; "We've met!"

Somehow, I finished dinner and escaped from the house. I was so embarrassed that I did not ask Audrey for another date and I never saw her again.

One night the Remac miners found they were not the only ones going to the lakeside house, when another group of men showed up. During the ensuing fight, much of the house's interior was wrecked. After this event the house got its nickname and was hence referred to as "The Stope." I have often wondered about the reaction of the owners when they returned the following spring.

Lee Bracy

I met Lee at Remac in 1952. I did not get to know him that well, but found him to be congenial. I never learned anything about his past and as far as I know, he was never married. I remember him getting into a fight with Rae Thomas once, but since Rae was very drunk, he had an easy time of it.

I was helping to estimate some highway work in Prince Rupert twenty years later when I ran into Lee. We had a great visit, reminiscing about the Remac days while sharing a few beers. Lee was now retired and had taken up lapidary work. I had earlier wondered why people collected rocks. When I saw Lee's shop, I learned why. Lee made beautiful jewelry that anyone would be proud to wear. He prided himself on the precision with which he cut his gems – he did not cement them into their settings, but cut them accurately enough for solid friction fits. As far as I know, Lee has now moved on to that big stope in the sky, but he left behind a few people like me who will never forget him.

Tranquille

Mining jobs were very scarce in 1953. At Kamloops I learned that there was a position available at the TB sanitarium at Tranquille, so I applied for the job. I also learned that more than just a few of the patients were ex miners. During the interview I was asked why I would quit high paying work in the mines to work for the government. I replied that I wanted to quit mining before I destroyed my lungs and wound up in Tranquille as a patient. I think that this reply is what got me the job.

I had been at Tranquille for only a month when my boss asked me to resign, saying that I did not really fit in there. An acquaintance told me I had gotten the job that this man's friend had also applied for. Meanwhile, I had substantial car payments that I could not afford on the wages I was earning there, so I quit and went job hunting again.

Chapter 13 - The Yukon

United Keno Hill

In Vancouver I made the rounds of the mining offices without any luck. Finally after I had pawned both my wristwatch and my suit, I found a job as a miner at the United Keno Hill mine near Mayo in the Yukon. The wages were $1.25 per hour – considerably less than the $1.68 per hour I had earned in the Salmo area. The company purchased the plane ticket and told me they would deduct it from my first pay-checks. I put my car in storage and flew north.

The trip to Keno Hill took two days. We left Vancouver in the morning flying in a DC-6 with stops at Prince George, Fort St. John, Fort Nelson and Watson Lake. After an overnight stay in Whitehorse, I continued to Mayo in a DC-3. I was picked up in Mayo and taken the 35 miles to the mine during the afternoon. It was a long drive up a winding gravel road to the mine. In some places there were small glaciers threatening to engulf the road. To counter this threat, a crew kept fires burning at the road edge to melt the ice before it reached the road surface.

When I reached the mine, I was housed in a bunkhouse consisting of one large room (ram-pasture) that I shared with about fifty other men. If ever there was a "UN" in Canada, then Keno Hill was it. There were over 300 men employed there and they came from nearly 100 countries. Theft of personal belongings posed a big problem – especially in the Ram Pasture, and I was fortunately able to move to a two-man room in another bunkhouse shortly after my arrival. There I roomed with Dick Waverick, a man I had known at the Paradise mine in 1949.

At the mine we had a small commissary where we could buy our everyday necessities. We could also buy beer there. It came in bottles packed in wooden barrels – 120 per barrel. The beer cost fifty cents for a twelve-ounce bottle and it was actually cheaper than Coca-Cola, which cost thirty-five cents for a seven-ounce bottle. We smashed the bottles after they were emptied so that they would take less space in the garbage dump - it cost more than they were worth to return them.

In the mine it was absolutely necessary to hide our tools between shifts, otherwise they disappeared and we would lose time getting new ones when we came back. Because the mine was so heavily timbered, there was no shortage of hiding places. I have often wondered how many axes, crescent wrenches and other small tools are still squirreled away in that mine.

At Keno Hill I encountered a miner named Bill Strynadka, who had also worked at the Paradise Mine when I was there. He was a fun-loving fellow and an excellent storyteller. On the same plane on which I arrived, were three young chaps just off the farm from around Winnipeg. Besides not being too bright, they were also naïve. Bill began telling them stories about bears and cougars getting into the mines to stay warm. While these young farmers did not quite believe Bill's stories, they did not quite disbelieve them either.

As luck would have it, one of these fellows (Kenny) became my helper. Our first job was to re-timber an old raise that had not been in use for some

A TIMBERED RAISE

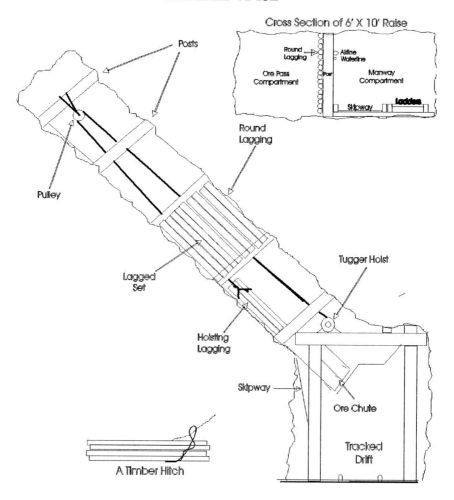

Cross Section of 6' X 10' Raise

Posts

Round Lagging

Airline
Waterline

Ore Pass Compartment

Port

Manway Compartment

Ladder

Skipway

Round Lagging

Pulley

Lagged Set

Tugger Hoist

Hoisting Lagging

Skipway

Ore Chute

Tracked Drift

A Timber Hitch

time. On our mine level there were only two parallel drifts connected by a short drift called a crosscut. One day I wanted to send Kenny to the main station to get some item we needed. He did not want to go because he was afraid of getting lost. I therefore went myself.

When I returned, Kenny was sitting on the platform immediately up inside the raise. Thinking to have some fun, I turned off my light, came over to the ladder and started scratching on the post while make grunting sounds to imitate a bear. Kenny, who had been humming softly, was suddenly silent. I began slowly ascending the ladder, while still grunting. Just as I was about to poke my head through the opening to the platform, I could no longer contain myself, but burst out laughing. It was a good thing that I did, for Kenny, his face as white as a sheet, sat poised with a raised pipe wrench ready to hit the first thing coming through the entrance.

Kenny was a hopeless helper. He appeared incapable of learning anything. He was hoisting round lagging to me (8-foot poles that were about five to six inches in diameter) with the tugger hoist mounted on the platform above the drift.

I was up in the raise signaling him when to stop so that I could unhook them and send down the wire cable for another load. It was taking him so long to do this simple chore that I switched jobs with him one day. I showed him how to swing the load out of the skip-way and signal for, slack by banging on the pipe, so that he could unhook the load and send the cable back down to me. This did not seem to help. He was just as slow at the top as he had been at the bottom.

After I had sent the final load up to him one day, I ran the hundred feet up the ladders to where he was still trying to unhook the last load. To

my astonishment, I saw that instead of swinging the load out of the skip-way as instructed, he was trying to unhook it right in the skip-way. I was lucky that he did not succeed for if he had, some pieces would surely have gotten away from him. They would then have hurtled down the raise and speared me because there was no way for me to dodge

Bill Strynadka and the author. Bill is sitting on the right. *Photo is from the author's collection* them. That was his last day with me. Bill Strynadka asked me to take him on as my helper instead because his cut in base pay was small compared to the bonus we could make as a good team.

Bill weighed only 145 as compared to my 169 pounds, but he was a smart willing worker and strong for his size. During the next two months, Bill

Emco mucking machine and an ore car – used to muck the ore off the track. *Photo taken by the author courtesy of the Britannia Mining Museum at Britannia Beach, BC*

and I did indeed make good money, but we remained in number two spot, close to, but still behind the two Finnish brothers who had consistently earned the highest bonuses.

During my last year in school (Grade X) I had learned some geometry. I was therefore able to pre-calculate the cut angles of the timber and planking on the chutes we were building at the bottom of our raises. Bill never ceased to be amazed by this, and our chutes were by far the best looking ones in the mine.

We quickly learned that in order to earn a decent bonus building these chutes, we had to install posts that were there for looks only, but did not serve any structural purpose.

In the cribbed raises we were getting paid just $8.00 per foot, a rate that was not conducive to making money since we could blast and timber only five feet per shift. However, we got extra money for any sections where the raise was oversize, as well as for the extra blocking required in these places. In order to increase our earnings, we therefore deliberately increased the size of the raise near the end of the pay period. When the surveyors came to measure our advance, they could check the size of the raise only at the top, so they paid us for the "over-break," as well as for the extra blocking, over its entire length.

On or about July 20th I was injured in a raise when a large slab of rock fell on me. It fractured two thoracic and one cervical vertebra. (See Chapter 26, "This Cat Had More Than Nine Lives"). During that month we finally surpassed the Finlanders and earned a bonus of over $20 per day, the highest in the mine for that year.

The Mayo Hospital

The ambulance took me directly to the hospital in Mayo where Dr. Clark was waiting for me. He put me flat on my back on a bed that had a one-inch thick mattress on top of a board and gave me no pillow. It was agony for the first week – partly due to my injuries and partly because my buttocks and my shoulder blades carried most of my weight and got no relief. Dr. Clark told me that I was quite possibly the first person in Canada to have a spinal fracture like this treated without a cast. He said that the theory was that given a chance, the spine would straighten and heal by itself.

The hospital had a kitchen, an eight-bed ward in which I stayed, and a three-bed isolation ward on the main floor. Upstairs was a maternity ward and the nurses' quarters. The staff consisted of a matron, three young single nurses and a cook. The three nurses were all attractive, but the black-haired, French Canadian nurse from Quebec especially entranced me.

I became constipated and glad of it because since the bedpan had no mattress to sink into, it felt like I was standing on my head when I tried using it. After my first try, I subsequently snuck out of bed at night on the rare occasions when I did have to go to the bathroom. I got a stern lecture over this when it became obvious to the nurses and to the doctor that I was not using the bedpan. Dr. Clark, who was brusque and lacked any pretense to a friendly bedside manner, threatened to cut me off WCB.

One of the patients in the hospital during the month I was there, was a young Czech who had Yellow Jaundice. He was getting two needles in his buttocks, four times a day and must have felt like a pincushion. He especially feared getting his shots from the one nurse, who was not skilled in this chore. She always admonished him to relax so it wouldn't hurt, but how could he when she was so inept with needles.

One day they brought in a drunk and put him in the Isolation Ward to dry out. Our doctor was short on patience at the best of times, but had none where drunks were concerned. I woke up during the night to find the guy teetering over my bed drinking from my water pitcher. I lay there paralyzed with horror as he rocked back and forth over me, threatening to fall on top of me and douse me at the same time. Somehow he managed to stay on his feet, and soon left. The doctor kicked him out the following day.

I was feeling much better after the first week in the hospital, but the time really dragged. I was able to read, but had to stay flat on my back. The young Czech was the only one allowed out of bed, so before long we got the idea of playing Blackjack. The Czech was our courier and delivered the cards to each bed where the recipient would say whether to hit or stay. When the hand was finished, our courier would move the money around as required, after which we would play the next hand. The nurses were a bit dubious about us gambling, but we assured them that it was okay and that other hospitals had allowed us to do this, (ha-ha).

I heard that Dr. Clark had left a career behind at the McGill hospital as well as a young wife in Montreal, to come to Mayo to get experience with broken bones. I don't know if this was true, but he had plenty of bones to work with at Mayo because the mine had a very high accident rate.

In the hospital was a young electrician who had crushed his ankle between two battery-operated locomotives. Dr. Clark had somehow put his bones back together with wire, plates and screws, despite having to work with primitive equipment. The electrician was able to leave the hospital with a walking cast after a stay of 5 months.

Bill Strynadka later told me that after I left the mine, Dr. Clark patched up a man, whose thigh was crushed in an underground rock fall, and sent him out to the hospital in Edmonton. In Edmonton the doctors were going to amputate the leg, so Dr. Clark wired out; "I could have done that here. Send him back!" Nine months after the accident, this man walked out of the hospital on both legs!

When I went to Mayo during a trip to Whitehorse in 1996, Dr. Clark was still there. I went to visit him, but was disappointed to learn that he was out on vacation. I was told that he was then living with an Aboriginal woman, and that he had trouble walking. I believe that he died the following year. He had spent 44 years in this small town and will be remembered by the many people he treated with his wizardry.

After I got out of the hospital I sat around the mine for two to three weeks recovering. I then went on light duty for a while, but that drove me nuts. When I asked to go back mining, they put me in a heavy timber raise where I had to wrestle with twelve-inch diameter posts that weighed two hundred pounds or more. I was not able to handle this, so I went back on light duty again. Not too long after this I was fired when the mine superintendent found me having a cup of tea while my partner was gone to fetch some mine cars. I suspect that it was a pretext to get rid of me for having a back injury. One company that I worked for later, had a policy of firing people with potential back problems.

During my time at Keno Hill, I regularly gambled and lost most of my earnings in the Black jack games. When I left in the mine in early November, my roommate, Dick Waverick, quit too. We were obliged to stay overnight in Mayo because the plane would not be in until the following day. That evening some of the local people invited us to a poker game at a private residence. I was doing quite well, but Dick wasn't, so I kept lending him money until his luck finally turned. When we left in the morning, we were up by over $500 each. That took a little of the sting out of my previous losses.

Chapter 14 - South Again

Vancouver

Dick and I stayed at the Abbottsford Hotel in downtown Vancouver for the month of November. While we were there, we regularly went to dances at the Commodore Ballroom on Thurlough Street. At our hotel, one waiter in the beer parlour often directed unattached women to our table when the place began to fill up. Dick, despite having a grotesque nose, (later corrected by surgery) was very successful with the women. I on the other hand was always too timid and afraid of offending to get very far with them. I did date a nice, attractive nurse from the Riverview Children's hospital a few times, but lost touch when I stopped writing to her.

Our money had begun to run low by early December, so we found work at the Kemano tunnel. The tunnels were almost finished then, but we were sent up as screed operators by the "Cement Mason's Union." Neither we, nor the Union man who hired us, knew what a screed operator was. We assumed that we could probably learn how to operate one quickly enough. Our jobs were at mid tunnel and we would be staying in the Horetzki Creek camp.

Kemano

The day before we left Vancouver, some friends from Keno Hill came into town. One of the fellows brought along a bottle of over-proof rum. We were visiting with them in the hotel room and I decided to drink the over-proof rum because no one else was touching it. I would take one large swig of the rum and then chase it with straight gin. Needless to say, when we boarded the ship for Kemano late that night, I was very, very drunk!

The following day we reached Banks Sound at the north end of Vancouver Island. The sea was rough with waves over thirty feet in height. Just about everybody on board was seasick. I was not so much seasick as hung over. It was the worst hangover I can remember having. I was also getting nauseated. I tried going out on the deck for fresh air, but that did not help. I finally discovered that when I stayed flat on my back, the nausea would subside, but if I got up or lay in any other position it would come back. I survived that day without having to vomit. The following day when I reached Kemano, I still had a severe hangover.

Kemano was the general name used to describe the huge power project being constructed by The Aluminum Company of Canada (ALCAN). The work included some dams in the Burns Lake area, a ten-mile long hydroelectric tunnel and power generating facilities. Water entered the tunnel at its eastern end, flowed through it and down a steep shaft to turn the turbines which generated the electric power. The power was transmitted to, and used at the aluminum smelter being built in Kitimat. The tunnel was shaped like a horseshoe and was over 30 feet in height and about 25 feet wide. The miners drove this tunnel from both ends as well as from the middle. In the process, they set production records that have never been equaled.

After we arrived at Horetzki Creek, we soon learned that the screed operators had to be in the "Operating Engineer's Union," not the Cement Masons. We were given the choice of shipping back to Vancouver, or joining Local 602 of the "Laborer's Union" and working as laborers. We both elected to stay and soon had jobs as "brake-men" on trains hauling concrete into the tunnel and refuse out. The man operating the Locomotive was a member of the Operating Engineers and hence earned a lot more than a brakeman.

I decided one day that I would write the exam to become a locomotive operator. This backfired. I have always had mediocre vision in my right eye, and when they discovered this, I was kicked off my job as a brakeman even though eyesight was not a criterion for that position. I therefore spent the next few months working on surface doing odd jobs and swamping for a dozer operator.

On Christmas Eve, I got into the Blackjack game at the camp and by late that evening I was up over $1,100. I left the game and went to bed, but was unable to sleep. I tried reading a book, but was unable to focus on it. I finally got out of bed, got dressed and went back to the game. By morning I was ahead of the game by $2,350. I went to breakfast and inquired about getting a boat to Vancouver, but learned that I was stuck in camp for the next several days. I went back into the game once more. One of the players there had lost $600 and was down to his last $100 when he got the deal. His luck then turned and he began winning. I tapped him (bet the amount in the bank that was available to me) three times in a row, the third time for over $700, and lost each time. Then I bet $200 three times in a row and lost. My money had suddenly shrunk to about $800 and I felt broke. Soon I had no money left.

I learned more about Blackjack when I wasn't playing than when I was. I soon found that there were always card-sharks in the game – men who came up from Vancouver and got jobs as flunkies in the kitchen, just to be there. One evening a friend brought a deck of cards to my room. It took us a while, but we discovered the cards were all marked. One ploy a crooked dealer often used was to have a silent partner sitting to his left. This man bet only nominal sums of money and took hits only if and when the dealer secretly signaled him to. The dealer could in this way enhance his own chances of getting a good card when it really mattered.

The general contractor at Kemano was Morrison-Knudsen (MK) from Boise Idaho. They were working for ALCAN on a "Cost Plus" basis. I soon learned that there was not a single grease gun on site. The sooner a dozer wore out, the sooner it could be replaced – at ALCAN's expense of course. I am certain that there were people with ALCAN who knew what was going on, but who were probably paid off to close their eyes to this wasteful practice.

At Horetzki Creek it seldom stopped snowing - it seldom got very cold either. On the road to Base Camp was a section of road prone to snow slides. The dozer operator keeping the road open had a swamper acting as a lookout for him. When a slide came down one day, this lookout man was buried. A large number of us spent several hours probing for him, but his body was not found until the dozer located him many hours later while it was clearing the slide off the road.

During the following spring, my foreman quit and went home. He told me that I would get his job, but management changed its mind when they found I was in Local 602. It turned out that there was a stipulation that all labor foremen had to be members of Local 168 of "The Tunnel & Rock Workers" Union. I promptly sent a resignation letter to Local 602 and applied for membership in Local 168, but it was ignored. I left Kemano in late June and headed for the Nelson country again.

Rodeos

In Tilley during my teen years, we had a rodeo on July 1st every year. By today's standards it was probably not much of an event, and I doubt that it drew more than mediocre talent, but to me it was the real thing. I never missed an opportunity to attend. Furthermore, there were other attractions as well. The year that I was sixteen, the Lions Club from Brooks had some gambling games on the fair grounds as well.

In addition to the usual Crown and Anchor type of wheels, they also had a .22 rifle set up. The object was to shoot down a lighted cylinder at a target. The target was a picture of Hitler with a bright red heart painted on his chest. To win, it was necessary to completely knock out all of the heart with three shots. The prize for succeeding was $25, which was a lot of money in those days. For $0.25 I got three shots and on my first attempt my first shot hit the heart right smack in the middle. This made it impossible to eradicate the rest of it with the two remaining bullets. Nevertheless, I took my other two shots to learn where the rifle was shooting. I quickly discovered that the front sight had been hammered off to one side a bit. This actually helped me because the front sight therefore did not obscure the part of the target I was trying for.

On my second attempt I thought I had succeeded, but when the attendant turned back the torn edges of the bullet holes, he found a faint trace of red. By this time there was quite a crowd watching me. When the attendant refused to pay me they all started yelling Crook! I then paid for a third try, but ruined it with a poor first shot. On my fourth and final attempt I finally succeeded. There was no way that the guy could find any red left where the heart had been, but he said he did not have the money on hand to pay me. He told me to come back after supper. The crowd went wild! They were convinced that the guy was going to cheat me, but when I returned after supper, he did indeed have the money and paid me forthwith.

The rodeo events included saddle and bareback bronc riding, wild cow milking, calf roping and wild horse racing. However, there were no chuck wagon races. I therefore promised myself that one day I would attend the Calgary Stampede specifically to see the chuck wagons in action.

In the early summer of 1954 I had just left ALCAN's tunnel project at Kemano. I picked up my, car from storage in Vancouver and first drove to Nelson where I visited a few friends. I also looked up Dixie and took her to a movie, but she was no longer interested in me - and small wonder. I had treated her badly when I had previously worked around Nelson, and took her out only when I did not have any other dates.

After a few days in Nelson, I left for the prairies and reached Calgary while the Stampede was in full swing. It was early in the evening as I headed south on 4th Street southeast from the downtown area. I had not gone very far when I saw three men in cowboy hats thumbing for a ride. Since I assumed they were going to the Stampede grounds too, I picked them up.

It turned out that one of the men was a bronc rider, one was a Stampede judge and the third some other kind of official. When I told them that I was on my way to see the chuck wagon races, the judge asked me to pull over to the curb and let him drive the car. He then pinned his badge on me and drove into the Stampede grounds and parked my car in a spot reserved for officials. After we got out of the car, he escorted me on to the grounds, and up into the Press Box.

I not only got to see the chuck wagon races, but I got to see them from the very best seat on the grounds. Furthermore, it did not cost me a single red cent for admission or for parking my car. This was the first and last time I watched chuck wagons in action, but it was an event that I shall never forget.

The following morning I drove north to visit my sister who lived west of Innisfail in a farming community called Dickson. While I was there I attended a dance at Caroline, a small isolated community some twenty miles farther to the west. I was wearing a suit, and was that ever a blunder. I stood out like a sore thumb and felt totally out of place. All the guys were not only in jeans, but they appeared to be wearing the pair with the least cow manure on the pant legs. There was so much dirt on the floor that whenever they played a polka or a fox-trot, a dust cloud slowly ascended from the floor. When the dance was over the dust slowly subsided to the floor again. I later learned that Caroline was then considered a veritable "Dogpatch" where girls were typically married at age fifteen or even younger.

Bill Strynadka

After a short visit in Dickson I drove on to Edmonton where I got together with Bill Strynadka for a few days. He had just come down from the United Keno Hill in the Yukon where we had worked together the previous year.

One day he, some of his friends and I were sitting in his hotel room having a few beer and shooting the breeze. I had been using a stale beer as an ashtray and had just dropped a cigarette butt in it, when Bill who was sitting beside me grabbed the wrong bottle and took a big swig from it. I could see his face turning green as he rushed to the bathroom with his hands over his mouth. He had swallowed the butt!

One evening the two of us were going dancing nearby. We first stocked the car up with liquor and then parked the car across the street from the dance hall. I said to Bill; "If you pick up a chick and want to take her out for a drink, just come over and get the keys from me.

We had not been there very long before Bill came over with a gorgeous woman on his arm and got the car keys from me. He was gone for only a few minutes before he came back without the woman and with a sheepish look on his face. He told me that as they were leaving the building, a huge black man stopped them and said; "You'se wasting your time Mac. I just took her out and fucked her and when I fuck em, dey stay fucked!" His dance mate was gone in a flash and we did not see her again.

I saw Bill infrequently over the next 30 years. He got married, quit mining and opened a service station in Edmonton. The next time I saw him; he had opened a second service station and had also gotten into the towing business. I heard from a mutual friend a year later that he now had four service stations. It sounded as though he was doing very well for himself. Many years later, in 1986, I saw him for the last time. He still owned one service station, but no longer had the towing business. He was clearly alcoholic and looked in poor health. When I tried to reach him in 2001, I was saddened to learn that he had died six years earlier. Although we had not seen each other very much over the years, I felt that I had lost a dear and valued friend.

Chapter 15 - Love & Marriage

Oil Rigs

From late July 1954 and until April the following year, I worked as a "roughneck" on oil-rigs. The first job was on a rig drilling for oil near Tilley where I did not stay long. This rig, I soon suspected was not really meant to drill for oil at all - but was there for show. Its real purpose was to mislead local people into investing in a company run by stock promoters. If this company had been serious about drilling a well, they would probably have contracted the drilling to a company with proven expertise in this field. Instead they had a drill rig that was down for repairs most of the time and inadequate for the job.

Since we did not work when the rig was down, I began looking for another job. I soon found one on another rig that was drilling near Suffield. Regent Drilling from Edmonton owned this one as well as forty other rigs working in the industry.

This particular drill was a "wildcat" rig - one that drills exploratory holes in an effort to find a new oil or gas field. As such, the rig moved a lot – spending about two months on each drill site. When we finished at Suffield we moved north to Cessford, and from there, south to Picture Butte, where we made an important find of natural gas.

Most of the crew-members on the rig were married and lived in house trailers on the drill sites with their young families. We single roughnecks found accommodations in the nearest communities. I soon learned that being a roughneck was not conducive to meeting nice girls in the community. Drill crews had a reputation for being wild, rough and uncouth, so we found the doors to the local social life were usually shut tight.

One day George Friesen (my fellow roughneck) and I were driving past a car lot in Lethbridge when we spied a gorgeous blue Pontiac convertible. We could not resist stopping to look at it, and of course, me being such an easy mark, I bought it. It was only a year old and was very classy. It was great for picking up girls, but I soon found I could not keep tires under it. Every second time I got a flat tire, it was ruined and I would have to buy a new one. It did not seem to matter whether I stopped quickly or whether I coasted to a stop, the tire would be destroyed. After we moved to Heisler nylon tires became available and I bought them for all four wheels and ended this problem. Those tires cost me a $50 each – nearly a month's pay in those days.

After finishing at Picture Butte, our rig moved north to Heisler, a village about forty miles southeast of Camrose. Here we were the first rig to drill in the area, so there was no sour reputation preceding us. The local townspeople treated us like celebrities, and we had no trouble getting dates. I was soon dating a nearby farmer's daughter (Frances) who became my wife the following year.

Everyone in Heisler was Catholic. The place was so Catholic that there were nuns teaching in the public High School. Later, when Frances and I became engaged, I decided to join the Catholic Church, since the Lutheran one meant nothing to me. I thought this was a better solution to family harmony than anything else I could think of.

We finished the well in Heisler in January and moved south to the Joffre oil field twenty miles east of Red Deer. Here we drilled in an established field and were no longer wildcatting. Instead of spending two months on a well, we were completing each one in ten to eleven days. Not only was the rock much softer here, but we were not doing extensive testing because we were drilling in a proven area. The moves between wells were also much quicker because we did not have to lay down and dismantle the derrick each time. Instead we jacked up the entire substructure with the upright derrick in place, and placed it on four tracked dollies and towed it from one site to the next with two bulldozers.

The Joffre field kept us all hopping until the road restrictions came on in April. Since it was no longer possible to haul in drill casing, and other heavy supplies, we temporarily shut the rig down. It appeared to me that I could expect to be out of work for at least a month and maybe two, so I took this opportunity to take my girlfriend Fran to meet my parents, and then to return to the West Kootenays to look for work.

Back Mining

When I returned to Salmo, that spring, I was immediately hired at the HB mine. I got my room and board with Rae and Doris Thomas in Ymir and worked together with Rae again for the first time in almost three years.

On the July 1st long weekend, I drove to Heisler and became formally engaged to Frances (Fran). She accompanied me

HB Mine: Flotation Cells in the ore concentrator. *Photo courtesy of the Nelson Chamber of Mines.*

back to Ymir and stayed with us for a few days until she found a job at the Maple Leaf Café in Salmo, where she was given a room upstairs. She was not there very long before she broke our engagement. She had become enamored with another miner rooming at the Café, a fellow I had previously known at Keno Hill. I convinced her to go back to Heisler - away from us both - to think things over. We got married later that fall.

The Remac Years 1955 - 1962

HB Mine: Flotation Cells in the ore concentrator.
Photo courtesy of the Nelson Chamber of Mines.

Meanwhile, the Reeves McDonald mine reopened at the beginning of September, and I was one of the first miners hired there, but Rae elected to stay at the HB. I applied for and got a company house at Remac. To me the house did not then appear that small, but its outside dimensions were only twenty feet by eighteen feet. It had a kitchen, a living room, a tiny bathroom and too small bedrooms. There was a cellar of sorts under the house in which was a makeshift furnace made of a "barrel heater" encased in sheet metal. The heat came upstairs through a large grate in the hallway floor. The house was not insulated and the interior walls were made of "beaver board." The company supplied the paint and I painted the entire inside of the house during the next month. During this time I also purchased furniture from the Sears store in Nelson.

During this period I was also taking instruction in the Catholic religion from Father Monaghan in Nelson and I was baptized a Catholic in early October. Fran and I moved into the house at Remac immediately after we were married in Heisler on October 25th.

During the following years a Catholic priest came to Remac regularly to hold Mass. The Masses were held in the community hall after which one of the families would invite the priest over for breakfast because in those days no eating was allowed before Mass.

During this time my Pontiac convertible kept impoverishing me with its problems so I bought a brand new 1956 Dodge sedan. Between the car and the new furniture I was truly in debt up to my eyeballs. Were it not for the overtime I was regularly offered, I would not have had any spare money at all.

Fran was meanwhile having difficult menstrual periods. They were painful, lasted a long time and came at intervals of anywhere between three and six weeks. Her doctor found that her womb was tipped and implanted a device to correct the problem. When she next saw her doctor, her womb was not only okay, but she was pregnant as well. The following year after sixteen futile hours of labor, our son Donald was delivered by cesarean section on November 7, 1956. Fran's doctor warned her not to get pregnant again for at least three years.

After the next Mass, we had the priest up for breakfast and told him what the doctor had said. The priest then gave us some literature on birth control, saying that in our case the rhythm method was permissible. The pamphlets indicated that the menstrual periods had to be regular and advised charting them for a year before trying to use this approach to family planning. When I pointed this out to the priest, he said something like; "You are both intelligent people, I'm sure you will figure out what to do."

Our daughter Pamela was born 19 days less than a year after our son Don! We decided then to use condoms, but after a few months of this, Fran was unable to handle the guilt. We decided to try the Rhythm method once more, but Fran was soon pregnant yet again.

This was a very difficult pregnancy because she had RH negative blood. She spent the final two months of the pregnancy in hospital and our second daughter Cheryl was delivered on May 27, 1959 - after a term of about seven and a half months. It took Fran five years to regain her normal weight.

I had meanwhile spoken to Dr. Carpenter, (my own doctor) about getting a vasectomy and the conversation went something like this:

Doctor; "Why don't you get Fran to have her tubes tied instead?"
Me; "She has a Catholic doctor. He isn't allowed to do that."
"Then let me take her over."
"Is that ethical?"
"No problem. I will speak with Dr. Beauchamp and arrange it."

The evening before the cesarean was scheduled; Father Monaghan got wind of it. Fran told me later that he came to her room and browbeat her for over an hour about her decision, saying that God would look after her, and even if she died, God would look after her children. Fran despite being sedated stuck to her guns and had her tubes tied during the operation.

Several months later, Fran was once more racked with guilt, so we had the priest up for breakfast after Mass. When we related the previous events to him, the conversation went something like this:

Priest; "Just go to confession and have it over with."

Me; "I was taught that we couldn't go to confession unless we were sorry for what we had done."

"That's okay, just go to confession."

"But we're not sorry for what we've done. We would make the same decision again."

"Never mind, just go to confession and that will be the end of it."

I suppose that I was too obtuse and idealistic to realize the priest's dilemma. To us it was obvious that he didn't really believe in what the Catholic Church was teaching. We stopped attending Mass, and when we did attend one a year or so later, the homily was so asinine that we were both permanently cured of the Catholic Church.

During my first summer at Remac in 1956, there was a surveyor's helper named Laverne Hesketh whose father worked in management for Cominco at the Trail Smelter. They had a lakeshore property on the north side of the Kootenay west arm a few miles east of Nelson. Laverne asked me to come out and blast some boulders on the lakeshore for them so they could build a pier. On my next Saturday off, I drove to Nelson and spent part of the afternoon breaking up the largest boulders for the Heskeths.

After we had finished the work we went for a ride in a rubber raft they owned. We had paddled well out on to the lake when we saw a speedboat coming towards us. It turned out to be Rutherglen, the local game warden, who immediately asked us for our fishing licenses. We explained that we had not been fishing, but he told us that the fishing gear in the boat was "prima facie" evidence to the contrary, and he seized the gear forthwith.

I was on night shift and Laverne being salaried, we did not lose any pay when we appeared in court the following week. We told the judge what had happened, and since he could not let us off, because carrying fishing rods without a license, was as illegal as using them, he was going to fine us each $5 but Rutherglen pointed out that the minimum fine was $15. Laverne's father paid the fines, for he could not very well let me get nailed while doing him a favour.

During the ensuing years at Remac, things went rather well for me. I became one of two miners driving "raises" and was consistently a top earner at the mine. I was also active in the Mine Mill and Smelter Workers Union and served one term as president of our sub-local. During this period I did have some narrow scrapes including one that should have killed me, (See "Chapter 26, This Cat Had More Than 9 Lives").

Chapter 16 - A Day In My Life As A Raise Miner

The house is very cold when I roll out of bed at 6:00 AM for it is not insulated and the outside temperature has dipped to –10° F. I quickly don my frigid clothes, go outside and down into the cellar to light the fire in the furnace.

The furnace is a makeshift affair and consists of a 45 gallon drum set on its side with a door attached at the front end and a stovepipe exiting at the top near the rear. The whole contraption is enclosed in sheet metal that directs the heat up through a floor grate to the upstairs level of the house. That grate can get very hot in a short time.

When our son Don was about one year old, Fran had just taken him out of the bath and dried him off. Before she could dress him, he ran for the bedroom, but when he stepped on the hot grate with his bare feet, he promptly sat down on it and got his buttocks burned. His rear end looked like a waffle iron for a long time after this incident.

It takes me only a few minutes before I have a roaring fire going for we burn wood only and I always have lots of kindling prepared. Heating with wood costs us little besides the labor of cutting it, but it is impossible to keep the fire burning very long without feeding it more wood. The fire heats the house quickly, but it burns itself out quickly as well. This allows the house to get cold before morning.

By the time I get back upstairs, the house is already warming up. Fran is by now busy cooking bacon and eggs for my breakfast. While the food is cooking, I have a cigarette and my coffee. Then while I am eating my bacon and eggs, she prepares my lunch. It is Monday and I am on day shift for the next two weeks after which I will work nights for two weeks. On days, we work from 8:00 AM to 4:00 PM and on night shift from 7:00 PM to 3:00 AM. This is a good arrangement for I can usually get a decent sleep during my night shift too. When I have worked on a three shift rotation, I have always found the "graveyard" shift to be a killer, for I could never get more than three hours sleep until near the end of the week when I would be tired enough to get five.

After breakfast I light another cigarette and head for the "Dry" at about 7:15. It is a good half-mile away and down a long hill. I am joined in my walk by other miners who also live in the town-site. The last part of the walk is down several flights of covered stairs that end at the Dry. A number of our coworkers live in the village of Salmo – some 22 miles distant. They get to the mine in their own cars, but carpool and take turns driving.

In the Dry, we undress and hang our clothes in our individual lockers. We then lower our diggers from near the ceiling where they have been drying and quickly dress. My woolen socks have large holes in the heels, so I turn them so as to get the old heel on top and fresh material at the bottom. In this way I can extend the life of my socks by a factor of 2 or 3.

Mattie who dresses next to me is short heavyset and very fat. Unlike most of us, he perspires heavily during work and his clothes stink to high heaven. I wish he would wash them a little more frequently. One of the trammers has his locker on the opposite side of the aisle a few feet away. He is as skinny as a greyhound dog and has the largest genitalia I have ever seen. His dick hangs there, the size of a dead gopher and his scrotum is just

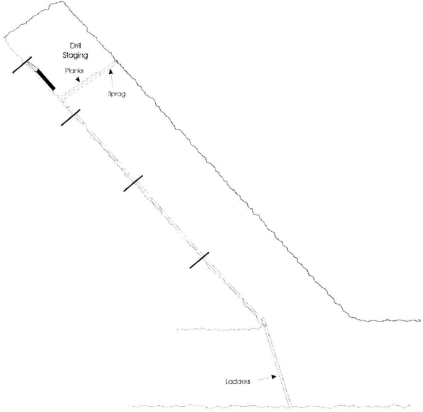

A typical "slot raise" at Remac. Sketch is by the author.

A miner drilling in a raise.
Photo courtesy of Andy Wingerak.

as immense. His wife is tiny and there is much speculation among his coworkers as to how she accommodates him.

After I have donned my "longjohns," shirt, trousers and rubber boots, I put on my "oilers," my hard hat and my heavy miner's belt. I light another smoke, then proceed to the lamp-room and get my underground lamp. I hang its battery on my belt and mount the lamp on my hat. On my belt I also carry a powder punch and a ten-inch crescent wrench. I then proceed to the shift boss' window and pick up my sharpened drill bits. Today I also purchase a new pair of neoprene gloves, which are charged against my commissary account. Together with the rest of the crew we proceed to the man cars for our ride into the mine.

At precisely 8:00 AM the train departs from the portal on the 1900 level and proceeds to the first stop about ¾ mile underground. Half of the crew disembarks here, but the rest of us proceed for another ¾ mile to the O'Donnel section of the mine. There I go to the fuse storage shed and pick up twenty-one 10-foot fuses and then enter the cage for a ride up to the 2250 level. I hang my fuses in a storage box erected at the station for that purpose, pick up an eight-foot section of ladder and a sprag and head down the drift to the raise I am currently driving.

It is 8:30 as I climb the ladders carrying the ladder, a pick and a slide-staff. When I reach the face forty feet above the drift, I hang the ladder on a steel peg and stash the pick and slide-staff for the time being while I grab the scaling bar out of the steel bucket where I had stored it. I then scale down all the loose rock I can find. Then I grab the water hose, open the valve and wash down the face to check for any holes that have not broken to bottom in yesterday's blast. As usual the only hole-sockets remaining are on the perimeter and they are no more than four inches deep. I wash them out thoroughly to ensure that there is no unexploded dynamite remaining in them. I shut off the water and with my slide-staff measure down 7 feet for my staging setup. Next I grab my pick and chop hitches into the rock for my sprags. The rock is hard, but with my sharp pick I am able to get decent hitches anyway. Next I use the slide-staff to measure for the two sprags I will use to construct my drill staging. There are still sprags in place from earlier rounds. I find one that is exactly the right length and insert it and then hammer in a wooden wedge to secure it. I descend to the level and grab the sprag I brought in with me, cut it to length and taper the ends with my axe. I then take my sprag and ascend the raise again. I quickly install it too, unchain the four 2" by 10" staging planks and set them on the newly installed sprags. On rare occasion I have been unable to cut a hitch where I needed it. Instead I have wedged the sprag in place and then drilled in a steel peg above it and chained it to the peg for safety.

Next I grab the 140-pound stoper (drill) off the steel peg it was hanging from and place it on the staging and hook up the water and air hoses to it. Then I take the steel oil bottle off the peg, open the "line oiler," fill it with oil and screw its cap back on. Last of all, I take my drill steel out of the steel bucket, throw them on to staging and put a carbide drill bit on each one. I am careful to put the newest (largest) bit on the starter steel and the oldest (smallest) on the longest steel because each drill steel must follow the previous one in the hole. I descend to the drift one more time to turn on the air and to hang the alignment plumb bobs (large washers attached to light chains) on their respective hooks. Back up on my staging and with the help of my "loading stick," I sight down on the plumb bobs and with yellow crayon, mark the centreline of the raise on both my staging and on the rock face. I am now ready to start drilling, but before I begin, I first light up a cigarette, the first since I got to my workplace.

It is almost 9:30 when I begin drilling my round. First, however, I drill a steel peg into the wall of the raise on which I hang my spare bits. I drill another one into the footwall on which I will hang the stoper, the steel bucket and the staging planks. It will also be used later for hanging a ladder. I expect to drill the necessary 26 holes in 4 to 4½ hours. I line up the stoper for the centre hole and check its slope with my "degree rule" to ensure that it is at the required 55° slope. I begin with the 2½-foot starter steel and drill it until the stoper leg is fully extended. I pull it out and insert the 4-foot steel next and drill it to bottom. I follow with the 5½-foot steel and the 7-foot one. If I am not behind schedule, I finish the hole straight a way with the 8-foot steel, otherwise I might postpone it to make sure I have time to drill all the holes to a minimum depth of 6½ feet, (6" of each steel is inside the stoper chuck).

Setting up a sound staging in raise mining is crucial to ones safety. There was a raise miner at Remac who fell when his staging went out from under him. Because he was on the same side of the raise as the ladders, his fall was arrested when his scrotum got snagged on a steel peg used for hanging the gear. He rode a locomotive out to the

First Aid room holding the contents of his testes together with his dirty hands. The doctor was able to save only one of them, but not surprisingly it became infected. He was off work for several months, but within a year he did manage to father another child. (Does this prove that we don't really need two?)

On the morning that my oldest daughter was scheduled for delivery by cesarean section, I was driving a steep (65°) raise. I was preoccupied and in a moment of thoughtlessness, I stepped on a sprag that had withstood two blasts. It went out from under me and I fell 35 feet to the level below, but escaped with a few bruises and a broken hard hat.

While I am drilling, the noise from the stoper is a steady deafening roar. When the shift boss arrives he brings a case of 70%Cilgel powder with him. He lets me know he is there by turning off my air for a moment and then back on again. I come down out of the raise and chat with him while I wolf down a sandwich and a cup of coffee from my thermos. Before he leaves, he gives me a proper sighting on the face for both line and grade. I adjust my alignment markings accordingly and get back to work.

I am very careful in lining up where I drill each hole. If one hole is too far away from the others, the round will not break all the way to bottom. If I make the raise too large, I will require more holes and explosives to break the round to bottom. If I can keep the raise uniform in size, I can often reuse my sprags several times. In short raises (60' or less) this is not so important because it does not take long to make an extra trip to the bottom. However, the following year, I drove a 350' foot raise where I was able to average only 2½ trips up and down the raise each day because I was always able to find at least one sprag near the face that was the exact length I needed. This allowed me to complete a full (if slightly shorter) round every single day, (and the highest bonus earned in the mine that year).

Once I begin collaring holes, the drill can be depended on to knock a lot of loose rock off the face. Together with the water and the drill cuttings, they quickly build up a thick layer of sludge on the staging. Therefore, once I have proper alignment, I usually drill the four lifters first. Since I am set up only seven feet from the face, I have to spread the planks to insert the 8-foot drill steel in the lower holes. This is much easier done before the sludge builds up on the staging. Next I drill the "burn" "shatter cut" (7 closely space holes) followed by the helpers, kneeholes and breast holes. I drill the back holes last.

Once I am finished drilling my round, I knock the bits off the drill steel and take them down to the level. Since I am on schedule, I grab another sandwich and a cup of coffee. I then turn off the air and water and carry the powder and fuses back up the raise. I bleed off the air and water and disconnect the hoses.

Using carbide bits has made a huge difference in drill production. I can normally drill a complete round with a set of five bits. Years earlier, I used a bucketful. The bits were made of steel and dulled quickly. Sometimes a bit would break inside an uncompleted hole. The options then were to drill a new hole or try to drill out the broken bit. If the bad hole was part of the "cut," it was usually necessary to drill out the broken bit. This was always time consuming and not always successful. In those days a good miner was lucky to finish even a short round each day, so it usually required two miners to drill a round every day.

I begin by loading the two corner holes in the cut. If too much powder is loaded into these holes, they will "freeze" the ground. Instead of ejecting the broken rock, it will remain squeezed in place and the other holes will not able to break to the bottom. If this happens, not only will I get a very short advance, but I will also have "bootlegs" (remains of drill holes) to contend with. Worst of all, in addition to a limited advance of just a foot or two, it will be very difficult to drill new holes where I need them. Experienced miners new to Remac often have a hard time learning how to break their rounds to bottom.

For the cut I break all the dynamite cartridges in half and alternate them with 8" wooden spacers. I always place the primer (cartridge with a capped fuse inserted in it) in the bottom of each hole. Next I load the cut helpers. I load them very lightly as well, but I do put a whole cartridge or two in the bottom of each of these holes. The rest of the holes are loaded with five cartridges each, and then filled to the collar by alternating with two wooden spacers followed by a half cartridge until the hole is full. By being so parsimonious I am able to blast nine rounds with only eight cases of powder. Since a case of powder is charged to me at $12, it represents an additional $12 - $13 on each pay check. This accounts for only 3%, but in our competitive environment, it is more about earning the highest bonus even if only by pennies. (My average advance last period was 7.25 feet per round. At $6.40 per foot I grossed $46.40 per day. After deducting $10.80 for powder, and $16.80 for wages, I earned $18.80 bonus per day).

To make up each primer, I punch a hole in one end of a cartridge with my powder punch and insert the cap end of a fuse. In clean holes I make it a practice of doubling the fuse over and inserting the cartridge, cap end first, into the hole. I usually crack the other end of the cartridge slightly so that I can push it and expand that part of it to fill the hole. I crack the rest of the cartridges along their perforations and tamp them thoroughly. The object is to get as much explosive as close to the bottom of each hole as possible to ensure that the round will break to the very bottom.

Each fuse has a blasting cap on one end of it and a "Thermalite" connector on the other. In earlier days we timed the sequence of detonation by trimming the length of the each fuse with the shortest to fire first and the longest last. The fuses were then lit in the same sequence – shortest first and longest last. The problem with this was not just the amount of wasted fuse, but it was easy to miss one during the lighting operation because the smoke from the burning fuses soon obscured ones vision. Furthermore we usually felt rushed and in a hurry to get out before the first shot went off. Using Thermalite connectors, we connect each fuse to the Thermalite cord in the desired firing order. Where firing sequence is crucial we space them out at least 8 inches, but for the rest the spacing can be a little less. This cord burns at a rate of 20 seconds per foot (3 feet per minute) and ignites each fuse as the flame reaches it. This allows us to light just one end of the Thermalite cord instead of a large number of fuses. Another feature of the cord is that it can be lit by striking it with a rock or piece of steel. This is handy if my matches have gotten wet.

Once I have the round loaded and the Thermalite cord connected, I begin hanging my gear. First I hang the stoper on the steel peg I had drilled earlier for that purpose. Next the steel bucket in which I place the drill steel and my loading stick. I then turn my drill planks over and pound them to knock off the sludge that is cemented on to them, after which I chain them together and hang them on top of the stoper to protect it from the blast. Last of all I tie the air hose to the planks so that I can blow air without the hose end whipping around all over the raise. I am now ready to light up the round. I carry whatever powder I have left over, down the raise and store it in my temporary magazine. If for some reason I am finished early I will go down to the 1900 level and hoist some sprags and ladders up for future use or find other ways of making the next day a little easier for myself.

At 3:20 I light the Thermalite cord and descend the raise for the last time that day. I turn on the air valve to blow air and ventilate my work area between shifts, pick up my lunch pail and the string of dull bits and walk out to the station. There I sit down with a fresh cigarette and wait for the

161

round to begin firing. I count each shot to ascertain that all twenty-one of them have gone off. After that I signal for the cage, ride it to the bottom level and get on the man-cars with the rest of the men for the trip back to surface. Since B.C. law limits our time to 8 hours a day underground, we must be out before 4:00 PM.

Once outside we pile off the man-cars and head for the Dry. It is easy to spot the miners, for unlike the other underground workers, their faces are as black as coal. This is from being splattered with drill cuttings from the lead-zinc ore. In the lamp room I shed my miner's lamp and place its battery on the charging rack so that it will be ready for the next day. I stop by the shift boss' wicket and report the number of holes drilled and blasted. At my locker I shed my dirty clothes, hang them on the hook and hoist them to the ceiling where they can dry. I then race to be among the first men in the large communal shower room.

After a hot shower, I don my street clothes and leave the Dry. Together with some of my co-workers, I retrace my steps back up the stairs, up the road and back to the town-site. We are usually home by 4:30 PM. On Saturday I will come down and wash my diggers.

When I get into the house, Fran immediately begins telling me all about her day, but my ears are still ringing from the unremitting noise of my stoper and it will be at least an hour or two before I will be able to hear properly again. Somehow, I am never able to get this point across to her. I suppose that she thinks I just don't have any interest in hearing how her day has been. I just want to be left alone with the "Nelson Daily News" until my hearing returns.

We have been invited by one of our neighbors to come over after dinner to watch TV. We are the only family in the town-site that has not purchased a television set. When the mine reopened in late 1955, we were newly married and I could not afford to buy one. Now that I can afford one, I am too stubborn to because I am disgusted with the way television dominates everybody's lives. In my opinion it has wrecked the community spirit that existed here in earlier days.

That evening, after we have eaten and washed the dishes, we walk over to our friend's house and watch the lone channel that is available. It is a CBS station and is broadcast from Spokane Washington. Our friends are all able to pick up the signal with rooftop antennas. There is one man in the town-site who has put up a home made rhombic antenna and is able to get three stations, but not clearly. We get to see "I Love Lucy," "The $64,000 Question" and "Have Gun Will Travel." The extent of the conversation is pretty much limited to; Hello. Do you take cream and sugar? Ssh, and Goodnight.

Chapter 17 - Life At Remac

Being a top earner invariably led to a certain amount of jealousy. It was mid February and some of us were sitting in the beer parlour one Saturday afternoon comparing T4 slips. Mine was not the highest one that year because I served on the Safety Committee where I earned only hourly wages one day every month. Sitting across the table from me was Mattie. He piped up and said he could not understand why I was not the top moneymaker and implied that I was "brown-nosing." I said to him; "Mattie, are you suggesting that I am "suck-holing," for if you are, I'll punch you right in the nose!" Mattie retorted; "Well you certainly do your share of it." I immediately drove him from across the table and we both jumped up. Mattie's nose spewed blood like a fountain, and I got in a couple more jabs before we were pulled apart. The bartender told us to go out on the street to settle our differences, so I told Mattie I would wait for him outside. I went out, and waited nervously, for Mattie, though shorter, was much stockier than me. I was very much relieved when he did not show up.

This was the first real fight I had ever been in, and during the next few weeks I got into a couple of other fights as well, before I stopped and had a hard look at myself. Since that time, I got into just one more fight and that was about four years later. In that one my opponent got a choke-hold on me and my mining partner had to come to my rescue.

When Fran and I were first married, she rolled cigarettes for me with a "Veemaster" cigarette roller. She could roll five at a time with it, but she refused to do it any longer after our son Don was born. I therefore started buying "tailor-made" cigarettes and before long my smoking had doubled. I went from 17 smokes a day to a pack and a half. I also began hacking and coughing a lot too. I was able to alleviate my cough by changing brands occasionally, but the respite never lasted long.

One evening after dinner I was sitting on the chesterfield coughing as usual when I said; "I think I'll quit smoking..." Before I could finish my sentence with "for a while," Fran started laughing at me. She assumed I had meant to say I would quit – period! I could not let her get away with that so I made a bet with her that I could quit until Christmas (It was January 5). I had promised to buy her a new coat, so I said; "I will still buy the coat, but it will be a year later if I win." However, if I lose, I will buy it immediately and spend $100 on it in addition to the $70 that we had budgeted.

It was tough, but I won my bet because my pride would not let me lose to her. At first it was a case of remembering not to accept a cigarette in the beer parlour. Several times I was almost ready to light one up when I would remember. The cravings reached their worst about three months after I quit, but I won my bet. I almost began smoking again the following year, but then one day I put my foot down and quit for good. I continued having occasional cravings over the next three years, but they eventually went away.

The morning that my daughter Pamela was scheduled to be born, I was driving a very steep (72°) raise. I suppose that my attention was not entirely on my job, for I carelessly stepped on to a staging timber in the raise that I had used the previous day. I immediately plummeted 35 feet to

the level below. The raise continued down past the level, but I had fortunately thrown some planks across it and they arrested my fall. I escaped with only a few bruises and a broken hard hat.

On another occasion I was starting a "drift" off a raise I was driving. I was using a stoper instead

A Jackleg Drill. Photo taken by the author courtesy of the Britannia Mining Museum at Britannia Beach, BC

of a jackleg because of the confined workspace and I was standing on solid rock when the 140 pound machine slipped from my grasp as I was changing steel. It fell on my foot behind the steel toe and bruised my foot above the instep. However, it was not the top of my foot that hurt so badly, but the ball of my foot behind the big toe. The pain was excruciating whenever I inadvertently put weight on it. A few years later when I had the foot x-rayed due to another injury, we discovered that I had a loose bone chip from the earlier accident. No wonder my foot had hurt so much at the time.

In the autumn of 1961 I was walking past a huge boulder at the bottom of a draw-point when a large rock hurtled from it. It struck my foot up against the boulder making several cuts through my rubber boot at the ankle. Surprisingly, there were no bones broken in my foot and ankle, but it mashed them together pretty badly. The skin was cut and my foot was soon infected. I spent two weeks with my foot up, changing hot compresses soaked in salt water before I was able to drive out the infection and walk on the foot again.

Al King

During the nineteen fifties and sixties the Mine Mill & Smelter Workers Union (Mine Mill) represented many miners in Canada, but its membership base was gradually being eroded by raids from the Steelworkers Union of America. During this period, Inco at Sudbury had the largest local, and I believe Consolidated Mining & Smelting Company (Cominco) at Trail had the second largest one. The Sullivan mine at Kimberley, also owned by Cominco, had a large Mine Mill membership too.

Al King: 1915 - 2003
Photo taken by the author in 2001

The Canadian Labor Congress (CLC) had expelled Mine Mill from its body because it was allegedly Communist led. This was a big issue during the McCarthy era. The CLC therefore sanctioned raids on Mine Mill by other unions. The Steelworkers Union posed the biggest threat to Mine Mill, because they had a huge war chest dedicated to that purpose.

I have no doubt that some of the top Mine Mill executive had Communist sympathies. I believe that one of its top leaders, Harvey Murphy was an avowed "Red." Nevertheless, Mine Mill was the most democratically run union that I have ever encountered. To the best of my knowledge the political leanings of the leadership never influenced the rank and file or the running of the Union's affairs. In this union every issue of importance, or to do with money, had to be ratified by the membership through referenda. I know of no other labor body that can lay claim to such grass roots involvement.

At Salmo the men working at the three major mines in the area, Cominco's HB, the Canadian Exploration, (Emerald) and Reeves McDonald (Remac) formed one local. There were also sub-locals at each of these mines. I first joined Mine Mill in 1955 while I was working at the

HB mine. When I moved to Remac later that same year, I began taking an active interest in union affairs. In addition to being a "shop steward," and being on the local executive, I served one term as the president of that sub-local.

It was during this time that I met Al King, who was then the president of the Trail Local. I believe that Trail had a membership of around five thousand men at that time. Al King in addition to his duties at Trail regularly assisted us with negotiations and other union activities. Although my association with him was always on a business footing, I learned to trust and respect him. He was a skilled negotiator whose word could be trusted by union members and management alike. He always carried himself with dignity and treated all around him with the utmost respect. It was not until I read his book, "Red Bait," that I learned that he had in fact been a communist for a while. Nothing he did back then led me to suspect him of being a "Red."

During the past year (2001) while I was visiting Rae Thomas in the Nelson area, he mentioned that Al King had recently published a book about the Mine Mill Union titled "Red Bait." I was unable to find this book in any of the Vancouver book stores so one day I decided to try and find Al King. When I searched the Internet for his telephone number, I expected that he would be living in either the Trail or Vancouver areas. I found one Al King listed in Vancouver and decided to try that number first. To my great surprise it was the correct number. He told me that his book was out of print but that he had a copy I could buy for $20. I arranged to visit him a couple of days later to pick up the book. Al was then eighty-six and though I had not seen him in forty years, I had no difficulty in recognizing him. To my disappointment, he did not remember me, but then of course he had dealt with a lot of miners and had met me only a few times.

I had a short visit with Al during which, we reminisced about the old days in the area and the people we had known. I left his house with an autographed copy of his book for which he refused payment. In return I gave him a copy of my poetry book, "A Way to Live." I felt greatly honored when he called me a few days later, told me he liked my book, but complained that I had not autographed it.

During our conversation that day, I mentioned that I had been to a Mine Mill convention in Vancouver in about 1957. I began to tell him about being stopped for speeding, when he broke into a huge grin. He said that he remembered the story very well – that it had gotten a wide circulation at the time. (Al King passed away at age 88 in mid April, 2003 shortly after suffering a stroke).

In 1957 my coworkers elected me as a delegate to the annual Mine Mill convention being held in Vancouver. My fellow delegates and I rode the Greyhound bus from Salmo to Vancouver and stayed at the Niagara Hotel, the convention venue. I don't remember much about the convention itself, which lasted most of the week. What I do remember was that on the evening before the last day, we went to a dinner and dance held for us in New Westminster. There was a bus available to take us there and back, but I rented a car instead and took along three of my buddies.

We had a steak dinner and like many others I ate two steaks. The meal included wine and various other drinks which were served both before, during and after the dinner. I drank a lot, but it did not seem to inebriate me – probably because of the huge dinner I had eaten.

The party was over, and my friends and I were on our way back to Vancouver, when one of them suggested we get to the Pender Street liquor store before it closed. Since we did not have too much time left before its closing time, I pushed my luck by driving well over the legal limit of 25 mph. We were cruising up Kingsway doing forty miles an hour when a policeman pulled us over. His first question was; "Why all the speed?" Without waiting for my reply, he ordered me out of the car and asked for my Drivers License. I explained to him that we were down from the West Kootenays for a union convention and that we were returning to our hotel after a dinner in New Westminster. He then repeated his first question: "what was the reason for all the speed?" I said to him; "To tell you the truth we were trying to make the liquor store before it closes."

The policeman looked at his watch and said; "Holy cow, you better get going or you won't make it!" I was not too sure of where the liquor store was, and I was also a bit nervous about getting stopped for speeding a second time if I rushed, so I said to him; "I'm not sure of how to get there, could you possibly lead us to it?" The policeman said; "Just follow me," jumped into his cruiser, and away he went! We followed right behind him (just as fast as before) and got to the liquor store with five minutes to spare. My buddies in the car did not hear any of the conversation and I was never able to convince them that I had not paid off that cop.

I well remember the morning after the party too, for we all had king-sized hangovers. Every time that the chairman, Thibault pounded the lectern with his gavel, we all jumped. He must have had a macabre sense of humor, for he took great delight in using the gavel energetically at every opportunity.

The Mine Mill Union sponsored a picnic each spring. Most of the men and their families from the local mines came to it. Activities included some sports as well as entertainment for the children. I will remember my first picnic well because I participated in the mucking contest.

The mucking contest involved shoveling a ton of broken rock from one section of a wooden box into the other. I made a strategic blunder by competing first. No one expected to beat big Nick (Bolinski) who was the biggest and strongest man around, but I did think I might take second prize, (there was no 3rd). Meanwhile as the contest progressed, more and more of the muck got spilled on the ground outside of the box instead of staying in it. When Tony Giza finally took his turn, he beat my time by only 3 seconds! The muck spilled on the surrounding ground was more than enough to make up the difference. I had worked so hard that it took me the rest of the afternoon to recover.

Wally and Terry Bunka

I first met Terry while I was chumming around with his younger brother Wally in 1952. They had both gotten married since then – to the two Zaleschuk sisters from Trail. Wally married Georgina, the older sister and Terry married Gloria, the younger one. Gloria was barely fourteen years old at the time and had five sons by the time she was twenty one! Wally and Georgina on the other hand had just one daughter.

We had a horseshoe pitch beside the Remac community hall where a few of us spent a lot of time. I played a lot of games with Terry Bunka, but he consistently beat me even though I threw a lot more ringers than he did. His shoes always came in with a downward tilt that caused them to stop very close to the peg, whereas mine came in tilted slightly up and tended to slide too far by. Since we always played for ice cream floats or similar treats, I paid for most of them. Don Clark and Terry's brother, Wally also played horseshoes, but they were not as good as us. Terry and I played checkers too, and when I suggested that we play this game for treats as well, I soon recouped my losses.

One summer there was a horseshoe tournament in Fruitvale (near Trail). I should have liked to enter together with Terry, but he and Wally had already registered together in the "A" event. Don Clark and I entered the "B" event. It was a "double knockout" competition, which gave each team two chances to survive. Poor Terry and Wally, they were humiliated because their competitors threw an average of 75% ringers. In the B event I averaged 50% ringers and that might have been good enough, except that Don Clark was off his game that day and played poorly. We all went back home with bruised egos.

I saw both Terry and Wally many years later during the-mid seventies, while I was living in the Vancouver area. I visited Terry in the house he had built at Squamish shortly before he broke up with his wife Gloria. He told me that he had been badly injured in the tunnel at the Granduc mine a few years earlier when someone had unbolted the valve on the main airline without bleeding off pressure first. The heavy valve struck Terry and fractured a number of his bones in the process.

I saw Wally only once during that same period. Some time later he too was injured at the Granduc mine when he drilled into some un-exploded dynamite and lost the sight in both his eyes. As of the spring of 2002, both Wally and Terry are living in Calgary.

Hollywood

I don't know how Hollywood got his nickname, but I suspect it may have happened due to his previous dislike of water. While I was working in the Dodger tunnels, he was there as well, but not in a mining job. At that time he never showered after work and those changing clothes beside him had to put up with his smell. Finally one day, a couple of miners grabbed a water hose each and cornered Hollywood by the showers. They gave him a shower from the hoses, but not with warm water. Hollywood supposedly went to the mine office to complain, but was promptly fired. During all the years that he worked at Remac, he showered after work every day.

Don Clark

Don was one of my good friends at Remac all the time we were there from the mid-fifties until I left in 1962. He, Ordie Jones and I hunted and fished together regularly. It was his brother that got killed while driving Hollywood's car. Don was easy going most of the time, but he had a short temper. One day we were up near the garbage dump sighting in our rifles. Don had purchased his new 308 a few days earlier and was adjusting the telescopic sights on it. Because he was flinching every time he pulled the trigger, his shots were going all over the place. He finally blew his cool and grabbing the rifle by its barrel, he smashed the stock against a large boulder. After he had cooled down somewhat, he returned the rifle to the hardware store where he had bought it, and they replaced it free of charge.

A few years after leaving Remac, I hired Don to work for me when I was a superintendent with Gulf Drilling at Revelstoke. He took over from me when I was moved to a different project. Over the following years our paths crossed occasionally. The last time I saw Don was when he stopped at my house in Prince George on his way to the BC Rail tunnels near Tumbler Ridge. I went to look up Don in Campbell River during the summer of 2001 only to learn that he had died two months earlier.

Car accidents amongst members of the mining community were common. Miners were notorious for frequently wrecking their vehicles. In 1952 when I was working at Can-Ex, my roommate, Harold Mulrooney (later the president of the Tunnel and Rock Workers Union) escaped with minor injuries when the driver of the car in which he was riding, went off the road and got himself killed. One Saturday afternoon, a few of us from Remac were in the beer parlour, when Don Clark's brother Jack borrowed Hollywood's car to go back to the mine for something. He missed a curve and did a somersault - the car flipping end over end, and killing him in the process. Later Willie McLean was killed and Rae Thomas crippled when he drove over a cliff while inebriated. While I was at Remac a guy named Thorburg was killed when the driver rolled his car two miles from camp on the way to Kaslo after work. After I left Remac, Doug Rozel and his wife were both killed when they went off the road on the "Creston Skyway."

Almost everyone at the mine's town-site heated their homes with wood that they cut in the adjacent forest. I bought a McCullough chain saw to cut my own wood as well as that for Ordie Jones, who worked with me on this. I also lent the saw to the Bunka brothers as well as to Ed (Alfalfa) Howes. The mine provided us with a flatbed truck at nominal rent for hauling the wood in.

One summer we had a forest fire nearby, so we at the town-site were all conscripted to fight this fire. I was pleased when I was able to bring my saw on to the job and get paid for it. I was disappointed and hurt though when I found that my friends were jealous of me getting paid for my saw, despite their having used it free of charge to cut their wood

When my brother Frank left the Air Force in 1959 after spending 10 years there, I found him a job as "timekeeper" at the mine. It was while he was there, that the Bunka brothers and we decided to learn how to play chess. We had many good games because we were all equally ignorant, but I managed to become and remain the champion of our group.

Frank and I joined one of two "Curling" teams from the mine that year. We played with Frank Thompson, the mine manager and Bob McDonald the surface foreman. Frank Thompson skipped our team, Bob played third, Frank played second and I threw the lead rocks. We curled in Salmo one night a week that winter.

There was a bonspiel held at Salmo late in the spring that year and we of course entered our teams. Since the rink had only two sheets of ice, and since there were a lot of entries, the bonspiel was run 24 hours a day. Our team had come off the ice at 11:00 PM on Saturday night and we were slated for another game at 3:00 AM on Sunday morning. Since we had to wait around, Bud Taylor, the local garage owner invited us to a party at his house. When we arrived Mrs. Taylor poured us each a drink and shooed us down into the "Rec. room" where someone was playing the piano and others were dancing. She told us that it was up to us to help ourselves to subsequent drinks.

When my glass ran empty I went upstairs for another drink of whiskey, but could not find the bottle, so I poured myself a drink from a "gin" bottle, but I could not find any mix, so I poured in some water. A person standing beside me saw this and said; "You can't drink that stuff like that, and poured some mix into it from freshly found bottle of ginger ale. I had one more drink of this gin before we went back to the rink.

When we got on to the ice, the skip was so drunk that he could not stand up, so we had to forfeit the game. Frank and I went to the hotel, got a room and went to bed. When I awoke a few hours later, my stomach felt as though there was a ball of red-hot lead in it. I was so sick that I contemplated seeing a doctor, but thought better of it, after all, who goes see to a doctor for a hangover?

By 11:00 AM I was able to eat some breakfast and I began feeling a little better even though my stomach still hurt a lot. We had left the room and were headed for the rink when we met a curler just coming from it. He immediately asked me if I knew what I was drinking the previous evening. I retorted; "Of course! I wasn't drunk. I had one drink of rye and two drinks of gin." "That wasn't gin you were drinking," he said, "That was picture developer!" It turned out that Bud Taylor's son Jack had been developing some film. He had stored the solution in a gin bottle and had accidentally left it on the counter together with the liquor bottles. It was no wonder that I had been so sick. Mrs. Taylor got a lot of teasing over the incident and I was often asked if my stomach was developing any photos.

Peligren And Kozar

Bill Peligren and John Kozar had worked together on a jumbo at the Emerald mine for some time. They were not only partners at work, but they had also become close friends. John Kozar came to Remac in the fall of 1955 as the mine foreman when the Reeves McDonald mine reopened. Bill Peligren followed him and hired on as a miner there the following summer. Bill also became the union president of the Remac sub-local, and in that position also served as a shop steward.

One day in early 1957 a young trammer was holding his train inside the mine while waiting for an inbound one to arrive. According to this guy, he phoned out and was told by Kozar that it was okay to proceed out of the mine. The result was a collision between the two trains. Kozar promptly fired him and denied having told him to proceed. Bill Peligren therefore laid a grievance against the company for unjustly firing the train operator.

That night there was a dance held at the mine's community hall. The train operator was there as was both Peligren and Kozar. Sometime during the evening (after everyone concerned were somewhat inebriated) a fight broke out between Kozar and the fired trainman. When Bill Peligren stepped in to break up the fight, Kozar struck him and then told him that he was fired too.

After the weekend was over, Bill Peligren promptly laid assault charges against John Kozar. The case was heard by a "Justice of the Peace" in Salmo, and Kozar was found guilty as charged.

The mine immediately appealed the verdict on John Kozar's behalf and won the appeal because Bill could not afford adequate legal counsel. The mine then blacklisted Bill so that he could no longer find work within the mining industry. Bill was fortunate in that he shortly thereafter found a mining job at the "Ripple Rock" project near Campbell River on Vancouver Island.

After the Ripple Rock project was over, Bill found work in the Campbell River area with the MacMillan Bloedel Timber Company. He spent many years with them operating a grader on the main logging road between Campbell River and the Franklin River area.

I first visited the Peligrens there in 1963 when I was working at Western Mines on the shores of Buttle Lake. He took me to look at a 10-acre piece of land that was for sale for $10,000 right in Campbell River. It was obviously a bargain and I wanted to buy it together with him. Neither one of us had the money, but I was sure I could borrow my share. Bill finally got cold feet so we let the deal slip away from us. It was not too long after this that a new school was built on the property. We could have made a killing if we had bought the property.

Later, I visited Bill and Molly again after they had purchased a motel and campground at Miracle Beach – halfway between Courtenay and Campbell River. I saw Bill yet again in 1970 when I was doing some work on a limestone deposit at Franklin River, but then lost touch with him.

While I was living at Sooke I ran into a miner who said he had a friend who visited Bill during the Ripple rock days. Bill supposedly took this fellow fishing (and drinking) one day and delayed a little too long before heading back to shore. By this time the tidal bore was racing down the narrow channel and creating huge whirlpools in the process. As luck would have it, the shear-pin on the propeller chose this moment to break, leaving them without power. By the time they finally got another shear pin inserted, they were already caught in a monstrous whirlpool. It was quickly sucking them down and death was staring them full in the face. Luckily the motor restarted on the first try, and with the throttle wide open they very slowly climbed back up to the surface, and before long they were safely back in Campbell River again. Bill's fishing buddy reputedly said to Bill; "This is the last time I will ever go fishing with you! As a matter of fact, I don't think I will even drink with you again."

In 2001 I found that they were living in Nanaimo so we visited them there. I had not seen Bill's wife Molly, since 1963, so it was a great treat to see them. Bill is now retired, but stays busy with his hobbies. He has become a wine maker and has a very large stock of various kinds of home made wine. He has also set up a lapidary shop in his basement and makes jewelry as well. My wife and I helped Bill and Molly to celebrate their 50th wedding anniversary on March 30, 2002.

John Kozar remained the foreman at Remac until the summer of 1960 while I was away selling vacuum cleaners. I was told that he had given notice that he was leaving and moving to Seattle to work for Boeing. A few days before he was to leave, he was carrying three cases of explosives in his pickup truck when it went off. The blast totally demolished the truck and

Bill & Molly Peligren with author's wife Erlinda in the middle. Photo taken by the author in March – 2002.

left a large crater in the ground. John was blown into small bits that had to be picked up piece by piece from the surrounding area.

The incident was judged to be an accident, but many people believed that it was suicide. There were rumors that John had been gambling on the horses, and that he in fact did not have a job at Boeing. There were also questions as to why he would quit Remac. Another unanswered question was why the dynamite exploded because it is almost impossible to detonate it without using a blasting cap. The true story will of course never be known – one can only speculate on what actually happened that day.

When my wife and I attended Bill & Molly Peligren's Golden Wedding celebration in Nanaimo on March 30, 2002, I saw John and Ann Mackave for the first time in 40 years. John told me that Kozar had actually been fired at the mine and was working his last shift on the day of the accident. He had in fact been told he could leave at noon, but insisted on working the full day and was killed the same afternoon. Mackave confirmed that Kozar was rumoured to have lost a lot of money on the ponies in Spokane.

John Mackave

John was a trammer for most of the time I knew him at Remac. He graduated to "longhole" drilling about the time that I left and stayed at Remac until shortly before they closed in 1972. He told me that he quit after Wally Bunka (who had become a shift boss by then) wanted to demote him to tramming again.

John told me he had a very close brush with death at Remac. He was blasting a hang-up at a draw point one day and had just lit the fuse when a lot of "fines" (finely broken rock) suddenly erupted and spilled down around him. He was immediately buried up to his knees and unable

John & Ann McKave at Peligren's Golden Wedding. *Photo taken by the author in March – 2002.*

to free himself. Unfortunately, he could not reach the burning fuse either. As John struggled desperately to free himself, he was finally able to reach the scraper cable that he had hung up above him so that they would not get buried when the muck came down. Using the cable to pull himself up, he was finally able to reach the burning fuse and yank it free of the dynamite before the cap detonated. A few seconds more, and he would have been history! John told me he suffered from nightmares for a long time after that frightening event.

After leaving Remac, John moved to Powell River and worked at the iron mine on Texada Island for several years. After the mine gave out, he worked for McMillan Bloedel for 19 years and retired at age 58. He and his wife now live at Thrums, near Castlegar (where they were both born). They have three grown-up children; Mark, who works for Tidy Steel in New Westminster, Len who is a photographer, and Kim, who has a small band which plays at the pub at the 6-Mile near Nelson BC.

John's wife Ann is a first cousin to Molly Peligren, so it was not surprising to see them at the Peligren celebration. John's first love was always music and since he retired has written a number of songs, some of which he recently sang to much acclaim at the pub where his son plays. It was a great pleasure to see them again after so many years.

Sid Gillies

I first met Sid while hunting deer in the Wardner area near Cranbrook. My friends, Ordie Jones, Don Clark and I had quit hunting for the day and were sitting at our campsite when Sid and another chap showed up. They both lived in the Wardner vicinity so hunted there regularly.

Sid hit it off well with us for he had a wry sense of humor that appealed to us. When someone exaggerated, Sid would retort with one of his favorite sayings; "Baloney is baloney, no matter how thin you slice it." He appeared to be very knowledgeable about firearms too, and hand-loaded the ammunition for his 7 x 61 Shultz and Larsen rifle. Since Ordie and I both hand-loaded for the .270 Winchester, we had something in common with Sid. Because Sid, like us, also knew his ballistics for all the popular rifles then in use, we regarded him highly.

Sid was an attractive fellow, but unlike the rest of us was still unmarried. Of course he was a few years younger as well, so that could be expected. He had a light complexion, light brown hair and was about six feet in height with a slim build. However, he was deceptively strong. One day he did half a dozen rapid one-armed push-ups in the beer parlour when I challenged him to on a bet!

Sid was not working when we met him so we suggested to him that he should come to Remac for a visit and we would try to get him a job at the mine. He did come and on our recommendations got a job as an underground laborer.

Over the following year he worked on a variety of jobs including miscellaneous labor jobs and tramming. Eventually he became a timberman's helper and worked with Axel Augustine.

I owe a debt of gratitude to Sid for having the courage to tell me one day that my friends sometimes found me difficult to have around because I was "always right." He said something like; "Jake, you are a very intelligent guy and I know that you are probably nearly always right in every argument. However, even if you are, your friends sometimes find it a bit tiresome to be around someone who is never wrong."

Sid Gillies. *Photo taken by the author in 2001*

Even though Sid was very diplomatic in the way he told me this, he nevertheless got his point across. I don't know whether or not I changed my behaviour much after this, but I certainly began to be more aware of what I was doing than I had previously been. During my life, I have not met very many people with the guts to tell a friend something like that, and do so in a way that did not produce anger or denial.

During the time Sid was with Axel Augustine they worked all over the mine. One day they were hauling some waste out of the 0'Donnel section of the mine. The adjacent ore body had been mined out from there on down several hundred feet. Some of the ore above had been removed in an open pit operation from the outside, so there was not a large amount of rock between the roof of the stope and the open pit floor above.

They were hauling some two-ton muck cars past the stope with a battery-operated locomotive when the entire roof of the stope fell in. The effect was like a piston descending rapidly down a cylinder. The displaced air had to go somewhere and it blew the two men together with their heavy equipment right out of the mine at high velocity. Axel collided with a timber near the adit and was killed. Sid was hurled outside, across the yard and over the embankment. Miraculously he escaped the accident with only extensive bruising. Although he escaped severe physical injury, he was pretty shaken up emotionally and quit his job a few days later.

It was not too long after this episode that Sid and I took on a contract (December 1961) to blast some rock in a granite quarry at Sirdar near Creston, BC. (See the section in this book called "This Cat Had More Than Nine Lives.") Sid then moved back to Wardner and I did not see him again until he visited me in Sooke in 1963. It turned out that in the meantime he had spent a year in the "slammer" for "breaking and entering"

(B&E). He had been out of work, out of money and had become desperate enough to be foolish. He worked briefly at a saw-mill in Sooke and I did not see him again until 1999 when I searched the Internet and found he was retired and living in the Fraser Valley. He and his wife have a double-wide manufactured home on a lot they have leased from the Band on the Seabird Reservation just east of Agassiz, BC.

When I looked up Sid we both recognized each other at once, even though it had been thirty six years since we had last seen each other. Sid had not only gotten married, but had grown-up children as well and was now retired from a Civil Service career. I found that we still enjoyed each other's company, so neither of us has changed that much during the intervening years. Nevertheless I was somewhat surprised to learn that he had been able to last for so many years in a government job. The Sid that I knew back in the fifties and sixties could not have done so, but on the other hand, it is not too surprising considering what marriage and family can do to a man.

Ordie Jones

Ordie came to Remac in 1956, a year after me and was my neighbor for a while. I met him when I helped him move some furniture into his house. He had a daughter, Evelyn who was about a year older than my son Don. Ordie's wife Maureen looked after Don when my daughter Pamela was born. She looked after both Don and Pamela for nearly two months while Fran was in the hospital carrying our youngest daughter, Cheryl.

Ordie was the mine surveyor and as such was salaried staff. In the mining community it was unusual for salaried people to associate socially with hourly paid employees, but Ordie was an outdoorsman so he felt greater kinship with those of us who also hunted and fished. He and his wife became our closest friends at the mine and he and I spent many weekends hunting and fishing together.

One Labor Day weekend we decided to go fishing in the lake in Kokanee Park (where Prime Minister - Pierre Trudeau's son was later drowned) and also hunt mountain goat on the same trip. We left the mine on Saturday morning and got well up the road past Kaslo when we came to an abandoned mining road. We decided to walk up the road as far as we could and camp there for the night. Since it was a beautiful sunny day, we took only our rifles, some food and our sleeping bags.

When we got to an old mine adit at the end of the road, we decided to sleep there for the night, so we threw our sleeping bags on top of some old ore sacks we found and turned in for the night.

I awoke at about 11:00 PM just as it began to sprinkle. We ignored the rain for awhile, but when it began to run into our sleeping bags, we finally got up and headed down the hill. The grass on the abandoned road was three feet high and by the time we arrived at the car, the only dry spot on either one of us was a small area on our backs that our pack-boards had covered. We were not only soaked through, but chilled as well.

We got into the car, stripped and put on dry clothes. Next I pulled out a bottle of "Cocktail 45" (a mixture of rum and wine). Ordie had never liked this drink before, but that night he learned to appreciate it.

After sleeping in the car for a few hours, we continued up the road towards the Kokanee Glacier. It was still pouring rain and we had not driven far before we encountered three men cooking breakfast under a canvas tarp. They turned out to be the star players of the Nelson Maple Leafs hockey team - Lee and Norm Hyssop as well as Ron Keller. They fed us breakfast and told us it had never stopped raining at the glacier since they got there early the previous day. We therefore decided to turn around and head back home.

On the way back to Kaslo, I broke the bell housing on my 1956 Dodge car. This car had little clearance and it hit a rock that was protruding between the two ruts that served as a road.

We made it back home despite the broken bell housing. When we got back to Nelson, we found that they had experienced nothing but sunshine the whole weekend despite being less than twenty miles from the glacier. I got an estimate of $150 at the Dodge garage for replacing the bell housing, but later, Boyce York, a rural mechanic welded it for only $70.

From Remac to Kootenay Lake was just over sixty miles, so after Ordie built his boat, he and I spent many hours fishing there. On one such fishing trip, we were trolling with the fishing rods resting in the rod holders. The weather was beautiful and I was slumped over snoozing after drinking too much Cocktail 45. Ordie decided to have some fun so he loosened the drag on my reel. I awoke with a start when I heard the reel screaming as the line peeled off. I immediately realized what he had done so I tightened the drag. Ordie stopped the boat because I was not gaining on the fish at all and most of my 300 yards of line was already out. After a seesaw battle, the fish suddenly seemed to give up and I began to reel it in. I was cranking away expecting to see the fish break water at any time, when I noticed there were a bunch of seagulls circling one bird that was lying on the water.

I had caught a seagull, not a fish! When I got it on board, I found one treble hook from my F7 Flatfish lure was in the bird's beak and the other treble hook had penetrated the webbing of its one foot. I took the hook out of its beak first and that was a big mistake because when I tried to remove the one from its foot, it bit me so hard that it drew blood on both sides of my wrist. That bird was lucky that I didn't wring its neck. Ordie took a few pictures of it and then we let it go. I don't think we caught any fish that day.

Ordie, Don Clark and I went hunting in the East Kootenays every fall. It was on one of these trips that we met Sid Gillies, who I have written about earlier in this section. Both Ordie and I had 270 caliber rifles, so on one weekend we made a trip to the "White Elephant" in Spokane where we bought hand loading equipment and supplies. From then on we hand loaded all of our own cartridges for these rifles.

One year Ordie decided to learn "taxidermy." I shot a raven at the nearby garbage dump for him to stuff. Being his first try at this sort of thing, he eventually goofed up, so he asked me to shoot him another one. In the weeks ahead, I gained a tremendous respect for these birds. There were always lots of ravens about whenever I arrived near the garbage dump without a fire-arm. However, if I had gun with me, the ravens would fly off long before I got there.

The Reeves McDonald mine was situated on the north side of the Pend-O-Reille river that flowed from Washington Stated into BC near Nelway Customs and emptied into the Columbia River at Waneta south of Trail. This was a very turbulent river that flowed past the mine at speeds of over 15 miles per hour in places.

One fall Ordie and I noticed that there were always two deer on the flats on the far side of the river in the early evening. We decided that we should try to shoot one and bring it back by boat. Accordingly we hauled his 12-foot boat down to the river and waited for the deer to show. As we were studying the far side with our binoculars, it seemed that every time one deer showed, the other one would stay hidden. It was getting dark when we decided we could not wait any longer. Ordie won the coin toss and got the first shot. When his shot missed, I shot next and killed the deer.

We got in the boat and motored to the far side without difficulty, but on the way back the boat was now heavier. With the 15 HP motor going full out, we could barely hold our own against the current. Then we hit a crosscurrent and almost swamped the boat. Ordie decided then that if we shot another deer over there, he would go over for it alone.

The following evening we decided to shoot from up at the mine dump. It was quite a bit farther, but the visibility was much better. This evening I had the first shot but missed. Then Ordie shot and he missed as well. My second shot hit the deer in the head and killed it.

We immediately went down and put his boat in the water. I hooked up the gas tank while he was readying something else. Ordie climbed into the boat, started the motor and roared out into the current just as the motor died. He grabbed the oars and got back into shore. We primed the engine again, started it and away he went for the second time, when the motor quit yet again. This time we decided to do a thorough check. I had forgotten to tighten the gas cap on the tank!

After that he got to the other side, picked up the deer and brought it back. He also accused me (somewhat in jest) of trying to do him in. When Ordie decided to triangulate the distances from which we had shot the deer, we were both astonished. Distances across water always look less that what they are, but we had shot those deer from 350 and 465 yards – it was no wonder that we had both missed a shot or two.

One fall Ordie and I went hunting up near the Paradise mine where I had worked many years earlier. We also carried along our fishing rods, which I had tied onto my pack-board. We were walking back down the mountain towards the mill camp when we discovered that I had lost the tip sections for both rods. Since one can't buy tip sections, we had to buy two new rods to replace those tips I had lost.

On one occasion, Ordie and I went hunting up west of Kaslo. It was a gorgeous evening, so instead of pitching our tent, we spread it out on the abandoned roadway and threw our sleeping bags on top of it. I left my loaded rifle and a flashlight beside me and was soon asleep. Some time during the night I came instantly awake without going through the usual transition from sleep to wakefulness.

I lay there listening intently for a while before I heard some faint rustling beside me. Then I felt an animal walk over my feet, up over my body and finally right over my face before climbing up the bank beside the road. I grabbed my rifle, shone the flashlight and saw a porcupine making its way up the bank and into the woods. Some part of me must have been aware and wakened me in such a way that I did not make any moves that would have turned me into a pincushion.

Once during the winter, Ordie and I decided to go ice fishing. There were some sloughs adjacent to the Salmo River that supposedly provided good fishing. I parked my car at the edge of the highway and we hiked in the better part of a mile to the slough. The fishing was excellent. As soon as it tapered off, we would chop a new hole and instantly catch a few more trout.

I got careless and stepped on some untested ice and immediately fell through with one leg – right up to my hip. The air temperature was –20° F, but the water soon warmed up inside my overshoe, so we kept on fishing.

It was just too good to stop. When we finally called it quits and hiked out to the highway, I got a rude awakening. While I had been standing still, the water in my shoe was tolerable, but when I started to walk, it got extremely frigid. The snow was two feet deep, so the hike out was no picnic. I was lucky that a friend lived very close to where I had parked the car. He lent me some dry socks and let me warm up before going back home.

Ordie eventually left Remac to go to work for CIL, the Explosives Company. Later he went to work for Peter Kiewit Sons Company (PKS) in Vancouver Washington, then back with CIL again before going to work for PKS in Vancouver, BC. After he left PKS the second time he became Construction Manager for Chinook Construction and Engineering in Vancouver. From this job he retired at age forty. I worked for him twice, first at PKS and later at Chinook.

Douhkobours

The Douhkobours were members of a pacifist group that was often in the news during my years in the West Kootenays. They had immigrated to Canada from Russia shortly after the turn of the century and had been promised religious freedom in Canada. They had settled first in Saskatchewan and later in the West Kootenay areas of Grand Forks, Castlegar, Krestova, and Nelson.

For the most part, they did not cause any problems, but the Sons of Freedom sect refused to send their children to BC schools because they felt they were taught militaristic values. The BC government therefore took these children into custody and placed them in a boarding school in New Denver. The parents began a campaign of protest that included public nudity, burning schools and their own homes, and later blowing up public structures.

The government's patience finally ran out after they bombed a 500-foot high transmission tower at Kootenay Landing. This cut off electricity in the area. At nearby Riondel, it also shut down Cominco's Bluebell mine

The out-of-work miners at Riondel were incensed and a bunch of them decided to burn down Krestova. They set out in their cars, but on their way there, they stopped at the New Grand Hotel beer parlour for refreshments and possibly to refine their plans. That was as far as they got! By the time the bar closed, they felt it best to wait until the following morning. The next morning, cooler and "hung-over" heads prevailed, and the miners returned to Riondel. It was shortly after this event that the provincial government prosecuted and convicted a large number of the Douhkobours and jailed them at a special facility near Agassiz.

Rolf Halvorsen

Rolf was a miner who lived in Ymir with his wife all the years I knew him. He was a notorious boozer until he finally joined AA. He fell off the wagon a few times as could be expected, but eventually stayed sober. Rolf then went on a health kick and stopped smoking. Next thing we heard was that he was into healthy eating too. It was not enough that he accomplished these difficult tasks, but he was a born evangelizer. He was forever trying to get Rae Thomas to attend AA meetings with him. One day Rae said to him; "I once knew a guy who first cut out smoking, next he cut out booze, then he cut out women. Do you know what he is cutting out now? "What?" asked Rolf. "Paper dolls in Essondale!" retorted Rae.

Don Dundas

Don was a colorful character. He worked in the mines around Salmo all the years I was there. He was a tall handsome man with black hair and a fairly dark complexion. He was a good miner, but like many of them developed a drinking problem. His family kept on growing and eventually Don wound up on Social Assistance for a prolonged period of time.

The following stories about Don typify not only him, but some of the miners who frequented the area back then:

In the late fifties the mine at Remac required all of us to wear safety glasses to protect our eyes. Many of the miners resented this because the glasses were such a nuisance and regularly got spattered with mud during drilling operations. Hence they did not wear them unless a supervisor was around and Don Dundas was no exception.

One day he was breaking up a big oversized rock on the "grizzly" with a sledge hammer when a rock shard flew into his left eye, bruising it. To create an alibi, Don laid his glasses on a boulder and smashed one lens with the hammer. Inadvertently he broke the wrong lens. In the accident report Don claimed that his eye got bruised despite wearing his glasses.

The mine management never tired of using this incident as an example to justify the safety glass policy. They speculated that if his eye was injured despite the glasses, it would have been much worse without them. No one in management even noticed that the broken lens didn't match the injured eye.

Late one evening a lady, who was walking by the liquor store in Nelson, noticed a broken window and a man sitting inside. She promptly alerted the police and shortly a constable was dispatched to the scene. He found a drunken Don sitting on the counter drinking a cheap bottle of wine. When the constable ordered Don to hand over the bottle, Don not realizing that it was a policeman speaking retorted; "Go get your own damn bottle!"

Tony Polaskus

Tony worked at Remac as a Raise Miner most of the years I was there. I first met him in 1952 and I remember that he drank Johnny Walkers Black Label Scotch Whiskey.

I was just leaving the bunkhouse to go to work on night shift one evening when I saw Tony who had been away on holidays. He stopped me and said; "Here, have a snort," as he proffered me a bottle in a brown paper bag. Assuming that it was his usual brand of smooth Scotch, I took a big swallow. I was startled for as the fiery liquid went down my throat, I could feel my insides drying up! It was not Scotch whiskey at all, but "Overproof" rum. Tony had just returned from Alaska.

When I returned to Remac a few years later, so did Tony. He was already well into his forties by then, but he still gave me a run for my money in raise production. I believe he was forty eight when he finally quit raise mining and went on staff as a shift boss.

I never saw Tony with a woman during the years I knew him, but I heard that well after I left the mine, he did too – with the wife of another man. Tony died from a heart attack while he was still in his fifties, so I never saw him again.

Doug Rozel

Doug came to Remac at about the same time as I did in 1955. He was a first-rate miner, both underground and in the beer parlour. As soon as Doug had a few beer under his belt, he would insert the phrase, "turn around and iron things out" several times into every statement he made, e.g. "We'll turn around and turn around and iron things out." Not surprisingly, he became known as "Turn-around Rozel."

His wife's name was Daisy, and she liked her booze about as much as did Doug. She was forever complaining that Doug would one day kill her with his drunken driving. Eventually, her prophecy came true. A few years after I left Remac, their car went off the road on the "Creston Skyway" and killed them both. They were not found until the following spring, by which time there was not much left of them.

Les Fry

Les worked at the mine concentrator all the time I was at Remac. The ore after it was crushed, entered the concentrator and was pulverized in the ball mill. This was a large cylinder about 10 feet in diameter that was loaded with steel balls that ranged from 4" to 8" in diameter. The cylinder rotated as crushed rock entered one end of it. The steel balls pulverized the ore by dropping on it as the cylinder turned.

One day Les was working inside the ball mill replacing the worn out liners. He was still inside when a coworker threw the switch and started up the ball mill. The drum fortunately made only one revolution before it was shut down and Les escaped with a number of severe bruises from being pelted by the heavy steel balls. A minute longer would surely have killed him. It is standard practice for the person inside such a machine to first lock out the switch and take the key with him. I don't know exactly what happened that day, but I doubt that Les ever got into a similar predicament again.

Pete Elias

Pete was working as a "timberman" at the Van Roi mine while I was there. He was a husky man noted for his immense strength. Pete drank little if at all and his great pride motivated him to stay in superb physical condition.

One miner who was building a house told us that he was skidding a log with a horse one day when the log got stuck. After several unsuccessful tries to free it with the horse, Pete came over and moved it so the horse could carry on.

When I returned to Remac in 1955, Pete came to work there looking after the lamps. He was no longer husky and he even appeared frail. He told me that after fracturing his leg, the Doctor in New Denver did not set it properly. Even I could see that the bones no longer lined up. He could no longer walk well or carry a load on that leg.

I got to know Pete well at Remac and found that this incident destroyed Pete's pride in his physical condition. He no longer had that "joie de vivre" of old. I was not very surprised to learn that he died not long after I left the area even though he was only in his late forties.

Justus Jobe

I first met Justus Jobe shortly after I was married. I was driving along a trail by the Salmo River when I had to pull over to let an oncoming Pickup truck by. The truck was sputtering and missing as it came towards us. I recognized the passenger, George Borden, who worked at the HB mine, so as the vehicle came abreast, I said; "Sounds kind of rough, eh?"

Some weeks later I was in the beer parlour when Jobe came over to my table. He was very drunk and very angry. He accused me of making disparaging remarks about his stature, his ancestry and his manhood. I sat there dumbfounded by his tirade. I had no idea what was going on until I realized that it was his truck I had remarked on a few weeks previously.

I have read a bit of psychology and I was intrigued by how my few words had been built into a diatribe that would have taken several minutes to deliver, whereas my remarks had taken all of three seconds.

A few years later, Jobe came to work at Remac and became my partner on "longhole drills." Since I took a real interest in him, we soon became very good friends. I learned that he had 25% native ancestry but he could have passed for a full-blooded Native Indian. I also found out that he had two brothers, who both looked white and were six feet in height as compared to Jobe who was dark and only five foot seven.

Jobe and I went hunting and fishing together a few times, and in September of 1961 we went on a week-long trip to the Flathead area and Justus brought along his son, Justus Junior.

We stayed at the McDougal ranch at the southeastern tip of BC where it abuts both Alberta and Montana. In those days there were very few hunters in this area because the road to it was not always passable. We drove to the Flathead in a 1949 Studebaker pickup that I had bought for hunting and fishing.

One day I was waiting for the two Jobes who were late coming back for lunch. I was getting very hungry, so at last I took a grouse I had shot earlier, gutted it and skinned it. I then put a stick through it and roasted it over a fire. I had some difficulty in eating it for I had no salt, but my hunger helped me overcome this shortcoming.

From that day on, we always carried salt, pepper, butter and some bread with us. We shot grouse every morning and ate one each for lunch every day. We learned cooking a grouse over an open fire makes it both tender as well as juicy. By the time the week was over, we had eaten enough grouse to last us for a long time.

Jobe and I both considered ourselves to be good woodsmen, but we were about to have that confidence tested. The Flathead River paralleled the road about a mile from it. It was snowing gently when Jobe and I decided to walk to the river one morning. We left the road about 400 yards apart in the hope that one of us might scare some game over to the other person.

I was walking towards the river at a leisurely pace, but expected to be there in 30 minutes. I was beginning to wonder why it was taking me so long when I converged on Jobe's tracks. I followed them for a few minutes before I realized that they were not his, but my own footprints. I had walked in a big circle! I had a compass with me but I was too stubborn to bring it out. Instead, I made sure that I was walking in a straight line. This time I walked briskly, but I still did not get to the river. Instead I encountered a road I didn't know was there. It took me a while before I realized I had reached the main road. I had not walked in a circle this time - I had walked in a big U. This time I pulled out my compass and made it to the river in fifteen minutes. However, I found no sign of Jobe. When I got back to the truck he was there. I asked him why he did not meet me at the river, and he replied; "A funny thing happened to me...!"

We realized then that the wind was turning us because it was blowing in a big circle. When we left the road the snow was coming from behind us so we unconsciously kept it there, not realizing that its direction was not constant.

Jobe's son shot a deer and I shot a Mountain Goat the first day there. The weather turned very warm, and by the time we got home the meat was spoiled. I had a very fine pair of goat horns, but someone stole them from my garage before I could have them mounted.

Jobe and I went hunting again in early December, but close to home this time. We crossed over to the west side of the Salmo River near the mine and left my pickup parked on a logging road. It was raining and the ground was bare, but as we worked our way up the mountainside the rain turned into snow.

I had been climbing hard through buck brush for an hour and was into snow that was over two feet deep when I spotted a White-tail Buck across a ravine and out in the open some 250 yards away. I was out of breath, so while I waited to get my wind back, I looked for a place from which to shoot. I wasn't able to find one, so I finally got up on my tip-toes to see over top of the brush. The deer was facing directly away from me and my shot broke its back, but did not kill it. I plunged down through the ravine with snow up to my waist and up the other side. When I reached the deer, my gun barrel was full of snow and my scope was fogged up. After cleaning the snow out of my rifle, I shot the deer in the head, but I did not kill it – I had shot it through its jaw! I was so mad at myself for this stupid stunt that I decided to kill it with my knife. I caught up to the deer, which was trying to run away and grabbed it by one hind leg. I slowly crawled up over its back and cradled its antlers with my left arm. Then holding its head back, I pulled out my hunting knife and slit its throat. The deer made a desperate lunge and almost threw me, but I managed to hang on.

After I had field dressed the deer, I had two choices; I could quarter it and fight my way back over the ravine the way I had come. Since this would require two trips I opted to drag the entire carcass down the hill until I reached the road. That was a mistake!

I was soon down out of the snow, but into a deep ravine whose bottom was crisscrossed with fallen trees. It was impossible to move in this jungle. I tried to drag the deer up the side of the ravine, away from the downed timber, but I always wound up down in the bottom again. I finally reached the road four hours after killing the deer.

When I reached the truck, Jobe was there. He had shot a deer as well and had also broken its back. With his next shot, he had also shot away part of its jaw. Having no more ammunition left, he had tied the deer top a tree and eventually gotten someone else to put the final bullet into it.

We loaded up both deer and headed home. When we arrived at the "Game Check," we found they were collecting the jaws for research purposes. We have often wondered what they thought about us, for we had two identical deer, each with part of its jaw missing.

Doctor Bob Miller

Bob came to Salmo to practice medicine in about 1960. He was an avid fisherman and spent much of his spare time fishing on Kootenay Lake. It was my privilege to accompany him on one of these expeditions.

Bob invited me to his house for breakfast at 6:00 AM. He immediately fried bacon and threw some eggs on as well. One of the eggs had a huge amount of blood on it and was obviously partly hatched. I was surprised when Bob continued frying it (I would have thrown it out immediately). When he dished up our breakfast he said; "I guess I had better eat that one," referring to the bloody egg. I suppose that being a doctor inures one to blood, but eventually it was too much even for him, and he finally threw it out.

I learned a good lesson about patience that day. We were using Bob's canoe, which had a square stern on which he had mounted a small outboard motor. We were trolling along, but the fish did not seem to be biting. However Bob eventually got a gentle strike. Instead of reeling the fish in forthwith, Bob took his own sweet time about it. I remember sitting there, thinking; "why don't you get on with it – the fish isn't putting up a fight." When Bob eventually brought the fish alongside, we saw that it was a three-pound Dolly Varden trout and that it was not actually hooked. One prong of the treble hook was around the fin beside its gills and the slightest resistance would have set it free. My impatience would never have allowed me to land that fish.

Doctor Miller disappeared one day while fishing on Kootenay Lake not too long after I left Salmo. No one ever found any sign of him or of his canoe. He left behind a young family, a thriving practice and many good friends.

Joel Ackert

I hardly knew Joel because he was much younger than me and worked at a different mine. He grew up in a mining family and his father was an old-timer in the area. His father had collected a huge assortment of mining memorabilia over the years and Joel has carried on this tradition.. Despite his having given much of it to the local museum, he still has the best collection in the area. He allowed me to use some of his photos in this book.

The author (left) together with June and Joel Ackert in front of their Salmo home.
Photo taken by the author's wife in 2002.

Chapter 18 - New Endeavours

Vacuum Cleaners

I have twice tried my hand at sales. In 1960 I left Remac in May and moved to Greenwood from where I tried to sell Electrolux vacuum cleaners for five months. I covered an area from Christina Lake in the east to Bridesville in the west. My training consisted of accompanying my sales manager one evening while he made a single sale as well as providing me with some written instructions.

I had no problem in getting into homes and putting on demonstrations, but I wasn't able to close enough sales. According to my sales manager, I should be able to sell one in three demos. My average was probably one in six. My problem was that I was too timid and afraid of offending people to ask them to sign the contract if they were hesitant. My concern about what people thought of me governed my life! I also felt intimidated by well-educated people, so I was hopeless when I called on teachers or doctors.

I sold an average of three machines a week, but this was not enough and I found my car expenses were taking too large a chunk out of my income. I needed to sell four machines a week, to make a living, and if I could have sold five, I should have made a very good living. It became obvious to me that if I could close one sale in three, I should have done exceedingly well in this business.

The St. Denis House

I finally gave up selling vacuum cleaners at the end of September. We left Greenwood and moved to Salmo where we rented a house from Melba St. Denis and I went back to work at Remac. Melba's husband Ken had been killed earlier that summer while pumping floodwater from the basement. He had been knee deep in water when the electric pump he was using shorted out and electrocuted him.

There was a small open porch on the kitchen end of the house. Its floor was over three feet above the ground and enclosed on two sides by four feet high walls. In the spring there were swallows' nests above the porch under the eaves. When the young birds are learning to fly, our house cat sits on the ledge of the porch watching them. One day I saw it suddenly leap out and swat down a bird in mid flight. I don't know how often the cat was successful, but I suspect that it got to eat a few of them.

On another day I was watching a robin in the garden looking for worms in the deep grass. The cat was watching it as well. It crept very slowly and deliberately toward the bird, which didn't seem to notice it. Just as the cat was getting ready for a final lunge, the robin just happened to fly to another spot a little farther away. As I stood there watching, the same scenario was repeated again and again. I am convinced that the robin was deliberately teasing the poor cat.

Fran's sister Madeleine and her husband Gordon arrived from Alberta one summer afternoon. They came with their two small children in tow and moved into our house for a few days. While I was helping them carry their luggage in, I spied a chamber pot on the floor in front of the back seat. It was full to the brim with urine in which numerous feces were floating. It was a ghastly sight! I asked Gordon and Madeleine; "Aren't you worried that the pot might spill?" They replied; "Oh no, we haven't had any problems with it at all." That same afternoon, one of them accidentally tipped it over and dumped its entire contents on to the floor of the car! I don't recall which one of them got to clean up the unholy mess, but I did not volunteer to help.

Andy and Bill Wingerak

The Wingerak brothers bought homes in Salmo and came to work at Remac during the late fifties. They had both previously worked at the Copper Mountain mine near Princeton. I did not get to know them too well until I returned to Remac from my vacuum cleaner sales fling and also settled in Salmo.

For a short period of time I worked with a Dale Foyle opening up a level for the longhole drills. Andy Wingerak and Big Nick Bolinski were our cross shift partners. I later cross-shifted Bill Wingerak in a new drift on one of the lower levels of the mine that had been opened up by a new inclined shaft. He and I set production records in that drift and earned the highest bonus paid during that year. Bill is long deceased, but I sometimes visit Andy and his wife Isobel in Kelowna.

Goodbye to Remac

After returning to Remac, my job at the mine was never the same, because the other miners resented me getting a heading where I could make good bonus. They felt that I had lost my seniority and shouldn't be entitled to such a heading. The company therefore put me on steady night shift so that no one else would covet my workplace. They wanted to keep me in a particular drift because production was very important to them, but they did not tell me their reasons at the time. When Bill Wingerak and I made top bonus there, it made me very unpopular with some of the other miners. I was meanwhile getting choked up about being kept on steady night shift and eventually I developed an ulcer.

In April that year, the Emil Anderson Construction Company moved into Salmo to begin building a new highway across the mountains to Creston. I applied for a job with them and was told they would hire me as soon as they got going, so I quit my job at Remac. I don't know what happened, but by mid April the job had not yet materialized, so I left Salmo and got a job with R. F. Fry and Associates at the Granduc mine near Stewart, BC. Justus Jobe quit too and came with me. I will never forget visiting another miner for breakfast after we left Salmo. The wife served us bacon and eggs and then proceeded to change her baby's dirty diaper right on the table where we were eating.

We flew to Prince Rupert with C P Air and from there to Stewart in an amphibious plane called a "Goose." From Stewart we flew up to the mine in a Beaver that was equipped with both wheels and skis. Our plane landed on the glacier and we found that the camp was set up on the glacier as well. Little did I suspect then that almost three years later, an avalanche would wipe out that camp.

Granduc mining camp. *1956 photo courtesy of Karran Panko nee Stensrud*

The snow slide struck the camp during the morning of February 18, 1965 and killed most of those who were not working underground. I later met the helicopter pilot in Whitehorse who had witnessed the event from the radio shack, which was spared. He told me that he was looking out the window, but did not see the snowslide. He remembers looking at the camp at one moment and not seeing it the next. He said that there was not a whisper of sound to indicate that anything had happened.

The avalanche killed 26 men, but a few were miraculously spared. The helicopter was demolished, so there was no way of getting out for help. The radio operator was able to send out one distress call before the power died, but this was to be the only communication with the outside world until rescuers arrived. When I met the pilot in Whitehorse during the Eighties, he told me that they were without communications and completely isolated for more than two days after the disaster.

After our arrival, my friend Jobe immediately got a job driving a drift from the surface near the camp. I was slated for a drift down in the shaft but we were unable to de-water it so I left after a couple of weeks and came back south. One day while I was still at Granduc, Jobe drilled into some unexploded dynamite and set it off. His eyes were peppered with fine dust, but he escaped serious injury. He was fortunate in not doing grave harm to his eyes.

Bunkhouse tent similar to one I occupied there in 1962. *1956 photo courtesy of Karran Panko nee Stensrud.*

After that we did not see each other until I visited him at Hudsons Hope 20 years later. In earlier times he had been considered a notorious womanizer. When I saw him in Hudsons Hope he had been treated for prostate cancer. He told me that his doctor had recently castrated him to arrest the cancer and I could not help but wonder at the poetic justice of this. The operation did not appear to have helped for long, for I learned that he died not too long after our visit.

Sooke

When I left the Granduc mine I found a job at the Cowichan Copper mine at Jordan River. I was not there long before I bought my first house - in Sooke, a village west of Victoria, and sent for my family, who was still living in Salmo.

The house had been moved on to the lot and set on a concrete foundation that enclosed a partial basement. Shortly after moving in, I replaced the antiquated coal and wood furnace with a new oil-burning one. The dealer installed it, including all the ductwork for a total cost of $600. I also bought a metal shower stall and installed that myself. It was my first attempt at plumbing.

The kitchen door was located at an awkward spot, so I had a carpenter move it. We found that the house had been constructed using square nails. This dated the house back to the 1890s, but the wood in it was as good as the day the house was built. There was fir flooring throughout, but some of it was covered with linoleum. After countersinking all the nails in the living room, I rented a belt sander, sanded the floor and coated it with clear urethane. It transformed the room.

The following year while I was working away from home at Western Mines, I bought a drill with a sanding attachment and Fran sanded all the wallpaper off the walls in all the rooms. It was a dirty job for there were several layers of it! She then painted them and the old house was transformed.

It was in this house that I first encountered carpenter ants. These insects do not build, as their name implies. They tunnel out homes in timbers and in our case it was in an 8" x 8" post in the middle of the basement that carried most of the weight of the main floor. I discovered them when I found a small pile of fine sawdust on the floor beside the post. On close inspection I found it was coming from a small tunnel opening part way up the post. We had a pest control company from Victoria come out and eradicate them before they caused serious damage.

The lot on which the house stood consisted mostly of gravel in front and natural ground covered with a few fir-trees and one huge maple in the back. We hauled in a few loads of sawdust and mixed it into the gravel. With the help of fertilizer and lots of water, we soon had a thriving lawn. We also had a contractor pave the driveway with asphalt. Our final investment was an automatic washer and drier from Sears that cost us $500.

Late that fall, we had a storm with winds up to 90 miles per hour out over the straight. When we got up the next morning, we found that a two-foot thick section of the maple had been torn off. It barely missed the house! It was large enough to have gone right through the roof if it had hit it. I shortly had Mangs Michelson, a faller, come over and cut down the rest of it as well as a few of the other trees.

The Cowichan Copper mine was situated at Jordan River and operated around the clock— three shifts per day and seven days a week. We worked six days on and two off and came back on a different shift each time. Instead of having only one or two crews in a heading, we always had four. The jobs at the mine had high contract rates but we earned very little bonus because out of four crews, there was always at least one crew that was inefficient

Peter Murray

Pete was working at Cowichan Copper in 1962 when I first met him. He and his wife Mary had purchased a small farm just west of Sooke. They had a cow or two plus some chickens that Mary looked after.

Pete had worked in a number of mines, chiefly in the north, in places like Yellowknife and Uranium City. He had been seeing Mary for a number of years, but for the longest time she had been unable to get him tied down. Each time he came down south to see her, he would wind up getting and staying drunk until his money was exhausted. For several years it appeared that nothing would come of their courtship.

Mary was a tenacious woman who saw something in Pete that was above the ordinary. On one of his trips out to civilization she managed to collar him before he could hit the booze and they were shortly married. Her belief in him turned out to be correct, for once married; she was able to persuade him to work in the south. There

Unknown miner with a jackleg and Pete Murray. *Photo courtesy of Pete Murray.*

he turned over a new leaf and has never looked back.

After leaving Sooke in 1963, I soon quit mining, so I did not see the Murrays for many years. I did hear about them from time to time however, and was told that they were doing well. They had really settled down and were finally raising a family.

I next saw them during the late eighties when I looked them up near Salmon Arm where they now live, and still farm. Pete had some years earlier started his own drilling and blasting company. Besides building logging roads he had done a fair amount of rockwork on the Coquihalla highway between Hope and Merritt. He had also partnered up with another man on a contract to drive a tunnel for the Greater Victoria Water District. This venture almost bankrupted Pete. Fortunately, he was able to harvest and sell a lot of logs from his farm to cover the disastrous losses he sustained in driving the tunnel.

Many of the good miners I knew over the years had problems with alcohol. Most of them eventually died, either from liver problems, or from car accidents suffered while drunk. A few however, like Pete, not only managed to turn their lives around, but went on to be very successful in new occupations. When I visited them during the summer of 2001, Mary was still looking after a few animals on the farm, and was still milking a cow regularly.

Fred Loutit

Fred was from Hay River in the Northwest Territories. I did not get to know him that well because he was usually on a different shift from me. A few years after leaving Cowichan I ran into Fred once again, this time in downtown Vancouver. Fred had come into some real money, for he had staked a number of claims adjacent to the important "Pyramid" ore body that was later taken over by Cominco. I believe that he got close to $200,000 for them – at a time when wages were under $5:00 per hour. He was very drunk when I saw him, and I have no idea how he has fared after that time. I was unable to find a phone number for Fred when I searched the Internet, but did find a number of Loutits in Hay River.

Don Ormrod

Don was a shift boss at Cowichan Copper when I arrived there in the spring of 1962. He stood about six foot, four inches, was lanky, and had wavy black hair. He had recently come to BC from Newfoundland where he had been a shaft miner. He told me that the "Newfie" women had snagged all of the bachelors on his crew, himself included. He maintained that the women there would marry anyone just to escape from the island. Except for his occasional bouts of heavy drinking, there was nothing wrong with Don as a husband and father.

Like most miners that I knew, Don was both a hard worker and a hard drinker. He told me, he had a curious trait when he got drinking. When he sobered up he would discover that in addition to making long distance telephone calls all over the continent, he would also have a new car. He could never remember how this had happened, or anything else that had gone on during his drunk.

Don was conscientious in his work. He was knowledgeable, had an easy-going nature and was also a good man to work for. Now that he was married, he controlled his boozing most of the time. When he did go on a bender, it was usually for only a day or two – hence not enough to interfere with his job too much.

One Saturday morning he awakened me at 3:00 AM with a telephone call. He said; "I think my foot is broken." Knowing that it is usually very difficult to diagnose broken bones in a foot without x-rays, I said; "We will probably have trouble finding a doctor at this time of the night – can you tough it out until morning?" He replied that he thought he would be okay until then. I then promised to come over after breakfast and take him to a doctor.

After breakfast I called Don. His wife, Irene answered the phone and told me that there was nothing wrong with him – that he was just drunk. Hearing that, I went about my usual Saturday morning activities. At 10:00 AM the phone rang. It was Don. He said; "My leg is broken. When I awoke it was lying crossways in the bed!" I immediately gathered together some material for splints and bandages, picked up a young friend named Cliff Campbell and proceeded to Don's house.

When I saw his leg, I could see at a glance that both the tibia and the fibula were fractured – the leg looked horrible! The entire calf area both front and back was an ugly purplish blue and the skin was broken where one of the bones was protruding. I cleaned up the wound and bandaged it. Then I had Cliff Campbell apply traction while I applied the splints and secured them. The pain must have been excruciating, but Don just gritted his teeth and bore the pain without complaining. Nevertheless, his face was as white as a sheet! We then loaded him into the back seat of my car and drove the fifteen miles to Colwood. We had no trouble in finding the clinic and delivered him to a doctor there. When the doctor saw the splints, he asked; "Who's the boy-scout?"

Don later explained to me that he had been at a party and gotten amorous with the hostess. Her husband objected and they went outside and got into a fight. When the husband gave him a push, Don fell over backwards but his foot got caught between a root and the boardwalk behind him. He heard the bones snap as he fell, but was still able to walk to his car, and later from the car into his house. It was no wonder it looked such a mess when I examined it the next day.

Don did not get a walking cast for over two months. Nevertheless, the mine management kept him on the payroll for the whole time he was recuperating. Obviously they held him in high esteem. Once he had a walking cast, he went back to work in an office job created specifically for him, but it would be over five months before he could resume his former duties.

Late that summer I got a very bad case of what I assumed was flu. It laid me low for a whole week. When I got back to work my legs did not recover their strength and my energy level remained very low. Meanwhile I had to climb 600 feet of ladders each day, so when Jack Start, a drilling contractor offered me a job as his helper on logging road construction, I accepted.

I worked as Jack's helper on his airtrac at $3 per hour for a while until he bought a drill mounted on a TD 25 International (dozer). I then went on this machine as a helper with another driller until Jack decided to replace me with his wife's son. I shortly thereafter found a job as the "blaster" for the Municipality of Saanich, a suburb of Victoria. I was paid $2.50 per hour, which was a lot more than the $1.70 they paid the labor foreman for whom I worked. My job was to blast rock on city streets that others had already drilled.

They assured me that the job was good for all winter, but by Christmas I had caught up to the drillers. I was allowed to stay on as a laborer, but my wages were slashed to $1.60 an hour. I stayed on at Saanich until mid January when I got a phone call from Western Mines at Myra Falls in Strathcona Park. One of their miners had been killed in a hotel fire at Campbell River, so I was hired in his place.

Western Mines is located inside Strathcona Park on the shores of Buttle Lake, some 50 miles from Campbell River. We had to drive 30 miles on a logging road and then take a boat for the last 20. There were only six miners at the camp - three on each shift. We were driving the main tunnel and were in about a half-mile. Our schedule was 10 days on and four days off. We worked either day shift (8AM – 4PM) or night shift (7 PM to 3 AM). It was a good job and our bonus earnings were excellent.

Mel Plager

I heard about Mel long before I met him. In 1951 when I was working as Rae Thomas' helper at the Van Roi mine at Silverton, he regaled me with stories about Mel, who typified a rare breed of men, one would meet only in such places as mining or logging camps.

Rae told me that he was walking past Mel's raise one morning when he heard a loud clattering and banging. He stopped and listened, when down came the stoper and the drill steel. Down came the staging planks and down came Mel! Mel uttered some choice profanities, picked himself up, grabbed the drill and climbed back up the raise.

Mel had grown up in Geraldton, an Ontario mining community and while still a teenager, found work in the mine where his father was employed. Every payday he would disappear for a few days until his check was spent when he returned home with a hangover. His father remonstrated with him ceaselessly about the virtues of saving his money and investing it in stock, but to no avail.

On one such occasion Mel returned home in his habitual post payday condition. His father began his usual tiresome tirade, but was interrupted by Mel with; "Dad, I invested my money in stock!" His father's face lit

Wetting down the muckpile after the blast. *Photo courtesy of Pete Murray.*

up and he asked; "Did you get any McLeod Cockshutt?" No, Mel replied; "I bought Old Stock, O'Keefe's Extra Old Stock!"

That was the end of Mel's stay at home - as his father promptly kicked him out. When I met Mel in 1963, he told me that this story was not true. However, in a way the story was more than true in the sense that it captured Mel's personality in a way that the truth could never have done.

When I worked with Mel at Western Mines, he, Ray Nelson and I worked together driving the main tunnel. The three of us would drill and blast a round and then go out for a quick sandwich while the smoke cleared. Mel however, would not wait to finish eating his lunch. He would grab his sandwich, jump on

Marking the tunnel outline. *Photo courtesy of Pete Murray.*

his "scootcrete" (diesel ore hauler) and head right back into the smoke. When Ray and I drove back in about fifteen minutes later it was through a foul, dense cloud that made us both gag. By the time we arrived at the tunnel face, Mel would have the scattered muck cleaned up, the muck pile watered down and the first load waiting for us to haul out.

Even with the fans exhausting the smoke for twenty minutes, the air was barely breathable! Mel however appeared to actually thrive on the poisonous vapors. With a constitution as tough as his, I was not surprised to learn a few years later that he had two nephews, who were also well known for their toughness – as hockey players in the NHL.

At that time Mel must have been in his mid forties. He was a tall, wiry, rawboned man who had one white eyebrow. His living habits had apparently not changed very much since his youth. On payday he could still be relied on to drink until his pay was exhausted. He was one of the few people that I have known who could do this and still do a good day's work every day regardless of how sick he might be.

I stayed at Western Mines until mid summer, when I learned that R. F. Fry and Associates were sinking a shaft at Cowichan Copper. I immediately applied for, and got a job with them so that I could be at home with my family. I worked in the shaft for only a short while before the foreman wanted to send me to work at their Craigmont operation near Merritt. He had a buddy to whom he had promised a job, and wanted me out of the way. I refused to go to Merritt and quit.

Real Estate

After I quit R.F. Fry & Associates, I decided to try to sell Real Estate. While I was taking the course by correspondence from UBC, Butler Brothers gave me a job setting chokers on their logging operation near Sooke. That was a tough job – it rained every day and we were soaked within an hour of coming to work, both from the rain and from our perspiration.

I wrote the Real Estate exam in late October of 1963 and promptly quit my logging job. I waited in vain for my license and finally learned that they would not issue it until I quit my job. I had neglected to tell them that I had already quit. Meanwhile I spent some time in the Realty (Northwestern Securities) office trying to learn something about selling houses, but received no training as such. During this time I sold my house in Sooke, bought one in Victoria and moved my family there.

Shortly after getting my license in late December I re-listed a house in Sooke that had been on the market for a long time. Another Realtor soon sold it so I earned a small listing commission. By being innovative on the terms I had made the house much easier to sell.

In 1964, during all of January I had viral pneumonia and found it very difficult to get out and show houses, but I did sell one. I also sold one in February as well as three in March. In April the weather turned gorgeous and the market dried up. Northwestern Securities was by far the largest real estate firm in Victoria with thirty-four Realtors, but we were getting at most one call a day. I learned later that the firm's reputation had been badly injured by a couple of unscrupulous Realtors before I came to work there. I did sell one house at the end of April, but it was a delayed possession, so I had no income from it until four months later.

By this time I had exhausted my savings, so I went back mining again. I realized that my biggest obstacle to being a salesman was my lack of self-confidence – and especially around people that I considered well educated, (I had completed only Grade 10). My fear of what people thought of me ruled my life.

Back Mining Yet Again

After giving up on Real Estate, I went back to work for R. F. Fry once more, this time at the Craigmont mine near Merritt. I was not there very long before I got a job at Noranda's Boss Mountain mine 60 miles east of 100 Mile House. This mine was at an elevation of 5000 feet and on July 1st, it snowed all day.

At Boss Mountain I was in charge of two other miners and assigned four trackless headings, which we drove simultaneously, using jacklegs and a rubber-tired Copco mucking machine. While one man was mucking out one heading, the other two of us drilled off a round at one of the other faces.

I no longer remember the names of these men, but one had the nickname, "Peanuts." We soon learned that Peanuts had a weak stomach, so during lunchtime the other fellow and I would regale him with the foulest jokes we could come up with. Poor Peanuts, he was by no means very clean, but he always lost his appetite and would have to abandon his lunch on these occasions.

I enjoyed my stay at Boss Mountain, but I missed my family. During July, I rented a cabin on the shores of Canim Lake and brought them up there for a few weeks. Shortly after they returned to Victoria, Jack Start called and wanted me to come back to work for him again, so I left the mine and went back home.

Shaft head-frame at Copper Mountain Mine in 1951. *Photo courtesy of Andy Wingerak.*

Chapter 19 - Goodbye to Mining

Art Brown

When I went back to work for Jack, he had replaced the dozer-mounted drill with another airtrac. I took over one airtrac and he operated the other one. His stepson Bill came to work as my helper for a few months until he quit and went into carpentry. I then got a new helper named Art Brown.

Art had recently left the Royal Canadian Navy. He was born in Selkirk, Manitoba and was of French ancestry despite the name Brown. I liked Art. He was not only a good worker, but he had a wry sense of humor as well. One of his traits was that he did not think it possible to eat anything unless he first smothered it in ketchup.

One day I took him to the Dingle House – the best steak house in Victoria. I had known the owners of this restaurant ten years earlier when they ran the Greyhound Bus depot café in Nelson. When I brought Art to the Dingle House, I immediately introduced him to the owners and told him where they had come from. This was not appreciated because the owners had adopted English accents and did not seem to want anyone to know about their humble beginnings.

While we waited for our steaks to arrive, we had a few drinks. When the food came, Art immediately asked for a bottle of ketchup. Our hosts were visibly offended and intimated that they had no ketchup. Art, who by now was a little inebriated, demanded in a loud voice that he wanted ketchup, and he wanted it right now. By then we had become the objects of stares from the other patrons. Art soon had his ketchup and we were not even finished eating our steaks when the bill arrived. The owner couldn't get us out of there quickly enough!

I worked for Jack for well over a year this time. He had hired me at my old rate of $3.00 per hour, but raised it to $3.25 in January 1965. Later that summer he raised it to $3.50 despite Union rates being only $3.10 for powder-men. Meanwhile, I was getting arthritis in my hands and wanted to get away from the wet climate. During the Easter week, I found a job at the Union Carbide mine near Bishop California. Since I expected to wait a long time for my work permit to come through, Art and I quit and went to the Mica Creek dam in September of that year.

After I left Jack Start, his other stepson, Wayne came to work for him running the drill. He was killed the following year by a premature blast. There may have been some confusion in his instructions to his helper.

Wayne had evidently gone back to check on something at the other end of the loaded section and the blast went off as he was walking by it. Perhaps the helper misunderstood him and lit the fuse thinking that Wayne would wait at the far end. No one ever learned just what happened that day, but it is practically impossible to set off dynamite without a detonator.

Mica Creek

The Mica Creek dam was being constructed on the Columbia River 90 miles north of Revelstoke. It was originally constructed as a part of W.A.C. Bennett's flood control treaty with United States and the electrical generating facilities were added much later.

Art and I took jobs as laborers at the dam with Perrini Construction just to get into the Rock and Tunnel Workers Union. We both felt that we could quickly get better jobs once we were on site. We were not there very long before I was promoted to "powderman" and looked after all the outside blasting on my shift.

Mica Creek gets its name because the rock in the area is 100% mica. It is not a hard rock, but it has a rubbery quality that makes it difficult to fracture. We eventually switched from dynamite to TNT based explosives. This was the only time I have ever used TNT and I had a weird experience with it one night.

It was a dry evening for a change, for it rained almost constantly. I had finished loading up a fair sized shot and set it off at shortly before midnight. As soon as I returned to the blast site, I was greeted by a burning muckpile! The entire rock pile was enveloped in flames and kept on burning for about fifteen minutes. I shortly learned that this was not uncommon when blasting with TNT. There were apparently unburned gasses escaping from the broken rock that caught fire as soon as they encountered enough oxygen to support combustion. The flames would probably not have been visible during the daytime, for I never saw this phenomenon again.

I was meanwhile looking for a way to bring my family up from Victoria to live with me. I met an engineer with IPEC, Hydro's engineering branch, who was trying to sell his 10-foot wide house trailer. We agreed on a price, but then found that I would have to move the trailer since the plot it was on was reserved for IPEC employees. I approached Perrini about a trailer lot, but they told me that their lots were reserved for management and supervision. I therefore went to Revelstoke, bought a new house trailer and arranged to set it up in the vendor's trailer park. We then sold our house in Victoria and prepared to move.

Meanwhile, I rose to the rank of foreman at the dam, and the company shortly asked me if I wanted a trailer lot. The opportunity came too late because I had bought a twelve foot wide trailer and it was too wide to haul over the "Bailey bridges" on the Mica Highway.

One day I ran into an old acquaintance from Salmo named Angus Nissen who was a carpenter at the dam-site. He told me about a small drilling contractor that was drilling and blasting for New West Construction, a road contractor near Revelstoke. He took me into town one evening and introduced me to the contractor. His name was Mel Abbott and his company was Gulf Drilling Ltd.

Gulf Drilling Ltd.

I started with Gulf Drilling as a powderman/driller on the Mica Highway in early December. Our job was on a section of road that stretched from thirteen to thirty miles out of Revelstoke. Shortly after going to work for the new company, I drove to Victoria, sold my 1965 Ford Fairlane car and bought a new 1966 F250 Ford pickup truck. I then brought my family back with me to Revelstoke and moved into our new trailer home.

It snowed constantly during the entire month of January. The wind blew steadily from the north and the temperature stayed at a constant –4° F. By month end there was six feet of snow on the ground. When February arrived, so did warmer weather. The ceiling in our new home began to leak. Some drifting snow had somehow gotten into the ceiling and with the warmer weather, it began to melt. It was not long before we had a different trailer, for the vendor was not anxious for our problem to become widely known.

Author's family in new 12' wide trailer –home circa 1966. *Photo is from the author's collection*

Mel Abbott had recently fired his job supervisor and was looking after the work himself, but he wanted to go back to Vancouver, because he had other work on the go. At about this time I was reading a book called Psycho-cybernetics by Dr. Maxwell Maltz. In this book I learned to look at my circumstances in an entirely new way. One important realization was that I need not be a victim of past circumstances and that I had the power to choose a new future. As a result, when Mel Abbott mentioned that he needed a superintendent to take over his operation there, I had the temerity to ask for a chance to try out for the job. In retrospect, I realize how ill equipped I was for the position, but somehow I managed to survive and pick up the necessary skills. This was the very first time that I had ever had the courage to ask a superior for something I wanted.

When I first began working for Mel, I quickly learned that some of the crew were intentionally keeping down their drilling production. They warned me on my first day that I had better not do too much work and make them look bad. One of them said to me; "We have a good thing going here, don't you dare spoil it!" It was not very long after taking over the reins that I replaced most of that crew. I began by hiring Don Clark from Salmo and Art Brown, who was still at Mica and got my first lesson in supervision. They were both hard workers, but when they came to work for me, they thought my friendship meant they did not have to work very hard. It took me a while before I got things turned around.

Being in charge of an operation for the first time was often very stressful, especially when things didn't go well. It might have gotten the better of me, but I developed the habit of asking myself; "What's the worst that can happen?" I found that the worst was always something I could live with. I also reassured myself by thinking; "If my work isn't good enough, let someone else try it. I can always go back to hourly work."

One man who stayed was a powderman named Len Zapshala. I did not get to know him well then, and when I met with Mel Abbott shortly after in the beer parlour in Langley, he told me that Len was ready to quit. I told him I had no problems with Len or his work, but Mel said to me; "That is not enough! You have to show him you appreciate him. You have to blow a little smoke up his ass!"

The following year Len and I worked together a lot and became close friends. Len was conservative and was always meticulous with his blasting and I appreciated that. A couple of years later Len was killed while working for Jack Start on logging roads near Sooke. He and his helper had driven out for a load of explosives during the day. On the trip back in, the helper was driving when they met a load of logs on its way out. It was a narrow road with only occasional "pullouts" to allow vehicles to pass. The helper threw the pickup truck in reverse but rolled the truck over the bank while he was backing up to the next pullout. He escaped without injury, but Len was killed.

There was a narrow spot on the road three miles north of Revelstoke in a slide area. The Department of Highways kept a D8 dozer there to clear off the snow whenever a slide came down.

One warm day in April, the dozer operator had just reopened the road, then pulled over to the side for a cup of coffee while he let the backed up traffic through. The dozer operator at that time sat on one side of a bench-like seat on his machine. When Mel Abbott and another man arrived a few minutes later, they found that a large slide had come down and closed the road. The dozer operator was buried up to his neck in snow that had solidified into ice. It was so hard that they had to chop it off from around him. If the dozer had been facing in the opposite direction, the operator would have been completely buried and smothered. The slide also shoved the dozer several feet toward the edge of the embankment. A few feet more and the machine would have tumbled down into the Columbia River.

That spring we put Don Clark in charge of finishing the work that was left at Revelstoke. I moved to Saturna Island with the Reich (rotary) drill we had used at Revelstoke. There we drilled off and blasted a 40,000 cubic yard shot in a shale quarry owned by B.C. Lightweight Aggregates. This material was later crushed and put through a kiln to make lightweight concrete aggregates. The quarry was very close to the beach and when the tide was out, the area was teeming with oysters. I frequently picked oysters for the crew, who ate them raw, with just a bit of vinegar and some pepper to season them.

On the Saturna project I had a powderman (I no longer remember his name) who had lost part of one arm just below the elbow. He had a steel hook to take its place and was quite proficient with it. He was even able to wire up the electrical caps almost as quickly as a person with two hands. He had lost the arm while changing the boom on his airtrac from the vertical to the horizontal position. Somehow, the boom fell on his arm during this maneuver.

He was born in Britain and when the German raids on London began, his father sent him to the Shawnigan Lake boys' school near Victoria to get him out of the country. He told me that he and many others were routinely beaten and buggered by the teachers. He ran away twice but was sent back. When he ran away the third time at age 14, he was able to join the merchant marine where he stayed until the end of the war.

After finishing the Saturna job, we moved the drill up to Brenda Mines near Peachland. Brenda was a large "open pit" molybdenum prospect owned by Noranda Mines. There we drilled 6½ inch holes for chip sampling the molybdenum (moly) ore. Our work was used to check the accuracy of the diamond-drill results and proved more reliable. The diamond drills were losing a substantial amount of their drill water (and its moly content) in the hole. They therefore tended to indicate lower ore values than was actually the case.

When we arrived at Peachland on July 1st 1966, the village was swarming with prospectors, mining promoters and Brenda people. Pete Spackman owned and operated the hotel there and its beer parlour was the social center of the village. Because the Brenda property was so large, it was not long before the Howe Street promoters had staked all the ground around it with the object of cashing in on the moly craze. This metal is not only used to strengthen steel, but is also an incredible lubricant that permeates the metal surfaces it comes in contact with. Judging from the prices some of the shares generated, one could easily be led to believe that some of these promotions had actually found something, but of course that was never the case. The only things these promoters ever mined were the pockets of the gullible.

Mel had meanwhile spent a lot of money to upgrade the rotary drill to high pressure air for the Brenda project. We began the job by using a "high pressure down the hole air-hammer." When this would not work, we had to revert to conventional rotary bits, but the revenue from our drilling did not even pay for the bits, let alone for the drill and the labor. This put Gulf Drilling in a tenuous financial position from which it did not recover. Gulf Drilling stayed in business until the January of 1967 when HB Contracting (HB) bought it for pennies on the dollar. I had in the meantime returned to Revelstoke to finish the job there and had been seriously injured. (See No. 8 of "This Cat Had More Than 9 Lives"). HB immediately took me off salary and let me collect WCB benefits. When I came off WCB, my salary was slashed from $1,000 per month to $800.

In April, HB sent me to Prince Rupert for a week to catch up on the blasting on a water main job they were doing there. It was the only time I have ever been in Prince Rupert for more than a day or two at a time. During that week, in addition to sunshine every day, we also had daily showers as well as some hail and snowstorms. During that week I ran into Lee Bracy, a miner I had known at Remac in 1952. He was now retired and had become adept at making beautiful rock jewelry

In June of that year we were pioneering the quarry in Pitt Meadows near where the Swanee-Set golf course is now located. That quarry is still operating today, more than 36 years later. I was working together with another powderman-driller named Len Zapshala and Don Keating was supervising the work.

It was at this quarry that I met Mike Cacic who was then with the BC Lions. He played defensive tackle for them for ten years – a long time to last in a tough game. Mike was a young giant, standing 6' 7" and weighing 270 pounds with no visible fat on his body. He still lived at home with his parents who had emigrated from Yugoslavia. I don't know whether Mike was born there or in Canada.

Mike's stated purpose in working for us was to get into condition for the Lions' summer training camp. What impressed me most about Mike was his phenomenal strength. He was swamping for a Caterpillar "D8" dozer that was skidding logs off the property and clearing brush. It was really something to watch Mike grab the big bull-hook with one hand and just run with it as he peeled the inch and a quarter thick wire cable off the dozer's winch as though it was a piece of string. I no longer remember what that hook weighed, but an ordinary man would have carried it with difficulty and worked laboriously to pull out the cable to which it was attached.

The weather that June was extremely hot all over the lower mainland, and at the quarry it was regularly up in the nineties (Fahrenheit). By the time we had labored in the sun for ten hours, we were thoroughly dehydrated and when we got to the Commercial Hotel each evening, our first order of business was to down a few glasses of beer to remedy that. Mike Cacic was no different from the rest of us in that respect, but he began by having the bartender set six glasses of beer in front of him. He then tilted his head back and alternating with his two hands, proceeded to pour down a glass of beer first with one hand, and then the other until the glasses were all empty. He did not swallow the beer; he literally poured each glassful down in two to three seconds. After that display, Mike would sit and sip his beer sociably with the rest of us.

I have met only one other man who reputedly had the ability to pour the beer down without swallowing it, but Mike was the only man that I actually saw doing it. The only other thing I remember about Mike was that he had bought a city lot adjacent to his parent's house supposedly for the express purpose of growing their potatoes, although I suspect that it was really for investment purposes. When I contacted Mike recently, he told me that after retiring from football, he went to work for the New Westminster School District as a plumber and welder and stayed there for thirty years. Mike did not get married until he was thirty-four years old, but he eventually raised two sons and a daughter.

Mel Abbott

Mel Abbott and I shared the same birthday (Dec. 9), but he was three years younger than me. His parents lived in Revelstoke where his father was a school principal. Mel's uncles, unlike his father, were all entrepreneurs, so Mel came by his talents naturally. While I was still at

Revelstoke that winter, Mel's mother died suddenly from an aneurysm while curling at the local rink. The wake held after the funeral was my first experience with how the Irish celebrate their dead – we all got drunk.

When Mel got into serious financial difficulties that fall, he kept looking for ways out. When he met Dick Addison, a mining geologist it was like a duck discovering water. Mel immediately began looking for a fast buck in mining.

One night we visited a prospector in North Vancouver who claimed he had a high-grade silver-lead-zinc property on a mountaintop east of Kootenay Lake in the St. Mary's River area. Mel and I drove to Nelson to investigate it. Because Mel got a severe bout of flu, I rented a helicopter and flew up to look at it alone. We landed on the peak of an 8,000-foot high mountain and I descended two hundred feet to the property. Previous owners had driven a fifty-foot long drift there in the early thirties. The ore at the adit was indeed very rich, but it was only the remnant of a thin vein that no longer existed. The original deposit had long since been eroded away and what was left did not amount to more than a few tons. There was absolutely no indication of any ore inside the tunnel.

The following month (Jan. 67) Mel and Dick picked up a molybdenum prospect near Boise Idaho. I travelled to Boise, rented an airtrac from the Morrison-Knudsen (MK) company and began chip sampling it. Mel allowed me to buy four thousand shares in the new company (Payette River Mines) for $0.10 a share.

Two years later, while I was working for Peter Kiewit Sons Company, the shares had risen to $1.80 each. I phoned Mel and asked about the possibility of buying some more shares and was assured that he would let me in at the "right" time. He then put me in touch with his banker who was in charge of the Langley branch of the Canadian Imperial Bank of Commerce (CIBC) where I borrowed $7,000 for buying the shares.

When I asked for the shares, they were trading at $1.80, but Mel did not sell them to me until they reached $2.00. The shares then promptly began a downward spiral and when they reached $1.45 I phoned the banker and told him to sell my stock. He tried to talk me out of it, but I insisted that he sell them. After the stock had dropped to $0.80 a share, I found that I still held all of my shares. I also owed $7,000 to CIBC and I learned too that the bank manager was in jail for "borrowing" the bank's funds to cover his own purchases. I finally got rid of my stock for $.25 a share and it took me two years to repay the bank. There was little that I could do about it for I had no evidence that the manager had refused to sell my stock. Mel quickly became a millionaire, but he too, like his mother, suffered an aneurysm and died at the ripe old age of 38. I am convinced that Mel was short selling the stock after all the suckers (like me) bought it.

Chapter 20 - Peter Kiewit Sons Company (PKS)

Grande Prairie, Alberta

My friend, Ordie Jones from my Remac days, had recently returned to work for PKS in Vancouver. He suggested to me that I should come over for a job interview. I was shortly hired as a rock superintendent for the Smoky Lake section of the Alberta Resources Railway 85 miles south of Grande Prairie, Alberta where Bob McEachern was the superintendent.

Since it will be some time before we will be ready to start drilling any rock, I am temporarily given the job of supervising a fleet of "641 scrapers" (large earthmovers). One evening we are building a large "fill" over a section of ground which is too soft to support a machine. The 641s are roaring down a steep hill at high speed, dumping their loads near the end of the fill and then laboring back up the hill to where the "push cats" will load them again. A young operator on a D9 dozer is leveling the material and pushing it ahead over the marshy area.

I stop him between scraper loads and tell him to have a cup of coffee while I spell him off. I am soon busy pushing the sandy material ahead to make room for the next scraper load. When that scraper comes flying down the hill, it hits the section that I have just leveled. The machine bounces so violently that the operator's hard hat goes flying off his head. I quickly realize that I might get someone hurt so I stop the dozer and tell the operator to get back to work and fix up my mess!

One afternoon we are constructing a fill through a section of muskeg. Before we begin, I wisely offset (referenced) the grade stakes to the right-of-way boundaries in case they get knocked over or moved by the equipment.

The following morning when I arrive at the fill, it has barely advanced from where it had been the previous evening despite the night-shift having hauled in three hundred and fifty loads. I am mystified! I first check the distances from my offsets to the fill stakes. The distances appears to be okay. Finally I measure the distance between the offsets on either side of the right-of-way. They have spread ten feet on one side and over thirty feet on the other! They have done this without trees being knocked over or even tilted from their vertical positions.

I radio Bob McEachern, the superintendent for advice and he comes out to have a look at the problem. It appears that the muskeg is very deep and that the material has been spreading below the surface and carrying the trees with it. Bob suggests that I doze out a wide pad to counter the outward push of the fill. When we have done that, we are able to construct the railway fill on top of this pad. We literally floated the fill on top of the muskeg.

After I have been on the job for two months, it becomes clear that we will be able to rip all of the rock on the project. I am sent down to a highway construction project some distance to the south. There we are building a section of highway towards the future town of Grande Cache where there is a large coal deposit.

Grande Cache

I arrive on the new job with the pickup truck that had been allocated to me at the Grande Prairie job. My first duties there are to supervise the erection of the construction camp. Jim Turner is the superintendent, and before long, he takes away my pickup truck and gives it to his foreman. He says I can use the flat-deck truck instead.

The Labor-day weekend is coming up and Jim Turner says we will let all the men who wish to, go home for the long weekend. One member of my crew asks me if he can take the weekend off, I assent. When Mr. Turner sees him packing up, he asks him who gave him permission to go home. The man says that I had. Mr. Turner tells him that I do not have the authority to give approval nor to give orders to anyone! He then comes to me tells me not to go around giving orders.

I was incensed! I immediately told him that I was leaving and for him to get another rock superintendent. My family was still living in our trailer at the Grande Prairie camp so I send word to them not to move the trailer down to Turner's job. I also got word to Ordie Jones in Vancouver that I was leaving.

The end result is that I stay on the job. Jim Turner and I have an uneasy truce, but we do manage to get along after that. I move my house trailer on to the job and get on with the work. In addition to supervising the rockwork where my crews drill and blast the rock at 30% below budget, I also supervise the culvert crews. I get on quite well after that except for one other episode.

We have a major rock cut not too far from the camp and it is on a long curve. As usual I offset my cut stakes before allowing any equipment on to the site. I also ask Jim Turner how he intends to move the rock once it has been blasted since I will blast it accordingly. He tells me that it will be loaded with a 988 loader and hauled with rock trucks.

After we have blasted the rock, Jim Turner changes his mind and decides to move the broken rock with the scrapers. I soon get a blast from the scraper superintendent for not breaking the rock fine enough. Jim Turner however does not complain to me directly.

The next problem is when the government surveyors try to re-survey the roadway through the rock cut. They insist that I have not shot the rock to the alignment they had given us. Fortunately, my offsets indicate otherwise. Eventually when a different crew surveys the line, there is no problem.

Our job is 85 miles north of Hinton, and adjacent to a small Native village on the shores of Grand Cache Lake. I have two crews, one crew installs the culverts and rip-rap and the other does the drilling and blasting on the project. Most of my men are non-status Aborigines. They had been evicted from the Jasper Park area at the turn of the century and the men were excellent workers.

Since I did not have anyone on the crew with a blasting ticket, I went to Edmonton to get one for myself. I figured it should be easy since I held an unrestricted BC surface blasting ticket. I was soon disabused of that notion. To get a blasting ticket in Alberta required me to hold a "Seismic First Aid" ticket as well.

The bureaucrat I met was very polite, but adamant that he could not issue me a ticket even if he wanted to, since I did not have the necessary First Aid ticket. I persisted for quite a while, but got nowhere. I was about to leave, when I mentioned that I held a BC Mine Rescue ticket as well and had brought it with me. His face lit right up because this was a ticket that meant a lot more to him than my BC Blasting ticket. Within a few minutes I walked out of his office with a blasting ticket, but with the proviso that I would come into Edmonton that winter and take their week-long First Aid course.

I was awakened shortly after midnight one night to tend to a mechanic who had been injured. He had jumped from a machine and slipped when he hit the ground. He fell across a frozen chunk of earth and fractured his femur (thighbone). He was crying out loud from his pain, but with assistance I managed to extend his leg and splint it. I accompanied him to Hinton in the ambulance. It was along drive. Hinton was eighty miles away on a gravel road and the mechanic cried like a baby during the entire trip.

The scraper crews have worked for much of the winter building grade. It was cold and when a new borrow area was cleared and stripped, it did not take long for the frost to penetrate the ground. Once the scrapers got into the unfrozen earth it no longer had time to freeze, so we were able to build road without incident. However we soon learned that it did not pay to operate the machines when the temperature dipped below −30° F. Below these temperatures the iron becomes brittle and breaks easily.

I continued with my rockwork for most of the winter as well. We had a large "through-cut" adjacent to our camp that took us some time to drill off. One morning while I was wiring a shot, (with bare hands) the temperature was −30°F. In order to warm my hands occasionally, I kept a pail partly filled with used oil burning by the side of the right-of-way. I found that I could wire eight caps before having to warm my hands. A few days later I was wiring another shot when the temperature was only −20°F. However, this day there was a slight breeze blowing and a few snowflakes falling. Despite being warmer, I was now able to wire only six caps before having to warm my hands again.

Jim Turner left project the following spring to take over another job in northern BC. Meanwhile he left his nephew, Gunnar Slack in charge of the job. Most of the grade had been built and it was just the finishing and gravelling that was left to do.

The work went very poorly for Gunnar. Wherever shallow grades had been built on frozen ground during the winter, the new road quickly disintegrated and had to be reconstructed. The project had been below budget when Turner left, but it quickly went over because we had to rebuild so much of the grade. Unfortunately for Gunnar, he got stuck with the credit for the cost over-runs. In my opinion, he did a credible job and should not have been blamed for the shortcomings of the winter construction.

The Truck Driver and the Grizzly

As the job neared completion we had a number of independent truckers hauling gravel. One of the truckers named Jack was a fellow who had huge chunks of flesh missing from one thigh and from one shoulder. He had been mauled by a grizzly bear a few years earlier. Jack told me this story of his encounter.

He had been hunting and had shot a bull elk late one afternoon. Since he did not have time to get it out that day, he just field-dressed the animal, quartered it and went home. The following morning he returned with a friend to pack out the meat.

They were hiking in from the road where they had left the vehicle. Since they were expecting to carry meet, Jack was carrying the only rifle. When they neared the kill site, Jack heard the grizzly so he cocked the weapon and was carrying it at the ready. The bear was on him so suddenly that he barely had time to point and shoot.

The next thing he knew, he was on the ground with the grizzly on top of him. He did not remember feeling any pain, but he could hear the flesh being ripped off him and bones cracking as the bear chewed on him.

He lost consciousness for a while and when he came to, the bear was gone. His friend had run back to the pickup and returned with another rifle. His friend drove him to the Hinton hospital where the doctor went to work sewing him up and setting his fractures. The local game warden came to see him and treated him with ill concealed contempt while questioning him about the incident.

The following day the game warden and the local Mountie went looking for the bear. The game warden armed with a rifle appropriate for a grizzly was well prepared. He heard the bear shoo its cub up a tree as they approached so he was ready for it. The grizzly was on him so quickly that he did not even have time to pull the trigger! The Mountie shot the bear, just as it was about to crush the warden's head in its jaws. The game warden escaped with four ugly punctures of his scalp, but a severely bruised ego. Jack said he did not sneer at him after that.

During that summer (1968), there were two women who lived in the Native village for a few months. They were employed under one of Prime Minister Trudeau's programs for "Young Canadians" and one of them was a 3rd year medical student from Edmonton. One evening Emil Moberly, who worked on my drill crew, came to me and said his wife was about to have a baby. He asked if we would take her in to the hospital in Hinton. I promptly got the ambulance driver and picked up Emil's wife. I also invited the medical student to come along and that turned out to be a fortuitous decision. We got only seven miles from camp when we had to stop and deliver the child. We were lucky for it was a quick and easy birth, but nevertheless, I was happy that I had brought along the "med" student who did most of the work.

I stayed on the project and looked after final cleanup and taking down the camp. My house trailer was the last item to be hauled out and I was the last person to leave the job. Before this happened we had bizarre incident late one night.

213

One of the aborigines came to my trailer looking for his sixteen-year-old daughter. We had not seen her so we went to see the trailer hauler who was sleeping in one of the camp units for the night. He said he had not seen the girl either. We then checked each camp trailer but still did not find her. We did however find an older Native woman. She was drunk and had an unfinished bottle of whiskey beside the bed.

The girl's father finally drove to a small place called Muskeg some fifteen miles away where he found his daughter. A supervisor who shall remain unnamed and whose wife had already left, had fled the camp trailer with her just ahead of the father after plying her with liquor. I have often wondered what that father would have done to the guy if he had caught him.

Yakima, Washington

I was the last person to leave the Grande Cache job. PKS moved me into their Edmonton shop for a short while, but then they sent me to Yakima for the winter to look after some shaft excavation for bridge footings that I had helped to estimate.

I was feeling some trepidation about working south of the border for I remembered the antipathy that many of us in Canada had felt towards Americans coming up and taking our jobs. My fears were groundless! The Americans practically rolled out the red carpet for me when I came and made me feel very welcome. They treated me as an expert on the work I was directing for no one else had any experience in underground excavation. Within a month of arriving in Yakima, I rented a house and moved my family down from Alberta.

Not long after arriving in Yakima, I attended a "Unitarian Fellowship" meeting. There I met a man, who as soon as he learned I had come down from Canada said;

"I was hunting in Canada this fall."

Me; "What part?"

"In Western Canada."

"Yes I know, but where in Western Canada?"

"Out in Alberta."

"But where in Alberta/"

"Oh just some little place that you'd have never heard of – a place called Muskeg."

Me; "I just left Muskeg less than a month ago!"

Jerry Nesteval was the "grading" superintendent on the bridge project. He was my immediate supervisor and we hit it off from the start. Our crews worked only from Monday to Friday, eight hours a day. We supervisors however came in on Saturday mornings for weekly planning sessions. After these meetings Jerry, the other supervisors and I usually stopped at a small bar called "The Oasis." The bar had a pool table, and I was soon the champion of our group. Since we always played for beer, I had to keep drinking as long as I was winning. My wife, Fran renamed this bar "the Stumbling Block."

One afternoon a young woman came into the bar and shortly challenged me to a game. She was just as good a pool player as I was, and my friends were barely able to suppress their anticipation of me losing a game to her. I did lose a game, but I got even with my mates, for the lady and I partnered up and challenged all comers. We didn't buy another beer all afternoon.

The Resident Engineer on our project would not allow us to pour concrete on the project if the temperature fell below freezing. As this was one of the coldest winters on record with lows down to $-20°$ F. we poured no concrete at all during January. Many buildings in Yakima had frozen pipes that winter because they were not insulated against this degree of cold.

I found the Americans very hospitable, but that trait did not extend to some of their doctors. I have since been warned that anyone moving to the States for any length of time had better find a family physician as soon as possible.

One cold winter morning when I went to start my pickup truck, the battery appeared to be dead. I pulled back the rubber cover from the battery post, scraped the green corrosion off both the cable connector and the post. I then took a deep breath and blew the stuff away. It deflected off the rubber cover straight back into my good (left) eye!

I immediately ran to the kitchen sink where I spent the next fifteen minutes splashing water into my eye. Next I got out the yellow pages and phoned the nearest doctor. I explained what had happened, but the receptionist whined; "But you are not the doctor's patient." I said; "I'm new down here and I don't have a doctor, what am I supposed to do, let the battery acid ruin my eye?" She responded; "I suggest that you go to Emergency at the nearest hospital."

After flushing my eye some more, I drove to the nearest hospital and went to the emergency room. After waiting for over two hours, I was finally given an appointment to see an eye doctor at his office in mid afternoon. If I had not done a good job of rinsing my eye, I might have had serious damage. While our medical services in Canada are not always ideal, I cannot imagine getting the kind of brush-off from any Canadian doctor.

By early March, spring was in full swing and the local golf course was open. Jerry and I went out one afternoon for a game despite gale force winds whipping down the fairways. When we approached the first green, we could not see the flag

Author & family at the PKS field office on the day they moved back to Canada. *Photo is from the author's collection*

stick. We found it lying down and we cursed the group in front of us for not putting it back in the cup. After finding this scenario repeated on the next three holes, we finally realized that the wind was blowing the flags out of the cups.

The project went very well, not least of all because my part of it was 31% below budget. The company invited me to stay with them down there, but I felt a loyalty to Ordie Jones and came back to Canada after Easter.

Walhachin

After I returned from Yakima that spring, PKS put me in charge of pioneering a new quarry to produce ballast for the Canadian Pacific Railway (CPR) at Walhachin. The work included opening the quarry, blasting rock and crushing it for railway ballast.

Walhachin has a haunting history. It is a small hamlet located on the south side of the Thompson River, about forty-five miles west of Kamloops, BC. It was built during the early 1900s by English "Remittance Men." It was also a watering depot for the CPR in the days before diesel, when steam locomotives still pulled the trains. "Remittance Men" refers to the black sheep of English nobility that were paid an annual stipend by their families to stay away from England, hence the term "remittance." Some of these men and their families settled in Walhachin. There they built houses, a few of which still remain almost a hundred years later. They also planted orchards and created an irrigation system to water them. The remains of the flumes that delivered the water can still be found on the hillsides above the Thompson River.

Although their families had disowned them, the men of Walhachin were still loyal to England. When World War I broke out, they all returned to Britain and joined the army. The story is that they all wound up in the same regiment, which was completely annihilated. Walhachin became a village of widows and children.

After leaving Walhachin, I moved to Kelowna to do a clearing job at a new distillery Hiram Walker was building there. It was a small project, but I was able to negotiate work worth eight times the original contract amount. In addition to the clearing, we also built the percolation basins, the rail spur and the site roads.

There were a lot of wasps on the site and everyone on my crew had been stung except me. Whenever wasps or bees buzzed them, the men tended to wave their hands at them until they eventually got stung. I would just stand still and let them fly all around me, and they never bothered me. But that changed one day.

It was a cold, windy, evening in late August when I came out after supper to check on the afternoon shift. I was wearing a green "Pioneer" brand rain jacket to cut the wind and I was standing about forty feet from the dozer as it pushed over some trees. Without any warning, a ground wasp flew into my right ear and stung me. Then another and yet another hit me on the neck. Before I could get away, I had nine stings – all on a small part of my neck!

The following morning I was out on site at 7:00 AM. It was a beautiful, but cold morning, so I was still wearing that same jacket. I was 100 feet away from the dozer when I got stung yet again. I am convinced that the wasps disliked the distinctive smell of my rain jacket.

Barry Eberle

George Larson and his brother-in-law, Barry Eberle owned the D7 dozer we rented to clear the distillery site. One of them started early in the morning and the other took over later in the day and worked until dark. George was the older of the two, and worked at a steady, methodical pace. Barry was his opposite - when he was on the dozer it was usually at full throttle in second gear. Between the two we got acceptable production. Barry later brought a log-skidder on site to skid the logs we had salvaged. It was the first time I had ever seen one and I was thoroughly impressed with its performance. I could hardly believe the way it climbed over logs and stumps at high speed without tipping over.

Not too long after the project was finished, Barry quit the partnership and began his own contracting company. He remained in the clearing business and had his ups and downs but managed to stay solvent in a very competitive business. When I was involved with Westcoast Energy on the Vancouver Island Pipeline project in 1990, Barry worked as a subcontractor on clearing work in the Nanaimo area. A few years later when we were doing pipeline work near Chetwynd, Barry worked together with a Native contractor for us again. In 2001 I saw him yet again when he and a Native contractor hired me briefly to help them on some clearing work for a Calgary oil company in the Kelly Lake area near Beaverlodge, Alberta.

Bob Goodall and Merv Lowe

Bob Goodall was the Engineer and Merv Lowe his assistant for Stone & Webster. This company was the construction manager building the Hiram Walker distillery at Winfield, BC. The three of us got along well together because we were all addicted to golf. Merv was a tall stocky man who had been the wrestling champion at the University of Saskatchewan during his student years. He was very strong and also very supple considering his build. He had an odd back-swing with his head coming up six inches and then down again on his downswing. When his coordination was on, he could drive the ball nearly 300 yards, but when it was off, he hit it all over the place.

One day while teeing off on the first hole at the Mountain Shadows golf course, Merv hit his drive out on to the highway. The ball bounced once, up under an oncoming truck. We could see it bouncing around underneath the vehicle several times before it suddenly shot out from under the truck and back on to the fairway. Although Merv lost a lot of distance off the tee on that drive, with his length, he was still able to reach the green with his second shot and par the hole.

Some time after I left the job, Bob took over as the Project Manager and finished the distillery – under budget. A few years later he came to Vancouver where he went to work for Associated Engineering. From then on we were once again golfing buddies until the company moved him to Edmonton. Eventually Bob came back to Vancouver as Construction Manager for Westcoast Energy Inc. (WEI). He was in charge of the Vancouver Island Pipeline project in 1990-91 and it was one of his chief inspectors that hired me on that job.

After the Island Pipeline project was over, I worked directly for Bob in the WEI office for the next five years. We did not get out golfing as often as before, but he was still determined to improve his game. The last times we played together, he was indeed hitting the ball farther than he used to in the old days. Bob is now retired and spends much of his time at his cottage, or aboard his sailboat at Sechelt. He bought a fifth wheel trailer when he left Westcoast and has been to Newfoundland and back as well as to the Arctic and back. His wife, Sandy continued doggedly pursuing her own goals and finally got her degree in music while continuing to teach piano lessons to a number of students. The Goodalls have three children who have long since flown the nest and the oldest now has a family of her own.

Jimmy Devins

I first met Jim Devins in 1968, but did not get to know him well until we both worked at the Walhachin quarry during the spring of 1969. I had come there to pioneer the quarry – to ready it for the "production" people. After we had done the preliminary work with a dozer and an "airtrac" drill, we brought in Jim Devins and a large "Robbins" rotary drill for the production phase of the project. The airtrac typically drilled blast holes of two and one half to three inches in diameter and was adequate for preparing the quarry for larger equipment. The Robbins, on the other hand, was capable of holes of up to nine inches in diameter, and was suitable for large volume rock production. Jim's stay on the project and mine overlapped by a few days while we produced rock for the large crushing plant that was being set up.

Jim and the Robbins drill stayed with the crushing plant for the next several years, producing ballast for both the CP and the CN railroads. Our encounters were usually limited to the PKS annual meetings, which were held each winter in Vancouver. However, in 1974, we were both working for the Chinook Engineering and Construction Company, when we again met. I had spent the summer looking after a "stripping" project at the Endako mine. Jim had been in charge of Chinook's mining project at Cassiar Asbestos in northern BC. I had come back into head office and had successfully tendered a job of replacing several wooden trestles with "multiplate" culverts for the CN railway in the Ashcroft area. Since Jim was finished at Cassiar, Chinook brought him in to supervise this project. It was an intricate little project that required detailed planning, but Jim handled it with ease and completed it on budget. Because I had bid this work, I visited him on the job a couple of times while it was underway.

Jim had spent two seasons at Cassiar as the superintendent for Chinook. His operation there was much more economical than that done by Cassiar's own forces. He therefore wound up doing all of their mining work. In the process he soon had a large spread of equipment that included a scraper fleet as well as three Robbins rotary drills. Jim made a lot of money for

Chinook – and also for himself on this project, for he was earning a bonus of 5% of the field profits.

While I was in Chinook's head office, I produced the final cost reports for the Cassiar job and was therefore privy to how much the project had earned in "field profits." (Field profits were based on project income, less out-of-pocket costs and internal rentals charged to the project for company owned equipment). At a time when Jim's annual salary was under $18,000, his bonus for each of the two seasons was in excess of $120,000!

I did not see Jim again for over twenty years. After his big paydays at Chinook, he had started his own drilling and blasting company in the U.S. and from the reports I heard, he had been doing quite well. In 1995 I was leading a workshop for small Native contractors in Chetwynd when I next saw Jim. He was working for Barry Eberle and they were assisting a small Native clearing contractor who was clearing right-of-way for WEI in the area.

Jim told me that he had strayed from the straight and narrow just once! He had picked up a young blonde in a bar one night and the next morning this girl phoned Jim's wife in Kelowna and asked her to divorce Jim. Jim's wife did not give him a second chance. By the time she and her lawyers were through with him, Jim had little or no money left.

Three years later during the winter of 1999-2000, I was helping a small Native based contractor named Dav-Jor, that was doing work for some energy companies north of Fort St. John, when I again saw Jim. He was operating a Dav-Jor dozer and building drill sites for Canadian Hunter Exploration. I supervised the project directly for a couple of weeks and shared a bunkhouse room with Jim during my stay. While there, I tried unsuccessfully to induce Jim to take over the job from me. He told me that he was quite content to operate a dozer and that he was no longer interested in supervision. I found this hard to believe, for I cannot recall previously knowing anyone with his level of ability who would willingly give up the power and responsibility that comes with management. Jim, however, appeared happy and content and was doing an excellent job for his employer, as well as for the client. He left no doubt in my mind that he had discovered contentment in doing a small job and doing it well. However I heard the following year that Jim was now supervising work for Dav-Jor Contracting.

Bert Norris

Bert Norris was nearing sixty, and the oldest person by far in the PKS Vancouver office when I began working for them. He was not in the least excitable, and his personality and calming influence had a positive effect on all those around him.

Bert had tendered the Hiram Walker Distillery work on which I became the superintendent so he oversaw the job from head office. I found Bert to be a great guy to work for. He was always supportive, and never lost sight of our long-term objectives. He seldom missed an opportunity to find something I was doing well and to compliment me on it. I found that very motivating. I also found that Bert was not only extremely honest, but fair as well and would never take advantage of anyone just in order to make a few extra dollars. He was the kind of fellow that I aspired to become. During the summers that we were both in the Vancouver office, Bert often asked me out for a game of golf in the evening. He was not a great golfer, but I always found him a joy to play with.

When Bert retired at age 65, the character of the office was profoundly altered. Most of our brightest young people left the company, and several of them went to work for Goodbrand Construction in Langley. These fellows changed that little company into one of formidable size with a large impact in the construction community. I last saw Bert when I visited him in Escondido, California a couple of years after his retirement. He had purchased a home in a golf course development and was able to play golf every day, but he died a few years after retirement.

Frank Taulu

In November of 1970, I went over to the Port Alberni area to get out a 1,000 ton bulk sample from a limestone deposit we had acquired there. We made arrangements for a local crushing and paving contractor to do the work for us, and I was there to make sure that the rock was crushed to our specifications.

The contractor hired a man to drill and blast the rock, but he did not seem to know what he was doing. Since I was just standing around anyway, I suggested to Frank Taulu, the foreman that he get rid of his driller and I would drill the rock for them at no cost.

We got the job finished and the material barged to Tacoma for testing. Ed Daly, a co-owner of the crushing outfit gave me a case of Canadian Club whiskey for the favour I had done. During the two weeks I spent at Port Alberni, I was at Frank's house twice – once on Sauna Night (Frank's family had come from Finland), and the other time I was invited to a party there.

Since the early Seventies I had not had occasion to go to Port Alberni again, so I lost track of Frank. During the summer of 2001, my wife and I were on a camping trip to the Island. My wife insisted that we visit one of her former colleagues who lived just south of Nanaimo. There was another visitor there when we arrived. He turned out to be Frank Taulu, and he remembered me and reminded me that I had done the drilling and blasting for them. I had completely forgotten it.

Don Long

I first met Don in 1951 while Ed Litviak and I were staying in Creston. He had just graduated from high school a month earlier. What I remember was that he was driving his father's brand new Ford sedan and that we discovered that it would go just as fast in second gear as in third.

A few years later I ran into Don several times on the streets of Nelson while I was working at Remac. Don had graduated in Civil Engineering and was working in a "soils lab" there for the B.C. Department of Highways.

After I went to work for PKS in 1967 I saw that Don had become their "Engineer" on the final construction phase of the Bennett Dam near Hudsons Hope. After that project was completed, Don moved into our Vancouver office in charge of Estimating, and he became my direct supervisor.

Our District Manager often missed being the successful bidder on construction projects because he, in our opinion, wanted to get too much margin on the job. I had related to Don the old adage from Wall Street; "Sometimes the bulls win and sometimes the bears win, but the pigs never win!" After that, whenever the manager wanted to add money to one of Don's estimates, he would retort; "Now John, don't forget that the pigs never win."

During the early "seventies," we were tendering on some railway relocation near Wardner, BC. Don and I flew up to Cranbrook one morning, rented a car and went out to look at the job. The project appeared pretty straightforward so we were finished early. Our return flight was not until 5:00 PM, so Don decided to take me for a tour of the region.

We drove up to Fort Steele and looked around for a while and when I suggested to Don that it was probably a good time to head back, he said; "No rush! I know a shortcut back to Cranbrook from here, so we have lots of time."

I replied; "I have spent a fair amount of time in this area too, and I am not aware of any shortcuts."

Don insisted; "Well I grew up in the East Kootenays, and I know there is a shortcut!" The so-called "shortcut" we took went right through Kimberley and was actually farther than going back the way we had come. We were still a mile from the airport when we saw our plane leaving.

Don had to be back in the office the following morning for an important meeting, so we decided to drive to Calgary and get a late flight from there. We were lucky, for when we went to the car rental company, another customer had just turned in a car he had rented in Calgary. We were able to return this vehicle and save the drop fees for both parties. We reached Calgary in time for an 11:00 PM flight and were back in Vancouver shortly after midnight.

On another occasion we were bidding a highway job in Prince George. Don sent me up ahead of him to look for a gravel source. I was able to locate a "gravel esker" near the top of the job, which would give us an advantage in bidding the work because it would be a downhill haul. I went into the Lands Office and found out that the owner was an Optometrist living in Kelowna and that her husband was a lawyer. Don gave me the go-ahead to rent a backhoe to check out the size of the deposit. When he arrived later in the day, he took over the exploration work while I caught a plane to Kelowna where I was able to negotiate an agreement with the owner and her husband. I was able to tie up the deposit for $1 plus a royalty of $.25 per cubic yard for any gravel we used.

Ben Ginter was the low bidder on the job, and he promptly inquired about buying the gravel from us. When he did not like our price or our terms, he tried to buy it directly from the owners, who then wanted to break our agreement saying that I had tricked them. Our lawyer at Davis and Company replied with a sarcastic letter ridiculing the idea that I, a layman, could have tricked him, a seasoned lawyer. That gravel was never used and lies there undisturbed to this day.

After Bert Norris, the assistant District manager retired, the head office staff began leaving PKS. Don took a job with the department of Highways as the "Construction Superintendent" in Prince George. He was killed a few years later when the plane in which he was a passenger crashed in poor visibility north of Terrace, BC.

Bob Squair

Bob was the Equipment Superintendent for the PKS Western Canadian District all the years I worked for them. He was five years my senior, but we became good friends and often had a drink together after work. His wife Marge was a shoe salesperson for one of the Vancouver department stores and her passion was Bingo. During my first years in Vancouver, they had me over for dinner more than once.

The one dinner I won't forget was during the Grey Cup football game that we watched during the afternoon. Between the two of us, we polished off two and one half bottles of "Canadian Club" whiskey. The following day I had to hike the new alignment for the "Upper Levels" highway that we were tendering. Needless to say, it was a very tough hike for I had a king sized hangover.

Bob retired from PKS before turning 60, after which he did consulting work for the Natives in the Dease Lake area as well as work for the Canadian International Development Bank (CIDA) in Africa. He finally hung up his hard hat for good when he reached the age of 70. Meanwhile he had moved out of Vancouver and bought a five-acre farm east of Maple Ridge in the Whonnoch area. He suffered a stroke in 2000 and was slowly recovering from it but passed away in 2003.

Bob McEachern

I got some excellent training in materials handling at PKS. The central lesson was that to move dirt, you had to build and maintain a smooth haul road so that the scrapers could travel at high speed. Bob McEachern was my first boss when I began with PKS on the Alberta Resources Railway grade south of Grand Prairie in 1967. I found him to be blunt, but a good guy to work for.

I was supervising a scraper spread one morning, building railway grade and was short of a grader operator. The operator I did have was afraid of working around the scrapers, so he did not keep the haul road smooth. When Bob came out to see how we were doing, I was on the seat of a D9 Cat dozer, pushing dirt. He reamed my ass royally for not keeping the haul road smooth. When I told him that the grader operator was afraid of the scrapers, he told me that I would get more production if I shut down one scraper and put the operator on the other grader. What I liked about Bob was that when he had something to say, he did so immediately, after which it was never ever mentioned again.

I learned another lesson from Bob several years later. I had successfully tendered a job of making and placing "riprap" (rock erosion protection) on the banks of Fraser River near Chilliwack. I was supervising the project and Bob was in overall charge of it from the Vancouver office. We had to use a vibrating grizzly to screen out the undersize rock and this machine kept breaking down. I was ready to give up on it and wanted to replace it, even though it would cost us a lot more than was allowed for in my estimate. Bob would have none of that. He persisted in repairing the thing and with a little more effort at fixing it, he got it to last out the job. My weakness has always been a tendency to give up too quickly when things got tough.

Chapter 21 - The Butterfly Effect

For want of a nail a shoe was lost.
From loss of a shoe a horse went lame.
For want of a horse a cannon was lost.
For want of a cannon a battle was lost.
For want of the battle the war was lost.
Based on an old adage common to several cultures (my words)

According to "Chaos" theory, the flapping of a butterfly's wings in Canada will eventually have consequences for the weather on the other side of the world.

Have you ever stopped to consider how some seemingly inconsequential action can completely alter one's life? We are forever making choices – some of which will have far reaching implications for our future? In "Chaos – the Making of a New Science," James Gleick describes how even the smallest irregularity in an otherwise stable system, will eventually render it unstable. Any change, no matter how small, will someday have huge consequences. On the following pages I will relate how my life was greatly altered by a number of seemingly inconsequential incidents.

During the winter of 1971, I was in the employ of PKS as an estimator and superintendent in their Vancouver office. My marriage had broken down and I had instituted divorce proceedings the previous summer. I had also met Rita, the woman who would become my second wife. Meanwhile work in the head office was very slack, so the manager wanted to send me up to hang out in their Kamloops mechanical shop for the winter.

Knowing that there was no work of consequence for me in Kamloops, and not wanting to leave Vancouver, I asked Bert Norris to have the company give me leave with half salary. PKS had a provision for paying half wages to salaried people who were not needed with the stipulation that they could work elsewhere as long as it was not for a competitor. I mistakenly assumed that it would be easy to find some temporary work and was also looking forward to the extra money as well. It would help me pay for the upcoming divorce.

As it turned out, it was a hasty and ill thought out request. With Christmas coming up, December is a poor month to seek another job. Most companies tend to defer hiring new staff until after the holidays. Another reality I had overlooked was the inevitable question of why I had left my previous employer. Who would want to hire me if I told them I was still on the payroll at PKS? Last, but not least, was the fact that I had only a Grade X formal education.

I sent out a lot of resumes without even getting acknowledgments from the recipients. I replied to advertisements and filled out job applications giving vague responses to the question of why I had left my previous employment. I was getting nowhere! Then one day I saw an ad, by a fellow I knew, for work in the Far East. I had two years previously attended a week-long "management seminar" that this man's company had put on for the "BC Roadbuilders Association." The ad was not very specific about the kind of work that was involved, so I phoned him to find out more about the job.

It turned out that the work was not in my field of expertise. I told the gentleman about my problem in finding some temporary work. I related to him my frustration in not even having my resumes acknowledged. He suggested that I go for career counseling with Dr. John Huberman, a consulting psychologist who was connected with UBC, and who had addressed our group at the Roadbuilders seminar.

I promptly made an appointment and began by taking the "Strong Vocational Interest" test to see what kind of people I shared interests with. From this test it appeared that I shared concerns with people in the human potential field, such as personnel managers, ministers and counselors. Meanwhile I put further tests on hold because I found a job at the Granduc mine near Stewart, BC.

The Granduc Mine

When I arrived at the mine this time, the camp was no longer on a glacier, but they had instead driven a ten-km tunnel to the main workings. I was partnered up with another miner loading long blast holes. It was brutal work for me for the first three weeks because I had not done much physical labor for several years. My partner was a smoker, and it did not seem to bother him to smoke while we handled the dynamite. What I minded most about him was that he also smoked while we were preparing the detonators. When the mine superintendent found out about my background he offered me a job as a shift boss. I had to turn him down and tell him that I was on retainer with PKS.

It was a "Trackless" mine and the hauling equipment was all diesel powered. There was an adequate ventilation system in place, but the Scoop Tram operators did not like the wind blowing on them while they were mucking, so they kept turning it off. The rest of us were therefore often stuck with breathing the diesel-smoke laden air. At the camp portal was a set of steps enclosed in a snow shed. There was one flight of 66 steps, a landing and another flight of 33 steps that provided access from the portal up to the camp. When I first arrived I could easily run from the bottom to the top, taking the steps two at a time. When I left three months later, I could make it only two thirds of the way up before my wind gave out. I coughed up black soot for over a month after I left the mine.

I was elected to serve as a Union Shop Steward soon after arriving. I had no shortage of grievances because the office staff was constantly making mistakes on the payroll. I was not able to convince the men that the company was not trying to cheat them. I really couldn't blame them for thinking that, for it always took a long time to get corrections made. I had an error on one of my first paychecks, and even though I knew the paymaster from before and felt comfortable with talking to the staff, it took me over a month to get the mistake rectified. The basic problem was that the office staff was poorly trained.

The weather at Granduc was pretty mild, but it snowed every day without let-up until early February. By that time the total snowfall for that winter had surpassed 960 inches! The company did not plow snow at the camp - they loaded it into trucks and hauled it away. The road to Stewart was kept open not by plows, but by large snow blowers. Mortars were set up to blast the snow down in areas subject to avalanches before it could build up to depths where it made the road dangerous.

The MBA Program

When I returned to Vancouver in late March, I again saw Dr. Huberman and took a battery of further tests. The results of these tests were impressive enough for him to get me an interview at Simon Fraser University for their Executive MBA program, (a Masters degree in Business Administration). When I wrote the required "GMAT" (standard admissions test for graduate studies in commerce) I scored in the 92nd percentile - high enough to be admitted into the program. This was despite my application being three weeks late, not having the required primary degree and competing with over 300 other applicants for the 60 seats available in the program.

Getting into the MBA program and holding my own (B+ average) with the engineers, accountants and other well-educated people there, boosted my self-esteem beyond measure. I should never have had the self-confidence to start my own consulting business a few years later, had this not happened. Since then I have never again felt intimidated by anyone as far as education or position were concerned.

Before commencing classes in September 1972, we first spent a weekend in a "T-Group" session at the Rosario resort on an island off the

227

coast of Washington. Its purpose was to build class cohesion to help us weather the heavy demands the program would place on us. I remember one session where we were encouraged to share private information with members of our group. One member of my group was a Chinese man who worked at the BC Fish Inspection Laboratory. He had grown up in Mainland China and was imbued with the ethic that the group was more important than the individual. He was not comfortable about sharing personal information and the professor began to pick on him until he finally walked out of the class. He did however come back for the next session. When the professor started in on him again, I finally blew my top and told him to stop it. As soon as I did this another student chimed in and soon several of us let our opinions be known. That put an end to the harassment.

At SFU we began the term with a course in "Small Groups Behaviour." One evening each one of us in our group was told to write down anonymously on separate slips of paper how we viewed each of the other class mates in our group. These opinions were then sorted and distributed to the subjects. I got quite a surprise that night. I got lots of nice comments that I did not think I warranted, but a surprising number of my classmates also saw me as a "loner." It had never occurred to me that I might be regarded as such, but on retrospection realized that I was.

I turned 44 during my first term and was one of only three people in their middle to late forties. The average age of my classmates was probably around 34. They were all people who were in management positions or aspiring to be. Many, if not most of their employers, were supporting them in their schooling. That was not so in my case. When I enrolled, I informed John Patterson, the regional manager of what I was doing but got no encouragement whatsoever. At PKS it was the practice to provide their own in-house managerial training that was tailored to its kind of construction work. However, my immediate supervisor assured me that they would indeed try to keep me in their Vancouver office if possible.

The MBA program required a heavy commitment. It was referred to as "The Divorce Course" because for the married students it put an end to their family life. In my job at PKS I averaged nearly 50 hours week during the off season. The MBA program required another 30 to 40 hours, so it left virtually no free time for other activities. I used a week of my two-week annual vacation at the end of each term to write my term papers. I then paid someone to type them for me.

I married Rita in February 1973 and the following summer I negotiated some logging road construction at Port Neville with Weldwood of Canada. I hauled up a barge load of equipment and kicked off the job in August. In

September another supervisor relieved me and I returned to Vancouver. It was not long before the job experienced cost overruns and fell well behind schedule. I was asked to take in more equipment and finish the project. Since I was the one who had picked up the work in the first place, I felt morally obligated to do so. By the time I returned to Vancouver, I was a month and a half behind in my class-work, so I dropped out for the rest of the semester and lost a full year. My only real complaint was that no one at PKS suggested reimbursing me for part of the tuition I had already paid.

The following year I re-enrolled in the second year classes and wound up with a different group of classmates. I therefore got to know twice as many people as I otherwise would have done. One of them was Fred Mandl, a young personnel manager from Canadian Pacific Airlines who became a close friend.

Fred Mandl

Fred was born in Germany but came to Canada while still in his teens. His father worked for CP Air in Whitehorse, so Fred finished his high-school education there before going on to UBC where he got his degree. At CP Air he worked in "Personnel" and was in charge of a typing pool where they had recently purchased the first semi programmable typewriters. The text was not only printed as it was typed, but also stored on tape. This enabled the typist to edit the work and then reprint it without having to type it all over again. These printers cost $2,000 (in 1973 dollars) and could print out the edited text at speeds of over 100 words per minute!

Having spent his late teen years in Whitehorse, Fred naturally loved the outdoors. He made it a practice each summer to spend a week or two canoeing and/or hiking in the wilds up there. Fred, who was married told me of one incident where he had made arrangements to meet a girlfriend at some lake. Fred's father worked at the Whitehorse Airport, so he did not dare take the girl in with him.

Fred had a plane drop him off at the remote lake and his girlfriend planned to come in a couple of days later. At the lake he found the remains of an old campsite and pitched his tent on a wooden platform he found there. He found an old rusty axe and began to chop firewood with it. The axe was extremely dull, and somehow it deflected off the log he was chopping and into the top of his boot.

He had seriously damaged his foot and could not walk on it at all. During his first night, a grizzly bear came on to the platform, but Fred was able to shoo it away by waving his arms and yelling at it. His girlfriend arrived two days later, but before he could signal to the plane that he was hurt, it was already on its way back to Whitehorse.

Fred decided that he could not afford to wait for their scheduled pickup ten days later, so they decided to hike out. It was a two day hike to the nearest place where they could get help and since there was a well stocked trapper's cabin half way there, they decided to leave almost all their food behind.

Fred made himself a crude crutch and they headed out. By the time he realized that at the rate they were moving, it would take two days to reach the trappers cabin, it was too late to return for the food. They managed to kill a porcupine, but the meat tasted awful. After two long painful days of limping along they finally got to the cabin, only to find that the shelves were as bare as Mother Hubbard's cupboard. It came as a severe shock for the cabin had always been well stocked for as long as Fred had known about it.

It took them two more long days before they finally reached civilization. They had not saved any of the porcupine meat because they had expected to find food at the cabin. They therefore hiked three full days without any food. When they finally reached Whitehorse, his acquaintances all knew that he was not alone. On the flight back to Vancouver, a friend of his wife came over to him and told him what she thought about him. His wife was probably the only person who did not find out about the incident although by now she must have had a good idea of what was going on.

Fred wound up as part of a group of software developers who produced personnel programs. In that role he made numerous trips to Russia and also to a number of African countries. He also became a permanent teacher for one day a week at the BC Institute of Technology.

Dr. John Gillies

In my class of 1972 was a doctor who worked for the Federal government at the Haney Correctional Centre. Until he enrolled in the MBA program he had been playing hockey in a commercial league three nights a week. After enrolling, he cut this to two nights a week.

Like many hockey players, John had trouble with fluid build up in his knees due to old injuries. However, he did not go to another doctor to deal with this problem. He inserted a hypodermic needle and drained it off himself whenever it became a problem! I can't imagine very many people who would be able to do this.

During his second year at SFU, John decided to open a private practice. I had by now learned that he never slept more than four hours a night, but I could not imagine how he handled the workload. He told me that his secretary was very efficient and knowledgeable. She not only typed all of his term papers, but was able to tend to most of his government work as well. He did however, cut his hockey down to one night a week.

Dr. Cal Hoyt

Years later while I lived in Whitehorse, I occasionally flew to Vancouver to attend opera. One person I encountered there every time was Dr. Cal Hoyt. He had been in charge of the MBA program for most of the years I was there, but is since deceased. He had taken on the top job at the Vancouver Opera Society. He had also been one of my favorite professors at SFU.

Dr. Vergin

Dr. Vergin taught the "Operations Research" course together with Dr. Bill Wedley and a third professor who played French horn at the Vancouver Symphony. Vergin had just finished working for Marlon Brando at an island near Tahiti.

Marlon Brando had decided to build a resort on this island and hired Dr. Vergin to supervise its construction. Whenever Marlon Brando ran short of money, he would just do some more film work. Dr. Vergin said it was as if he just went and turned on a money tap whenever he needed to.

As the work was nearing completion, Dr. Vergin began entering into contracts with people in the tourist industry in order to make the resort well known and get it up and running profitably as quickly as possible. When Marlon Brando learned of this, he ordered him to stop and to cancel all the arrangements he had already made. Marlon could not stand to have his resort sullied by ordinary tourists. It was to be a get-away for him and his friends.

In my final year at SFU, in addition to taking a course in "Research Methods," I was expected to complete a research project. I was able to get Dr. Bill Wedley to be my mentor and I was going to test the "Delphi" research method. This method seeks to build consensus in a group by feeding back its collective opinions in some specific study. I was going to see if group opinion could be influenced with biased or false feed back. The implication, if such proved to be correct, would be to discredit this consensus building technique.

By the time I completed my research design, Dr. Wedley had moved to Waterloo, Ontario. He was however very pleased with my work and I was ready to start the project by the time he left SFU. I was first obliged to find another professor to oversee my work, but by then they were all spoken for. I finally did get Dr. Gary Mauser to agree to supervise my research, but he did not approve of any of the work I had already done. His opinions were diametrically opposed to those of Dr. Wedley.

Since my wife was a schoolteacher at Eric Hamber Senior Secondary school, I thought that the Teachers Federation might cooperate with me by giving me access to a group of teachers to use as my test subjects. They soon disabused me of that hope and informed me that they did their own research. They were not at all interested in anything a non-teacher might wish to do.

By this time I was finding it increasingly difficult to keep up with my work at PKS. I was getting one bout of flu or cold after another. The manager had begun to ask me pointed questions about my health. I was allowed five years from when I first enrolled in the MBA program to complete my project. Since I had already lost a year when I was at Port Neville, my time was running out. I could have applied for a short extension, but I could not see how I was going to finish the project considering the opposition from both my advisor and the teachers, so when my health continued to deteriorate I finally let the project die.

By this time I had been on thyroid medication for over six years, but it had not occurred to me to be retested. When I was finally referred to a specialist, I was shocked to learn that my T4 level registered 4 on a scale where a normal range was between 7 and 13. The doctor recommended I keep it near the top of that range. He then increased my dosage by 250% and my health slowly returned, but too late to resume my research project. Nevertheless, the self-confidence I developed during this period was by far the most important achievement of my life.

Chapter 22 - A Memorable Holiday

Have you ever considered the consequences of the way you pack for a trip, or what flights you book when you have a choice amongst alternatives?

In 1975 Rita and I decided to take a trip to the Canary Islands for Christmas. We were to fly from Vancouver via Seattle to New York with United Airlines, and from there to Madrid and then to Tenerife with Iberia Airlines. However, a week before our scheduled departure, United went on strike. Iberia switched their flight from New York to Montreal, and got us seats to Montreal with Air Canada, but a day early.

The morning of our departure dawned clear and cool. That is, it was clear at 1,000 feet but cool and very foggy at ground level. We were up at four - in our seats at seven and still in our seats at eleven when they finally cancelled the flight. By mid afternoon we might have given up scrambling for other flights, but we had already paid for the holiday so I was afraid it might be difficult to get our money refunded. By late afternoon we were somehow able to find seats on a flight out of Abbotsford for late that night. It was to Toronto, not to Montreal, but nothing to worry about, they said.

We almost missed our bus due to a mix-up over the tickets, but somehow we got on that plane out of Abbotsford at 2:00 A.M. Sleep was out of the question for me. After the near miss, I was too tense. We landed in Toronto the next morning in a raging blizzard! Of course there were no flights leaving for Montreal under those conditions. Somehow the weather cleared sufficiently for us to leave and we got to Mirabelle Airport just nicely in time for the Iberia flight that was to leave at 9:00 P.M. Thank God for booking a day early from Vancouver!

We boarded the airport bus and headed for the plane that was parked out on the runway. We didn't get there! The bus stopped on the runway and we just sat there. The minutes ticked away - half an hour, then an hour, and finally two hours. Two hours spent waiting while they cleaned up a fuel spill at the plane.

We were two hours late out of Mirabelle, and two hours late into Madrid. It was 45 hours since leaving home and 45 hours without a wink of sleep. I couldn't relax! I was still in the same clothes too and without a decent wash.

We missed our Tenerife flight of course. Soon we were scrambling again. Have you ever been in the Madrid airport? The line of wickets seemed to stretch at least a quarter of a mile from one end to the other.

The bored attendants shunted us back and forth from the wicket at one end to the one at the far end. Each agent insisted that the person at the other end of the line was responsible for us. We finally found a sympathetic attendant who spoke English fluently. She found us a flight for four o'clock that afternoon.

Waiting, endless waiting, from 10 A.M. to 4 P.M. without a place to rest. Then at 4:00 P.M. our flight schedule was postponed to 6:00 P.M., and two hours later it was put off yet again, to 8:00 P.M. Despite somehow missing our bus out to the plane, we did get on it and we did get to Tenerife by about midnight.

What a relief, we were finally there! It had been sixty hours without sleep and sixty hours without a decent wash or a change of clothes. By this time it seemed that my clothes might easily walk away under their own steam. Fortunately we would soon be in our hotel room. I drooled at the thought of a nice hot shower. What a foolish thought! We had arrived but of course my luggage had not! By the time I had negotiated the line-ups and registered my missing luggage, another hour and a half was gone, and so had our ride into town.

We were lucky. We found a cab and got to the hotel by 2:00 A.M. No one showed us to our room. We groped around in the dark until we eventually found the master switch which let us turn on the lights. At last I could get out of those filthy clothes and climb into that nice hot shower. Did I say hot shower? The water was ice cold! I didn't know that the pilot light was out and by that time I was really too tired to care. I was soon asleep, asleep for the first time in over sixty hours.

In the morning we got the pilot light for the hot water lit and we finally had hot showers, but I could hardly endure putting on those same filthy clothes again. I walked bravely out on to the street, and into the first store I saw. Of course I managed to find the only store in town where no one understood a word of English. Nevertheless I did find some clothes. Furthermore they fit, and unbelievably, I had a great time getting them. My luggage showed up five days later and we had a wonderful holiday despite what one might call a "trying start".

I learned a couple of useful things on that trip. One was to keep a few clean clothes with me, and the other was to choose our flights carefully during peak travel times. When we flew to Copenhagen three Christmases later there were no direct flights from Vancouver so we chose a flight that made connections in Seattle (close to home). This turned out to be a wise choice for the worst snowstorm in memory shut down the Copenhagen airport for two days. When we finally got back to Seattle, we had of course missed our connecting flight, but the airline was able to bus us back to Vancouver.

Chapter 23 - The North Country

Fort Nelson

I left PKS in the late spring of 1974 and worked first for Chinook as a superintendent and estimator, next for Standard General as their Chief Estimator, then for Jack Cewe Contracting as a superintendent in charge of replacing temporary repairs with permanent ones for BC Hydro. There my crews did over 5,000 repairs throughout the Greater Vancouver area in just 5 months. I returned to PKS in the early summer of 1976 to work as an estimator full time. In January of 1978, I tendered a 16-mile road-surfacing project at Fort Nelson for the Department of Public Works (DPW).

I had first flown through Fort Nelson on my way to United Keno Hill mines in 1953. This time I flew up in January to look at the surfacing job before estimating it. The first person I saw after stepping off the plane was George Dvorak. George had been the mine foreman at Cowichan Copper while I worked there 16 years earlier. It was he who had kept Don Ormrod on full salary for several months after he had fractured his leg in a drunken brawl. George now owned and operated an oil-field supply business and his wife taught at the local high school. I saw George just one more time, when he invited me to a party at his house. He was killed the following winter when he got caught in a snowstorm while flying his own small plane.

We turned out to be the low bidder on the road surfacing project and I went back up to supervise it. I arrived in Fort Nelson in early April just as the oil-rigs were moving out. I remember seeing large trucking rigs parked along both sides of the Alaska Highway from one end of town to the other. The place was so busy that I should not have been able to find accommodation, had I not booked it well in advance.

he near end of my project was 25 miles south of town – too far to commute. I therefore had to set up a camp on the project. Meanwhile I stayed in a motel unit that was adjacent to and owned by the Fort Hotel. When I arrived, the bars were crowded with oil men but within a couple of weeks, these people were gone and Fort Nelson returned to a more leisured pace. Nevertheless, the bars on Saturday night were still busy places during most of my stay there.

The first social function I attended was "Oliver," a play staged by the local high school. It was the first time I had seen it, and I was awestruck by the quality of the acting! It is a wonderful story and I have since seen both the stage version and movie versions of it, but they have not affected me as deeply as that first time in Fort Nelson. This experience left me with a warm feeling for this little northern town that might otherwise have seemed pretty ordinary.

The Stewart-Cassiar highway had been completed a few years earlier and one of the principal contractors on it was Keene Construction from Fort Nelson. I met many equipment operators who had worked for Bob Keene, but I had not met him personally until shortly after I arrived at Fort Nelson. In his heyday, Bob Keene had owned much of the town, but when I arrived he owned only the Fort Hotel, and was shortly to lose it too. Meanwhile it seemed to me that he was one of his own best customers. He appeared quite inebriated each time I saw him. He invited me out to his ranch, but I never felt inclined to go. When I left Fort Nelson, Keene was reputedly doing poorly, but I have since heard that he had gotten control of his drinking and was once again doing well.

Our surfacing project entailed the crushing and placing of 4 inches of gravel as well as producing and placing a like quantity of asphalt. The job therefore included a sizable amount of trucking. At the local truckers insistence I attended a meeting with them to which I brought Ray Wood, who was my Job Sponsor from the Vancouver office. The locals all owned heavy-duty trucks, but since we were limited to legal sized loads by our contract, these trucks were not economically feasible – especially since they did not have trailers. Those truckers were most unhappy when we told them that we could not afford to use them, and that we would be using a trucking contractor from the Fraser Valley. This contractor had trucks especially suited for the work and could haul the gravel at a much lower cost. Ray and I both had some misgivings about getting out of that meeting with a whole skin. He was not too happy with me for getting him into such a meeting in the first place!

A couple of months later I was having dinner with Len Shumlick, the project supervisor from DPW, and his wife. We were seated at a table next to two local truckers who were both drunk. During the meal, in addition to verbally abusing me, they threatened to catch

Crushing gravel on the Fort Nelson pro-ject.
Photo from the author's collection

me in a dark alley some night and beat me up. This never came to pass, but I did watch my step whenever I came into town for an evening.

We set up our construction camp in the gravel pit where our sub-contractor was crushing our gravel. We dug a shallow well in the pit to provide our camp with water. We tested the water and found it was very hard, but fit for human consumption. Despite installing a water softener to reduce the mineral content, it was not suitable for washing white clothes as one of the women from DPW soon discovered when her wash turned yellow. The water tasted fine, but it had a queer characteristic – when mixed with rye whiskey, it turned the drink as dark as rum and coke.

One day a black bear wandered into our camp in search of food. The door to the "Rec." trailer had been left open and a card table stood just inside the doorway with a plate of cookies and an urn full of hot coffee on it. In trying to get the cookies, the bear tipped the coffee urn over onto itself and got scalded. Instead of going out the way it came in, it jumped through a window – through both glass and screen and in the process knocked over the TV stand smashing the TV. You might think that being scalded would deter it, but that bear was fresh out of hibernation and it was hungry. It was back within an hour. This time it went under the cookhouse trailer and tore a propane line apart. That could have been disastrous. A spark might have blown the kitchen into orbit! We phoned the game department in Fort Nelson and got permission to shoot the bear.

My gravel spread foreman's first name was Sherman. He told me that he made a good living as a trapper during the wintertime, but he surprised me when he told me that his trap line was located in the Richmond-Delta area. I had always assumed that trapping was done in the far north, but he reputedly earned close to $30,000 a season at a time when few people earned that much in a whole year.

One night a few of us were in town for drinks and dancing at the local oasis, when a young prostitute propositioned me. She wanted $70 for her services, which I graciously declined. However, I told her I would be glad to pay her that amount if she could take out Sherman without his knowing that she was a hooker and that I was paying for it. She tried but failed because she was far too direct and did not take her time. Sherman had ridden into town with me. On our way back to the camp that night he told me about it. He was so elated that he was almost walking on air! Poor Sherman, his elation was short lived. I had told the others at our table what I had done, and the next morning one of them let the cat out of the bag and quickly deflated Sherman's ego.

We had two graders on the job. One of the operators was very slow, but he had superb eyes and was able to spread the gravel to the exact depths required. The second operator was faster, but could not control his blade well enough to meet the exacting standards. I therefore had him laying out the gravel to the approximate depth while the better operator came behind and finished the job.

We placed and compacted the gravel in two 2-inch lifts. It should have been pretty straight forward work, but I soon learned otherwise. Spreading and placing the gravel was not the problem, compacting it was! There was a dearth of fines (<200 sieve) in the product. Ideally the fines should account for about 2 – 3% of the total and ours was under 1%. This made it almost impossible to compact. We literally wore the gravel out trying to compact it. We had asked for permission to add some fines to the gravel, but had been denied. When we were almost 60% complete, DPW finally allowed us to spread some fines and mix it in with the crushed gravel. From then on, it was a snap, but we were already well over budget for this part of the job.

Asphalt paving is not done in the rain. Once the asphalt has been mixed, it must be used before it cools off, or be wasted. It was therefore important to halt mixing well before a shower stopped our laying operations so that we could use up the asphalt already en route to the paving machine before the rain hit. Our plant was set up at the gravel pit – 4 miles from the near end of the project. Summer showers were frequent and unpredictable. Furthermore, it could be pouring rain at the plant, but be sunny at the paving site or vice versa. Sometimes a thunderstorm would head directly for the paving site, and then abruptly veer off to one side or the other. Trying to second-guess the weather became a constant preoccupation for us.

Our paving plant was decrepit. The company was planning to upgrade it from a batch to a drum mixing process and was therefore reluctant to spend any money overhauling it. This led to constant problems for us. A day seldom went by without a mechanical breakdown. On one single day we once had eleven such interruptions. Fortunately, I didn't have much hair, so there wasn't much to pull out or to turn grey.

On one of Ray Wood's visits while I was still at the motel, I fried T-bone steaks for us the night before he returned to Vancouver. I seasoned them with salt, pepper and lots of garlic. Ray appeared to relish the steak, but he later complained to me that his wife would not let him near her for two days afterwards on account of his breath.

A company called Miann Contracting Ltd. from Prince George was reconstructing a section of the Alaska Highway north of, and adjacent to our project. The owners were two Dutch brothers named Joe and Frank

Welling. They had both been "Project Residents" for BC Rail a few years earlier. I had met Frank when we were bidding a piece of the Dease Lake extension near Takla Lake. He had taken a liking to me and both he and Joe kept after me to come to work for them. I finally agreed to do so, but only after the paving job was finished. When the paving completion kept getting deferred because of our mechanical problems, I finally quit PKS and turned the job over to my assistant.

Miann Contracting Ltd.

My first job with Miann was giving notice of "claim" for changes in their contract. Unfortunately I was too late for a number of items for which we could have claimed substantial amounts - the deadline for claiming them, having already elapsed before I got there.

The previous year I had convinced the manager of Plateau Mills sawmill that they should rebuild their mill yard because their log loaders were bogging down badly in it. I had brought out a couple of engineers from Associated Engineering in Edmonton to look at it. The mill finally called tenders for this work just before I quit PKS. I was able to get Miann on to the bidders list in time to tender it. We were the low bidders and the Welling brothers asked me to supervise it since they were still busy at Fort Nelson. Since none of Miann's equipment was available to me, I rented everything I needed from dealers in Prince George.

Doug Melinchuk, my night-shift foreman and I were on the site late one afternoon when a representative of the equipment owner arrived and began to inspect the machines. Doug said; "Holy Cow! Frank and I came out and disconnected the hour meters last Sunday." The equipment representative soon found out that the hour meters weren't working, but he did not ask me anything about it. He probably suspected that it was no accident that they were unhooked. I managed to settle the final number of hours with them because I had kept meticulous records. I was pretty shaken up by this and got Miann's promise that nothing like this would happen again. Despite having to use rented equipment to construct the entire project, I was still able to complete the job on budget.

That winter I successfully tendered a "starter dam" for the Lornex mine near Ashcroft. It required the excavation of unsuitable materials down to where there was good solid clay. Keeping the excavation dewatered was a challenge. There was so much peat floating around on top of the water that it was constantly plugging the pump's inlet. Finding a pump that could handle the suspended solids was another challenge. Nevertheless, we completed the job and since the equipment would normally be idle during the winter, it provided a positive cash flow, even though it did not meet the budget.

The following spring another incident made it obvious to me that the promise of the previous fall had been an empty one. In preparing to sell their earthmovers, the two brothers obtained and installed some second hand hour meters that gave the impression that the machines had fewer than their actual hours. It was equivalent to turning back the odometer on a car. I knew then that I would have to quit. Meanwhile, Rita who was teaching at the Eric Hamber High School in Vancouver had given notice she was leaving. We had sold our Vancouver house and had bought one in Prince George, so we were committed to moving there.

That same spring (1979) we picked up a job building a forest road at Burns Lake that was jointly funded by BC Highways and the Forest Service. Ralph Wood, a young technician from the Forest Service at Smithers supervised the job. He turned out to be a godsend for me the following year when I incorporated my consulting business.

During the summer of 1979 I developed a gut problem that took me nearly a year to get diagnosed. I quit my job with Miann in September to remove the aggravation that I felt had brought on the problems. My doctor, like so many others, never really examined me. How could he? The average visit lasted only five minutes! He asked me very few questions - just sent me for this or that test. Next he referred me to a specialist of Internal Medicine who didn't examine me either – just sent me for more random tests. As the problem worsened, I experienced severe pain with every meal, to the point where I developed an aversion to food and began losing weight. During this time I decided to incorporate my own consulting business and did so on January 17, 1980.

PART IV

THE CONSULTING YEARS

Chapter 24 - Prince George

Prince George

When Rita and I moved to Prince George, it had a population of 68,000. The city sprawled from the College heights area in the west to the industrial area in the south and up to Chief Lake road in the north. From the north end to the south is a distance of over 20 kilometers. We bought a three-bedroom house in the "bowl" - an area in the lower part of the city. From our house to the city centre was just over a mile and a half. The Prince George Golf and Country Club was a mere three miles away. One thing I liked about this city was that I could reach the downtown or the golf course in five minutes, or I could be out of town in ten minutes. That is very different from living in a place like Vancouver, where it normally takes over an hour to get out into the countryside even when the traffic is not heavy.

Prince George is at the geographical centre of BC. It boasts three pulp mills and several sawmills. Without the woods industry, it would be only a fraction of its present size. Because it is situated at the crossroads of Highways 97 and 16, it is also a transportation center. When we lived there it had two colleges, a Roman Catholic one called the "Prince George College" as well as the "College of New Caledonia." Now it is also home to "The University of the North."

Being a "blue-collar" town, one would not expect to find a lot of cultural activities, but it did have a playhouse that hosted four productions each winter. It had a small art gallery as well. For me the most important feature was the volunteer symphony orchestra that performed under the baton of a paid concertmaster. It staged several productions each year. Although it sometimes sounded a bit ragged at the beginning of its opening number, it was not too bad once the musicians got warmed up.

I incorporated my consulting business (Wapiti Consulting Inc.) on January 17, 1980 in Prince George. I chose this name because I wanted something western that had a nice ring to it and was not already in use. I wrongly assumed that everybody knew that wapiti was the proper name for elk and that the stress is on the first syllable (wop'-i-tee).

Over the next eight years, I prepared cost estimates and project bids for small contractors – companies that did not have this kind of expertise.

In addition to this I also provided supervisory, administrative, training, **preparation of contract claims and other typical construction services.**

When I first began my business, I hand delivered a flyer to each prospective client, which outlined my services and my charge-out rates. This produced exactly one client, a timber company located at South Hazelton, but I did only one job for it before the provincial government purchased it.

My former employer gave me very little work during my first year, but they had previously been bragging to a lot of people about what a smart "engineer" they had hired, so a few contractors began to call on me. In addition to this, the people at the local Finning Tractor branch also referred clients to me. Even so, my first year in business would have been mediocre, were it not for landing a two month contract with the BC Forest Service at Smithers.

Shortly before leaving Miann Contracting to begin my own consulting business, I had successfully tendered a unique road project that was jointly funded by the Ministries of Forests and of Highways. The Forest Service was in charge of the project and they sent out a young chap named Ralph Wood to oversee it. Until then he had never seen large earthmovers in use. Being very inquisitive, he had many questions for the contractor, but the owners did not bother to give him the time of day.

Because no one on the job would help him, he began phoning me with his questions. The following year when I was no longer working for Miann, he continued calling me for advice. Since I was not that busy, and also because I can't turn down someone asking me for help, I returned his (long distance) calls - usually at my own expense. Miann derided me for wasting my time with the guy and told me I would never get anything out of it.

I of course wasn't expecting anything, but to my big surprise, it did come! Ralph Wood brought Art Sherman, the Regional Engineer to see me with an offer of two months consulting for the Forest Service in Smithers, BC. That job made a huge difference for me. It made my first year's financial results outstanding!

Art Sherman

When I met Art, he lived by himself on the south side of the Bulkley River between Smithers and Houston, BC. I was told that he had been married once, but that it lasted for only three weeks. Art not only held a degree in Forestry Engineering, but in law as well. He originally came from the U.S., but he also spent a number of years in the Far East.

Art was somewhat strange. A few years earlier he had actually fired shots in the general direction of some tourists who had dared cross the footbridge over the river to his land. I went to visit him one evening, but he did not hear or see me coming. When I knocked at his door, he yelled; "Get out of here!" As soon as he found out it was I, he ordered me to come in for a visit and have tea

A forest road being built near Houston BC. *Photo taken by the author.*

with him. His house looked as though a tornado had recently been through it, but he was obviously comfortable in it.

During my stint with the Forest Service, I once accompanied Art on an overnight excursion to New Aiyansh and Greenville and thoroughly enjoyed his company. I don't think I would have liked to be his superior though. On one occasion Victoria sent him a directive on a new policy. Art wrote back and gave them an engineering, as well as a legal critique on it, neither of which was complimentary.

Art was an expert at handling the Forestry's finances. His political masters would typically send him a directive in February to spend a large amount of money by the end of the fiscal year on March 31st. Doing so at that time of year would have been a huge waste, so he found ways of hiding the money until it could be spent judiciously.

Sha-Nor Contracting

Len Rushton and his brother-in-law, Earl Liston came to see me in Smithers while I was still working with the Forest Service there. I had earlier (unsuccessfully) bid a job for them at the Noranda mine at Boss Mountain. They wanted me to help them get subcontract work on a highway project in Prince George on which Columbia Bitulithic was the contractor. I had earlier bid this project for L.G. Scott and Sons of Kitimat, so I was very familiar with it.

I provided them with suggested prices, but told them that I would need to know how much of the work would carry on into 1981, since we would have to make allowance for cost inflation on that portion. Unfortunately, they were so anxious to get the work, they forgot to do that, furthermore, they cut their unit price for providing water for gravel compaction. This was an important bid item, so I was quite concerned about their price for it.

The finished forest road.
Photo taken by the author.

After they were awarded the work they asked me to come and run the project for them. I agreed to do so for that fall (1980), but said I would gradually withdraw my services the following spring because I did not want to tie myself to a single client. I shortly learned that they were both truckers and had neither road building nor any previous contracting experience of any kind. Had I known this earlier, I would never have helped them get the work. Nevertheless, I was obliged to train them as construction progressed.

I put Len in charge of keeping the equipment maintained and fueled, and I made Earl the foreman in charge of the earth moving. Len's wife looked after the office for us, and Earl's wife became a flag person. I also hired my son to come and supervise construction of "binwall" retaining walls. Len's wife would probably have been the best supervisory trainee, but I doubt the crew would have been ready for a female boss.

Sha-Nor's work consisted of earthwork and gravelling for widening Highway 97 from two lanes to four through part of Prince George. The project began at the Nechako Bridge and proceeded up a short hill, then through an industrial section and terminated at the Chief Lake Road intersection.

After the slide. *Photo taken by the author.*

Near the top of the hill was a steep embankment that dropped off to a creek over one hundred feet below. Our first operation was to strip the topsoil off this embankment so that it could be widened for the additional lanes. We used a 225-Caterpillar backhoe to excavate and load the topsoil into trucks that hauled it into stockpile for reuse.

On the morning of the second day the hoe had just been fired up. It was waiting for the first truck to back in for a load, when suddenly and without warning, the ground slid out from underneath it! The hoe hurtled down the embankment on top of a large mass of mud and wound up in the

245

creek below. The operator had the presence of mind to swing the hoe's boom to the low side and interpose it between the machine and a large tree that it snapped like a dry twig. The operator was barely out of the machine's cab when a second slide came down and almost buried the backhoe. A minute longer and the operator would have been imprisoned inside the machine for several hours.

Binwall construction.
Photo taken by the author.

It turned out that the Highway Maintenance Division people were aware that there was water seepage in the embankment, but the Highway Construction Branch was not privy to this important information.

Getting the hoe out of the creek and back up the hill was a big problem. We sent a D8 dozer down to the creek to dig out the hoe, but then neither machine was able to climb back up the steep slope because the ground was too soft. We actually broke the dozer's inch and a quarter winch line while trying.

An improperly secured culvert on the back of a truck ruined a holiday for these people.
Photo taken by the author.

The local Fisheries officer had been on site before lunch and he promised to be back right afterwards. When he did not show up by 3:00 PM, I gave the go-ahead to walk the machines up the creek a hundred and fifty yards to where they could get them out on to an adjacent road. During this maneuver, we also cleaned out the old tires and tin cans that littered the stream-bed. The cost to the contractor for having the whole equipment spread sitting idle for a day was far greater than any likely fine we might have had to pay.

When the Fisheries officer returned the following morning and found out what we had done, he was livid! He immediately laid charges against the company, but when it finally got to court, the judge threw out the case. Not only had the officer been remiss in not returning to the site as promised, but we left the stream-bed in a better condition than we found it.

This episode turned out to have a silver lining. Sha-Nor had been short of operating capital and the bank refused to provide any unless the principals put up their homes as collateral. This they were loath to do.

The slide necessitated a major revision in the road embankment design that included drilling, blasting, hauling and placing a large amount of large rock adjacent to the creek on which to place the fill. I was able to negotiate a price for this work that provided us with a healthy profit. This profit provided the operating capital and it made the difference between a profit and a loss on the overall project.

It took a while, but by early summer the following year, Earl was beginning to supervise the work effectively. Whenever Earl just stood by and watched the equipment performing ineffectively, I would ask him; "Earl, do you think you can afford to let them operate that way when you are getting only $2.40 per cubic yard?" It was a strange situation. They were my bosses and were paying me to supervise them. I tried to teach Earl how to check the grades with a hand level and a survey rod. He seemed to be afraid to use them until he had over-excavated a few times too many and had to replace the material without getting paid for it. On two occasions the scrapers ripped holes in a six-foot diameter storm sewer. Even though it was covered by insurance, it was still expensive. After these episodes, it did not take Earl very long before he mastered the art of shooting grades.

There were other mishaps due to inexperienced construction workers. A man was hauling a small culvert on the back of a flat-deck truck without securing it properly. As luck would have it, the culvert pivoted on the truck bed just as the driver met a pickup truck towing a holiday trailer. These people were on their way out of town for two weeks of vacation. When

I let this inattentive operator go after he almost rolled his packer over the bank the second time.
Photo taken by the author.

the culvert poked a hole in the trailer wall it resulted in a delayed vacation. On another occasion a packer operator almost rolled his machine off the embankment. When he did it the second time I did not dare keep him on for he would surely have killed himself.

The following year, I got involved in bidding highway and railway jobs in to the Tumbler Ridge area so I eventually left Earl and Len completely on their own. It was with some trepidation that I visited them the following Christmas. They put my concerns to rest when they told me that the job had actually worked out well for them. They had not only provided all the family members with well paying jobs, but they had also gotten a fair amount of equity in two pieces of equipment. Just the same, from that time on, I always checked out my clients' in-house expertise before bidding any work for them.

Frank and Joe

Frank Welling on the Fort Nelson job in 1978. *Photo taken by the author.*

Frank and Joe came from Holland where they had both worked briefly in underground coal mines. They both had technical diplomas and both of them had worked for BC Rail as "Project Residents" on railway construction before starting Miann Contracting Ltd. They had an older brother named Al who owned a Honda car dealership in Holland. He probably helped them out financially when they first began contracting.

When I began working for them in 1978, Joe was 31 and Frank 41 years of age. Although Joe was ten years younger than Frank, he was the undisputed boss. However, Frank's presence in the partnership was vital for he was an eternal optimist and could always see the rosy aspects of a job, whereas, Joe could see nothing but doom and gloom. This was especially true whenever water played a significant role on a job. When we built the starter dam in the Highland Valley for the Lornex mine in 1979, Joe was beside himself with worry and might have pulled off the job were it not for Frank putting things in perspective.

Although I worked for them for just over a year, my association with them continued much longer. Except for the first year in my consulting business, I bid all of their work for them until late 1987. I also prepared successful contract claims for them on several occasions in addition to helping them with other engineering aspects of their work.

Westmin Resources

Twenty-one years after I left Western Mines in Strathcona Park, I was back. This time it was to bid on a tailings dam and for relocating Myra and Lynx creeks. The company had changed its name. It was now called Westmin Resources Ltd. We bid the earthwork portion of this project as a "joint venture" between Miann Contracting and Edgeworth Construction to Farmer Construction of Victoria who was the general contractor on the project.

As sometimes happens, we did not meet our budget on the Tailings dam work because we could not attain the production I had estimated for the scraper fleet. The ground was so soft that the scrapers could not move at a

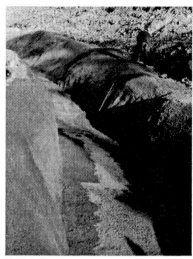

Lynx Creek relocation. Channel is lined with shotcrete. *Photo taken by the author.*

decent pace. Furthermore, some of the equipment was breaking down frequently, so our costs were substantially over budget. However, on the creek relocation work the rock quantities were much greater than anticipated so we were able to drill and blast the rock far below the cost I had allowed for. What we lost on the tailings dam, we more than made up for on the Lynx Creek relocation.

The mine management was most unhappy about our rock price on the creek relocation and refused to pay when the money was due. They were hoping to pressure us into reducing our prices by starving our cash flow. They of course turned a blind eye to our losses on the other portion of our work and to the fact that they had accepted our unit prices and did not have a legal leg to stand on.

I am not certain how we did in the end. My clients probably took a substantial cut in pay in order to get the job over with and get their money. In dealing with government agencies, collecting on agreed upon quantities is never a problem. You get paid for what you have done. Mining companies however, are notorious for trying to bargain with the low bidders after the tendering process is over.

Tumbler Ridge & Alaska Highway

In 1981, I had successfully bid two major BC Rail projects that turned out to be financially rewarding for Miann. The following year the brothers both bought new Mercedes cars and Joe bought out Frank's share in the company. Frank retired to Vancouver Island where he built himself a lovely home in Central Saanich. However, three years later when I picked up a job for Miann on the Alaska Highway north of Pink Mountain. Frank came back to run the job because he was already bored with retirement. The following spring, they started a new company that I had the honor of naming Exco (short for excavation contractor).

For all his optimism, Frank was very negative in some ways. He was forever criticizing everyone and everything. It got so that I did not want to be around him if I could avoid it. However, following the Pink Mountain job, I bid a lot of jobs for them in Alberta and Frank who by then had split up from his wife, drove me out to look at many of them. Being together with Frank on long car trips afforded me the opportunity to really get to know him well. He loved good classical music and was actually a very cultured person. During these trips I not only got over my antipathy to him, but also grew to respect and like him very much.

A Bear Story

Pete Olexyn, author's son Don and Tina Welling. *Photo taken by the author.*

In 1985 while we were doing the Trutch Bypass job on the Alaska Highway near Pink Mountain, my son Don was back at UBC taking his Engineering degree. When school was out in early April, he came up and looked after the surveying duties for us. Frank Welling's son John, who had also finished his studies for the term, was on the job as a laborer.

One Sunday morning John and Don decided to go for a hike. They took along John's Black Labrador dog and drove to the base of a mountain some miles to the west of our camp. They were hiking up a steep hillside with John in the lead, when Don saw a black bear crouching down behind a boulder above them. He whispered urgently to John: "Stop! John, stop! There's a bear up ahead." John replied; "Yeah, sure," and kept on walking. Don, his voice more urgent repeated his warning and John sensing that urgency finally stopped.

The bear then emerged from behind the rock and began walking down the hill directly towards them, but the dog had still not noticed it. Don scrambled up a nearby tree but John passed him on his way up, as he too got anxious to get off the ground. The dog finally saw the bear and tried to chase it away, but the bear ignored it and kept coming. Don pulled out his belt axe and sat poised to defend himself, but the dog was finally able to divert the bear away from the tree and it eventually left the area. Don and John both stayed in the tree for another twenty minutes and were just preparing to descend when a grizzly bear walked by a few yards away. The dog saw it immediately and barked at it, but the bear ignored the dog and maintained its direction and its pace as though it were not there.

On their way back down the hill they almost stumbled over yet another bear, but this one was gone in a flash with the dog in hot pursuit. When they returned to camp they were still pretty shaken up over their experience. After that incident they did not go on any more hikes.

The event might not have been so scary except that a few weeks earlier, a deranged black bear had killed and eaten a tree planter a few miles to the north near Prophet River. On that occasion, the bear attacked a party of four tree planters. Two of the planters ran, and the other two scaled a nearby tree. The bear went up the tree and dragged one of them down and ate him. The following day when the game warden arrived in a helicopter, it charged the machine and was shot from a distance of only ten feet. An autopsy on the bear revealed that it suffered from worms in its brain.

Chapter 25 - The Yukon

Whitehorse

In January of 1986, I successfully tendered a stretch of the Alaska Highway for Exco. The job was 50 miles west of Whitehorse in the Yukon. Frank went up to supervise the work and I went along to help with engineering and administration. During our trips to Alberta, Frank began complaining about indigestion and after we got to Whitehorse it got worse.

Placing a culvert in new road alignment.
Photo taken by the author.

Finally in May when Frank developed great difficulty in eating, he went in for exploratory surgery and the doctors found that he had widespread cancer. I took over supervision of the work, but when Joe came out and changed everything around without first telling me, I told him to run it himself. Things went downhill from then on for Joe did not have his heart in his work and he did not spend enough of his time at the site.

Joe Welling unloading a hoe on the Kusawa road. *Photo taken by the author.*

Frank was shortly admitted to the Cancer Clinic in Vancouver and was treated with chemotherapy, but died in September. With Frank's passing, I lost a very dear friend, but for his brother Joe, the loss was calamitous! He was unable to function well without Frank's presence and lost a lot of money on the jobs.

After Frank's death, Joe quit construction and for a while owned a garage in Prince George, but he did not do well there either. He tried his hand at a few other things, but with dismal results. Eventually he left his wife and moved in with a girlfriend in California where he still lives. He was employed as a dealer at a gambling casino at Reno for a while but is no longer doing that either. The last time I spoke with him he told me he was unemployed.

Frank's wife Mia, developed severe paranoia and was unable to function well for several years. A year after Frank died, she called me and asked me to come over to see her – she needed someone to talk to. While I was there she showed me Frank's will. Joe's lawyer in Prince George (Gary Brown) had prepared it just before Frank died. It was exceedingly long and may have been difficult for Frank to read since he was literally on his deathbed. Frank left the house to Mia and the rest of his estate to his two children. Joe was the executor and was to turn everything over to the children, but there was no deadline for when to do this! I wonder if there was anything left to inherit.

Mia was eventually prescribed medication that returned her to normal and she is now in a long-term relationship with a new partner. I believe that their son John lives in the Victoria area. Their daughter Tina is married, has a couple of children and lives in Whitehorse where her husband works for Northwestel. When I last saw her in 1996 they were just returning to Whitehorse from Fort Nelson where Tina had run a very successful "H & R Block" franchise.

Pete Olexyn

Pete was a salaried foreman with PKS (and a good friend) during most of the years I worked for them. He finally left PKS when they had little work and after a short stay with Goodbrand Construction, came to work for Miann. Pete was an excellent foreman on regular as well as on "multiplate" culverts. While he worked for Goodbrand, he assembled a huge culvert for a train underpass near Quesnel, BC. He also worked on all of the jobs that Frank and Joe Welling did while I was involved with them.

Pete began having health problems about the time that Miann and Exco went out of business. I heard that he had gone

Pete Olexyn and his crew installing a multiplate culvert in Stony Creek 40 miles west of Whitehorse. *Photo taken by the author.*

in for Prostate surgery and was continuing to have severe problems. When I stopped to visit him a few years later, he was in good health again. He told me that he had had his prostate scraped several times and had suffered agonizing pain and ill health for nearly three years. His doctor had finally wanted to castrate him to clear up the problem. Pete's wife put her foot down. She insisted that he get a second opinion before allowing such radical surgery. When Pete saw another doctor, he soon learned that he had diabetes, and his problem had never been with his prostate gland at all. His pain and suffering was all due to a sloppy investigation and a poor diagnosis.

Lyle Henderson

Lyle was my son's classmate when they went to school in Kelowna. After getting his degree in Commerce, he tried to sell Real Estate in the Vancouver area, but got into the business during an economic downturn. At the time I was doing a lot of work for Miann Contracting in Prince George and on my recommendation they hired Lyle to look after the field office on construction projects. Lyle stayed with them for the next half dozen years.

Lyle was not very keen about learning to use computers, but he had a great personality and got along well with everyone. It did not seem to me that he liked office work very much either, and it was sometimes difficult to get him to complete some of the chores associated with his job. Nevertheless, he stayed on and Joe Welling was reasonably satisfied with his work.

Lyle's true calling was in public relations, not clerical work and I saw an example of his flair for dealing with people one day

We replaced the Bailey Bridge in the top photo with 3 ten and 1 four foot diameter culverts. *Photo taken by the author.*

on the job near Pink Mountain. I don't recall what had happened, nor why, but we had one very irate local citizen threatening violent action. Lyle listened to him, and before long he was able to mollify the man who soon regained his composure. Whatever the problem was, Lyle was able to quickly settle it to the satisfaction of both parties.

My son told me that during his university years Lyle played a leading role in planning and implementing stag parties for prospective grooms. On one occasion, they got the groom drunk and put both him and

Lyle Henderson watching two airtracs at work. *Photo taken by the author.*

his car on to a BC ferry, heading north to Prince Rupert. This man became sober in time to somehow return in time for his wedding. Another victim was not as fortunate. They put this man on a plane to Toronto minus his money and his ID. This guy did not get back in time for the wedding! His fiancée was unable to see the humor in the situation and promptly broke the engagement. When Lyle got married in Whitehorse he kept it a deep secret and none of his former classmates learned of it until well after the event.

After we finished the construction projects near Whitehorse, Lyle got a job with the Yukon government in its "Lands Department." The following year when the Director moved on to another appointment, Lyle took over his position. His ability to calm troubled waters has stood him in good stead and he is still in that position as this is written in late January 2002.

The Mounties Get Their Man.

One evening a prisoner in Whitehorse escaped from the RCMP. They cornered him in a trucking company's compound in the industrial sector of the city. However, the fugitive jumped into a highway tractor (truck). He tore through the fence and out on to the highway with the Mounties in hot pursuit. When he got to our project, he almost ran over the night shift flag girl as he sped through the project. We estimated that he was driving at speeds of up to 90 miles per hour as he hurtled down the freshly gravelled highway.

He might have given the police a much longer chase, but when he hit a freshly dumped load of gravel, he lost control and flew forty feet through the air before the truck came to a violent stop on its side in a muskeg swamp. The cab was embedded so deep in the bog that it was almost out of sight. Needless to say, the law enforcement officers met little resistance when they arrested him. We did not get to see him, but I suspect that he must have taken quite a bruising. The owners of the truck did not fare too well either. The vehicle was pretty badly damaged from its sudden stop.

The City of Whitehorse

While I was working with Exco in 1986, we did three jobs in the Whitehorse area; the section of the Alaska Highway, a piece of the Kusawa Lake road adjacent to our highway job, and a landfill project in the city. As soon as the road jobs were finished, I moved into town and shortly bought a half duplex on Green Crescent in the Riverview area. I went south for Christmas and then moved my belongings into my new home right after New Year.

Whitehorse had a population of approximately eighteen thousand people in 1987 – at least that was what it was during most of the year. During the tourist season it swelled considerably as the campgrounds and the hotels filled with tourists on their way to and from Alaska. It is a city that depends largely on government funds for its existence. Ottawa accounted for about 65% of Yukon's total income while I lived there. Mining and tourism accounted for the balance, but now there is no longer any mining left.

Robert Service wrote a poem called; "The Men That Don't Fit In," in which he implies that the men of the Yukon were people who did not fit in with ordinary society. I think that is still true. I suspect that Whitehorse has more artists per capita than any other city in North America. Artists are in my opinion, mavericks – people who don't fit in, and who march to their own drumbeat. It is a city that staged eight plays every winter while I lived there. That is twice as many as in Prince George despite being one quarter its size!

Whitehorse does not boast a symphony orchestra, but it is very active in the arts. In addition to staging eight plays each winter, its volunteers also produce one major musical event - I first saw "The Mikado" there. One winter, the entire Toronto Symphony put on a concert there as well. They performed in the local high school and took up a large part of its gymnasium. I got to sit on one side, just a few feet from the bass violins, but the sound so filled the room that it was still a wonderful experience.

We were entertained on another occasion by a Calgary pianist who turned out to have been one of my niece's instructors. She was scheduled to begin her concert at 8:00 PM in the school auditorium. When the piano tuner arrived he found that a leaky roof had been dripping water on the instrument for an extended period of time. The piano was soaked! The organizers mobilized and went to work with a number of dryers to make the piano playable. The concert began shortly after 9:00 PM and was still a great success. The pianist told me the next day that she had been forced to improvise because two keys on the instrument did not work at all.

The Talisman Cafe

I found a neat eatery shortly after moving to Whitehorse. It was called "The Talisman" and it was run my two Baha'i members; Robert LeBlanc and an Iranian man named Yadi Kazemi. In addition to serving tasty and healthful meals, it was also home to the local chess club. Robert sold Real Estate and together with Yadi did some development work as well. I was introduced to the Baha'i faith by them, but I found that I am just not capable of accepting any dogma no matter how benign it may be. Nevertheless, I came to have a very high regard for the people who practice this Faith. It is a religion that has no hierarchy, but depends on establishing consensus in all matters. They treated women as equals decades before anyone else even thought of it.

One of the first social events I attended in Whitehorse was a film called "Doctor, Lawyer, Indian Chief." It was followed by a reception at which I was seated directly across from two beautiful young women whom I got to know very well. One was Lu Penikett, the wife of Tony Penikett, who was then the government leader of the Yukon. The other was a young single girl named Gaylene Carver who promptly adopted me as her surrogate father.

Lu Penikett

Lu was born of Aboriginal parents at Snag – not far from Beaver Creek in the Yukon. (Snag holds the record for the lowest temperature ever recorded in North America $-85°F$) Despite being a mother of three children and the wife of a busy politician, she was actively involved in Band affairs at White River and Beaver Creek. These two bands had been amalgamated by government fiat many years earlier. This resulted in ongoing tensions between the two factions. Whoever was in power, tended to hire their family and friends and ignore members of the other group. Lu was successful in having the two bands separated again and now each runs its own affairs. She later went to Victoria to study law. I don't know how she managed both this and her family. Tony moved to Victoria to work for the BC government after the NDP was defeated in the Yukon. I have since been told that they are no longer together.

Janie Loney

Shortly after coming to Whitehorse, I saw an ad for reflexology. I went to have my feet treated and was astounded to learn that the young lady massaging my feet was related to my sister Ester. Janie's mother is a sister of Ester's late husband, Henry Hindbo who lived in Dickson, Alberta.

I actually met Janie in 1950 when she was a young child and I stayed overnight at her parents house. When I met her in Whitehorse, she was married to a local Mountie, but is now separated from him and living in Red Deer, Alberta.

Gaylene Carver

Gaylene suffered from epilepsy and fought a long battle trying to find the right medication and the proper dosage to control it. Despite her difficulties, she was an enthusiastic young lady who was always involved in community activities. She loved gardening and was interested in the things I was trying to grow in my little greenhouse. Being her adopted father filled a void in my life since my own children were scattered down the West Coast in Vancouver, San Francisco and San Diego.

Gaylene grew up in the lower mainland and returned to Vancouver while I still lived in Whitehorse. She came back to Whitehorse again, but stayed for only a brief period before going south once more. By the time I came south to work on the Vancouver Island pipeline project in 1990, she was married to a young man named Gary Harrison who now manages an equipment dealership in Coquitlam. They have two children aged eight and almost six (2002) and she seems to have her health problems under control too. Gaylene is still actively involved in community activities and does volunteer work regularly as well as helping Gary one day a week in his business. She is another one of those people who I seldom see, yet consider a close friend.

Gaylene Harrison nee Carver.
Photo courtesy of Gaylene Harrison.

Klondike Toastmasters Club

I joined one of the local Toastmasters (TM) clubs shortly after moving to Whitehorse. In all of my earlier years, I had met only two women named Irene. The first one was a classmate in Grades one and two. The second one was the wife of Don Ormrod, whom I met in 1962 in Sooke. When I joined the Klondike club in 1987, I promptly met three Irenes. By the time I left the Yukon in 1990, I had met ten more!

I remained a member of the Klondike Toastmasters club all the years I lived in Whitehorse. During 1988, I led a "Speechcraft" project where we trained four Aboriginal leaders in public speaking and leadership skills. One of the people in my class was Paul Birckel's sister Lucy who was a schoolteacher. Another one was Vera Owlchild who was exceedingly shy, but made great progress. Rosemary Trehearne was the third woman and James Allen was the only male in the class. I don't remember much about any of them except that they all stuck it out for the entire course. I found it very rewarding to work with every one of them.

During my years in the club, I made two trips to Anchorage to attend spring conferences. On one of these visits I competed in the "Evaluation Contest" and managed to take third place, but I did not do nearly so well in the Speech contests. My most memorable experience was driving to Anchorage during the early morning in April. The Aurora Borealis (Northern Lights) were so bright that they were still visible until just before sunrise.

Willie Zatkovich

One of my first jobs after starting work for Miann in 1978 was preparing a contract claim for them on a road project they were doing for the "Department of Public Works Canada" (DPW). When we submitted it to Willie Zatkovich, the local manager, he just ignored it. I finally wrote a letter to our Member of Parliament, Frank Oberle, and got prompt action. Two high ranking officials came out from Ottawa and met with us in Willie's office. They told us what they would, and what they would not entertain, and then directed Willie to settle the claim with us. Willie was not only big enough not to harbor any resentment about this, but from time to time he sent a client to me that he was unable to help for one reason or another. I will always be indebted to him for that.

After Willie left DPW, I saw him a few times on projects he was supervising, but I have not seen him since I moved back south in 1990. The last time we met, he was raising Huskies and racing them. I don't know whether or not he can still keep up with them.

Larry G. Jacobsen

Champagne Aishihik

During my second year in Whitehorse I did quite a bit of consulting work for the Champagne-Aishihik Band before deciding to go on staff with their construction company. I felt that I needed an understanding of them that I could never get as an outside consultant.

I was on their construction company's payroll during 1988 and 1989, during which time in addition to administering and supervising work, I found both Federal and Territorial funds for training programs that I initiated and led. Working for them was a unique experience. Paul Birckel, the chief was a man, but it was the women who ran the band office. Except for two of them, the rest treated me as if I didn't exist. It took almost two years before I felt that they accepted me. Paul Birckel on the other hand was a great guy to work for. I spent most of my week working in his office in Whitehorse and usually spent only a day or two at the Band's headquarters in Haines Junction. Paul was innovative and stayed on as the chief for many years because no one else wanted to run against him.

The government of Canada had given the Band $1million to help them get into the construction business. Despite this gift, they found it very difficult to compete. I believe there were a number of reasons for this;

- Although many of them had a strong work ethic, their culture seemed to get in the way. The men often started late in the morning, took 30-minute coffee breaks and quit early in the day.
- The manager had pretty good mechanical skills, but they had no full-fledged mechanic. The third year apprentice was pretty fair for an apprentice, but not yet a mechanic.

One incident that highlighted the second problem was when they sent a truck engine into Whitehorse to have it rebuilt at a cost of $18,000. The shop foreman told the man who picked it up that they should be sure to flush the engine cooler before installing it. I don't know whether the message got lost or ignored, but the cooler was not flushed. The truck drove just 20 miles before the metal cuttings in the oil wiped out the rebuilt engine.

One area where the Band had been losing a lot of money was in new housing construction. While I was with them, they hired a carpenter foreman who helped train their workers and also inspected the units being built by a Native contractor. For a while we also had a "Drywall" expert training a few of their members in this aspect of construction. I saw remarkable progress in cost control of housing construction during my time with them.

260

Dr. Brannigan

One of the colorful residents of Whitehorse was Doctor Brannigan. He was very popular with the Aboriginal community, but not with the Medical Establishment, which had been trying for several years to revoke his license. During my stay in Whitehorse, he was so popular that he captured the Liberal nomination, but was defeated by the NDP candidate in the federal election that followed.

Dr. Brannigan's clinic at Atlin BC. *Photo taken by the author.*

One of the reasons for the antipathy of his fellow doctors (to put it mildly) was the fact that Brannigan held unconventional views. One summer he brought in a so-called "psychic healer" from the Philippines to his clinic at Atlin, BC. This clinic itself was controversial. It was built in the shape of a pyramid with the idea of capturing the healing powers such shapes were said to possess. Out of curiosity I went to Atlin while the psychic healer was there. As far as I was concerned, it was just "snake oil" treatment, but of course many people believed otherwise.

I had Dr. Brannigan as my personal physician for a short while. After he tried a chiropractic maneuver on me without first giving me any warning and hurt my back, I did not visit him again. In addition to considering himself as having chiropractic skills, he had also become an acupuncturist. I did not find it surprising that the medical establishment were trying to revoke his license.

Westcoast Energy Inc.

I left the Band in early 1990 when most of their Federal funding dried up. Since I did not think there was enough consulting work in Yukon to keep me busy, I came down to Vancouver and went to work as a cost control inspector for Westcoast Energy on the "Vancouver Island Pipeline Project."

They originally hired me for a term of one month to stabilize a slide at Squamish, but I stayed 17 months - until the project was completed. I then went to work for them in Head Office on a consulting basis, first to liaise with the Aborigines on pipeline clearing, and later to do cost analyses on contract claims as well as administrative and research work.

I stayed with Westcoast for over 6 years, but when they restructured the company in September of 1996, they wiped out the Construction Division. Since then I have done only a few minor jobs for them, but my association with them has led to work for other companies in the Fort St. John area.

During the winters of 1999 and 2001 I worked for Pioneer Natural Resources from Calgary from January 1st to past mid March each year. My job was "Cost Control" – keeping on top of costs and verifying the contractors' expenditures on Extras. During the winter of 1999 – 2000 I worked for a Reserve based contractor named Dav-Jor Contracting during December and January. I tried without much success to help them improve the level of organization in their operations.

As this is written (Feb. 2002), I am pretty much retired, but still doing a little occasional work for Westcoast Energy (now Duke Energy). During my consulting years I did work for about fifty five different clients.

PART V

THIS AND THAT

Chapter 26 - This Cat Had More Than Nine Lives

Introduction

During the first half of my life I was miraculously spared from death nine times in accidents from which I had no business coming out alive. I have had other narrow escapes as well, but none of the same calibre as those I am relating here. One such close call was being a passenger in my own convertible that failed to negotiate a curve at 70 miles per hour. Another was falling 35 feet down a near vertical raise (mine-shaft). Later, when I first began in construction work, I was supervising a "scraper spread." We were dumping in a congested area when I was almost run over by a large earthmover backing up. I could not hear it due to the noise in the area. I turned my head just in time to see an eight-foot diameter tire coming at me a few feet away, but I was able to jump out of its way. These foregoing examples, I consider to be close calls – not miracles. The instances narrated here are different. I am convinced that I ought to have had little or no chance of surviving any of them.

No. 1 – The Combine

In September of 1945 I was 16 years old. A friend of my father's was combining barley for us during the morning, (a combine is a mobile threshing machine). My father told me to climb inside the back end of the machine during the lunch break and clean barley beard out of the straw walkers. There were three straw walkers (course screens with sharp spikes protruding from their rear). They were connected to a crankshaft and their purpose was to separate the grain from the straw. These screens were so densely plugged that much of the grain was being ejected out on to the ground together with the straw.

I had nothing to stand on so I had to lie on my stomach on top of the screens while laboriously cleaning the barley beard out of each individual hole in the screen. It was slow tedious work and I was not even

A combine similar to the one in which the author was injured.
Photo taken by the author.

close to being finished when my father and the combine owner returned from lunch. I heard them fire up the engine, but assumed that they were merely warming it up. Meanwhile, having completely forgotten that I was still inside the combine, they threw it into gear to augur the grain out of the hopper and into the truck parked alongside. (This combine was an early "Massey Harris" and it required the operator to run the entire machine just to operate the augur). I was still lying on my stomach on top of the straw walkers with my legs dangling when the machine suddenly leapt into action. I got the ride of my life! The spikes stabbed me repeatedly in my chest and abdomen with the speed of a machine gun. By the time I was able to push myself off the straw walkers and out of the combine, my clothes had been shredded and my abdomen and chest riddled with holes. You can imagine the surprise the two men got when they saw me fall in a heap on the ground behind the machine.

I was carried into the house, put into bed and my wounds dressed with Raleigh's ointment. No doctor was called (we were too poor to even consider it). While most of the punctures were superficial, a number of them did penetrate both my abdomen and chest walls. It was a miracle that none of my abdominal wounds became infected. This would have caused Peritonitis, which in those days was deadly, for this was before penicillin became available.

When I arrived at school a few days later my schoolmates were shocked! They had heard that I had gone right through the combine, from one end to the other, and assumed that I was dead.

No. 2 – A Mining Mishap

My first underground job was at the Paradise lead-zinc mine near Invermere, B.C. in the fall of 1949. I had heard two versions of how the mine came by that name. The first was due to its elevation – the main adit at 7800 feet above sea level was perhaps as close to heaven as any mine in Canada. The second version held that the original name was "pair-a dice" and had to do with gambling - all mines contain a large element of that. I had worked briefly at the mill camp the previous winter before being laid off. Now I was back and told I would be working inside the mine.

I think that everyone who goes into a mine does so the first time with some trepidation. This was certainly so in my case, but it did not last more than a day or two. I was shortly given a job as a miner's helper with a miner who had just six months of underground experience. Our job was to rehabilitate an old "drift" (a horizontal tunnel) by scaling (removing unstable rock) and timbering it. Any rock that we pried loose with our scaling bars had to be hand shoveled into a mine car and trammed to the nearest ore-pass. The miner, whose helper I was, did not believe in scaling more than absolutely necessary because he did not like to hand muck (manually shovel) the rock off the track afterwards.

We timbered the drift by placing 8 foot long 8" x 8" fir posts eight feet apart in both directions and capped them with timbers of the same dimensions. On top of the caps we placed a floor constructed of 3" x 12" fir planking called lagging. On top of these sets we set other posts of varying lengths to shore up the roof of the drift. The back (roof) of the drift was generally about three to five feet higher that the top of the main sets.

The ore in this mine was very high grade, running at about 25% lead and zinc combined. Pure lead is especially heavy, having a specific gravity of ten, (ten times the weight of water). A chunk of ore therefore does not have to be very large to do a lot of damage. The rock in this mine had one unique characteristic. An imminent rock fall was often preceded by minute pieces falling a second or two before the main event.

One afternoon my partner and I had just finished lagging a set when we stopped for a smoke. He was standing on the lower rungs of the ladder and I was sitting on top of the newly lagged set with my feet dangling over the edge when I felt a small rock hit my back. I instantly leapt onto the ladder just as several tons of rock fell right where I had been sitting. It smashed the heavy planking as well as the timbers to which it was spiked. Had my reflexes been just a trifle slower, I would not be writing about it.

After this fateful episode I got to work with an experienced miner, one who was also safety conscious. This event proved to me how important it is to get proper job training and learn to recognize unsafe conditions.

No. 3 – A Rolling Experience

In the summer of 1951 I was working for Pacific Diamond Drilling from Vancouver as a "diamond driller" near Spillmachine in the Columbia valley. We had a single-axle flat-deck truck that was needed in Vancouver, and I was entrusted with delivering it there.

I stopped at Cranbrook to pick up two lengths of 8 inch casing pipes, so I stayed there overnight. I promptly got together with a good friend and spent the evening partying at my motel. The next morning I put the partially consumed bottle of whiskey into my suitcase and continued on my way to Vancouver.

It was early July and the temperature was 100° F when I came through Rossland. There I caught up with a man who was towing a heavily loaded utility trailer behind his car, which not surprisingly was overheating. He turned out to be a carpenter moving to Vancouver from Winnipeg and his trailer was loaded with heavy power tools as well as a few furnishings. Since we were both going to Vancouver, I offered to take a few crates from him to lighten his load and he gave me an address to which to deliver them. We made the transfers and were soon on our way again.

The road from Rossland to Vancouver included a long tortuous section that led up over the Monashee Mountains, down through a deep valley, then back up over them again before finally descending to Cascade near Christina Lake. It was referred to as the "Cascade" route even though it did not come anywhere near the Cascade Mountains. Except for the section between Chilliwack and Vancouver, none of the highway was then paved, and the Cascade stretch was no exception. This section was heavily "wash boarded" over much of its forty miles. The main feature of this part of the route was the number of switchbacks. On the Rossland side there were probably only half a dozen, but from the first summit to the valley below, there were at least fifteen.

The passenger door on the truck refused to stay closed and flew open at frequent intervals. I would repeatedly have to reach across the cab to pull it shut. The casing pipe on the truck was also giving me some trouble. Because I did not have the facilities to tie it down properly, it rolled from one side of the deck to the other.

I had reached the first summit, started down the other side, when I looked back to see how the pipe was faring. At this moment the truck door swung open for the umpteenth time. As I reached over to close it yet again, I got too close to the edge, and with the roughness of the gravel surface, literally bounced off the road and over the edge.

Over I went! As the truck began to roll I dove for the floorboards and clung to the gearshift. I had just two thoughts – one was that the bottle of liquor in my suitcase would be smashed and the resulting smell would make everyone think I was drunk. The other was; "how am I going to get the truck back on the road?"

The truck made one complete roll and slammed into a large tree that stopped it instantly. After the initial shock, I gathered my wits and slowly clambered out of the truck amazed at my good fortune. It turned out that the tree that arrested my roll was the only mature one in sight for hundreds of feet. All the others were small immature ones of up to six feet in height. Were it not for that lone tree, there would have been nothing to stop the truck from rolling for hundreds of feet down the mountainside. The truck had also been spared major damage. The decking behind the cab had absorbed the impact of that first roll and was broken, but the cab was intact. The impact with the tree had dented and jammed the right door shut so that it could no longer be opened. This saved me a lot of aggravation for the remainder of the trip.

I hitched a ride back into Rossland where I got a wrecker to come and pull the truck back up on the road. After checking the oil and radiator levels I tried unsuccessfully to start the engine. However, a quick check under the hood revealed that the coil wire had come out of the distributor cap. I reinserted it, hit the starter and the motor fired right up! Our toughest job was gathering up the casing pipe and all the carpenter's equipment that had spilled out of the broken crates and scattered down the mountainside. Once that was done I was once again on my way and reached Vancouver that evening without any further incidents.

The only injury I received was a small puncture wound in my back, of which I was completely unaware. Because I was drenched in perspiration from the heat, I did not notice that the back of my shirt was saturated with blood until a gas station attendant pointed it out to me in Grand Forks. I have often wondered how and why I came to hit the only tree large enough to stop the truck. Without it I would surely have been killed.

Number 4 – Another Mining Mishap

In the spring of 1953 jobs were very difficult to find in B.C. Fortunately I was able to find a job at the United Keno Hill mine some 35 miles from Mayo in the Yukon. The flight was from Vancouver to Whitehorse in a four-engine DC6 and from Whitehorse to Mayo the following day in a two-engine DC3. The one-way ticket cost $135, paid for by the mine and then deducted from my first paychecks. That was a lot of money considering that a miner's rate was then $1.25 per hour. The fare was reimbursed if one worked 250 shifts. If one stayed for a whole year, the return fare was also reimbursed.

One significant aspect of working so near to the Arctic Circle is the amount of daylight during the summer. Towards the end of May, one could read the newspaper at any time of day (or night) without needing any artificial light. Then it did not matter whether one worked the day shift or the night shift, because it was broad daylight all the time.

The mine produced ore from two adjoining properties; the Calumet mine and the Hector mine. This ore was trucked to the concentrator at Elsa - eight miles closer to Mayo. After processing, the ore concentrates were bagged and trucked three hundred and fifty miles to Whitehorse from whence it travelled to Skagway via the Whitepass Railway and to the Tacoma smelter by ship. If my memory serves me correctly, the sacks each weighed 140 pounds, so the handlers had to be in excellent physical condition to manually load the trucks day after day.

Within a month of arriving, I was able to get a premier job – driving crib raises. There was just one other two man crew so employed – two brothers from Finland. This job provided me with the opportunity to compete with the Finns for the highest bonus earnings in the mine. The raises followed the ore veins and therefore varied greatly in steepness from one section to another.

The first raise we drove went uneventfully, but not so the second. This raise was vertical for the first sixty feet, before flattening off to a gentler incline. The ore in a short section too had a very strange characteristic, instead of breaking up into coarse rocks, it broke up as fine as flour.

One day we had blasted a round and had gone for lunch while waiting for the smoke to clear. Meanwhile the tramming crew drew down the muck from the ore-pass side of the raise so that we would be able to get access back inside. My helper took a mine car and went to get a load of cribbing while I went up the raise to open up the bulkhead. I knocked out a plank from the side of the timber and crawled inside to shovel the broken muck off the bulkhead. The high-pressure air hose we had left blowing in the raise after the blast should have driven the noxious gasses out of the raise. As it turned out, this had not happened due to the flour like quality of the broken muck. It was so fine that it formed an airtight seal and had trapped the gases inside.

I had barely begun shoveling when I suddenly felt my knees go weak. In a flash I realized what had happened, and immediately crawled back out into the manway rushed down the ladders as fast as I could go. My coordination quickly became so bad that my feet did not even touch the ladder rungs, but I somehow got to the bottom without letting go and falling the remaining distance. I staggered along the drift to where I could find fresh air. I was so disoriented that I kept bumping into the timbers on either side of the drift. These timbers were six feet apart, but not wide enough apart for me in my drunken-like state. The last I remember was collapsing as I reached the fresh air.

By the time my helper returned, so had my consciousness together with fits of vomiting. They immediately put me on a stretcher and sent me to the Mayo hospital 35 miles away, where I spent a day under observation. I quickly made a full recovery and was back to work two days later. However, if my response in that raise had been even a few seconds slower, I should never have escaped the deadly carbon monoxide fumes from the blast, nor have been here to tell you about it.

No. 5 – Still Another Mishap

In late July we were driving yet another raise, this one in the most unstable rock that I have ever encountered. When we were quiet, we could hear the rock crackling as it constantly shifted. In order to drill it safely, we had to timber right to the face, bulkhead the man-way compartment over, and then drill between the bulkhead timbers. The rock was so bad that a foot or two of it would slough off the face while we were drilling it.

We were using electric detonators for our blasting. After loading and wiring a round, we had to race to the bottom to detonate the blast before a rock could slough off and break the circuit. Sometimes we lost that race and had to climb back up the raise, crawl inside and repair a broken wire before we could blast the round.

The raise we were driving this time was vertical for the first forty feet, it then flattened off to about 35 degrees for a long section, before it steepened up to over 60 degrees. In the flat area the muck would not run down the ore-pass by itself, so we had to shovel it down the manway. The tramming crew would then load it into ore cars with a muck machine at the bottom of the raise.

After blasting the first round in the steep section, we still had to muck it out by hand for one last time before we could timber the raise. We had finished scaling down the loose rock and had just begun shoveling when the geologist's helper yelled that he was coming up. Bill Strynadka, my helper and I sat down, he on one side and I in the middle and waited for the young chap to come up the ladder. I was leaning ahead watching his progress when a large slab of rock weighing several hundred pounds broke off the face and slammed my head down between my knees.

If I had been sitting upright, the rock would have driven my head into my chest and that would of course have been the end of me. As it was, I had severe fractures of my fourth and fifth thoracic vertebrae as well as a hairline fracture of one cervical. I was very fortunate. I spent just over a month in the hospital, flat on my back on a board covered with a mattress one inch thick. The discomfort of lying on that bed for the first week was almost as bad as the pain from the fractures and the torn muscles. Bill and I did earn the highest bonus for the year in that raise!

No. 6 – A Penetrating Experience

Seven years of my mining career was spent in the Reeves McDonald mine south of Nelson BC and adjacent to the U.S. border. This mine was generally referred to as Remac, because we had a post office there by that name. It was a mine that typically produced about twelve hundred tons of low-grade lead-zinc ore per day. It was while working at this mine that I got married, moved into a tiny bungalow in the company town-site and began raising a family.

I was working night shift in a stope in the O'Donnel section of the mine. This part of the mine was about one mile farther into the mountain than the main workings. Normally there were three of us in that section on night shift, but on this night the other two men,

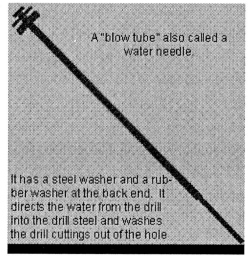

A "blow tube" also called a water needle.

It has a steel washer and a rubber washer at the back end. It directs the water from the drill into the drill steel and washes the drill cuttings out of the hole

who were on the bargaining committee, were meeting with management. One man was working the afternoon shift (4:00 PM to midnight), but after he was gone, I was the only person left in that part of the mine.

When drilling on surface, the rock cuttings are removed using compressed air. When drilling underground, to minimize dust, water is used instead of air for the same purpose. The drill steel has a small hole down its centre to accommodate either. Inside the drill is a tube referred to as a blow tube if air is used, or a water needle when water is used. This tube penetrates a few inches into the drill steel in order to force the air or fluid (as the case may be) through the steel.

On this night I was busy drilling with a "jackleg," drill when the drill water failed to exit from the drill hole. I immediately checked the drill steel and found that the back end of it was riveted (flattened) to the extent that the steel was completely plugged. I quickly disassembled the drill and removed the water needle. It was about 16 inches long and a quarter inch in diameter. The riveted steel had drawn the end of the water needle into a long needle-like shape with no hole left through which to discharge the water.

On the back end of the tube were two washers; one made of rubber, the other of steel. I decided to remove these before heading out to the drill doctor's shop for a replacement. Sitting on the muck pile and forgetting that the tube was now as sharp as a real needle, I held it against myself and tugged at the washers to remove them. As I tugged on them I felt the tube suddenly give way. Oh-oh, I thought; there goes a hole in my slickers (rubber rain suit)! When I looked down I immediately saw to my horror that only about 4-5 inches of the tube was still in sight. The rest of it was embedded in me between my abdomen and my thigh.

I quickly yanked it out as two alternatives went racing through my mind. Should I remove my clothing immediately and try to stem the bleeding, or should I first get down to the telephone on the main level? My concern with the first alternative was that if I had punctured my femoral artery, I might lose consciousness while trying to control the bleeding, before getting to the phone. I therefore plunged down out of the stope, over to the main shaft and down seventy feet of ladders to the telephone. As I raced down the ladders I could feel the blood running into my left boot. I was able to contact the shift boss on the phone immediately and tell him what had happened. Then I quickly peeled down my rubber pants, then my regular pants and finally tore open my heavy woolen "long johns" to see how bad it was.

I found that the blood was not spurting, just flowing slowly from the wound. The blood had saturated an area of my underwear about 12 inches long and 4-6 inches wide. There had been no blood pouring into my boot! My over-excited imagination had created that illusion.

By the time I got out of the mine the first Aid attendant was waiting for me with the ambulance. He hauled me into Salmo and awakened the doctor. Before sending me on to the hospital in Nelson, the doctor examined me and marveled at how lucky I had been. He told me that it appeared that I had not only narrowly missed my femoral artery, but also my bladder and my colon – any of which could easily have killed me. I spent a week in hospital with ice packs and pumped full of penicillin, then another week at home before returning to work. From that day on, whenever I saw the doctor he marveled at how lucky I was to be still alive.

No. 7 – Getting a Bang Out of Life

In early December of 1961, I was still working at Remac, but now living in Salmo. One day my friend Sid Gillies came to visit me. I had first met Sid while hunting with two friends in the Wardner area near Cranbrook.

We had found him a job at Remac as an underground laborer, but he had quit immediately after his partner, was killed in a major cave-in, (Sid escaped the accident with only bruises). He was now between jobs and came to me for advice on blasting a quarry at Sirdar near Creston. He told me the new quarry contractor was ready to hire him as a blaster and he wanted advice on how to do the work. His experience with dynamite was nil! He was totally unqualified to do the work, but he had somehow gotten the Mines Department to issue him a Metalliferous mines (underground) blasting certificate. Since this was a quarry, the work was governed by the Mines Act, and not by the WCB, where he could never have acquired a ticket.

From talking with him it quickly became apparent that the contractors at the quarry knew even less about blasting than Sid did. I suggested to him that perhaps we could do the work on "contract." He checked it out and shortly thereafter we had negotiated a sub-contract price with the quarry contractor. I took a week's holidays and we moved into a motel at Sirdar.

Our contract was for blasting 1000 tons of granite. Part of that tonnage was contained in a twenty foot high pile of already broken rock, but numerous pieces in it had to be re-blasted because they were too large for the crusher. The main face of the quarry, where most of the rock would come from, was also a mess! It entailed the tricky job of cleaning up a number of misfired charges before we could proceed with regular drilling and blasting.

I put Sid to work on the pile of broken rock with a jackhammer and showed him how much dynamite to load into each drill hole. We were using "safety fuse" with caps for detonating our shots since the rock pile was directly under a high-tension power line could not use electric detonators. We were also very close to some buildings, so we had to be circumspect in the use of dynamite. I showed Sid how to make up the detonators and told him that the minimum fuse length under the regulations was 3 feet, but that I wanted a minimum length of 4 feet! I further suggested that we shoot only a dozen holes at a time. I then went to work cleaning up the main quarry face.

The daylight was beginning to fade and a light drizzle was falling when Sid came over and asked me to help him light the blast – he had not 12, but 42 shots ready to go! We called over the cat-skinner and asked him to give us a hand too. He was a huge young giant; about six foot seven in height, weighing over 275 pounds. Each one of us armed with a "hot wire" lighter, began at the bottom of the muck pile and worked our way towards the top, lighting one fuse at a time. Because of the drizzle, it was difficult to get the fuses lit. I had a knife and was able to cut off the damp section of each fuse first and thus light each one on the first attempt. Sid and the cat-skinner had no knives and were much slower. I was almost at the top of the muck pile and had lit about twenty fuses before my hot wire lighter burned itself out. The cat skinner was at the top of the pile as well and Sid was just carrying away the jackhammer at the bottom when I shouted; "That's enough, let's get out of here!"

The words were barely out of my mouth when the first shot went off with a BANG! Chunks of rock went whizzing past our ears as we ran down the muck pile. On the way down the cat skinner ran right over me and we both went rolling to the bottom just as the second shot went off, not twenty feet away. As we picked ourselves up, yet another charge went off sending rock flying in all directions. By now it was getting quite dark, so I elected to duck into a shallow depression in the quarry wall where I was partly sheltered, but far enough away to see any rocks coming my way and still have time to evade them. The cat skinner just kept running until he was out of range.

Sid had been exposed to just one blast, but the cat skinner and I had been exposed to three! Except for a small cut on my finger gotten when I rolled down the muck pile, no one had been injured in the slightest. How we were all able to come out unscathed with rocks flying around our ears will always remain a mystery to me.

It turned out that Sid had not only ignored my advice about the number of shots to set off at one time, but also about the length of the fuses. He had cut them only two feet long, not four feet as I had requested!

The rest of the work went as planned, and although we did not do the work as quickly as expected, we still earned good wages for that week.

No. 8 – Rolling Stones Gather No Moss

During 1966 I was working as a superintendent for Gulf Drilling Ltd., a small company that specialized in drilling and blasting jobs. I had recently finished up a job at Brenda Mines near Peachland, BC. Earlier in the year I had supervised blasting work on the Mica Highway north of Revelstoke, BC for the same company. The Department of Highways requested that we come back to one huge rock cut that was now unstable. They asked us to drive a bench about thirty feet above the road to intercept rock rolling down from higher up the slope. My old friend (Don) from my mining days, whom I had hired for Gulf Drilling, was supervising this work. He was almost finished and I was sent up to make sure the work was satisfactorily completed. The drilling and blasting was complete, and only some scaling work was left to do. We decided that the two of us could easily finish that in a few days and therefore laid-off the rest of the crew.

On December the 15th, we were finished except for a couple of hours of work. There was one large slab on the floor of the bench that we were unable to move without blasting. Don who was living at Salmo wanted to get away early so he could get the ferry across the Arrow Lakes and get home that night. We decided that he could leave and I would come out and finish the job by myself in the morning, before returning to my home in Peachland.

The next morning I got a few sticks of dynamite and a detonator. After blasting off the loose slab there was a gaping depression left in the bench. All that was left for me to do was to scale the loose rock around that hole. I could easily have done the work without working off a safety rope, but decided to use one anyway.

I was standing on the floor of the depression, and had no more than ten minutes of scaling left to do when I felt a jerk on my rope. I looked up and could hardly believe my eyes. The rock wall above the bench was giving way! Rocks came flying through the air all around me. One huge boulder about three feet in diameter came right at me, but I was able to side step it.

The slide had almost stopped when I felt another jerk on my rope. I looked up, and there directly above me, teetering on the bench on top of my rope was a gigantic cube of rock about four feet on each side. For a moment it appeared that it would stay there, but then over it came! There was no way that I could dodge it because it was squarely on top of my rope.

I did not see my entire life flash by me during that second or two before it hit me, but I remember thinking; "it is either going to mash me into the rock, or it will take me with it down to the road below." Neither happened! My scaling bar and my hard hat were the only things that went down. I was still there on the end of the rope of which only one strand was still holding. My only injuries appeared to be bruises to my knee and my elbow.

The rock, which must have weighed about two tons, would surely have killed me had it been round instead of angular. Because it was a cube, it had somehow flip-flopped right over me. It took some time for it to sink in and what a miracle it was that to be still alive. As I drove back to Peachland I became wildly exhilarated with the feeling that nothing could kill me!

As it turned out, I did not come out of that incident unscathed. I suffered a severe lumbar disc and a pinched nerve that gave new meaning to the word agony. This injury was to plague me for many years and eventually became arthritic.

No. 9 – No Old Bold Pilots

An old saying has it that there are old pilots and there are bold pilots, but there are no old, bold pilots. Since I never did become a pilot, that statement probably still holds true.

While working on the Mica highway in the spring of 1966, I began taking flying lessons at Revelstoke. I was shortly thereafter dispatched to a quarry job on Saturna Island, and not long after that, to Brenda Mines near Peachland. After my accident at Revelstoke described above, I was flat on my back for two weeks. My doctor had me on a heavy dosage of Valium to relieve the muscle spasm in my back, which in turn was pinching my sciatic nerves. My back was soon feeling much better, so the doctor advised me that I could do just about anything I wanted as long as I didn't do anything to jolt my back.

Meanwhile the Revelstoke flying school had moved to Vernon for the winter because at Revelstoke the snowfall was too heavy to keep the runway open. I decided that I might as well get in a few hours of flying time, and with that in mind drove to Vernon on December 30th. I logged three hours in the air that day, before getting a room at the hotel. The next day I had already flown for three hours, when it occurred to me that it might be an opportune time to do the mandatory cross-country flight before returning to Peachland. The weather was still good, although a dark front was looming in the north, and the winds had picked up somewhat.

The flight was usually flown from Vernon to Penticton, thence to Kamloops, and from there, back to Vernon. I decided to fly it in the opposite direction because in the event that the front came in faster than expected, I would have the wind on my back coming south from Kamloops. This would make it easier for me to return to Vernon if I had to abort the flight.

I was flying a Piper Colt, a two-seater that cruises at only 85 miles per hour. In my flight plan I had chosen an altitude of 6000 feet, but once underway found it too turbulent at that height, so I went up to 8000 where it was only slightly better. When I reached Kamloops, there was a cloud lying over the entire city, so I could not land as required for the flight. Since I needed the air time anyway, I decided to continue on to Penticton even though the flight would not qualify as the "cross country" one. As I neared Merritt, the front still hung threateningly in the sky to the northeast. It did not appear to be moving at all, but I noticed that a fairly large cloud had appeared in the southwest, and then suddenly another one in the east. I knew then that I had to cancel the rest of my flight, and that I should land at Merritt. The problem was that I had hardly any money with me, and it was New Year's eve. I wanted to get home.

I turned the plane eastwards and headed up over the mountains towards Vernon. The sky suddenly became completely overcast, but I felt that I still had enough time to make it before the weather closed in. As I headed east the ceiling kept dropping at an alarming rate. I still had time to turn

276

around and go back to Merritt, but I did not begin to suspect the danger I was in, so I kept on flying towards Vernon.

By the time I reached the summit of the highest mountains between Vernon and Merritt, the ceiling was down under 500 feet (legal minimum is 1000), and still dropping quickly. But now it was too late to turn around. The air had become extremely turbulent, but instead of cutting my speed, as I would normally have done, I increased the rpm to takeoff levels to get a few more miles per hour out of the plane. Meanwhile the turbulence was buffeting the little plane violently all over the place, but I dared not slow down for the clouds were now right on top of me. In order to stay under the overcast, I was now flying down a gully and almost skimming the treetops.

Have you ever ridden a bucking bronco? If you have, you will have a good idea of how rough my ride had become. I was in agony because my back was literally killing me, but I dared not slow down. I did not think I was going to make it, but I was in such pain that I did not dwell much on the thought. Then, suddenly below me was the most beautiful sight in the world – Okanagan Lake! I had made it, and fifteen minutes later I was back on the ground at Vernon.

After several days of physiotherapy my back was not improving so I finally checked myself into the Kelowna hospital and spent a week in traction. I have not piloted a plane since that fateful day. My employer, whose plane I had hoped to fly, went into receivership so I saw no point in continuing my lessons. Since that long ago episode I have had a couple of other near misses, but none that I would define as a life used up.

Chapter 27 - Hobbies

Golf

Golf is a game that has become very popular in recent years. If golf is a disease, then considering the rate with which it is now infecting people, it should at the very least be classed as an epidemic and perhaps even a pandemic!

I was introduced to golf in the spring of 1962. I had recently quit my mining job at Remac and was waiting for a job I had been promised. The job was on new highway construction between Salmo and Creston. I later came to suspect that the fellow who offered me the job (in the beer parlour) was not sincere, for the job kept being postponed. I had quit my job because I had developed a duodenal ulcer. It was probably from being choked up over being on permanent night shift.

It was a gorgeous spring morning in April and I was sitting with some friends in the beer parlour having my one glass of tomato juice my ulcer diet allowed. It was far too nice outside for us to be in the pub so someone suggested we go play golf. I pooh-poohed this idea, saying it was an old woman's game - that it was like grown-ups playing marbles. The others however prevailed on me to come along. One fellow even lent me some golf clubs. Since my doctor had told me not to drink alcoholic beverages while he was treating my ulcer, I finally gave in and joined them.

The Salmo golf course consisted of nine holes with "sand greens" situated on an old airstrip belonging to the federal government. When my turn came to tee off, I confidently stepped up on to the rubber mat, teed up a ball and took a vicious wing at it with the "driver." I missed the ball completely! Somewhat embarrassed, I took another big swing at the ball and missed it again! By then I was getting angry, but nevertheless, I swung at the ball once more with dogged determination. This time I actually hit it off the tee – almost thirty feet.

At this point one of my buddies said; "tee it up again, keep you head still and your eyes on the ball. We will watch where it goes for you." Heeding his advice I tried to hit it one more time. This time I connected solidly. From then on I was able to hit the ball every time I teed it up, but with a big slice. The ball would fly toward my selected target, but then veer sharply to the right. This was not too bad because the trees bordering the course were consistently on our left.

After this first try at golfing, I could not quit because my pride had been too severely wounded. I bought a "half set" of golf clubs at the local Marshall Wells hardware store and became a regular at the golf course. Hitting the ball off the tee was no longer a problem, but hitting it off the grass was something else. I was able to hit the ball off the grass about 50% of the time, but the other times, I usually hit the ground first. Any time I tried to hit the ball forcefully off the grass I hit the ground as much as six inches behind it. If I tried to concentrate on not doing this, I would "gut shoot" the ball – hitting it in the middle instead of the bottom. When this happened the club would usually cut the ball cover wide open, making the ball unfit for further play. As I slowly gained more confidence, I sometimes tried to compensate for my slice by aiming to the left of my target. Whenever I tried that, the ball would invariably go straight – straight into the trees where I aimed!

Shortly after this episode I left Salmo and after a brief period at the Granduc mine near Stewart, moved to Sooke on Vancouver Island. There I worked for Cowichan Copper in their mine at Jordan River. I promptly purchased a house in Sooke – right beside the nine-hole golf course. I could step over my back fence and be on the fourth tee.

The Sooke golf course was an old sheep farm with some small greens placed on it together with a few sand traps. Only the greens were watered, so during the summer the fairways were usually brown and hard. It had one water hazard – a small lake in front of the men's first tee. . To me who had never seen another course except the one at Salmo, it seemed like a good course. Since it was relatively inexpensive, I soon became a member.

To clear the lake off the first tee required a shot that carried about one hundred and thirty yards in the air. At first this was not a problem for me and I was able to get across most of the time. Gradually I started to hit more and more balls into the lake though. Then it seemed that the harder I tried, the more often I failed. It would be a while before I learned that golf is counter-intuitive, for example, the harder you swing at the ball, the less distance you tend to hit it. If you want the ball to go high, you must hit down on it. You can't correct a slice by aiming to the left for it guarantees that you will continue slicing.

On one occasion an older gentleman was standing beside the first tee watching me as I drowned one ball after another in the lake. Trying to be helpful he made a number of suggestions. He stood off to the side a few feet while I tried to do what he suggested. I almost missed the ball, which flew off at right angles to my aim and smacked the old fellow right on the ear. Fortunately for him he was not really injured, but he did not give me any more advice either.

One day I stopped at the Colwood Golf Course near Victoria to look around. I spotted a used set of golf clubs with a "Sale" tag on them. The set included a "Bag Boy" pull cart, a full size golf bag and thirteen stainless steel shafted Spalding Elite clubs. The price was $200.00, which was a lot of money in 1962, but only about half of what a new set would have cost. When the Golf Pro noticed me eyeing the clubs he came over and said: "tell you what, you buy those clubs and I will throw in four free golf lessons!" I don't remember whether I bought those clubs the same day or not, but I did buy them.

The first thing the Pro told me when I came for my first weekly lesson was that if I played golf during the period I was taking lessons, I would be wasting his time as well as my own. During that first lesson he had me hitting balls gently with a seven iron. He made a big issue over the correct way to grip the club. I found the grip very awkward, but tried my best to do what I was told. He also emphasized that I had to hit the ball on my

The author playing golf. *Photo is from the author's collection.*

downswing so that the club first struck the ball, then the turf. Following his instructions, I practiced hitting a minimum of 150 balls on the Sooke course every day when I was not having a lesson.

Over the following three weeks he gradually let me progress to longer irons and to fuller swings. It was not until my fourth and final lesson that he let me use a three wood. His parting advice was to go ahead and play golf now, but to keep practicing as well.

I played at Sooke for two summers before moving into Victoria where I joined the Gorge Vale Golf and Country Club in the spring of 1964 and I was soon playing to a thirteen handicap. I have never been able to hit the ball much over two hundred yards, but my accuracy and consistency partly made up for it. To play anywhere near par, one must be able to hit the ball at least 250 yards off the tee.

When I joined the Gorge Vale, the annual fees were about $90 and the initiation cost me $100. Its members, who were mostly servicemen and ordinary workers, owned the course. This is no longer the case. Well-to-do people have gradually displaced the old members, and very few wage earners are still members. Today ordinary people can no longer afford to join the Gorge Vale – I believe the initiation as now around $30,000 and annual dues around $2500.

I finally quit mining in 1964 and got into construction. This was not conducive to playing golf for I was usually out on jobs in remote areas. This changed in 1969 when I worked near Kelowna and was able to play on most weekends. The following year I spent the summer at Smithers where there was a nine-hole course with sand greens. After that I spent much of my time in the Vancouver area and was again able to play quite often.

In 1974 I finally had my moment in the sun. I spent the summer at the Endako Mine near Fraser Lake in central BC. I was in charge of a stripping job at the mine, but had a lot of free time because a sub-contractor was doing the entire project for us. For the first while the mine management was very concerned that we meet an agreed upon schedule. Later the schedule lost its significance and since the sub-contractor did not want any input from me, I was able help out on the local golf course and to play a lot of golf as well.

The Moly Hills Golf course was constructed on the shores of Francois Lake not too far from the mine and only about fifteen miles from the town of Fraser Lake. Jerry Wreggitt, a man I had met years earlier when he was selling drill steel, was the owner. He was still working for the Endako mine and building the course in his spare time. The mine had given him the land in return for him turning it into a golf course.

The course was hilly and had a beautiful view of Francois Lake. The greens were tiny and were built of "tailings" sand. No green was level and during that first summer the grass on them was exceedingly thin. This made them very difficult to play. Once a ball began rolling downhill on a green, it never stopped until it was off the putting surface. To have any hope of scoring well it was imperative that the approach shot stop below the flagstick. If one was chipping or putting uphill, there was a good chance of the ball stopping near the cup. Downhill or side hill chips or putts invariably ran off the greens. On one occasion my uphill putt on the first green ran by the cup about two feet, then reversed itself and rolled back down the slope and into the hole for a birdie!

Jerry Wreggitt held several tournaments that summer. I not only won all the first prizes, including a wrist watch and a putter, but quite a bit of cash as well. At the completion of each tournament we always had a "horse race." This game began with each competitor throwing a couple of dollars into a pot. We then all played each hole together. The person(s) with the high score for each hole dropped out. Whoever lasted the longest, (usually me) won the pot.

Many of the local golfers were either just learning to golf or had very little experience. Since I was the best player there that summer, I was called on for a lot of instruction. I have never since been as popular as I was during that summer of 1974.

My final achievement that summer was winning the first "Moly Hills Open Golf Tournament." There were many golfers from nearby towns competing. Although some of them were better golfers, my knowledge of the course stood me in good stead. This was also the one course where placement of shots was far more important than distance off the tee.

I visited Jerry Wreggitt again in the early eighties while I was on my way to Kitimat to see a client. He was killed the following day when his tractor flipped over backwards while he was dragging a big culvert. His wife eventually remarried and sold the golf course. His son Andrew completed a Fine Arts course at UBC and won the Governor General's award for poetry the following year. I recently watched a movie (Jan. 29, 02) and saw that it had been written by Andrew Wreggitt.

In 1978 I moved to Prince George and was again able to become a member of a decent course. There my handicap stayed at ten except for brief dip to nine. For those of you who don't know what a handicap signifies, a handicap of ten requires the best half of one's games to average about 79-80 strokes.

In 2001 I joined the golf course at Mission, BC. I am once again playing quite a bit of golf, but alas, not to a 10 handicap - it's now 20. I can say with total honesty that the older I get, the better I used to be.

Holes-in-One

A hole-in-one is an uncommon occurrence that consists of holing the tee shot. It happens almost exclusively on par 3 holes because they can be reached from the tee. They have happened on very rare occasions on par 4 holes as well when a powerful golfer with the wind at his back gets incredibly lucky.

For the average golfer, making a "hole-in-one" is an unforgettable experience. Many golfers play the game for their entire lives without having one. Because the event is so rare, when it does happen, it is cause for celebration in the club's lounge. However, rather than the lucky golfer being treated by his fellows, it is his duty to treat everybody else with a drink of their choice. This may seem grossly unfair, and I have no idea how this practice originated, but since the game has its roots in Scotland, perhaps that has some bearing on the matter. Needless to say, having a hole-in-one can be financially disastrous for the (lucky?) golfer!

In many golf clubs it is now customary to offer hole-in-one insurance. For a fee of about $25 or more, the club will take on the burden of buying drinks. This relieves the member of the risk of destroying his budget, while at the same time providing the club with an added source of revenue. The law of averages will of course favour the insurer – in this case the club.

During my golfing years I have never bothered myself about taking out insurance and despite having made two holes-in-one, (25 years apart) I have escaped unscathed. The first was in early October of 1970 I was on Vancouver Island on business for my employer. I decided to stay over for the weekend and play golf at Sooke where I had first learned the game. On October 3rd I was out on the course alone on late Sunday afternoon. There was a Scotch mist falling and I had finished playing the first nine holes. The owners had closed the clubhouse and everyone was gone except for one couple. I therefore teamed up with them to play my second nine.

The fourth hole was 160 yards long and slightly downhill. Since the fairways were hard, one could expect a lot of roll after the ball landed. The green was on a hillside that sloped away from the tee and the best way to play the hole was to make sure to be long rather than short, even if it meant being in the sand bunker on the lower side. Being long meant having an uphill chip that had a chance of stopping near the hole. A downhill chip was impossible to stop on the green.

On my first round I had used a seven-iron and been too far past the green. This time I used my eight-iron instead. When we got to the green, my ball was nowhere in sight. From the green to the heavily vegetated ditch below was about forty yards and I assumed that somehow my ball must have reached it. I was searching down along the ditch when my male playing partner asked; "Have you looked in the hole?" I just laughed at him, but when I looked up at the green I saw a trail through the dew that led right into the cup!

It was my first hole-in-one and since the clubhouse was closed I could not buy the couple drinks. Back in those days the pubs were not open on Sundays either, so I escaped with buying coffees at the only café that was open. The Golfcraft Company rewarded me with a nice trophy since I was using their clubs and their ball. I also got a case of ginger ale from Canada Dry.

My male playing partner told me that this was the third ace he had witnessed. A few years earlier he had been playing at the Oak Bay course in Victoria with a fellow Scot. This man was very parsimonious and always played with old beat-up golf balls. My friend scolded him for being so cheap. He said; "If you can't afford to buy a new ball, I'll give you one." He pulled out a brand new Dunlop 65 and handed it to his playing partner. They were on the sixth tee – a par 3 hole that was about 185 yards long. The man teed up the ball and pulled out his "3 wood." With a mighty swing, he launched the ball well to the left of his target and straight at the ocean. The ball caromed off a rock, flew towards the green, ricocheted of a tree and ran into the cup! The following weekend they were once again playing at Oak Bay when the fellow holed his sixth tee shot, but legitimately this time, and with the same ball. I had been a member of the Gorge Vale golf course at the time and I remembered seeing a blurb about the event in the Colonist newspaper.

Twenty-five years later (less three days) I had recently been married again and was living in Vancouver. On October 1st of 1995, I was playing golf at the Fraserview course and was striking the ball rather well. My playing partners were all rank beginners, so I was getting a lot of oohs and aahs whenever I hit a good shot.

The seventh hole was a 208 yard long par three that I always had difficulty reaching. I pulled out my driver and hit the ball solidly. The ball flew through the air straight towards the flag. It landed on a bit of an up-slope that slowed its momentum, hopped onto the green and rolled right towards the cup. My eyesight was not good enough to see the ball at that distance, but my playing partners were certain that I had holed it. When we got to the hole, sure enough, there it was in the cup.

After we finished the round, the one fellow had to leave immediately. The other two accompanied me into the clubhouse where I was able to buy a beer for one, but only a coffee for the other chap. I loudly announced that I had made a hole-in-one and asked if anyone would like a drink. To my astonishment, I did not get a single taker! All it cost me was one beer and one cup of coffee. Unlike my first hole-in-one experience, this time I did not receive any mementos for my achievement.

My third hole-in-one occurred on July 2, 2003 at Lake Padden Golf Course in Bellingham, Washington. I hit a six iron rather poorly on the 140 yard twelfth hole, but it landed short of the green, rolled up and into the cup. This one cost me a dinner for my lone playing partner.

Toastmasters

Toastmasters (TM) is an International organization dedicated not only to help people speak in public, but to foster leadership ability, overcome shyness and improve thinking habits. It began in California in the Nineteen Twenties, and now has clubs in scores of countries around the world.

I first encountered this wonderful organization in 1969 while I was in Yakima. I was able to attend a few meetings before returning to Canada that spring, but did not actually join a club until after I moved to Prince George in 1978. When I moved to Whitehorse in 1986, I became a member there as well. I was also a member of a club in Vancouver during the mid-Nineties, but left after I got married again and moved to Port Coquitlam..

During my membership in the Prince George club, I witnessed firsthand how two members who were both hobbled by intense shyness, came out of their shells. One lady who worked for the Justice system was promoted three times during the year after she joined this club. Another was a young man who did not stay too long because he had other over-riding commitments. He was still very shy when he left, but he told me that for the first time in his life, he could speak to his boss at work.

While I worked for PKS in their Vancouver office, we had a fellow named Roy Paton in charge of Safety who I thought was a good speaker. Nevertheless, he followed my advice and joined a TM club in which he stayed for several years. His speeches, which had been good before, became outstanding. When he left PKS to become the president of Continental Explosives, I was sure that it was his TM experience that helped him prepare for this position.

The typical TM program begins with a business meeting where its members have an opportunity to learn how to conduct meetings in conformity with "Robert's Rules of Order." This is a valuable asset for members who may chair meetings in other areas of their work. Next is a session called "Table Topics," in which the Table Topic master asks members to speak briefly (3 minutes), and without preparation on a subject that the topic-master provides. Trying to master this hurdle provides training in thinking quickly on ones feet. It is especially useful for people in public leadership positions.

Prepared speeches follow under the auspices of the Toastmaster of the evening. Members deliver prepared speeches of 5 to 7 minutes in length that strive to fulfill certain requirements set out in a manual. One speech for example will afford the speaker an opportunity to focus on improving his grammar and word usage. Another might focus on logical structure, while still another is tailored to the use of gestures or tonal quality. Each speech criterion is designed to help the speaker improve one aspect of speech making.

Everything in a TM meeting is timed and evaluated. One member is in charge of timing. A Grammarian listens for both poor and exceptional use of grammar. A personal evaluator is assigned to each speaker. His role is to provide feedback to the speaker on what is being done well and how to improve the speech. The Evaluator does this by pointing out specifically what the speaker has done well and how it can be improved even further.

The General Evaluator evaluates everything in a TM meeting, including the evaluators. Learning effective evaluation is probably one of the most challenging tasks, for it is mandatory to be both constructive and supportive in this role. What makes TM so effective is that it provides a safe and supportive space for its members to grow. Every member, regardless of experience, soon realizes that "they are all in this together."

There are three general levels of achievement in TM. After successfully completing 10 designated speeches, one earns the title; "Competent Toastmaster."

In the next tier are several levels of "Able Toastmaster," each of which requires 15 designated speeches. In addition to the speeches these levels also require certain community involvement outside of the club.

The pinnacle of achievement is attaining "Distinguished Toastmaster," and to reach this lofty plateau, one has indeed to be distinguished. This level, in addition to the speeches, requires extensive community involvement including starting a new TM club or rescuing one that is foundering. Only the most dedicated members achieve this level for it has to be done within a certain time frame.

In my opinion, Toastmasters is truly one of the greatest service clubs in existence. A few years ago I emceed a wedding reception (180 guests) on short notice and with almost no preparation. I should never have been able to do this had it not been for my involvement in Toastmasters.

Crisis Centre Volunteering

I was a volunteer at the Prince George Crisis Centre for most of the years I lived there. A Crisis Centre is a place where people in crisis can call and know that someone is taking them seriously. The centre in Prince George had a full time and a part time paid position whose duties included enlisting volunteers and seeing to it that they were trained. The volunteers manned the telephones 24 hours a day and seven days a week. From midnight to eight AM and all day Sundays, the calls were routed to the home of the volunteer on duty. The balance of the time one or two volunteers manned the phones at the Crisis Centre office. People were also free to come to the centre for counselling during normal office hours.

All the volunteers received thorough training before being allowed to handle calls. The training was usually done over a couple of weekends and each trainee followed up by working under the direction of an experienced volunteer for a minimum of five shifts. In addition to this, refresher courses were held yearly. The training focused on developing skills to listen to a caller without passing judgment and to use empathy as opposed to sympathy in dealing with clients.

The most important element in dealing with a caller was to let the caller know that he or she was actually being listened to. This could be done by asking the caller to clarify a problem or by asking other pertinent questions.

The one thing we were trained never to do was to offer advice. We might ask the caller if they were aware of certain resources in the community that was available to them, but the focus was always on the clients making their own choices. All volunteers were required to remain anonymous and not develop personal relationships with any callers.

People in crisis are often people who don't want to face up to certain issues, but expect someone else to fix them. The problem with giving advice is that it gives the caller an escape from taking responsibility for his or her own decisions. It allows them to blame their woes on others instead of dealing with them. If advice is given on how to deal with a problem, the caller can make a half-hearted attempt to follow it and then blame the advisor for the failure that ensues. By assisting the callers in finding their own solutions, there can be no buck-passing. It is not very often that a volunteer feels he or she has made an important difference for someone, but it does occasionally happen.

The Crisis Centre in Prince George also acted for the Ministry of Social Services, and in this capacity was authorized to dispense emergency aid when Ministry offices were closed. This help usually consisted of a room for a night or two plus a voucher for meals until the client could visit the Social Services office the next day that they were open. A large percentage of these claimants seemed to have arrived in town just as the bars closed on Friday night. I never enjoyed dealing with such cases, but fortunately they were a minority.

Another type of person was the chronic repeat caller who seemed to have no intention of changing his or her lifestyle. Nevertheless, occasionally such a one actually did make progress and eventually stop using our service. What made the job worthwhile was the fact that on occasion you felt that you had been able to make a difference in someone's life.

One caller I shall never forget began the conversation with the statement; "My husband has only a few more weeks to live." My first assumption was that she was having great difficulty coping with this and needed to pour out her grief. She quickly let me know that they had both known for many months that his time was limited. She was calling me because her husband had made her promise that she would not give him a church funeral because he was an agnostic. Since the caller was a devout Catholic from a large equally religious family, she was having great difficulty in dealing with her promise. I asked her; "Who do you think the funeral is really for, the dead person, or the survivors?" There was a short pause and then it was almost as though a light bulb was being switched on as the realization of this hit her. Her voice took on a fresh confident quality and she ended the call shortly. It left me feeling great too because I felt that my question had made a telling difference. I am willing to bet that her husband had a grand church funeral.

After I moved to Whitehorse I volunteered for the Crisis Centre there too. Being a much smaller city, we had no office from which to work. The Telephone Company rerouted all the calls to the home of the volunteer on duty. I was not overly impressed with the training I received in Whitehorse, so I volunteered to lead the next session. The next time I was in Prince George, I was able to obtain a copy of the training manual from the Crisis Centre there. I subsequently led two training sessions in Whitehorse. The one was exceptionally encouraging for volunteers from it stayed on much longer than average. I felt well rewarded for my efforts.

Anne Jeffries Ginouves

I met Anne soon after moving to Prince George when I became a volunteer at the "Crisis Centre" there. Anne was in charge of the centre and we soon became close friends, especially after we both joined the same Toastmasters Club.

Anne Jeffrey Ginouves.
Photo is from the author's collection.

Anne had first come to BC and had lived on the Queen Charlotte Islands for a time while she was researching the painter, Emily Carr. She was twice married, first to a lawyer, then to a doctor. She had two children by the former and they were living with their father in Ontario. She had also written a book that had been published by the Canadian Broadcasting Corporation (CBC). Anne shortly left the Crisis Centre and became involved with "Women's Studies at the College of New Caledonia. I was teaching part time in the Construction Technology program at the same college, so we saw each other frequently, both there and at Toastmasters meetings.

Anne left Prince George for a while and moved to Montreal, but she returned to Prince George a couple of years later and went to work for Canada Manpower. When my marriage broke down I left Prince George and moved first to Vancouver, then back to Prince George for a year and then to Whitehorse. Anne meanwhile got married for a third time – to an American financial consultant and moved to Florida where she still lives. This marriage did not last long either. She finally got her Master's degree in History and is working at a University there.

Teaching

In late 1980, Allen Dumas at the College of New Caledonia in Price George asked me to teach part time in their "Construction Technology" program. I taught "Estimating and Bidding" the first year and "Equipment Economics" for two subsequent years, but declined to teach after they stretched the sessions from January to June instead of ending them in April.

The first year I had a class of 15 that included a young man who did not seem very interested in the classes. I warned him twice that he would have to pull up his socks if he wanted to pass, but my words fell on deaf ears, and I gave him a failing grade.

He called me a few days later about his failing grade. He ranted and raved and accused me of picking on him. I finally hung up the phone, but before long, it rang again. This time it was a woman who said she was his sister. She lit into me about hanging up on her brother. I tried to explain why I had not passed her brother, but she wouldn't listen – just kept on heaping abuse on me. I finally shut my mouth and let her carry on. When she had finally finished her tirade, she calmed down and began asking questions. I was then able to give her the history of event.

She then told me that she had an older brother who was a top student and was now at BCIT. The parents had a habit of comparing the younger brother unfavorably to the older one. The younger one was not academically gifted and being compared to his older sibling did not do anything to motivate him. His father had already rented an apartment for him in Burnaby, so he was infuriated when the boy failed. By letting the sister spout off until she ran out of steam, gave her the space to listen to me. We finished the call with an acceptance and appreciation of each other's point of view and I learned yet again that self-defense is not an effective way of promoting understanding.

I have been doing some teaching again these past years. In January of 1988 I developed a week-long workshop on the basics of contracting that I then led for the Champagne-Aishihik Band at Haines Junction in the Yukon. While I was consulting for Westcoast Energy I scaled down this workshop to two days and presented it at the Blueberry Reserve in 1992. During the following years I presented it at Chetwynd and Fort St. John as well. This year I developed and presented another workshop to Aborigines at Prince George and Kamloops on the behalf of Westcoast Energy (now Duke Energy).

As a volunteer, I have been teaching computer courses to people at the Wilson Senior Centre here in Port Coquitlam for the past five years. My students have ranged in age from fifty to eighty five years. Now that e-mail has become so common, many older people have been urged by their grandchildren to correspond with them in this medium.

Chapter 28 - Follies and Personal Development

On Marriage

I was married to my first wife for over 17 years. In 1969 when I was with PKS, I supervised a small job on the Hiram Walker distillery at Winfield near Kelowna. We sold our trailer home and bought a house in Kelowna, and when I later wound

The author's first wedding in 1955.
Photo is from the author's collection.

up in the Vancouver office full time she refused to follow me. Part of the problem was the way I had dragged her and the children around from one job to another - we had moved 13 times in nine years. Our relationship was already on tenuous grounds for other reasons as well. I am sure that she always found me overbearing, so when she finally put her foot down and

told me she was not moving again, I was not too surprised. I have read quite a bit of Carl Jung's work and it was something he wrote that helped me see myself in a new light. I had been having dreams about being pursued by Grizzly bears for many years. Carl Jung suggested that if you dreamt too much about bears, you were perhaps "overbearing!" I still dream of bears occasionally, but they no longer chase me.

Rita helping the author cut the wedding cake – Feb. 10/73. *Photo is from the author's collection.*

My second marriage was doomed from the start, but it still lasted 11 years. My wife Rita, seemed very insecure, and had never had a close relationship until she met me when she was 38. I was the last person she should have married, because I like women too much. Shortly after meeting her, we visited Art Teske, an old friend who had worked for PKS. He had a book on astrology and even though I put no stock in such stuff, I looked up our horoscopes. What I found was quite intriguing. As I remember it, the book predicted that we would have an intense relationship that I would find emotionally draining.

We had been married for only two months when one day I came home from work, and noticed a peculiar chill in the air. I was mystified when Rita refused to talk to me. She finally flounced over to the chesterfield, picked up a long blonde hair and accused me of having had a woman in our apartment. I was flabbergasted. I was head over heels in love with her and could not understand how she could even begin to distrust me. Our only visitors had been my children and the hair had obviously come from my daughter Pamela's head.

From that time on it seemed to me that the anger in her would slowly rise until after a few months it would erupt and she would need only some pretext on which to attack me. I came to believe that she carried a deep-seated anger towards her father that she was unable to acknowledge, let alone express. When the resentment built up to a certain point, I would always be the recipient of it. Nevertheless, we managed to live together for over ten years and it seemed to me that her anger was slowly subsiding.

We had moved her parents to Prince George and found them a house on the same block where we lived. Her father was in the early stages of Parkinson's disease, but things were going quite well for them until her mother had a moderate stroke that hospitalized her. Soon she had another stroke and it became obvious that she would never leave the hospital. Her father's health also deteriorated and he too was hospitalized. The stress from these events seemed to be too much for Rita, and I once again became the scapegoat for her anger and resentment. It reached the point where I could no longer live with her so I moved out. We were divorced two years later.

Shirley and her son "Red" – Nov. 1988. *Photo is from the author's collection.*

In 1988 I went to the Philippines and brought back a wife (Shirley) who was 35 years my junior. It was an interesting experience. I knew that I was being extremely foolish, but her four-year-old son and I really hit it off well together. During the ceremony while my rational self told me how utterly stupid I was being, I experienced a feeling of being merely an observer and at the same time playing a role as if I was in a play.

Shirley told me on at least two occasions that we would get along just fine as long as I obeyed her. She certainly found my buttons quickly and soon knew which ones to press. When we moved to Nanaimo for my work on the Island Pipeline, I bought a house there since it seemed to be a good investment. After the project was over, Shirley refused to move to Vancouver – she thought I should commute back and forth on weekends. There was no way that I could afford to keep two places, so I applied for a legal separation and got divorced just over five years after we were married.

I had met a number of Filipinos in Vancouver during my marriage to Shirley. One of them introduced me to a nurse named Erlinda who is now my fourth wife. She was a single mother too, who has raised a son who now works for a Vancouver software company. In 2003 we celebrated our eighth anniversary – perhaps there is still hope for me to settle down.

Erlinda comes from a family of twelve children as do I. I am the third oldest in my family and she is the third youngest in hers. Except for two brothers still in the Philippines, her brothers and sisters are all in Canada or the USA. There are now six women and five men surviving in each family.

She was a high school teacher in the Philippines, but when she came to Canada, she first got a job for three years as a Nurse's Aide at the Beacon Hill Lodge. After getting her diploma as a Practical Nurse, she worked at St. Paul's Hospital for twelve years. She then went back to school and graduated as a Registered Nurse in 1993 and is still working at St. Paul's Hospital.

Erlinda & the author. *Photo is from the author's collection*

The EST Training

In the early-eighties I got involved with Werner Erhart and his "EST" training. I took part in three six-day training sessions near Santa Rosa, California. What I learned there has stood me in good stead, for I have learned to understand myself and accept myself as never before. I got to see how my fear of what people thought of me has so often kept me from succeeding in my endeavors. I have often given up when if I had persevered just a little longer, I might well have succeeded. I have come to see that I tend to be a very impulsive person (it runs in the family), and have been slow to use that to my advantage.

An important learning I got in California was the ability to sometimes see myself in action as though I were a bystander. This has on occasion helped me keep my sense of humor when I might otherwise have lost control. The most important thing I learned has been to thank people for their criticism rather than defending myself. As well as being very useful to me in growing, it is also a very effective way of disarming opponents. I have been able to apply this knowledge in most situations except in my marriages, but perhaps I shall one day learn to apply it there as well.

Another useful learning was to treat pain (both physical and mental) as a gift. Whenever I have been able to do this, it has lost much of its power over me. I originally learned this concept from George Leonard, the founder of "The Institute for Humanistic Psychology" at Big Sur California, but it was Werner Erhart's training that drove it home. Without the knowledge I gained from the training sessions mentioned above, I should never have had the courage to divulge some of the personal experiences that I have included in this book.

Bank Holdup

In February, 1998 I took part in a bank hold-up. When I say I took part in it, it was as an unwilling bank customer who was made to lie on the floor while a lone bandit brandished his pistol about and made a bank employee fill his bag with money.

I had just entered the Vancity branch at the Pinetree Centre in Coquitlam and was waiting for an open wicket. I was awakened from my reverie by a shout behind me; "This is a holdup! Everyone hit the floor." I whirled around, thinking it was some kind of joke, but was instantly disabused of that notion, when the bandit pointed his gun at me and repeated his demand.

As I got down on the floor, I saw that everyone else was already there. The gunman strode up to the wicket beside where I was lying and commanded the teller to fill his bag with money. In a quavering voice she said; "I don't have any money here." The gunman snarled; "You know where to get it - now move!"

After some more demands by the robber for the bank employee to hurry up, I was startled by several bangs, but they did not sound like gunshots. As I looked around I saw the door to the outside closing and the remains of a couple of Roman Candles still emitting smoke from where the fleeing gunman had thrown them as he fled the bank.

The RCMP (police) finally arrived and like everyone else, I was required to wait and provide a statement to them. I found it amazing how poorly I was able to describe the assailant. I had somehow assumed he was black, but why I don't know, for he was wearing a balaclava. I also learned that the police had been called immediately, but that they deliberately waited until the robber was gone before coming. I expect that this was to preclude the possibility of the man taking hostages.

I expected to see an account of the robbery in the newspaper and got another surprise. It did not appear. I presume that the banks don't like to publicize these events because it might not only scare away customers, but also encourage other potential thieves to try it too. This was my first and only experience of this kind and I was somewhat surprised to realize that I did not even consider the possibility of intervening during the holdup.

Chapter 29 - Health

Store Teeth

As a child growing up in a destitute family, we did not see the dentist (Dr. Robinson) very often. If and when we did see him, it was invariably to get a tooth extracted. We could not afford to have them filled.

After leaving home, I spent a fair amount of time on jobs a long way from the nearest towns. By the time I got to see a dentist, it was usually too late to save a tooth, so again I usually had the bad ones pulled.

At Halloween while I was working on a drilling rig near Picture Butte, Alberta, my friend George and I attended the local dance. Later in the evening (after we had done some serious drinking, he said; "Lets go to the dance at Taber." I replied; "Sure, as long as you do the driving."

I was half dozing on the passenger side of my Pontiac convertible when on opening my eyes I saw George was taking a curve at 70 miles per hour. He was on the wrong side of the gravel road and I remember thinking; "You'll never make it!"

He didn't! We went off the road sideways and bounced around a while before coming to a stop. I remember looking up and seeing George. He was outside looking in at me. He told me that he did not remember falling out of the car, but came to, sitting on a big rock. He had a bump on his temple the size of an egg. He said that when he came over to the car he heard me saying; "George, where are you. You are supposed to be driving this thing."

We were very lucky that the car had stayed upright, for there was a five-foot drop off where we went over. There was no serious damage to the car. The windshield was cracked, the radio buttons were bent and so was the steering wheel. We both looked awful. I had knocked 4 teeth loose, one of which was broken off at the gum and another one was broken off half way down.

After getting the car pulled back on to the road, we returned to the dance hall we had just left. We must have been some sight – George with the big lump on his head and me with blood all over my face and two teeth missing. It's no wonder that drill crews got a bad name for we certainly did our share to maintain that reputation.

The next mornings were pure agony for me, for I had a cracked rib in addition to my other wounds. Somehow, I managed to tough it out and go to work every day. Eventually I was back to normal except for my teeth.

The following spring we were drilling in the Joffre field near Red Deer when the tooth that had broken off at my gum became abscessed. I went to see a dentist to have it pulled. When he stuck the needle up into the abscess, he lifted 170 pounds on the point of that needle! He did not realize that the tooth was abscessed, and I had neglected to tell him. The Novocain didn't freeze my mouth and when he pulled that tooth, I broke into a cold sweat. When I rose to get up out of the chair, he said; "Better sit and wait for five minutes." I probably waited two minutes and left the chair. My legs almost buckled, but I managed to get out of his office without further incident.

Within the next three years, I had another tooth or two pulled. I was by then married and working at Remac. When I went to see a dentist in Nelson I found that Dr. Robinson from Brooks was now practicing there. By this time I may have had a dozen teeth left, so I decided to replace them with dentures. In 1958 I paid Dr. Robinson $25 to pull them in the hospital under a general anesthetic and then went without teeth for a few weeks while my gums healed. During this time I had bone slivers constantly working their way out of my gums. A few slivers continued to come to the surface even after I got my new dentures.

The new dentures cost me $125. I will never forget the evening when he inserted them. After having nothing in my mouth for several weeks, it felt like my mouth was full of marbles. I thought I was going to choke on them. When his receptionist asked me how much I was going to pay her that day, I was unable to utter a word. Dr. Robinson interrupted and told her that I had already finished paying for them.

I replaced my dentures in 1969 while we were living in Yakima. This time I had them made by a dental mechanic and they cost me US$150. I got my third set in 1984 from a dentist in Prince George. This time I paid $800, but I was then covered by my schoolteacher-wife's dental plan, so I paid only about one third of the cost. In 2000 I got my fourth set of dentures, and again had them made by a dental mechanic (now called a Denturist). This set cost $1,200, 60% of which was covered by my nurse-wife's dental plan. It has been my experience that denturists do as good a job as dentists, but cost considerably less. The increase in prices was mostly due to inflation.

There is no doubt in my mind that I have saved an enormous amount of money by wearing dentures, but knowing what I do now, if I had to do it again, I would certainly try to save my teeth. The biggest problem with dentures is that as the gums shrink, it becomes increasingly difficult to hold lower dentures in place.

Doctors

I first visited a doctor when I was sixteen and my eye was injured by a "softball." Since then I have seen a fair number of them and found a few excellent ones as well as a lot that I considered mediocre or lazy. In this section I have described a few incidents. The doctors that stand out in my memory as being both smart and dedicated are; J.V. Clark of Mayo, Carpenter of Salmo, Brian Finnemore of Kelowna, DeRosario of Prince George, Nona Rowat and William Irvine of Vancouver.

During my mining years, I was required to have an annual medical examination. I found that some of the doctors were meticulous and did a thorough examination every time, but others seemed to do no more that look in one ear to see whether or not daylight was coming through from the far side. If it wasn't, they shooed you out of their office within a few minutes. The thorough doctors first checked my chest expansion and listened to my breathing. Next they checked my pulse and blood pressure several times between bouts of exercise. Lastly, they sent me for a chest X-ray.

The Workers Compensation Board (WCB) paid the doctors for doing the medical exams in the mining industry and the chest X-rays were supposedly done to check for silicosis. During my mining years I was not aware of any doctor ever making a diagnosis of silicosis. There were rumors that if a doctor did this, he would no longer be retained for WCB work. Subsequent events appear to confirm this. My friend Rae Thomas did not have his silicosis diagnosed until he was in the Shaughnessy Veteran's hospital being treated for injuries suffered in a car accident. After the doctors there confirmed he indeed suffered from silicosis, he soon got a pension from the WCB. Al King, the former president of the Mine Mill union at the Trail smelter told me that he knows of many such cases. He was responsible for getting WCB pensions for a number of former miners or their widows.

Thyroid Problems

My legs had been giving me a lot of trouble since I had that flu during my Cowichan Copper mining days. They ached constantly as from severe fatigue, and nothing I did seemed to alleviate it. After I moved into Victoria to sell real estate I saw both a regular doctor as well as a specialist in internal medicine. Neither of them could diagnose my problem (five-minute appointments probably did not help either). The specialist had the gall to tell me that I had a "neuro-muscular syndrome" and that I would just have to learn to live with it. It was just a fancy way of saying that I had a problem with my nerves and my muscles. After I left the coast I found that my symptoms were usually less severe, but sometimes they still came back to bother me.

After coming to Kelowna in 1966 and while working at Brenda Mines near Peachland, I met Dr. Brian Finnemore. He became my personal physician and it was he who had treated me when I injured my back at Revelstoke. (See episode 8 in "This Cat Had More than Nine Lives"). In 1969 when I told him about my leg problems, he immediately checked my T4 level (thyroid) and found it was far below normal. He prescribed thyroxin, which I have been taking ever since. A few years later when I was going to SFU, I was again plagued by ill health – I seemed to get sick all the time. When I finally had my thyroid checked again, my T4 level was once again very low. I had my daily dose more than doubled and was soon feeling great once more. Since then, I have monitored it very closely and managed to keep it within acceptable bounds.

Tonsillectomy

Aside from having my teeth pulled in a hospital under a general anesthetic, I had never had surgery until January 1968. I had been plagued for years with chronic tonsillitis, so I decided to have them out. I was then working on a new road into Macintyre Mines at Grand Cache Lake north of Hinton, Alberta. I checked myself into the Hinton Hospital in the evening and had them yanked the next morning.

When I woke up I learned that they don't cut out you tonsils – they snare them with a piece of wire and pinch them off. For a youngster, it is not much of an operation, but for someone who is 39, it is a wee bit more. The left side of my throat healed nicely, but because the doctor did a messy job on the other side, my throat was much worse than before for a couple of months afterwards.

Vasectomy

My next experience with surgery was shortly before I married my second wife, Rita. Since she got bad side effects from birth control pills, I agreed to have a vasectomy. Accordingly, in December of 1972 I took a day off work and went to the surgeon's office for the procedure.

The surgeon did the operation in his office with just the two of us there. He gave me a local anesthetic and proceeded with the job while explaining to me what he was about. Even with the anesthetic, it was quite painful. I would sure hate to think what it would have been like without one. After he was done I went straight home and spent the rest of the day with ice packs on my scrotum. I went back to work the following day, but if I had been doing manual labor, I should not have been ready to do that for it remained quite painful for several days.

A Nose Job

In 1973 I came down with a severe infection of the right side of my head. After it cleared up, my doctor sent me to see an "Ear, Nose and Throat" specialist for a check-up. This doctor recommended that I get the inside of my nose straightened out. He told me it would make my breathing much easier

I checked into VGH in the evening so that I would be ready for the surgery early the next morning. In the morning they sedated me heavily and then wheeled me into the operating room where the surgeon gave me a local anesthetic. He then proceeded to cut out some cartilage with what looked like a pair of side cutters. That part was not too bad, but he next inserted a chisel into my nose and began striking it with a mallet. Despite the sedation and the freezing, it felt as though my head was going into orbit. Several assistants pinned me to the table while he finished chiseling bone out of my nose. He finally administered a general anesthetic but only after he was finished with his chiseling job.

I woke up in the recovery room – or at least I thought I did, but I had some weird experiences. Rita was sitting beside my bed and I was telling her that they kept the dead bodies in the basement. I was also telling her something about there being devils down there.

When I next saw the doctor, he pulled the cotton batting out of my nose. I was awe-struck, for he kept on pulling it out by the yard! I could not believe the amount he had managed to stuff in there, but it must have been over thirty feet long.

My breathing did indeed improve markedly and stayed that way – for about five months. After that it gradually deteriorated to the same as it had always been. The doctor followed up for only a few months, so he never learned that his operation was a waste of time. The worst part was that mucus in my nose now adheres to the scar tissue that he left behind and is always difficult to remove. It has been an aggravation ever since. I should have known better than to believe that straightening out the air passage in my nose would make much difference.

Spastic Colon

During that summer of 1979 I developed a gut problem that I could not get diagnosed for nearly a year. The doctor I had in Prince George, like so many others, never really examined me. How could he? A typical visit lasted for only five minutes. He spent very little time asking me questions, just sent me for tests. He next referred me to a specialist in Internal Medicine who didn't examine me either – just sent me for more random tests. Meanwhile, I began losing weight. I had developed an aversion to food because of the pain that accompanied every meal. During this time I decided to start my own consulting business and incorporated it on January 17, 1980.

Eventually Frank Welling from Miann got me in to see his doctor - DeRosario. What a difference! This visit lasted about 30 minutes! He first questioned me about my history for at least 20 minutes. Next he had me lie on his examining table while he probed my abdomen with his hands. It was not long before he found exactly where the pain was coming from. A barium enema then confirmed what he already knew – I had a spastic colon. This was not surprising to me – it was a direct result of the bind I had gotten myself into by going to work in a job I couldn't "stomach." After a few weeks on Lithium, everything was back to normal.

Prostate Biopsy

The last surgical procedure I had was a biopsy on my prostate in 1986. I checked into "Day Surgery in the morning and came out in the afternoon. I was told to have someone come and get me, but this time there were no noticeable after effects except for a bit of burning the first couple of times I urinated. The remarkable thing was that the growth disappeared on its own within a few years and has never come back.

An experience that I have found incredulous, is the hole left in my memory while I am under a general anesthetic. In each case I was told to clench my fist while the doctor injected the anesthetic into a vein. When he was finished, he said; "you can unclench your fist now." Meanwhile I am lying there waiting for them to begin, when I realize that I am in the recovery room and that the operation is long since over. There was absolutely no sensation of losing consciousness, nor of coming to.

Naturopaths

In 1996 my daughter Cheryl and her daughter Alexandra (Alex) went to Dr. Krupowski, a naturopath for food sensitivity tests. Alex had been suffering from chronic tonsillitis for some time and her doctor wanted to remove them. The testing was done electronically with a machine similar to a galvanometer that had been developed in Germany. It tests for electrical resistance in the body while one electrode is held in one hand and the operator touches an accu-pressure point of the other hand while placing various ampoules of food on the machine.

According to the results, they were both intolerant to sugar and most grains, and especially to wheat. When she told her doctor about this, he laughed at her. However, after being on a diet that excluded the offending foods for a while, Alex's throat cleared up. Cheryl found it too difficult to keep both Alex, and herself away from sugar and baked goods, so before long the tonsils were acting up again. This time her doctor told her to get Alex back on the diet. Because they could not seem to follow through on this, Alex eventually had her tonsils removed.

I decided to see the same naturopath and get tested too. I found I was especially intolerant to milk products, wheat, sugar, gluten and oysters. In addition to this I had an extremely high Candida (yeast) level. I already knew that I had developed a severe allergy to oysters over thirty years previously and that milk did not agree well with me. The other items were a surprise to me!

By eliminating the offending foods from my diet, I was able to reduce their impact fairly quickly and eat most of them again. When I got tested again one and two years later, the wheat and sugar were right up there again. Four years ago, the effect of these foods took much longer to be alleviated, so I had kept them out of my diet for about three months when one day I noticed that all of my arthritis was gone.

I have had two severe back injuries many years ago, 2 fractured thoracic vertebrae in 1953 and a severe lumbar disc in 1966. These old injuries had been giving me constant pain for at least a dozen years, but they are no longer doing so. X-rays had confirmed that these injured vertebrae had become arthritic. Meanwhile my weight began to gradually drop. After eight months my weight had dropped from 217 pounds to 172. I have since found that wheat intolerance is a family trait. I have a brother and a sister who have both stopped eating it and feel much better.

Giving up wheat and sugar products has been the most difficult thing I have ever done. One does not realize that one or both of these products pervade almost all our popular foods. I have found that being completely pain free, after so many years of having it as a constant companion, is a great motivator. Not only am I pain-free now, but I have lost my joint stiffness as well! Losing the unwanted weight was an added and a most welcome bonus. I have tried breads made from other grains, but they are no substitute for wheat bread. Bread made from rice is readily available, but it is very dry and unpalatable. I finally found a pure rye bread that is available from Irene's Bakery in Victoria. It is carried by "Save-On Foods" at all of their major stores. They even carry it in Fort St. John!

Last Christmas I began to backslide and started eating a few baked goods like cinnamon buns and cake. When I tried to stop, I quickly found out just how addictive sugar is. It has become obvious to me that I cannot eat these foods in moderation. I am now off them once more, but it was very difficult. Once I began eating sweets, my joint stiffness returned very quickly, followed shortly by some tendonitis in my left hand. It has become evident to me that I need to keep wheat and sugar out of my diet for the rest of my life.

Chapter 30 - My Family

My Parents

Dad stood 5' 11" and weighed between 240 and 250 pounds all the years I was at home. He had a good-sized gut, and since his initials were P.B. (for Peter Boesen) our classmates referred to him as "Pot Belly Jacobsen."

I remember Dad as always being an impatient man who had strong opinions on a number of issues. When I got old enough to drive the tractor and do general farm work, he was often at organizational meetings involving The Alberta Wheat Pool or other cooperative associations. By the time I was in my teens, I had begun to question some of his opinions. One incident I will never forget was during the war when I saw an article in the newspaper about the Bristol Bomber. The article indicated that it required 54 men to keep it flying (including the ground crew). When I mentioned this at the supper table, Dad instantly retorted; Twelve Danes could do that!" Dad always had a low opinion of Englishmen. Where it stemmed from I don't know, but he never doubted that Danes were far superior to them.

Dad & Mother in Denmark circa 1970. *Photo is from the author's collection.*

During the winter we always had lots of free time. Dad taught me to play Danish Checkers and a card game called "Sixty six." Danish Checkers was almost the same as the kind that is played here. The only differences were that the king could move across as many unoccupied squares as the player wished and could jump an enemy checker in the process, (It had to come to rest in the square directly behind the piece it jumped). The other rule was that the king could not be forced to jump an enemy checker that was en prise. We played Sixty-six with a deck stripped of all the cards from the deuce to the eight inclusive. I believe the rules for it can be found in Hoyle's book of card games.

We spent many hours during the winter playing these games, and I can't remember ever winning. I also remember the only time I saw Mother lose her temper at Dad. It happened one wintry afternoon while we were absorbed in our usual card game and Mother's request fell on deaf ears once too often. She stormed past our card table and "carelessly" knocked it over!

Dad was a racist and seemed to honestly believe that Danes were superior to other races, and especially to Germans and Englishmen. They were always the butts of the many jokes he regaled us with. I don't recall how he reacted when the German army overran most of Denmark in one day during World War II. I do remember my sister Gerda being ashamed of being Danish.

In addition to having a great sense of humor, Dad tended to be very impatient as well as sarcastic – a trait that I learned well. We got into trouble at school more than once when we repeated remarks Dad had made about something we had been taught. When one of our teachers stated that the average human head weighed thirty-five pounds, Dad made fun of this statement. He told us that the heads of the sows he butchered weighed less than that. I believe it was Gerard that reported this information back to the class the following day. He did not earn any brownie points for that!

When my brother Frank reached his mid teens, he and I were constantly noticing how Dad seldom did what he preached. Dad also seemed to be a sucker at auction sales, bringing home pieces of machinery that could never be made to work. I realize now that during the teen years it is quite normal for boys to reach a rebellious stage, but of course we knew nothing of that then.

My father's total fall from grace happened one day when I was with him in town. The local garage man had done some work on a tractor for us, and Dad accused him of sloppy work and implied that he was cheating us as well. The garage man blew his top! He threatened to give my dad a licking, at which point Dad back-pedalled in high gear, denying that he had accused him of anything. I was flabbergasted! I could not imagine Dad backing down from a smaller (but younger) man. I felt terribly ashamed of him. I now wonder how Dad felt about doing it in front of me. It must have been pretty tough for him to have me witness him having feet of clay.

Mother was a short woman – barely 5' 2" tall, but quite stout from carrying so many children. I think she weighed about 100 pounds when she married Dad but later weighed as much as 160. Her personality was the opposite of Dad's and that probably helped them get along. She always seemed soft to me, but I suspect now that she was much the tougher of the two.

One image of Mother that has stayed with me over the years was Mother in front of the sewing machine. She often sewed until after eleven at night to finish some garment she was making. I suppose she found she could get more done once we were all in bed. It appears to me now that unlike me, she must have been an evening person for she was never an early riser. Unless we were visiting friends, she could be counted on to take an afternoon nap every day between three o'clock and four.

The other memory is of Mother sitting on a milk stool picking black currants. We had two large bushes of them and they always yielded huge quantities of berries. Mother made them all into jam, which she usually stored in two-quart jars and sealed with wax.

Mother was able to be the centre of attention without expending any effort. One time we (my wife, children and I) were visiting my sister Ester. Dad, Mother and my brother Frank were there as well. Frank was attending the University of Alberta at the time, and I think Ester was back in school too. The conversation was about education and Dad was trying his best be the centre of attention. However, despite all his trying, it was Mother who got it all.

In 1972 Dad and Mother celebrated their golden wedding anniversary in Bassano, Alberta. All we siblings except my sister Eunice from Tucson

Golden Wedding on Sept. 1, 1972. Standing; left to right; Frank, Inger Gerda, Dad, Mother, Ester, the author and Gerard. Seated; Eva, Ray, Linda, Fred and Julie. *Photo is from the author's collection.*

Dad and Mother at the Golden Wedding. *Photo is from the author's collection.*

Arizona were there. (I had been the lone absentee at their Silver Wedding anniversary). At about this time, or shortly before, Dad had moved his bed out into the garage. Not too long after that, he moved out of the house and into an "Old Folks Home" in Calgary. I think it was his way of opting out of competition with Mother. She saw it as a failure on her part to keep their marriage going.

While Dad was in his late sixties, he had been very sick and almost died. The doctor insisted that it was his heart that was causing his problem, but refused to listen when Dad told him that pernicious anemia ran in his family. Dad was finally able to get his family doctor to have him tested. He did have Pernicious Anemia and after a series of Vitamin B-12 shots, he was restored to health. Dad became a Raleigh product salesman after selling the farm, and he soon replaced the vitamin shots with Raleigh's vitamins and stayed healthy for another dozen years. This was despite the doctors' insistence that he had to continue with injected Vitamin B-12.

Mother in her late eighties. *Photo is from the author's collection.*

I had a good visit with Dad shortly before he turned 81 and about 10 months before he died. By that time his heart was giving him trouble, but he controlled it with nitroglycerin. During our visit he apologized to me for not letting me carry on with my schooling, saying that he just could not afford to. I realize now that I got something more valuable than schooling from my parents, and that was a love of reading and a questioning mind. When Dad died the following October, I was very much at peace with our relationship.

Mother sold the house in Bassano and moved into an apartment building owned by the "Odd Fellows" service club. She lived there until the age of 90, but when she developed severe dementia she became a resident of Father Lacombe's Nursing home (a long term nursing facility) and died there at age 96. Up until she was ninety, she was in remarkable health and rode a bicycle fearlessly around the streets of Calgary. I recall going for a walk with her when she was 87. She not only walked with vigour, but she actually hopped off the curbs at the intersections. I only hope that I can maintain her degree of health into my eighties.

When I visited Mother the Christmas before she died, I was very impressed with the quality of care she received at Father Lacombe. I found the staff there to be exceedingly kind and attentive. Mother left each one of us with a small inheritance, which I spent wisely. I bought a good bicycle and gave the rest of it to the nursing home that had looked after her so well.

Mother never wore make-up during her entire life, but she could not impose her will on the undertaker. She wore lipstick for the first time when she lay in her coffin. There were a few odd coincidences in our family. Ester, the second oldest and Eunice the second youngest daughters were both born on September 17. Mother died on her oldest daughter's birthday and Dad died on his youngest son's birthday.

Where are we all now?

In a family with twelve children, one can reasonably expect them to scatter somewhat. That has certainly been the case with us though none of my siblings have been as footloose as I. My oldest sister lived in Van Kleek Hill, Ontario. She died around age 61, but the rest of us are all healthy and active. I now have three sisters living in Alberta; two in Calgary and one in Olds. There are two sisters and two brothers on Vancouver Island, three of whom are in Victoria and the other in Nanaimo. One brother lives in Ottawa, Ontario and one in Vancouver, BC. There is also one sister in Tucson Arizona and I live in Port Coquitlam, BC. We have never been a close knit family, but I do see a few of them now and then.

My own children have also been far flung. My youngest daughter has one daughter and has remained in Vancouver. The older daughter has been in California for over 20 years. She and her husband have one daughter and they have recently moved to Sacramento after many years in Mill Valley. My son (the oldest) and his wife have lived in Southern California and Arizona for the past 17 years, but have now returned to Vancouver. They have two young children, so now 3 of my 4 grandchildren are close by.

In early 1984 I found it necessary for me to quit drinking. My consumption had been slowly increasing and I was unable to reduce it, so I quit completely. In 1998 I gave up coffee, wheat products and refined sugar (I had been off milk for many years) and have been free of arthritis ever since. I found that giving up wheat and coffee was more difficult than giving up alcohol. It seems that as my body ages it becomes more sensitive to a variety of agents - it is also very sensitive to the glue in freshly laid carpets.

In my personal relationships, things seem to be improving as well. It is almost 10 years since I met my present wife and we have now been married for 9.5 of those years. I have now been in the same residence for 9 years, the longest under one roof since I left my parent's house. Am I finally settling down, or is it just that I am slowing down due to old age? I don't know whether I am becoming more patient or whether it is all due to a decrease in energy due to aging.

Erlinda's son Eric circa 2001. *Photo is from the author's collection.*

ABOUT THE AUTHOR

Larry came to Canada from Denmark when he was a baby and grew up on farms in, BC and Alberta.

He worked in farming, logging, sawmills, diamond drilling, and on oil-rigs, as well as brief periods in sales. Before getting into construction work, he spent thirteen years as an underground "hard rock" miner

In 1980 he incorporated his own consulting company, which has done work for over fifty clients in BC, Alberta and Yukon.

Larry is the third oldest of twelve children, but has only three of his own. He and his wife live in Port Coquitlam. In addition to writing, golfing and teaching computer courses, he plays bridge and snooker. He is also a scrabble player and a crossword puzzle fan.

Contact the author at:
Larry.Jacobsen@gmail.com
Tel: 604.552.0004
Cell. 778.235.1566

Printed in the United States
60060LVS00003B/49-87